Ever After High™

Fairy Tail

Ending

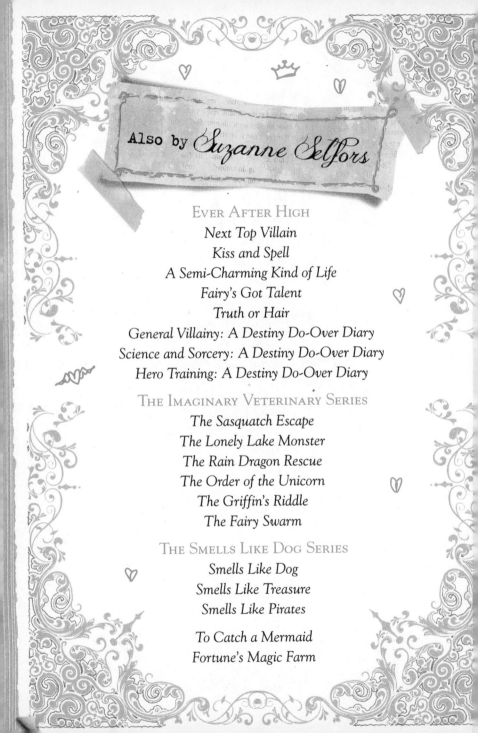

Also by *Suzanne Selfors*

EVER AFTER HIGH

Next Top Villain

Kiss and Spell

A Semi-Charming Kind of Life

Fairy's Got Talent

Truth or Hair

General Villainy: A Destiny Do-Over Diary

Science and Sorcery: A Destiny Do-Over Diary

Hero Training: A Destiny Do-Over Diary

THE IMAGINARY VETERINARY SERIES

The Sasquatch Escape

The Lonely Lake Monster

The Rain Dragon Rescue

The Order of the Unicorn

The Griffin's Riddle

The Fairy Swarm

THE SMELLS LIKE DOG SERIES

Smells Like Dog

Smells Like Treasure

Smells Like Pirates

To Catch a Mermaid

Fortune's Magic Farm

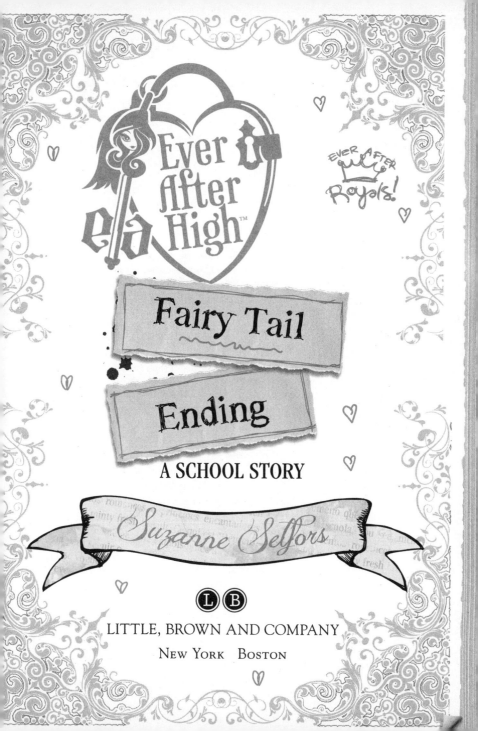

Ever After High™

EVER AFTER Royals!

Fairy Tail

Ending

A SCHOOL STORY

Suzanne Selfors

LB

LITTLE, BROWN AND COMPANY

NEW YORK   BOSTON

This book is dedicated to Kara Sargent,
for being my compass and friend as we
made our way through magical waters.
Thank you.

Little, Brown and Company

Hachette Book Group
1290 Avenue of the Americas, New York, NY 10104
Visit us at lb-kids.com

Little, Brown and Company is a division of Hachette Book Group, Inc.
The Little, Brown name and logo are trademarks of Hachette Book Group, Inc.

The publisher is not responsible for websites (or their content)
that are not owned by the publisher.

First Edition: October 2016

ISBN 978-0-316-38408-7

Library of Congress Control Number: 2016945003

10 9 8 7 6 5 4 3 2 1

RRD-C

Printed in the United States of America

Contents

A Magic Wind

The view from the ship's bow was breathtaking. In the east and in the west, a calm turquoise sea stretched to the horizon, the perfect flatness interrupted only by diving seagulls and dancing porpoises. But to the south, which was the ship's direction, the sea met an expanse of jagged white cliffs. Tall trees grew atop the cliffs, forming a dense forest. And rising above the forest, as if trying to touch the cloud-dappled sky, were the turreted towers of Ever After High.

For students who arrived by boat, this first glimpse of the school was a welcoming beacon. To know that the sea journey was about to end was a relief to many. And to know that a new year was about to begin, in the most famous and most prestigious school in all the fairytale lands, induced shivers of excitement. But on this particular day, the girl standing on the bow felt neither relief nor excitement.

Meeshell gripped the railing so tightly her knuckles turned white. She held her breath for so long, she nearly turned blue. There it was. Her school. Her future.

Her story.

Like many before her, Meeshell had traveled from a faraway kingdom. But hers was a land that most had never seen and would never see. It was shrouded deeply in mystery. A place of fable. A place of unequaled beauty. A place nearly impossible to reach, unless one had the correct physical attributes.

She might as well have come from the moon, for

that is how strange her world would seem to her fellow students.

She didn't, however, come from the moon.

She exhaled, then shifted her weight. She'd been standing so stiffly, her knees had begun to ache. *Knees,* she thought. *Such weird, knobby things. Will I ever get used to them?* She reached down and gave them each a good rub, then returned her focus to the distant turrets.

"There is no better education than the one you'll receive at Ever After High," her father had assured.

"You'll learn much more than we could ever teach you," her mother had said.

"You'll do great!"

"You'll be fine!"

"You'll fit right in."

Ever After High was her father's alma mater, so it made sense that he was super enthusiastic about his daughter attending the same school. And her mother wanted the very best for her children, so she was excited, too. But Meeshell's heart ached from

leaving family and friends behind. And doubts churned. What if she couldn't figure out how to adapt to this new world? What if she didn't understand their strange traditions? What if she stood out, like a crab in a bed of starfish?

As the ship slid gracefully through the water, Meeshell closed her eyes and held her face up to the cool breeze. She liked the way it felt as it tickled through her long, pink hair. The breeze was too gentle to fill the ship's sails, but she'd remedied that little problem. Using her magic touch, she'd created a little wave and had aimed it at the boat's stern. The wave never crested; rather, it continued to push them along. The ship's captain had been grateful for her help. The narwhal he usually employed to pull the ship on calm, windless days was on vacation.

"Lass?" A man's voice interrupted the silence. Meeshell's eyes flew open. Captain Greenbeard stood beside her. "You want one of the crew to fetch your coat? You'll be catching a chill out here."

She shook her head. Cold air didn't pierce her, as

it did others. Besides, she didn't own a coat. They didn't have coats where she came from. It had been difficult enough finding a dress. Luckily, her mother had a vast collection of objects that had fallen from ships, or had been stolen off of beaches by rouge waves. Those objects included the plain yellow dress that fell to Meeshell's ankles, the white ribbon tied around her waist, and the bag that now contained her few precious belongings.

"You're certainly a quiet one." The captain leaned his elbows on the railing and stared straight ahead, toward the white cliffs. He was a rugged-looking fellow, with deep lines around his eyes and mouth. He'd been kind to her during the voyage, as had the rest of the crew. "I'm finding it difficult to believe you've never been on a ship before. Never?"

She shook her head again.

"Well, you handled yesterday's choppy weather like a true sailor. Didn't turn green or get sick. Takes most landlubbers weeks to get their sea legs."

Sea legs? She didn't know what that meant. She'd

gotten her legs three days ago and they were supposed to be for land use. Were there special legs for the sea?

The captain glanced at a purplish bruise that glowed on Meeshell's forearm. "All that stumbling you've been doing, all that bumping into things, that's to be expected. The ocean swells can be as unpredictable as Poseidon's moods."

The captain was right. She'd certainly been struggling to walk gracefully. Because she'd been stuck on a ship since getting her legs, she'd had little chance to learn how to use them, other than walking up and down the deck, or up and down ladders. The physical bruises would go away. But what about the bruises to her confidence? Only time would tell.

Though only three days had passed, the journey from her kingdom had felt like eons. Too shy to talk to the crew, and too distracted to focus on a good book, Meeshell had tried to make the hours pass faster by watching for sea creatures. But alas, no matter how many pods of dolphins or seals she spotted, time moved as slowly as a sea slug. Fortunately, her mother had packed her favorite foods. "It will take you a while to get used to what they eat on land," she'd told Meeshell. So, while the rest of the crew munched on salty smoked herring and dry cornmeal biscuits, Meeshell ate seaweed-and-kelp-berry salads.

"Never seen that kind of food before," the cook had commented with a shrug. He was a troll, with huge ears and a nose to match. "You should try my fish chowder." He shoved a bowl right up to Meeshell's nose. She grimaced at the sight of the fish tails and fins floating in the creamy stew.

"No, thank you," she politely told him. Her voice came out quieter than she'd intended.

"What's that you say?" he asked.

She cleared her throat. "No, thank you." It was very difficult to get the words out, not just because of her shyness, but because something was different about her voice. No matter how hard she pushed the words, they still came out quiet. Hopefully it

was just a temporary ailment, and her voice would be back to normal before classes began.

"She said no, thank you," one of the crew told the cook.

"No fish chowder? But my chowder is famous."

"Famous for its aftereffects," another crew member said with a snicker.

The cook dismissed Meeshell with a wave. "Suit yerself." Then he scratched his rump with his wooden spoon.

Meeshell had eaten the last of her salad that very morning, and she'd been worried that she'd have to eat some of the cook's food. But now, with Ever After High in sight, there'd be no reason to risk an upset stomach. Fish was not on her menu. Never!

The white cliffs and stone towers loomed closer. "Land ho!" Captain Greenbeard hollered. Commotion arose on deck. Crewmen and women streamed out of the galley, wiping crumbs from their beards, braids, and shirts. Captain Greenbeard took his place next to the ship's wheel. As the ship sailed around an outcropping, a quaint harbor came into view. A few smaller boats were moored at a dock that jutted out from a white beach. The sand sparkled, as if made from glitter.

"Drop the main!" the captain ordered. A large rope was untied and the billowy sail, with its narwhal emblem, collapsed onto the deck. Without any wind, it must have been some kind of magic that had held the sail aloft. The magic wave that Meeshell had summoned was no longer needed, so she waved it away.

Captain Greenbeard gripped the wheel as the ship glided toward the dock. "Man the lines! Rudder hard over!"

Meeshell stepped aside as a crewman grabbed the bowline. As the ship neared the dock, three crewmen jumped onto the rough planks, ropes in hand, then guided the ship to a standstill.

A sign stood at the end of the dock:

WELCOME TO STORYBOOK HARBOR
THIS WAY TO MIRROR BEACH

THIS WAY TO
EVER AFTER HIGH

Meeshell took a long, steadying breath. She'd arrived.

One journey had ended, but another was about to begin.

Fairest Feet

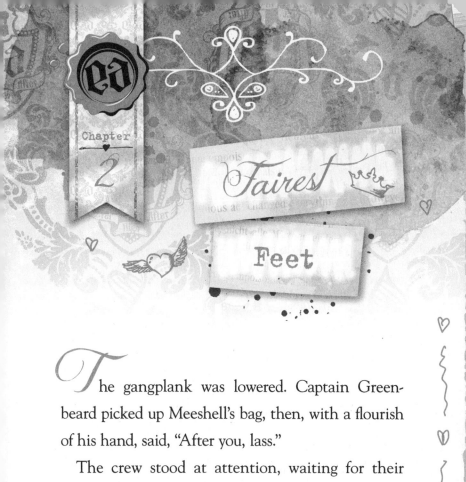

The gangplank was lowered. Captain Green-beard picked up Meeshell's bag, then, with a flourish of his hand, said, "After you, lass."

The crew stood at attention, waiting for their only passenger to disembark. All eyes were on Meeshell. Did they suspect her true identity? If so, were they waiting to see if she could navigate that narrow piece of wood, or if she'd stumble and fall into the water? That would be quite a scene, and one she wanted to avoid!

"Thank you for the ride," she said to the crew, trying to be heard above the shrieking of a pair of seagulls, who'd swooped onto the deck to pilfer whatever crumbs they could find. Meeshell took a few steps forward. Then, ever so slowly, she made her way down the plank, telling herself to place one foot in front of the other. She didn't take her eyes off her new feet. The captain walked behind her.

"You're unsteady because you've been at sea," he told her. "You'll get used to land again in no time." She was glad to know that he still didn't suspect the true reason why she was unsteady, and she certainly hoped she'd quickly get used to land.

Upon reaching the dock, she sighed with relief. The dock was solid and steady, no movement from the waves. She pressed her toes against the wood and found her balance. Then the captain hollered, "Hello!"

A gentleman was walking down the dock. He appeared to be a dapper fellow, wearing a crisp black suit, a striped waistcoat, and a tie. His thick gray hair and mustache were embellished with white streaks. A heavy key ring hung from his belt. Upon reaching her, he extended his arm. "You must be Ms....Ms...." He hesitated. "Ms. Meeshell." She nodded and shook his hand. "I am Headmaster Grimm. Welcome to Ever After High. I hope your journey was uneventful."

Uneventful? She wouldn't have chosen that word to describe what she'd been through over the past three days. Having never left home before, having never traveled alone, the journey had been the biggest event of her life! The headmaster must have noticed her confusion at his comment for he added, "No *major* events. Storms. Shipwreck. Giant squid attacks, that sort of thing. In other words, you appear to have made it in one piece."

She nodded again.

"We did get a touch of bad weather, but the wee lass fared well," Captain Greenbeard said.

"That does not surprise me." The headmaster gave Meeshell a knowing look. Then he glanced around. "Do you have luggage?" He glanced down at her feet. Her bare toes peeked out from under the dress's hem. "A pair of shoes, perhaps?"

"She travels light. Just herself and this bag." The captain handed it to the headmaster. "She's a quiet one. Only a sentence here or there, during the whole trip."

Headmaster Grimm took a small velvet pouch from his waistcoat pocket and handed it to the captain. "Thank you for your service," he said.

"Yes, thank you," Meeshell said, smiling shyly.

"You're very welcome." He took off his blue knit cap and bowed like a gentleman.

"Good-bye!" the crew called. Meeshell waved. Captain Greenbeard strode back onto his ship and ordered his crew to get underway. The gangplank was raised. Meeshell wondered if she should use her magic touch again, and give them a friendly push, but a gray head and long twisted horn poked out of the water, next to the boat. The captain's narwhal had returned.

"Follow me," the headmaster said.

As the narwhal pulled the ship from the harbor, Meeshell followed the headmaster up the dock. The boards were not evenly spaced, and some were thicker than others. She winced as a sharp pain pierced the big toe on her new left foot. "Ow."

The headmaster took her arm and led her to a log. She sat. She held out her foot. Her toe throbbed with pain. "A sliver," he informed her with a shake of his head. "Tending to students' medical needs is not my usual duty." He took a small device from his waistcoat pocket. Even though they didn't use such devices in her kingdom, she knew all about phones. He tapped the screen. "I have summoned a nurse fairy." Then he frowned in disapproval. "Why are you not wearing the correct apparel for your feet?"

Meeshell gulped. There'd been no time to get shoes before she left. The decision to send her to school had happened so quickly. Her mother had placed clothing orders, but they hadn't arrived before her departure, so the packages were supposed

to be delivered to her at school. She held her foot. "I..." How was she to know that feet were so delicate? She'd never worn them before.

In a burst of blue light, a tiny winged creature appeared before her. It zipped around her head, then perched on her foot. Oh barnacles, did that ever tickle! Meeshell gritted her teeth and held as still as possible. The fairy peered over her big toe. Then it touched a wand to the sliver and, voilà, the pain was gone. In another burst of light, the fairy disappeared before Meeshell had the chance to say thank you.

"Better?" the headmaster asked.

Meeshell nodded. The pain was gone and there wasn't even a red mark where the sliver had been.

"Our nurse fairies do a very good job," he told her. "Let us hope you won't have to call upon them again." Then he resumed their walk.

She followed the headmaster across the beach and up a sandy trail. He walked with long strides, and didn't stumble or wobble the way she did. "Do

you think there's something wrong with my legs?"
Meeshell asked.

He peered down his long nose at her. "I beg your
pardon but I'm having trouble hearing you." The
gulls were no longer screeching, and the waves
lapped gently in the distance, so there wasn't much
to compete with Meeshell's voice.

"I'm sorry." She put her hand to her throat. "I
can't seem to speak very loudly. It's…odd."

He raised an eyebrow. "Indeed."

She cleared her throat and tried again. "Do you
think there's something wrong with my legs?"

"How so?"

"They feel so unsteady. Maybe I didn't get the
right kind."

"I'm sure the Sea Witch gave you perfectly adequate legs. She has no reason to do otherwise. She
wants you to be successful here."

The headmaster possessed a commanding voice
that was reassuring in its confidence, but also a bit
frightening in its authority. This was the man who'd

summoned Meeshell to Ever After High. He'd sent a letter to her parents insisting that she attend. And he'd convinced the Sea Witch to help by giving her a pair of legs.

She looked down at those legs, hidden beneath the long, yellow dress. There was no reason to suspect they were faulty or badly formed. It was, as the headmaster pointed out, in the Sea Witch's best interest that Meeshell and her new legs succeed at Ever After High.

For Meeshell had something the Sea Witch wanted.

Watery

Witch

The events that led up to Meeshell's journey happened as quickly as a riptide. First, Headmaster Grimm's message arrived in a bottle, carried by United Manta Ray. Her parents read the message, then they summoned her. "Meeshell," her mother said. "We have news. You are going on a trip tomorrow morning."

"Tomorrow morning?" Meeshell asked, both surprised and confused. "But I've got school."

The family had gathered in the castle's main room. Meeshell's mother and father were the queen and king of the Merpeople, which made Meeshell a princess. But their palace was not a sprawling fortress. Unlike land-dwellers, the Merpeople did not build immense structures. Rather, they lived in harmony with their surroundings, down deep where fishermen's nets and lines did not go. This castle was an elegant cave, lighted by magical jewels that were embedded in the walls. Hermit crabs made little trails in the sandy floor, and butterfly fish swam gracefully near the entrance. Storms did not rage that deep, and sharks did not prowl. It was a lovely, peaceful place, with no dangers to speak of.

Well, except for the Sea Witch.

But she lived in her own cave, on the other side of the kelp forest. And she'd made a pact with the king and queen. She would not bother them as long as they stuck to the story and gave her their first-born daughter's voice. Meeshell's voice.

Meeshell's mother was the famous Little Mermaid. As a young woman, she'd agreed to give her beautiful voice to the Sea Witch in exchange for legs and the chance to live on land. And so the deal was made, and the Little Mermaid went to live among the land-dwellers, leaving behind the most beautiful singing voice in all the Merworld. But as is true in many fairytales, there is often a way to elude a witch's dark magic: true love. In the Little Mermaid's case, when she found the true love of a prince and he agreed to live beneath the sea with her, the curse was broken. Her voice returned to her.

Which left the Sea Witch without a beautiful mermaid voice to complete her collection. This sent the witch into such a rage that the sea roiled and frothed like a witch's cauldron.

So now the Sea Witch had to wait for the day when the Little Mermaid's firstborn daughter would live the story her mother was supposed to have lived—to permanently exchange her voice for legs and life on land.

And wait the Sea Witch did, counting the days until she got Meeshell's voice.

"You will not be going to Merschool tomorrow

because you will be going to a different school," her mother explained.

"Why?"

"You have been invited to attend Ever After High," her father said, a proud smile on his handsome face.

Meeshell pondered this news. Ever After High? Her father often spoke of the school he'd attended. He'd loved it. She remembered many bedtime stories about his days fighting dragons in Dragon-Slaying class and climbing towers in Hero Training class. How he'd been co-president of the student body, and captain of the Track and Shield team. The world above the waves was so very different. For Meeshell and her Merfriends, school studies focused on learning about the other creatures that inhabited the sea. There were no class presidents or clubs or teams. Her people considered themselves the guardians of the waters, and thus, taking care of other creatures was of the utmost importance.

"But Ever After High is *on land*, and I'm not supposed to go onto land until I'm older," Meeshell

said. "My story isn't supposed to start yet. Is it?"

Her mother swam over and handed Meeshell the message-in-a-bottle. It had been written on waterproof paper.

From the desk of
HEADMASTER GRIMM

Dear Philip and Pearl,

I believe it is in your daughter's best interest to begin her studies, posthaste, at Ever After High. While Merschool is suitable for those who will live out their lives in the sea, I believe it is not the best choice for a young princess whose destiny is to eventually live on land. Ever After High will provide Meeshell the everyday experiences that will prepare her for her future life as a land-dweller. Fall quarter begins in three days. A dormitory room shall be waiting for her.

> Yours ever after,
> Headmaster Grimm

P.S—I have sent an urgent message to the Sea Witch, asking her to help with Meeshell's transformation.

"The Sea Witch?" An icy feeling darted up Meeshell's spine. The scales on her tail shivered.

"Unfortunately, she is the only one who possesses the magic to give you legs," her mother explained.

"I know but..." This was all so very confusing. When Meeshell woke up that morning, she'd been looking forward to learning stingray songs. But now her life was being turned upside down. "But..."

"Sweetheart, I know you must feel like you've been hit by a tidal wave," her mother said gently. She took Meeshell's hand. "But this isn't bad news. It's good news. This is a wonderful opportunity. When I went onto land, I barely knew anything. I'd only observed people from a distance, so it was very difficult for me. But you'll get the chance to live with people, to learn directly from them. And when you make that final transition to living permanently on land, it won't be so shocking."

That all made sense, but it didn't change the fact that Meeshell wasn't ready to leave. "But that means

I have to go away." She tried to bravely hold back her tears.

"Only for a while. You'll have long weekends and holiday breaks to come home. And there's summer, of course." Her dad took her other hand. "You'll have so much fun, the time will fly by."

But how could she have fun without her friends? And then another thought struck her.

"What about Finbert?" Meeshell asked. She reached out her hand. A tiny narwhal swam over. She stroked his back. Finbert had been her beloved pet since she was a baby. She couldn't stand the thought of them being apart for such long periods of time.

"Finbert can join you after you've settled in," her father replied with a smile. "You will see that several of your classmates at Ever After High have pets."

Well, at least that was something. "Did you hear that, Finbert?" she asked. "You can join me later." He nodded, then chased after a puffer fish.

Suddenly, the water turned cold. A sharp current shot through the castle, swirling around Meeshell and her parents. The hermit crabs tucked into their shells. The butterfly fish darted into a crevice. Something was coming.

The Sea Witch entered. Her tail differed from most of her fellow Merpeople. Not made of glistening scales, it was built of red armor, like a crab's shell.

At the sight of the witch, Queen Pearl pulled her daughter close. King Philip grabbed his trident and rose into a protective stance. The Sea Witch stopped swimming and waved a hand at him. "Oh, calm down, Philip. I'm not here to stir up the waters. I got a message from Milton Grimm, same as you."

The king lowered his trident. "You'll help us?" he asked warily.

"Help *you*?" She cackled as all witches do, whether on land or in water. "I'm not here to help *you*! You two and your true love kept me from adding a beautiful mermaid voice to my collection."

"If you're not going to help us, then why are you here?" Queen Pearl asked.

"I'm here to help myself, of course!" Her voice was as rough and scratchy as sand. Her long, tangled black hair floated around her head. A few crabs peeked out from among the tangles. She pointed a finger at Meeshell. "If I give you legs, and you go to school, and you make lots of friends, and you meet a dashing prince, blah blah blah, then you will fall in love with living on land and you will embrace your destiny. And I will have your voice!" More cackling.

"You can't have her voice until she decides to stay on land permanently," Queen Pearl pointed out. "And that won't happen until after she's graduated."

"Yeah, yeah, details, details. Whatever." The Sea Witch rolled her black eyes. "I only care about one thing: completing my collection!" Then she hollered, "Coral! Where are you?"

Another mermaid swam into the palace. Coral, daughter of the Sea Witch, was a few years younger

than Meeshell. She had dark, blue-black hair and a red tail like her mother.

"Seeing as this is a special request, I'm going to let my daughter cast the spell. She could use the practice."

Coral smiled nervously. "Yeah, my last spell didn't go so well." Meeshell's parents shared a troubled glance. Coral's botched spells were well-known in the Merworld.

The Sea Witch chuckled. "Never mind that, darling. That stupid shark seems fine with his new head of hair. We all make mistakes. That's part of learning." The Sea Witch patted her daughter's head.

"Do you think this is a good idea?" King Philip asked the witch. "Shouldn't you be the one to cast the spell?"

"Of course it's a good idea!" the Sea Witch bellowed. "Coral is perfectly capable of replacing a Mertail with two human legs. Right, Coral?"

It took Coral a few moments before she nodded, and even then, she didn't look confident. Meeshell

gulped. Her hand flew to her tail, to its soft, blue scales.

The Sea Witch spun around, then swam toward the entry. "Meet us at dawn, on the shore of Turtle Island." And with another blast of cold current, she was gone. After a little wave good-bye, Coral followed.

"Is this really happening?" Meeshell asked her parents.

"Yes," they both said. Which was not the answer she'd hoped for.

Flotation

Device

*S*and and pebbles crunched beneath Meeshell's bare feet as she followed the headmaster up the path. "Are you still resolute about hiding your true identity?" he asked.

"Yes." She'd thought about this during her sea voyage. And she'd discussed it at length with her parents before leaving the Merworld. If her future was to live on land, and to be two-footed, then it was important for her to gain acceptance among the

students as an equal. To not be treated differently. If the students and teachers knew she'd spent most of her life with a tail, they might not expect as much from her. She didn't want that. She wanted the true experience. If everyone thought she was a human, they'd treat her as a human.

The trail rounded a corner and the beach disappeared from view. The headmaster folded his arms behind his back as they walked. He didn't try to force conversation. She couldn't tell if he agreed or disagreed with her decision to hide her true identity. They continued in silence, up the path and onto a cobbled road.

She'd just been getting used to the sandy terrain, but cobblestones were a totally different sensation. Her ankles twisted as she stepped into the ruts between the stones. How did people do this? Swimming came naturally to Merpeople—they didn't need to be taught. But walking was so weird! "How long does it take someone to learn to walk?" she asked.

The headmaster turned, glancing at her from beneath his bushy brows. "Some start walking after nine months, but for others it can take more than a year." More than a year? What had she gotten herself into?

They traversed a pretty wooden drawbridge, then stood at the entrance to the campus. An elegant archway loomed overhead, its face carved with the words: *Welcome to Ever After High.*

Meeshell's skin got all tingly. It was as if she'd just discovered a new world. Certainly she'd seen parts of this world up close. She'd encountered many boats, both those run by fishermen, and huge cruise ships overflowing with land-dwellers. And she'd watched humans walking along the beach, swimming, sunning themselves. But to stand in their world...it felt like a dream.

The school was so much larger than she'd imagined. The stone buildings looked big enough to fit giants. Wide walkways wound between colorful gardens where everything was in bloom. The flowers

were all unfamiliar to Meeshell, but they were beautiful. A unicorn fountain stood at the center of a pool, where white swans nibbled on water bugs between lily pads. But what struck her most was that there were mirrors everywhere she looked. On the trees, on the walls; one even hung from a tiny white cloud.

The campus was oddly quiet. She'd expected lots of people and activity. Her father had always described it that way. She looked around.

"The students are gathered in the Charmitorium for a School Spirit assembly," the headmaster explained. "The cheerhexers are leading the assembly, to show support for our athletic teams." Right on cue, a loud cheer rose from a nearby building. A dreamy, faraway look filled the headmaster's eyes. "Back in my day, I played center on the basketball team. I held the record for most baskets of food dunked in a single game. Those wolves could never catch me. Ah, I remember those days as if they were yesterday."

Meeshell tried to imagine a game like that, but her attention was diverted by a large brown rabbit sitting on a bench. Meeshell had seen rabbits before, hopping about on shore, but this one wore glasses. And was reading a book! And were those horns sprouting from his head? Then she squealed as something bumped into her foot. She stepped aside as three roundish creatures, covered in prickles like sea urchins, waddled past. They made funny snorting noises at her. She shielded her eyes with her hand and looked up at the sky as a large shape passed overhead. "Was that a dragon?" she asked.

"Indeed."

Her father had told many stories about dragons. They terrified villagers and stole treasure. They reminded her of sharks.

"You have no reason to be concerned," the headmaster explained. "All the Ever After High dragons are friendly. We don't allow dangerous dragons here. There's a protective spell to keep them away."

That was a relief. It was bad enough encountering

a shark, but having to worry about something swooping down from the sky seemed unbearable. Meeshell followed the headmaster up a wide stone stairway. As the headmaster approached, a pair of doors flew open. He and Meeshell stepped into the Administration Building.

A tree grew in the center of the building, its branches reaching into the corners and its trunk disappearing right through the ceiling. Birds nestled in the branches. A pink squirrel scurried around the trunk. There was a mirror on this tree, too.

Up a staircase Meeshell and the headmaster went, spiraling 'round and 'round until they reached the upper floor. They passed through another door and into a room, where a lady sat at a desk. She had extremely large ears and an oversized nose from which long, black hairs sprouted. The sign on her desk read:

NO STUDENT SEEN WITHOUT AN APPOINTMENT

The headmaster spoke to her. "Mrs. Trollworth, this is our newest student, Meeshell. Do you have her student file?"

"Does she have an appointment? She can't be here without an appointment." She tapped the sign with a stubby finger.

"There's no need for an appointment. I just met her at the dock and now we need to find her new student file."

"Yeah, okay, it's here somewhere." The troll lady shuffled through a very large stack of papers, tossing some over her shoulder onto another large stack. It was quite messy behind her desk. She found what looked like an old sandwich, took a bite, then tossed it aside. After riffling through another stack of papers she exclaimed, "Got it!" She handed over the file. Then she stared at Meeshell's bare feet, which had picked up quite a bit of dirt during the walk. "You part troll?" she asked. Meeshell didn't understand the question, until she noticed that the

troll lady's feet were also bare. Except hers were hairy, with gnarly yellow toenails.

Meeshell shook her head.

"Oh. Too bad for you." She plopped onto her chair and began to eat noisily from a bag of salted cockroach crisps.

"Right this way." Headmaster Grimm escorted Meeshell into his office. A massive carved desk sat in the center of the room. The walls were covered with framed photos of various members of the Grimm family. But what really caught Meeshell's attention was the elderly woman who was sitting on a cushion and floating about four feet off the ground. She looked very comfortable. Meeshell suddenly missed the sensation of floating—missed the way the water held and cradled her.

"Hello," the woman said. Her voice was craggy with age, but kind. Snarled gray hair peeked out from a scarf she wore over her head. A pair of golden bangles hung from her earlobes.

"Meeshell, this is Professor Baba Yaga. She is the department head for Spells, Hexes, and General Witchery classes. Because you are not a witch, you will not likely find yourself in one of her classrooms. However, she volunteered to keep an eye on you during your stay here."

"I have a keen interest in you. I was your father's advisor when he attended this school. I remember him well." She floated closer. "You have his eyes."

Meeshell gulped. This professor knew her identity? She looked questioningly at the headmaster.

"You can't hide the truth from Professor Yaga," he said. "And she feels it is very important to monitor your health."

"My health?"

"Yes," Professor Yaga said. "Please, sit." She motioned toward a chair. Meeshell sat. She went to tuck her tail beneath the chair, but then remembered the new legs. She crossed them at the ankles, imagining that they'd once again become a tail.

The headmaster walked behind his desk and sat in a chair so large, it looked like a throne. Professor Yaga pressed her fingertips together and floated a bit higher, looking down at Meeshell. "Your health is of my utmost concern. Leaving the water is not a simple feat. Your body is not used to gravity."

"Oh." Meeshell thought about this for a moment. "Is that why I feel heavier?"

"Exactly. You are used to the buoyancy of water. I noticed that when you walked in, you were a bit wobbly on your legs. I wouldn't worry about that. You're young and strong; you should adapt quickly."

"Coral, the Sea Witch's daughter, cast the spell, and she said that when she tried it on an eel, the eel's new legs fell off. Do you think that might happen to me?"

"Let us hope not!" Professor Yaga gave Meeshell a very lengthy stare. "I'm wondering about your voice. Is that as loud as you can speak?"

"Yes, I'm having trouble. My voice feels…weak."

"Ah, another effect of being out of water. Your vocal cords are used to both air and water, but not to air one hundred percent of the time. It's having a negative effect on them."

"Could the air *damage* my voice?" Meeshell asked, her brow furrowed.

Professor Yaga narrowed her eyes. "It is a possibility." Then she gave the headmaster an odd look. Meeshell uncrossed her legs and sat up straight. Was it possible her voice wouldn't be fine? This could be a very big deal because her story centered on her voice!

"I can see that you're concerned." Professor Yaga floated closer again, then patted Meeshell's shoulder. "Let's not panic. Perhaps all your voice needs is time to adjust. I will keep a close eye on you and check in with you often. But if anything changes, let me know right away." And off she floated.

Once again, Meeshell's hand flew to her throat. If this trip to Ever After High ruined her voice, the Sea Witch would be furious! And without a voice to trade, Meeshell's story line would be ruined.

"I have the highest confidence in Professor Yaga," Headmaster Grimm told her. "You are in extremely capable hands. When Faybelle Thorn cast an evil spell and it backfired, taking away Faybelle's ability to fly, Professor Yaga guided her through the recovery process. And recover she did. That young fairy ignores the campus flying speed limit every chance she gets." He cleared his throat, then opened Meeshell's file. "Now, there is some business we must attend to. Because you wish to keep your identity a secret while you're here, we think it would be best to give you a single room."

Meeshell agreed that things might be easier if she had total privacy, but it felt like special treatment. "Do other students have single rooms?"

"No."

"If I get my own room, won't that make other students suspicious?" Her throat felt tickly as she spoke. "I want to be treated like everyone else."

"Very well." He leaned forward and hollered, "Mrs. Trollworth!"

The troll lady poked her large head into his office. "What?"

"Meeshell needs a roommate assignment."

The troll lady disappeared, followed by more sounds of papers being flung about, then she stuck her head back in. "There's an empty bed in room twelve-C."

"Twelve-C?" he asked.

"Yeah. Farrah Goodfairy."

"I see." He stroked his chin for a moment. "Farrah Goodfairy is not royalty. Will that matter to you?"

Meeshell shrugged. "Should it?"

At her school in the Merkingdom, most of Meeshell's classmates were not princes or princesses. In fact, none of her closest friends from her old school were royalty. Things like that simply didn't matter to her.

"It has long been a tradition, here at Ever After High, to house royals together. It makes sense, based on their shared school curriculums and traditions. But lately we've been embracing diversification. I

think Farrah might be a good match for you. She's very intelligent and exceptionally friendly." He wrote something into Meeshell's file. "Very well. Twelve-C it is. Now that we have that matter settled, a member of the Welcoming Committee should be here shortly to show you around."

And at that very moment, a girl stepped into the office. She smiled so brightly at Meeshell that, for a moment, all of Meeshell's worries faded away.

An Apple a Day

*H*eadmaster Grimm stood and a wide grin spread across his face. Whoever this girl was, she was very well liked. "Well, this is a lovely surprise. What can I do for you?" he asked.

"She doesn't have an appointment!" the troll lady hollered from the other room.

The girl called out to the ornery receptionist, "It's okay, Mrs. Trollworth. I didn't make an appointment because I'm not here to see the headmaster."

She turned and smiled again at Meeshell. "Briar Beauty usually greets new students, since she's head of the Ever After High Welcoming Committee, but she couldn't leave the Spirit assembly, so she sent me. I've applied to be a member of the committee. You're my first official new student." The girl's cheeks were round and dimpled, and her blue eyes twinkled. They *actually* twinkled. She held out her hand. "I'm Apple. Apple White."

"Hi." Meeshell shyly reached out and shook her hand. "I'm…Meeshell."

"No last name?" Apple asked. Meeshell shook her head. "Oh, how enchanting! One name, just like Cinderella. Well, Meeshell, I'm fairy, fairy happy to meet you."

"Are you…?" Meeshell's voice was barely a whisper. She knew that she'd be meeting all sorts of well-known students, but this girl was related to the most famous woman in the entire fairytale world! "Are you *Snow White's* daughter?"

"Yes, but don't let that sway your opinion of me. Seriously, my mom is wonderful, but in most ways she's just like everyone else's mom. She checks in on me all the time, wanting to know if I'm getting enough sleep, if I'm flossing, and if I'm eating healthy. And she always wants to know if I have a *boyfriend*." She giggled. "I'm much too busy studying to worry about that sort of thing." She reached into a book bag and pulled out a red apple. "This is a little welcome gift for you. Don't worry, it's not a *poisoned apple*." Apple giggled again. "I don't poison apples; I just eat poisoned apples. At least, I'm supposed to, one day."

Meeshell took the apple. It certainly was beautiful. She'd eaten apples, but only the golden kind. There was a place near her home where an ancient apple tree grew close to shore, its branches hanging out over the water. She and her friends would wait for the fruit to fall, then sit on the beach and eat their fill. But she'd never tasted a red apple.

"Go on, give it a try. It's a hybrid, grown special in my kingdom. Mom ships crates of them to me."

Meeshell took a bite. She was surprised by the combination of tart and sweet. "Yum," she said. She wiped a bit of juice that dribbled down her chin.

"I know, isn't it the best?" Apple took another one out of her bag and set it onto the headmaster's desk. "Headmaster Grimm, what is Meeshell's dorm assignment?" she asked.

"She shall be rooming with Ms. Goodfairy," he said.

Apple clapped her hands. "Oh, you'll love Farrah! She's a spelltacular girl, and a hexcellent student! Come on, let's go. I have so much to show you. Good-bye, Headmaster Grimm. Charm you later!"

The headmaster grabbed Meeshell's bag and handed it to her. "Good-bye, Ms. White and Ms.… ahem…Meeshell. Remember, Professor Yaga will act as your advisor, should you need anything."

"Thank you."

Apple placed another apple onto Mrs. Trolworth's desk. "I don't like apples!" the troll lady bellowed, reaching for a handful of cockroach crisps.

"Oh, Mrs. Trollworth, haven't you heard the saying—an apple a day keeps the doctor away?" Apple asked sweetly.

"What's that supposed to mean?" Mrs. Trollworth asked grumpily.

"It means apples are good for you."

As they left, Mrs. Trollworth called, "Hey, this one doesn't have any worms in it. Next time you bring me an apple, I want one with worms!"

When Apple led Meeshell down the stairs, her red skirt flounced with her excited footsteps. "I like your yellow dress. It's very...old-fashioned," she said diplomatically. "But what happened to your shoes?"

"Um, well, I came by boat and..." Meeshell wasn't sure what to say.

"Oh dear." Apple gasped. "Did a giant squid take them? That happened to my aunt once. She took a cruise to the North Pole and a giant squid ate the whole boat. Luckily, he spat out my aunt, but he kept her shoes. Isn't that mean?" Meeshell didn't respond. She'd met a few giant squids and they were the opposite of mean. In fact, they were the shyest creatures in the ocean. But she knew that legends often portrayed them as dangerous beasts. The very last thing giant squids wanted to do was to attack anyone or anything. They preferred napping and weaving. And they certainly didn't eat boats or shoes. "I'll help you get a new pair. We have the best shoe store in the village."

"Thanks," Meeshell said.

"So, how come you're whispering?"

"There's something wrong with my voice." Meeshell felt her cheeks burn. Apple must think she was so strange, with her whispery voice.

But Apple just gave her a sympathetic smile. "I'm royally sorry to hear that. If it gets worse I can pick up some throat lozenges at the infirmary. The pickled pepper lozenges taste terrible, but they work great."

The doors to the Administration Building flew open and the girls stepped outside. The campus was still quiet. "Since this is my first official Welcome Committee assignment, I need to check my list," Apple explained. She pulled a little piece of paper from her pocket. "Let's see, first I meet you, then I'm supposed to take you to the bookstore to get supplies. It's right over there."

As they walked across the quad, Apple chatted happily. "I remember my first day at school. I was super hexcited because I'd requested Raven Queen for my roommate and I got her. I spent most of the morning decorating our room. She didn't like it, not at first. And I think she was shocked that the girl she's supposed to poison was her roommate and wanted to be her friend. It took her a while to get used to me but now we're BFFAs. That's best friends forever after." She smiled at Meeshell. "You'll make friends right away. In fact, that's one of the things

on my list. Look." She pointed to the list and read. "'*Help the New Student Make Friends.*' Everyone here is really nice. Well, not *everyone*. There are some villains, but a fairytale wouldn't be a fairytale without villains." She stopped in her tracks and raised her eyebrow. "Are you a villain?"

Meeshell shook her head.

"I didn't think so. I'm a fairy good judge of people and you don't strike me as a villain. What is your story? Oh, wait, never mind that right now because here's the bookstore."

Hoping to avoid more conversation about her "story," Meeshell darted into the bookstore. It was a crowded place, with floor-to-ceiling shelves. Besides books, there were all sorts of things to buy, each adorned with the Ever After High emblem—water bottles, socks, and hoodies to name a few. There was an entire section dedicated to Daring Charming. Meeshell had read a lot about Prince Charming, but she wasn't familiar with his son. Daring's handsome face adorned T-shirts, book bags, and key chains.

"Daring's got a whole fan club," Apple explained. "We dated for a while but, right now, I'm way too busy for romance. What about you? Do you have a boyfriend back home?"

Meeshell shook her head. She had friends, lots of friends, but never a real boyfriend. There'd been that one time, when Splash, a boy she went to school with, had held her hand. And had kissed her cheek in the moonlight. But she didn't feel anything deeper than friendship for him.

Apple picked up a Daring Charming water bottle. "I figure there will always be boys to date. But we only get to go to this school for a short time, and I want to make the most of my education while I'm here." She set the bottle aside, then walked up to the counter. The cashier had green hair and pointed ears. "Hi, Birch. This is Meeshell, a new student. She needs to pick up a MirrorPad."

"Welcome to Ever After High," he said. Then he handed Meeshell a black square thing.

"What is this?" Meeshell asked.

"You don't know?" Though Apple sounded surprised, she didn't seem to judge Meeshell, which was a huge relief. "Well, here at Ever After High, we have a Mirror Network. That's the fastest way to communicate. With this MirrorPad, you can watch the latest MirrorCasts, communicate with other students, get your class thronework assignments, send hexts to your family, basically everything. Yesterday my mom sent a photo of our family cat. Isn't she cute?" She pulled out her own MirrorPad, touched the screen, and a snow-white cat appeared, wearing a cute jeweled red collar. Meeshell suddenly missed Finbert. "Oh look, I have a MirrorMail from Ashlynn. She wants to meet up for lunch."

"Wow," Meeshell said, amazed by the technology. The Merkingdom didn't have anything like this. If she wanted to meet up with her Merfriends, she used the conch shell to call them, and then they'd meet at their favorite kelp grotto.

"Thanks, Birch," Apple said.

"No problem."

Outside the bookstore, Apple and Meeshell sat on a wooden bench. "Okay, now that we have your MirrorPad, let's look at your class schedule." Apple opened Meeshell's MirrorPad, touched the screen a few times, and a schedule appeared.

Student: First Name: Meeshell.
Last Name: Withheld.

Apple pursed her lips and glanced at Meeshell. "Why does it say 'withheld'?"

"Uh, some kind of mistake?" Meeshell suggested.

"Well, you definitely have a full schedule and, oh look, you're in Princessology. I didn't know you were a royal. But where's your crown?" Apple touched her own crown.

Meeshell didn't normally wear a crown. Instead, she preferred a pearl headband, which she'd tucked into her small bag, along with a few of her very special belongings.

Apple looked concerned. "Oh dear. Did that

giant squid take your crown, too? We'll be sure to get you a new one. We can probably order it and have it delivered. What kingdom are you from?"

Even though she'd had those three days on the ship to ponder all the potential questions, Meeshell hadn't quite worked out all the details of her alias. She'd been distracted by her new legs, and the great effort it took getting used to them. "I'm from very far away. Across the ocean. You've never heard of it, I'm sure."

"I took Geografairy last year and aced it. We had to study *all* the kingdoms. Let me guess." Apple scrunched up her face as she thought deeply. "Since you came across the ocean, is it…is it the Kingdom by the Sea?"

Meeshell nodded. She felt bad about starting her friendship with a lie but if she told Apple where she came from, then Apple would immediately know she was a mermaid. As warm of a welcome she was getting from Apple, Meeshell still believed that, in the long run, it would be best if everyone at

Ever After High thought she was just a normal, two-footed princess.

Apple placed a hand on Meeshell's shoulder. "This is probably your first time being away from home. We all get homesick at first. But it will pass, I promise. You'll start to feel as if this is your second home in no time. And one of the best ways to fight homesickness is to make new friends." Meeshell was speechless. This very nice student, whom she'd just met, was being so kind. Would everyone be like this? Apple glanced at her list. "It says here that I'm supposed to get you signed up for at least one club or sports team. What are your interests?"

Meeshell wasn't sure what to say. Back home, she really loved riding manta rays. In fact, she was a champion, having won first place in her age group in the manta ray race. She also loved combing the seafloor for treasures. While the Sea Witch collected voices, Meeshell collected shells of all shapes and sizes. And she was really good at sea languages, having mastered Porpoise *and* Dolphin. But none of

those interests seemed right for Ever After High. "Well, I'm not really sure what my interests are," she said. Then she coughed. Her throat felt so scratchy.

"*Oooh*, we need to get you those lozenges."

Sounds arose in the distance. The doors to the Charmitorium flew open and students began to emerge. "Oh look, the assembly is over. It's time for lunch. Come on, let's get you something to eat and you can meet some of the other students. And then I can cross one more thing off the list: help the new student make friends."

Tea

Trouble

$\mathcal{A}$pple was taking her Welcoming Committee role very seriously: Each time she and Meeshell passed something she'd say, "Welcome to the drinking fountain." "Welcome to the wishing well." "Welcome to the exterior hallway of the Student Union Building." She certainly seemed very nice, and her desire to make Meeshell feel at home at Ever After High seemed genuine. Her warm smile put Meeshell at ease. But it was a bit unnerving for Meeshell to think that one day Apple would be poisoned by an apple and lie in a coma, waiting for true love's kiss. The truth was, many of Ever After High's students, including Meeshell, had stories that would require sacrifice and courage.

"Welcome to the Castleteria!" Apple exclaimed, throwing her arms wide.

The Castleteria bustled with activity as hungry students hurried in from the assembly, eager to grab lunch. There was so much commotion, and so many people, Meeshell wished she were a hermit crab and could disappear into a shell. Some of the students cast curious glances at Meeshell's old dress. One student, a human-sized fairy with blond hair and iridescent wings, flew up to her and said with a sneer, "I didn't realize that today was Wear Your Grandmother's Old Dress Day." Then she flew off. Meeshell felt her cheeks go red for the second time that day.

"Don't mind her," Apple said. "Her name is Faybelle and she *never* says anything nice. Besides, wearing old clothing is called being retro and it's very in style right now."

Lots of students said hello to Apple, who in turn introduced Meeshell, but the names and faces came so quickly, Meeshell was certain she wouldn't remember a single one. Her gaze darted around the dining hall. Large trees grew along the walls, their branches reaching high above tables that were arranged in tidy rows. The kitchen area was its own vast room. Another tree grew in the center, copper pans hanging from its branches. Cauldrons bubbled on dragon-fire hearths and baskets overflowed with colorful vegetables and fruits. Students grabbed trays and lined up at a long counter to choose from a wide array of foods. Apple handed Meeshell a tray. Meeshell tried to forget the mean fairy's comment but as she looked around, it was quite obvious that her dress *wasn't* in fashion.

A hunchbacked woman stood behind the counter. She held a ladle that overflowed with something gray and gooey. A box labeled LUMPS sat at her elbow. Apple whispered in Meeshell's ear, "That's

porridge. Hagatha serves it all day long. Blondie Lockes likes it a lot but I suggest you avoid it. It's the worst." When they reached the woman, Apple introduced them. "Hagatha, this is our new student, Meeshell. Meeshell, Hagatha is our Castleteria cook."

"Got any food allergies?" Hagatha asked, wiping her hand on her greasy apron. Meeshell shook her head. "Got any special dietary needs?"

Meeshell hadn't noticed any sea-lettuce salads or barnacle stew in the food choices, but she didn't want to make special requests. She needed to eat the same things the other two-footed people ate. But there was one thing she couldn't stomach. "I don't eat fish."

Hagatha grunted. "I don't blame ya. Fish are slimy things. I don't eat them neither." *Slimy* wasn't a word Meeshell would use to describe the ocean's most beautiful creatures. Her eyes widened as Hagatha dumped a ladle of porridge into a bowl, then set the bowl onto Meeshell's tray. The porridge jiggled a bit, as if it were going to jump out of the bowl, but then it settled into a mound.

"This will make it taste better," Apple said as she grabbed a honey bear. The bear giggled as she picked it up and squeezed.

Because Meeshell was obviously overwhelmed and a bit confused, Apple helpfully selected a few more items for Meeshell's tray—a cucumber sandwich, a miniature thronecake, and a glass of fairyberry iced tea. Then she led her to a table. "Everyone, I want you to meet our newest student, Meeshell. She's a princess from the Kingdom by the Sea."

One by one she was introduced. "This is Ashlynn Ella, daughter of Cinderella. She works at the Glass Slipper, which is the best shoe store in all the kingdoms. And she speaks to animals, which comes in handy if you get stuck in a tower and you need a griffin to come and rescue you."

"Yes, Griffinglish is my favorite animal language,"

Ashlynn said. A delicate crown was nestled on her long, strawberry-blonde hair, which flowed over her shoulders.

The next girl had wavy, milk-chocolate-colored hair and a pair of crownglasses perched on her head. "This is Briar Beauty, daughter of Sleeping Beauty. She's the best party planner on campus, and even though she tends to fall asleep *a lot*, don't let that fool you. She's always up for a fun adventure."

Briar waved. "Welcome to—" Her words were interrupted by a huge yawn.

A shiver ran up Meeshell's spine. She was meeting the daughters of the best-known fairytale characters ever after! This was amazing.

"And this is Madeline Hatter, daughter of the Mad Hatter. We call her Maddie."

Meeshell paused. She didn't recognize the Hatter name. Must be from a story she'd never read. The girl was very colorful, with stripes and polka dots and swirls on her clothing. Her hair was equally

colorful, with stripes of turquoise, purple, and blue. An odd little teacup hat sat on her head.

Maddie grabbed Meeshell's hand and shook it quite vigorously. "Hello and good-bye. I like to say both those things because it saves time. When we save time in Wonderland, we put it into a jar so we can use it later." Her personality was as exuberant as her outfit. Meeshell liked her right away.

"It's nice to meet you," Meeshell said. There was so much noise in the Castleteria from all the chatter, she could barely hear her own voice.

"Uh, what was that?" Maddie asked.

Briar cleaned her crownglasses with a napkin. "I think she said it's nice to eat stew."

Maddie nodded. "Well, who can argue with that?"

Apple squeezed in next to Maddie. Ashlynn scooted down the bench to make room for Meeshell, who placed her tray on the table and sat.

Ashlynn glanced down and gasped. "Your feet," she said.

Meeshell bit her lower lip. Was it obvious that

her feet were brand-new? Or was something actually wrong with them, as she'd suspected.

But Ashlynn was smiling. "They're the prettiest feet I've ever seen. No wonder you don't wear any shoes."

"She lost her shoes on her journey here," Apple explained. "They were stolen by a giant squid."

"Awesome," Briar said. "I've always wanted to see one of those."

Apple stirred sugar into her tea. "I thought you could take her to the Glass Slipper and help her choose some new ones."

"I've got a better idea," Ashlynn said. "We'll use the new app and order a pair right now. What size do you wear?"

Size? Meeshell gulped. How could she possible know a thing like that? She must have looked very confused because Ashlynn smiled kindly.

"Oh, I get it. You probably always have your shoes ordered for you, so why would you know the size?"

"Uh, yes, that's it," Meeshell said.

Ashlynn placed her MirrorPad under Meeshell's feet to measure their size, then selected a few pairs to be delivered to her room. "Easy as pie."

"Hey, wanna see my tea-rriffic new talent show trick?" Maddie took off her hat and began to pull out a stack of teacups. The stack got taller and taller. How could all those cups fit inside that tiny hat?

"It's a magic hat," Apple explained. "She keeps *everything* in there."

Maddie held the wobbling stack of teacups, which now reached to the ceiling. "Look," she said proudly. "It's the Leaning Tower of Tea-sa!" Right when she said that, the tower collapsed, spilling tea all over the table. A giant puddle formed and began to move toward Meeshell. She dropped her porridge spoon, her eyes widening. If the puddle rolled off the edge, it would land in her lap. It would land on *her legs*! She shrieked, jumped to her feet, and stepped away.

Maddie frowned. "Well, that didn't go as planned, but you know what they say in Wonderland—there's no use crying over spilled tea when you can sing over it instead." As she started to hum a little song, a pair of cleaning fairies flew over and began mopping up the mess.

"You okay?" Apple asked Meeshell. "You look startled."

Meeshell checked her legs. They were perfectly dry. She let out a long, relieved breath. "I'm fine."

"You didn't get tea stains on your dress, did you?" Ashlynn asked.

"My favorite color is tea stain," Maddie said. "It's pretty *and* it's delicious at the same time."

"No, there aren't any stains," Meeshell replied. The fairies cleaned the bench, then flew away with their little mops.

"You sure you're okay?" Briar asked. The girls were all looking at her, probably wondering about her strange behavior. Who shrieks when tea is spilled? Was Meeshell already getting a reputation as an oddball?

"Are you afraid of tea?" Maddie asked.

"No, I'm...I'm not afraid of tea." Meeshell's heart beat quickly. That had been a very close call. Too close for comfort. And because she was quite flustered, she said the first thing that she could think of. "I'm...I'm afraid of water."

It was absurd, of course, to think that a mermaid could be afraid of water. But, for the first time in Meeshell's life, there was some truth to this statement, because the spell that had given Meeshell the ability to walk on two legs had a flaw.

And it was all because of Coral, the Sea Witch's daughter.

Coral's

Spell

Three Days Ago

They met at dawn on the shore of Turtle Island. The turtles were a bit annoyed by the interruption. They narrowed their bulbous eyes and munched on sea grass while the Merpeople gathered at the water's edge.

Meeshell hadn't slept a wink. How could she? So much was about to happen. Not only was she going to leave her family and travel to a new world, but she was going to change the shape of her body!

The Sea Witch parked her rather large self onto a boulder. Then she sipped a cup of briny brew. She looked as if she'd come to watch a special show. "Coral, are you ready?"

"Hold on a minute," King Philip said. "I still have some concerns about your daughter casting the spell. She's very young, after all. Can you guarantee that nothing will go wrong?".

The Sea Witch took another sip, then cackled. "Philip, my dear, you know there are no guarantees where magic is concerned." She reached into the water, pulled out a wiggling eel, and ate it whole. Then she dabbed at the corners of her mouth with a piece of kelp. "But Coral is my daughter, which means she's extremely talented and intelligent, just like me." She paused, as if waiting for Meeshell and her parents to confirm what she'd said. But they said nothing. She glowered and the air around her turned stormy. But her anger faded quickly and she took another sip. "Anyhoo, as I was saying, Coral is

perfectly capable of changing a tail into legs, aren't you, darling?"

Meeshell and her parents looked at Coral, who thus far had said nothing. She swam next to the boulder, chewing nervously on her lower lip. She was so different from her mother, quiet and with delicate features. Was she Sea Witch material? "Well, actually, I've only practiced the spell on eels—you know, since they don't have legs—and it did work but then…" She held up an eel, who glanced worriedly at the Sea Witch. "But then the legs fell off after a day."

"Fell off?" Meeshell cried, her hand flying to her mouth.

"That's alarming," Queen Pearl said.

"Oh, it's really not that bad. The eel hated having those legs." Coral let the eel go and it swam into the depths before the Sea Witch could eat it.

"I can't have legs that fall off," Meeshell said. "Dad, do something."

"Why are you asking your daddy to do some-thing?" the Sea Witch said snippily. "He has no magic. We're the witches. Talk to *us*."

Meeshell swam closer to the Sea Witch than she'd ever been—so close that she could see the bar-nacles that grew on the witch's earlobes. She felt so nervous, her tail trembled. But she knew that the Sea Witch had as much to lose as she did. "It's in both our best interests that this spell work," Meeshell reminded her. "If you believe that Coral can do it, then I shall also believe. Because if this doesn't work, and I'm a failure on land, then you will never have my voice."

The water around the Sea Witch grew stormy again, and she rose onto her tail so she towered over Meeshell and her parents. "I *will* have your voice!" Her face turned as red as her tail. Even Coral swam backward, to keep clear of her mother's wrath.

While the Sea Witch was having a temper tan-trum, Coral glided up to Meeshell and said, her voice lowered, "Mom's making me do this. Just wanted you to know, in case things go wrong."

"Got it," Meeshell said. She didn't add that her mom and dad were also making her do something she didn't want to do. Why couldn't Ever After High wait for another year? There were so many fun things going on in the Merkingdom. She'd miss the next manta ray races. And her friends were planning on surfing the outer reef next week.

"Let's do this!" the Sea Witch hollered. She settled back on her boulder.

Meeshell kissed her mom and dad, trying very hard to hold back tears. They said all sorts of comforting things to her. They'd send letters. They'd send care packages. She'd have fun. She'd be home at the end of the quarter for a visit. But none of those things made Meeshell feel better. Choking back a sob, she swam into the shallows, until she was sitting in the sand. A pair of turtles waddled away, leaving a little trail of footprints.

"Go on, Coral, cast the spell. You know it by heart." The Sea Witch waved her daughter forward.

Coral, looking as if she was about to face a great white shark, slowly swam into the shallows next to Meeshell. She lifted her hands into the air. One hand held a slender wand, made from carved abalone shell. Meeshell couldn't help but notice that the hand was trembling. As Coral spoke the words that would change Meeshell's life, everyone and everything held perfectly still and in absolute silence. Even the waves halted their course.

"Through the power vested in me,
By the wild magic sea,
Two legged shall she be."

Meeshell looked at her beautiful tail, with its blue shimmering scales. She wanted to squeeze her eyes closed, just in case something terrible happened. But she mustered her courage. Right before her eyes, her beloved tail faded away, and when she reached out, she found not the familiar texture of scales, but something soft and smooth.

It was a leg. And right beside it was another leg. Two legs! Meeshell kicked, as she would with her tail, and the legs flopped awkwardly.

"Marvelous!" the Sea Witch cried. She began to applaud. "Well done, my dear!"

Coral smiled, just as surprised as everyone else that her spell had worked.

It took a long time for Meeshell to get to her feet, and then to keep her balance. Luckily, the sand was a soft place to fall. By the time she'd mastered walking a few steps, a ship appeared in the distance. The *Narwhal* had come to take her to Ever After High.

It had already been decided that Meeshell would hide her identity, so there were quick kisses goodbye, and words of comfort. King Philip and Queen Pearl disappeared beneath the water, as did Coral and the Sea Witch. Meeshell made her way onto the dock, her bag in hand, watching as the ship drew closer and closer.

"Oh, I forgot to tell you something." Coral popped out of the water, then floated next to the dock.

"What?" Meeshell asked.

"There's a little thing you should know about the spell."

Meeshell's entire body stiffened. "A little thing?"

"You're really lucky that you get to go to Ever After High. I hope I can go there one day. Do you think you'll meet your prince?"

"My prince?"

"The one in your story. The only one you'll give up your voice for and live with happily ever after."

Oh, *that* prince. With all the emotional upheaval of the last twenty-four hours, Meeshell hadn't thought about her future prince. He was supposed to be a land-dweller, so it was possible that he went to Ever After High.

"I don't know if I'll meet him," Meeshell said. "But, Coral, what is the little thing you forgot to tell me?"

"Oh right." She reached out of the water and pointed at Meeshell's legs. "You can't get them wet or they'll turn back into a tail. But then once the tail dries, it'll turn back into legs. See ya." And then she disappeared.

That was not a *little thing*.

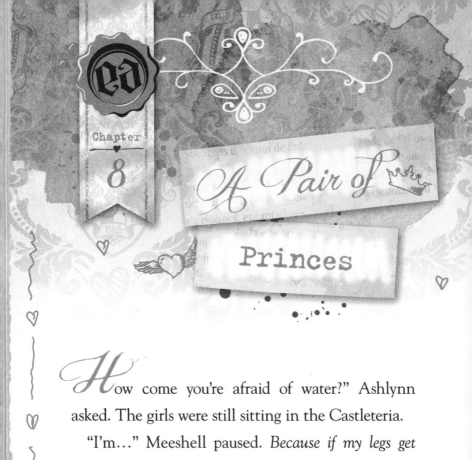

A Pair of Princes

"How come you're afraid of water?" Ashlynn asked. The girls were still sitting in the Castleteria.

"I'm…" Meeshell paused. *Because if my legs get wet, then they will turn back into my tail and you'll all know the truth about me.* "I'm not sure. I just am."

"Well, we all have our fears, don't we?" Apple said in an understanding way. "Actually, I've never told anyone this, but I used to be afraid of apples. When I was little, of course. Because I didn't realize that only one of them would be poisoned."

"I don't like storms," Ashlynn said. "They upset the birds, you know."

"I got bit by my horse when I was little," Briar said. "I didn't ride for three years after that."

"I prefer to be afraid of things on Fridays," Maddie said, as if this were perfectly normal. She reached into her teacup hat and pulled out a platter of tea cakes. "Oh, I almost forgot. Dad sent these over from the shoppe."

The girls each ate a tea cake. While Meeshell hadn't enjoyed the porridge, she added tea cakes to her mental list of delicious new foods. Ashlynn and Maddie hurried off to class, and just as Meeshell finished her last sip of tea, Apple said, "Oh look, here comes Daring."

Meeshell recognized the handsome prince immediately, having seen his face plastered all over the bookstore merchandise. But the surprise was that he was even better looking in person. That regal nose, that chiseled jaw, those dreamy eyes! Meeshell's heart skipped a beat.

"Hello, ladies." He swept a plate aside and sat on the corner of the table. And then he smiled. Briar Beauty quickly slid her crownglasses into place, then threw her hands over Meeshell's eyes.

"You can't look directly at him when he does that," she informed her. "His smile is so bright that if you look at his teeth, you'll see spots for days."

Good to know.

As soon as the light faded, Briar removed her hands. Meeshell stole a shy glance, then quickly looked away as her heart skipped another beat.

Apple made the introductions. "Meeshell, this is Daring Charming. Daring, this is our newest student, Meeshell. She comes from the Kingdom by the Sea."

"H-h-hello," Meeshell stammered.

Daring pushed his thick blond hair off his forehead. "No need to say it. I know you're enchanted to make my acquaintance." He whipped out a photo from his pocket and handed it to her. "It's already signed."

She looked at the photo.

It was inscribed:

To my loyal fan, from the prince you adore,
Daring Charming. xoxo

"You're welcome," he said.

Seriously? Meeshell's heart stopped skipping beats. Yes, he was eye candy, but he was way too full of himself. She knew boys exactly like him back home. He was definitely not her type. She politely tucked the picture into her book bag. He took a long look in a nearby mirror, then strode away. Briar slid her crownglasses back onto her forehead. "You'll get used to him," she said.

Apple neatly folded her paper tea cake holder and set it aside. "Daring might spend a lot of time talking about himself, but he kind of can't help it. I mean, he's spent his whole life knowing that he's destined to become Prince Charming. That can give a guy a healthy ego!"

Meeshell watched as Daring sauntered from the Castleteria, catching eager glances from girls along the way. He stopped two more times to check his reflection. She remembered Coral's question. Would she meet her future prince at Ever After High? If so, she hoped they wouldn't all be like Daring. She had no idea how to relate to a guy like that. She wanted someone who didn't care so much about how he looked. Someone who liked to talk about interesting things.

Someone smart.

Apple waved. "Hey, Humphrey, can you come

over here for a moment? I'd like you to meet our new student."

Another boy walked toward the table. From first glance, the only thing he had in common with Daring Charming, physically, was that a crown sat on his head. He was of average height and average build. He wore a button-down shirt, suspenders, and bow tie. He didn't walk as if he owned the world. Rather, he seemed hesitant to approach the table. No girls sighed as he passed by.

"Humphrey, this is Meeshell. She's a new student and she's not familiar with MirrorPads so she's going to need your help signing into the network, etcetera." She turned to Meeshell. "Humphrey Dumpty is the president of the Tech Club, so any tech troubles you have, he'll know how to solve them."

"Uh, hi," Humphrey said. He made eye contact for only a moment, which was fine with Meeshell because she was starting to feel overwhelmed by all the introductions. He shuffled in place. "So, yeah, uh, I'm always happy to help. But right now I have a Tech Club meeting. Can I help you later?"

"Sure," Meeshell said.

"Okay." He fiddled with a collection of pens and pencils that were crammed into his shirt pocket. "I'll see you later." Then he hurried away, but just before he reached the exit, his foot met a chair leg and he stumbled forward. *"Ahhh!"* he cried, his arms reaching to break his fall. As he tumbled onto the floor, the few students who were still lingering in the Castleteria gasped with alarm. Meeshell stared at Humphrey, who was now sprawled, facedown, on the Castleteria floor. But before anyone could move to help him, he scrambled back to his feet. "I'm fine, I'm fine," he said, brushing off some toast crumbs. Then he used both hands to feel all over his head. "Yeah, I'm definitely fine. No cracks. It's all good." He cast an embarrassed glance at Meeshell, then exited.

Oh, he was from *that* Dumpty family.

Thus far, Meeshell had met two very different princes. She hoped that somewhere in between the overly confident hero who handed out signed pictures of himself and the shy, clumsy guy who'd barely spoken to her, there'd be a normal prince for her.

The next thing on the Welcoming Committee to-do list was: *Check New Student into a Dormitory Room.*

The girls' dormitory and the boys' dormitory were separated by a large Common Room, where the students spent lots of time socializing, doing throne-work, and sometimes just relaxing in front of the river-rock fireplace. Getting to the dorm room required climbing more staircases. Meeshell's legs began to ache. She felt envious of the fairy students,

who zipped past, their wings leaving cool breezes in their wake. "I know," Apple said, as if reading her mind. "If only we had wings."

They stopped at room 12C. The sign on the door read:

FARRAH GOODFAIRY AND MEESHELL

The words twinkled. Apple knocked gently. The door flew open and a girl with blue hair and large blue eyes stood before them. "You must be Meeshell," she said with a big, welcoming hug. "I'm so happy to finally get a roommate. Come on in." When she flew around, Meeshell realized that her roommate was a fairy. How hexciting!

The room was a good size, with two canopied beds, two desks, two dressers, and two closets. This fairy clearly had a favorite color because the bedspreads, pillows, overstuffed chairs, and paint were all variations of blue. "These boxes arrived for you from the Glass Slipper." Three shoe boxes sat on Meeshell's bed. She set her MirrorPad and book bag next to them. "Where are the rest of your things?" Farrah asked.

"Yes, I was wondering the same thing," Apple said. "Why haven't the trolls delivered your luggage? I could call my dwarf network. They do a great job with deliveries."

"This is all I have for now. My mom ordered some new clothes for me, but I guess they haven't arrived," Meeshell explained.

"Oh, that's no problem. Farrah happens to be a future fairy godmother, so I'm sure she can help you if you need an outfit."

"Yes, of course. What do you need? How about a jacket?"

She grabbed a silver wand from her vanity and waved it through the air. A little trail of sparkles appeared. Suddenly, Meeshell was wearing a cropped jacket that perfectly matched her dress.

"Thank you," Meeshell said gratefully.

"Just so you know, my spells don't last very long. That jacket will disappear at midnight."

It would seem that Farrah, a future fairy godmother, and Coral, a future sea witch, had something in common—their spells had glitches.

Meeshell opened the shoe boxes. Then she sat on the bed and began trying them on.

Farrah pulled Apple aside. Even though Farrah had lowered her voice to a whisper, Meeshell could still hear the muffled conversation. "How come she speaks so quietly? Is she shy?" Farrah asked Apple.

"Well, she does have a sore throat. But yes, she's very shy. I bet she's homesick, too. I think it might take a while for her to feel comfortable with us."

"Oh, I remember feeling that way when school started."

"Me too. But I'm her Welcoming Committee representative, so I'll do everything I can to help her settle in."

89

"Hi!" three voices called.

Ashlynn, Briar, and Maddie all walked into the dorm room. "Oh look, the shoes arrived. Those are adorable." Ashlynn pointed to the pink sneakers that Meeshell had on her feet. These were the ones she found the most comfortable. Ashlynn held a vase, with a strange-looking flower. "We thought maybe we got off on the wrong slipper so we brought you this flower for your dorm."

"It's a snapdragon," Briar said.

Meeshell had never seen a snapdragon before— they didn't grow under the sea. The flower was pretty, with large petals that folded over one another. But when Meeshell leaned forward to smell the flower, the petals unfurled and a cute little dragon face appeared. It opened its mouth and roared at her! Ashlynn laughed as the vase shook in her hands, spilling some water.

Meeshell jumped away. Luckily, the water missed her, landing on the floor instead.

"Oops," Ashlynn said. "Sorry about that." The

little dragon flower began to snap its mouth at her. "I'll just put it over here." Ashlynn set the flower next to Meeshell's bed.

Meeshell wondered if the little dragon would move around during the night. What if it splashed water on her while she was sleeping and her tail came out for her roommate to see? "Is it…safe?" she asked nervously.

"Oh, never mind, you don't have to keep it," Ashlynn said quickly, picking the flower up. "I didn't know you were afraid of snapdragons! Or is it the water? Are you afraid of flower water, too?"

I'm not really afraid of cute little flowers…or water! she wanted to explain. *I just can't get my legs wet.* The girls were looking at her, waiting for her to say something.

Apple sensed her discomfort and jumped in to try to help her new friend. "You don't have to explain." She grabbed a towel from the bathroom and mopped up the spill. Then she began to usher everyone from the room. "I think we should give Meeshell some

time to herself. It's been a long day, and she's probably tired." She motioned to Farrah, who followed her into the hallway. Then Apple poked her head back into the room. "We'll let you rest. And I'm going to get you some lozenges for your throat. See you soon." And with that, she gently closed the door. Meeshell overheard their conversation as they walked away.

"I don't think I've ever met someone so shy before," Briar said.

Then Maddie said, "I'm pretty sure it's my hat. She doesn't like my hat."

Their voices faded, leaving Meeshell alone for the first time since arriving.

It was a relief to be alone. She sank onto the bed and let the soft pillow cradle her head.

So many feelings swirled inside her. Everyone had been so nice, and they clearly thought she was a two-footed land-dweller, just like them. But now they thought she had some kind of phobia of water—*all* water. What if she got thirsty and needed

a drink? What would she do? How silly it was—a mermaid pretending to be afraid of water.

She rose from the bed, then walked onto the balcony, looking out over the campus. Students mingled in the quad. Swans swam around the unicorn fountain. A forest spread to the south and the sea spread to the east. There was no sign of the *Narwhal*. How she longed to be back on that ship, heading home. Back to the watery world she loved. Back to her family and friends.

Back to her beloved tail.

A chime sounded somewhere nearby, pulling Meeshell from her musings. She turned and walked back into the dorm room. The chime sounded again. Was it coming from the MirrorPad? She picked it up. The screen lit up.

Welcome to the Ever After High Mirror Network. You have a message from StoryTeller2. To respond to your message, please set up your Mirror Network chat room account.

A keypad appeared, asking her to fill in her code name for access to the chat room. She sat on the bed and thought a moment. What type of code name should she choose? The answer came quickly. She typed **Seashell**.

Welcome to the Mirror Network chat room.
New message from StoryTeller2.
StoryTeller2: Hi.

Because they didn't have MirrorPads in her kingdom, using her fingers to type was as difficult as using her feet to walk, so it took a while to get the hang of it. But soon she mastered the two-finger method.

Seashell: Hi.
StoryTeller2: How are you doing?
Seashell: Fine. Who is this?
StoryTeller2: I'm a student. I know what it's like to be the new kid. It's overwhelming at

first. If you have any questions about school,
I'm happy to answer.
Seashell: Thanks.

There was a long pause. Meeshell wasn't sure what to do. Was it rude if she didn't ask questions? How did this work?

StoryTeller2: Okay, well, I'm here if you need me. Bye.
Seashell: Bye.

The screen went dark. She sat back against the headboard. What an odd way to talk to someone. She didn't know who StoryTeller2 was, but he or she seemed very nice. And apparently, he or she knew her. Had they already met?

The sound of beating wings drew Meeshell's attention to the open balcony door. Four tiny fairies flew into the room, leaving trails of sparkles in the air. They carried an enormous package, which they

dropped onto the bed. The label read: *From Fashionably Ever After...For Meeshell.*

"Thank you," Meeshell told the little creatures, amazed they could carry such weight. They all zipped away.

She eagerly untied the twine and opened the package. A note inside read:

> Dear Meeshell,
>
> I loved Fashionably Ever After when I lived on land. They always provided me with the loveliest outfits. Hope you enjoy these.
>
> Hugs and kisses,
> Mom

Meeshell opened the box. It was stuffed with clothing—dresses, pants, tops, pajamas, and a swimsuit. Well, the swimsuit wouldn't be needed, since she couldn't get her legs wet. She set that into a drawer, along with the pants and shirts. She hung the dresses in her closet. Then she opened her bag and took out her precious belongings—a brush and comb, seashell clips for her hair, a princess mermaid arm bracelet, her pearl headband, and her favorite pink coral necklace.

"Oh, that's gorgeous!" Apple said when she returned with lozenges. She was referring to an asymmetrical dress with lightweight ruffles, which looked, to Meeshell, like waves. The dress had a coral top with scalloped fish-skin texture. "And this is adorable!" Apple pulled a teal sea-horse-shaped purse from the Fashionably Ever After box. Then she smiled. "It's kinda funny that you're afraid of water but you have a total sea theme going here with your clothes."

"Yeah, that is funny," Meeshell said sheepishly.

"I hope these work." Apple gave Meeshell the box of pickled pepper throat lozenges.

"Thanks. Me too." While her feet were content in their new sneakers, her throat was feeling more ragged than ever. She didn't want to think about what would happen if her voice didn't recover. She popped one of the lozenges into her mouth. Then, for good measure, added another. She nearly gagged. They tasted disgusting!

"I know you're feeling a bit overwhelmed," Apple said, "but tomorrow will be great. It's Club Day. That means you can walk around and check out all the clubs until you find one or two to join. Or three. There's no limit. One quarter, I joined twenty-two clubs. Was I ever busy! But you do whatever works for you. And I'll be there so you don't have to worry about getting lost. It will be spelltacular."

Meeshell hoped so.

Becoming a land-dweller was her destiny and she wanted to make the best of it. She hoped the lozenges would work. Because it didn't matter if she had no shoes, or if she wore the same yellow dress for the rest of her life. What mattered was her voice.

It needed to heal because it was the key to her future.

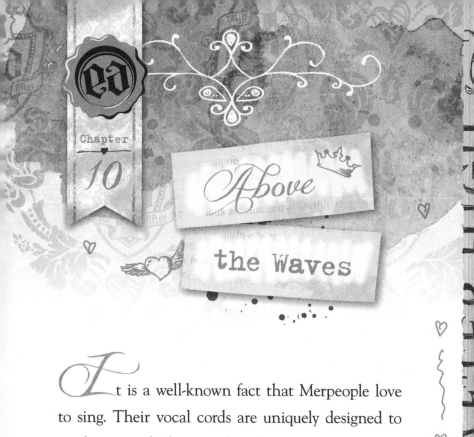

Chapter

10

Above

the Waves

It is a well-known fact that Merpeople love to sing. Their vocal cords are uniquely designed to produce sounds that travel underwater.

In Meeshell's kingdom, Merchoirs existed for every age group, and while not everyone joined, everyone could sing. And sing well. So while under the water, Meeshell's voice sounded similar to the other mermaid voices—perfectly in tune and fluid like the water itself. And like her friends, she mastered many sea-creature languages, which required a

variety of sounds that human vocal cords cannot produce. So even though she was a princess, when Meeshell sang in the kelp grotto with her friends, she was simply a member of a choir, equal in tonality and harmony.

However, when Meeshell surfaced, which Merpeople often do, her voice changed in a unique way. It sounded...*human.* According to the Sea Witch, an avid collector of voices, Meeshell's above-water voice was magnificent. Breathtaking. The most beautiful voice the Sea Witch had ever heard. It was something to be coveted.

But none of the other Merpeople seemed impressed with this discovery. It was tradition to sing underwater, and that is where they made most of their music. So the fact that Meeshell sounded human above the water did not cause a commotion. Except with the Sea Witch.

"Why does your mom collect voices?" Meeshell asked Coral one day. Coral often swam behind

Meeshell and her friends, never joining in, but always there, watching.

"She hates her own voice," Coral said. There was good reason. The Sea Witch, who was only part mermaid, had a voice dark as a storm and prickly as a sea urchin. "So she likes to try on other voices, like trying on a new hat. Your mom's was once her favorite."

The Sea Witch had possessed Queen Pearl's voice, but only for a short time. That changed when the story went in another direction and Prince Philip fell in love with his Little Mermaid and agreed to live below the waves with her.

"True love always breaks spells," Coral said. She looked slyly at Meeshell. "Do you know why my mom wants *your* voice?"

"She likes the way it sounds," Meeshell said simply. Everyone knew that.

"Yes, but that's not the only reason." Coral swam a little closer. "Mom told me that she's sick of being the Sea Witch. She wants to become a famous singer and travel the world. She thinks your voice will make that happen for her."

"Really?" Meeshell tried to imagine the Sea Witch living on land, traveling from town to town, putting on concerts. Would someone have to push her around in a tank of water? Or would she be able to magic herself a pair of legs?

Coral and Meeshell swam under a coral arch. "My only regret about being half Sea Witch is that I inherited my mom's bad voice."

"No, you didn't," Meeshell said honestly. "Your voice is nice."

Coral laughed. "Nice? Have you ever heard me sing?" Meeshell shook her head. Come to think of it, Coral had never participated in any of the choirs. "I'm terrible. The worst!"

"You can't be that bad," Meeshell said.

"You wanna bet?"

They swam to the surface. It was a calm afternoon. The water was as smooth as glass. Coral swam to a reef and sat on a rock. She opened her mouth and…

That wasn't singing!

Meeshell's fingers flew to her ears. The sounds coming from Coral's mouth were unlike anything Meeshell had ever heard. The noise started out screechier than a gull, then dipped deeper than a seal's bark. "Okay, okay," Meeshell said. "Stop. Please stop."

Coral closed her mouth. Then she laughed. "I told you so."

Meeshell climbed onto the rock next to her. "Do you think your mom might give my voice to you instead?" Meeshell brightened at that idea. To give up her voice was a sacrifice she'd been born to make, but to give it to the nasty Sea Witch had always seemed unfair. Giving it to Coral, a nice girl who'd never done anything mean to anyone in the ocean, seemed much more palatable.

"That's a nice idea, but Mom definitely wants your voice for herself. Besides, I don't care about

singing. It's totally not my thing." She dipped her hand into the water and scooped out a little fish. Meeshell cringed, wondering if Coral would eat the fish whole, just like the Sea Witch always did. But Coral got a dreamy look on her face, then released the little creature. "If Mom becomes a famous singer and leaves the ocean, that means that I'll take her place as the Sea Witch, and you know what I'm going to do with all that power?"

"What?"

Coral sighed, her shoulders slumped. "Drat. I thought you'd have a good suggestion. I'm not really sure what I want to do."

"That's okay," Meeshell said. "We have a long time before we have to make those big decisions about our lives."

As they sat on the rock, looking out over the water, both girls knew that destiny was at work. Coral's magic would get stronger. And Meeshell's voice would not always belong to her.

chime sounded. Meeshell opened her eyes and rolled over in bed. It took her a moment to remember where she was. Then the chime sounded again. The noise was coming from her MirrorPad. She reached out, grabbed it, and read the screen.

Good morning. Time to get up.

Apple had set the alarm for her. How odd to wake up in a bed that was surrounded by air. And stranger still, to be covered in so many blankets. Usually, the first thing she did after waking was to feed Finbert. Then she would swim into the dining room to have breakfast with her parents. But she had no idea how her mornings would go at Ever After High.

She sat up. A note lay on her bedside table. It was from Farrah. *I had to leave hextra early this morning to help set up the Fairy Club booth. See you later.* Meeshell was surprised she hadn't heard Farrah getting ready. She must have slept like a sea log, as her mom would say. She stretched out her arms and yawned. Then she stretched her tail, but when two feet popped out the end of the blanket she nearly shrieked. She pulled back the covers.

Right. She'd momentarily forgotten about those two things.

Her MirrorPad chimed again.

New Message from StoryTeller2.

StoryTeller2: Good morning.

Seashell: Hi.

StoryTeller2: Did you know that today is Club Day?

Seashell: Yes. I'm supposed to find a club to join.

StoryTeller2: I hope you find something that you really like.

Oh, *how nice*, she thought.

Seashell: Will you be there?

StoryTeller2: Yes. Oops, I mean, maybe.

Seashell: Since you know who I am, will you introduce yourself to me?

Super-long pause.

StoryTeller2: I gotta go. Good luck today.

Meeshell frowned. It was so odd not to know who was on the other side of the conversation. Was this normal on land? Did people often hide their identities and talk to one another?

A knock sounded on the door. "It's just me," a familiar voice called. Apple entered the room, as cheerful as ever. She wore a lovely red dress. A pair of bluebirds was tying a ribbon in her hair. "How's your voice?" she asked.

Meeshell hadn't spoken a word since waking, so she didn't know the answer. And she was a bit afraid to find out—partly because of what it might mean to her story, but also because she didn't want to eat any more of those horrid pickled pepper lozenges. She put a hand protectively to her throat. "I...I'm not sure." Then she smiled. Her voice sounded quite normal. What a relief! "I guess it's better."

"It sounds spelltacular! Those lozenges must have done the trick."

Perhaps it had been the lozenges, or, as Professor Yaga had said, maybe her vocal cords had needed time to get used to being in the air 24/7. While Apple waited, Meeshell went into the bathroom and changed into one of her new outfits that her mom had sent. When she emerged, Apple laughed, but not in a mean way. "How come you're wearing pajamas?"

Meeshell looked down at the pants and top, both made from soft cotton and covered with little sea horse designs. She tried to play it cool. "Uh, well, we sometimes wear pajamas back home. Don't you do that here?"

"Only on Pajama Day." Apple sat on Meeshell's bed. The bluebirds had flown away, but a pair of yellow songbirds was running a comb through Apple's hair. "But today isn't Pajama Day. It's Club Day. All the clubs on campus will have booths set up in the quad and they'll be looking for new members. This is the perfect opportunity for you to find the perfect club. Or two. Or three. Go ahead and change, and I'll go with you."

Meeshell appreciated how patient Apple was being with her, but she didn't want to take advantage of her kindness. "Oh, you don't have to keep being my Welcoming Committee. You must have more important things to do."

Apple laughed again. "Nothing is more important than doing my duty. And right now, that is to find you a club." She held up her Welcoming Committee list. "It's the last thing on the list."

"Oh, okay. Thanks."

Meeshell picked another outfit from her closet. This dress was similar to the one she'd worn the day before, with a scalloped texture and with ruffles along the hem that looked like waves. She held it up, and received an approving nod from Apple. Then she went back into the bathroom. She stood in front of the mirror, staring at her reflection, but not in the way that Daring admired his. Rather, she felt as if she was looking at a stranger. *Who are you?* she asked herself. Who is this land-dweller, standing in a dorm room, with two feet, attending the most prestigious school in all the kingdoms? Her parents were expecting her to do her best, which meant getting good grades and making new friends. And if that wasn't enough to cause one's scales to tremble, she'd be trying to get those grades and friends while hiding her true identity as a mermaid. How would she pull this off? She leaned against the wall, her chest tight, her breathing quick. Suddenly, she felt as if she'd been tangled in a fisherman's net!

"Meeshell? You okay?" Apple asked gently from the other side of the door.

"Yes. I'm almost ready." Meeshell told herself to snap out of it. The good news was that her speaking voice was back to normal. Did that mean her singing voice was back, too? She'd have to find a safe, private place to give it a try. In the meantime, she should stop worrying so much and brave the day. It was all going to work out. She was going to live her destiny!

After dressing, Meeshell arranged her pearl headband and chose a lovely statement necklace that sparkled with shells and coral. Then she grabbed her MirrorPad and sea horse purse, and followed Apple.

Walking down one flight of stairs, then another and another, was much easier than it had been yesterday, which was a very good sign that she was getting used to her legs. And when she and Apple stepped into the quad, they were greeted by a chorus of "hellos," which was a very good sign that the other students were getting used to Meeshell. Apple stopped at a coffee cart and got them each a mocha frappé, which Meeshell loved. "Can I have one of these every morning?"

"Sure, if you want. The cart is from the Hocus Latte Café in the village. You can get all sorts of drinks there, too."

The world was full of so many new flavors. As she sipped the chocolaty goodness, birds sang in the branches above. A dragon glided over distant tree-tops. A boy and that rabbit she'd seen with the glasses walked past, both their noses stuck in books. The boy was quite handsome, and wearing a crown. Then she saw two more boys with crowns. Wow, there sure were a lot of princes at this school.

Was one of them destined to be part of her story? Maybe the one who was currently staring at her?

"Whassup, ladies?" he called. He had piercing green eyes and freckles. He was dressed in khaki shorts, a velvet jacket, and bow tie.

Apple, once again, made the introductions. "Meeshell, this is Hopper Croakington II. Hopper, this is our newest student, Meeshell."

Hopper wagged his eyebrows at her. "Well, hello. You can be *me* shell anytime." Meeshell wasn't sure what that meant but she smiled politely. Was he trying to flirt with her? He leaned against a tree. "What brings you to—?" He turned suddenly. "Briar," he whispered. Briar Beauty was walking across the quad. She waved at Apple and Meeshell, and at Hopper. A blush spread across his face and…

Poof!

Meeshell looked down at the ground. Where Hopper had once stood, there was now a green frog. The frog adjusted his little gold crown, looked up at her, and said, "Delighted to make your acquaintance. If you ever find yourself in need of companionship, I am a skilled conversationalist. Good day." He bowed, then hurried away on his little bowlegged green legs.

How odd. Meeshell was about to ask Apple what was up with this Hopper guy, when she saw another boy with a crown. She'd met him yesterday in the Castleteria. What was his name? Oh yes, Humphrey.

He was carrying a stack of MirrorPads. He noticed her looking at him and stopped walking. His face turned red. He fiddled with his bow tie, waved, then backed into a hedge, landing on his rump. "I'm okay," he called as he jumped to his feet. He collected all the MirrorPads. "Nothing cracked!" Then he hurried away.

She hadn't meant to stare at him. Poor guy. Was it possible that he and Meeshell were equally shy? And equally awkward?

The far side of the quad was crowded with white tents. A sign was posted on each tent:

PEGASUS-RIDING CLUB

WAND-MAKING CLUB

FAIRY CLUB

Representatives for each club sat at tables that were piled with informational brochures. Apple and Meeshell walked between the tents, with Apple stopping to give Meeshell a brief description of each club. "And that's the Oversleepers Anonymous Club." Briar sat inside that tent, her chin resting in her hands.

"There's no shame in being sleepy," Briar called out. "Join today and get a free pair of wide-awake glasses so you can fall asleep in class without being caught." The glasses were lined up on the table. Each had a pair of eyes painted on the front— wide-awake eyes that blinked occasionally.

Farrah was tending to the Fairy Club booth, which was covered in so much fairy dust, passersby started sneezing.

Ashlynn and Maddie walked up. "Hi, Meeshell," they both said.

"Hi."

"Hey, you're not whispering anymore," Ashlynn noted with a smile.

"My sore throat is gone."

"I'm helping Meeshell pick a club to join," Apple explained. "Do you have any suggestions?"

"I'm in the Forest Club," Ashlynn said. "We sweep the forest floor to keep it nice and tidy. If you joined, we could sweep together."

"I'm in the Wonderland Club," Maddie said. "It's supposed to be for people from Wonderland. But most people get to Wonderland by mistake, so it doesn't seem fair to say just because you haven't fallen down a rabbit hole, you can't join. So we let anyone join. Do you speak Riddlish? That helps. It's our club's language."

"I really like the Library Club," Apple said. "We don't do much, just study together. It really helps me keep my grades up. Oh, and you could always join Daring's fan club." They'd stopped at the Daring Charming Fan Club tent. Five girls and one guy sat at a table covered in Daring Charming memorabilia. And right next to it was the Tech Club. Humphrey sat at a table covered in all sorts of gadgets. He looked away when Meeshell looked at him. *Yep*, she thought. *Painfully shy.* She wondered if there was a Shy Club they could both join.

None of the suggested clubs sounded like the right fit to Meeshell. She was about to move to the next tent when a mirror on a nearby tree lit up. A girl with blond curls appeared in the mirror. Her curls bobbed as she talked. "Hello, fellow fairytales! Blondie Lockes here to give you the latest scoop. I'm happy to announce that we have a new student. She arrived by boat yesterday, from the faraway Kingdom by the Sea. Her name is Meeshell and she's rooming with Farrah Goodfairy, and from what

I've heard, they are getting along swimmingly. So please give her a big Ever After High welcome." All the students who were hanging out in the quad turned toward Meeshell and clapped. Meeshell wasn't sure what to do. She gave a little wave, then tried to disappear in the shadows beneath one of the tents. Blondie whispered to someone offscreen, then looked back into the camera. "In other news, it's just been confirmed that our very own glee club, the Happily-Glees, are going to give an impromptu performance in the quad right now. They will be performing a brand-new song directed by our very own Melody Piper."

A glee club? Meeshell stepped out from the shadows. Maybe this could be the club she joined.

Six singers gathered beneath an oak tree. A girl with a pair of headphones stood before them. "That's Melody," Apple whispered in Meeshell's ear. Melody clearly loved music because she was adorned with musical notes—on her leather vest, her silver tights, and on her black leather booties. She took a pitch pipe from her pocket and blew a single note. Each of the singers hummed, trying to match the note. Melody shook her head, then blew on the pipe again. The singers hummed again. Melody's shoulders slumped. No one had found the note. Meeshell frowned. That wasn't a good sign.

Melody raised her hands and the Happily-Glees began to sing.

"Looking for my ever after
Don't wanna see my dreams get
* shattered*
Everybody says I have to, got to,
Wait around just to be rescued.
Not gonna sit alone in a tower.
I'll show the world my princess power.
I'm standing up 'cause I am stronger.
Listen to my heart; it's getting louder."

It was…terrible. Not the song—the song itself was great. The lyrics were brilliant. But the singing

was…well, it was like listening to a pod of elephant seals. Okay, maybe not *that* bad, but Meeshell was used to Mer-singing, the most beautiful singing in all the kingdoms. She winced, then tried to force a smile. Perhaps she was being overly critical. Perhaps this was considered good singing in the land-dwelling world. She glanced at Apple. The fairest-in-the-land princess was also trying very hard not to wince, but a tiny scowl had formed between her eyebrows. So it was true—they *were* terrible.

One of the singers was clearly off-key, while another singer was way too loud. The harmony wasn't working, and the choreography, well, it was just a mess.

When the song finished, everyone smiled and politely applauded, then went on about their business. The singers ambled off and Melody lingered, her expression one of frustration. Apple tried to console her. "That was really…interesting," Apple said.

"It's not supposed to sound like that," Melody explained. "There were a lot of wrong notes."

Maddie giggled. "I thought it was tea-rriffic. In Wonderland, the wrong notes are always the right notes."

Melody sighed. "We really need more practice time. And we could really use new members."

Apple's eyes lit up. "Hey, Meeshell is looking for a club to join."

Melody looked hopefully at Meeshell. "Do you sing?" she asked.

Meeshell wanted to shout *Yes! Yes, I sing! I love singing.* But now that she'd heard these singers, she realized that if she sang with them, her voice would totally stand out. If she joined the Happily-Glees, surely someone would figure out her true identity, for her voice was even more famous than her tail. She sighed with disappointment. This was the one club she truly wanted to join, but she'd have to pass. "No," she said. "I can't carry a tune."

"That's too bad. We really need a soloist. Your speaking voice is so pretty I would've bet you could sing beautifully. Well, see you all later." Melody set her headphones back over her ears and headed toward the coffee cart.

"Don't fret," Apple said. "Something will pop up. It always does." At that, a mouse popped out of Maddie's teacup hat and squeaked.

"Tomorrow is Sports Day," Ashlynn said. "Maybe you can try out for a team. I'm on the cheerhexing squad. Maybe you'd like to join?"

"That's a spelltacular idea," Apple told her. "All the teams will be having tryouts, and my Welcoming Committee list says I'm supposed to get you signed up for at least one club or sports team. Tomorrow is a new day! We can still make this work!"

Down the Drain

It had been a long day. Meeshell felt a bit of a failure, having chosen no clubs. And while classes had gone okay, she'd been too shy to speak up in any of them. And during dinner, there'd been so many new faces and introductions, her head was swimming. When she got back to the dormitory, she overheard a conversation in the hallway. It was Apple and Briar.

"I don't think I'm right for the Welcoming Committee," Apple said to Briar.

"Why?"

"I haven't been able to help Meeshell find a club."

"Well, helping the new student find some sort of activity is really important, that's true. And the Welcoming Committee does have a one hundred percent success rate."

"One hundred percent?" Apple gulped. "You mean, I could mess that up? That would be an epic fairy fail."

"You won't mess it up. You're Apple White. You can do anything you"—Briar paused for a huge yawn—"anything you set your mind to."

"Thanks for the vote of confidence," Apple said. "I'll keep trying. Meeshell deserves to feel like she belongs. We all do."

Just as the conversation ended, Professor Yaga called Meeshell on her MirrorPad and was happy to hear that her speaking voice had returned to normal. And that her legs were working better and hadn't fallen off, which was a real plus! "Remember,

if you have any unusual symptoms or concerns, call me immediately. Otherwise, how are things going?"

"Fine." Her answer didn't sound very convincing.

"I hear homesickness in your voice. It might be worse for you than for others since you are hiding your true nature," Professor Yaga said. Luckily, Meeshell was alone in her dorm room, which meant that no one overheard the conversation. "My advice to you is, whenever you are able, let your true self out. Otherwise, you'll always feel like a fish out of water." The MirrorPad screen went dark as the call ended.

Yes, that's exactly how she felt. What a perfect description. She wanted, very badly, to let her true self out. To see her tail again. That would make her feel better.

She stepped into the bathroom. Unfortunately, there was no bathtub. The shower was pretty, however, made of pink tiles and a unicorn faucet. It would have to do. She locked the door and turned

on the water. When she entered the shower, the change was immediate. Her legs disappeared and her beautiful tail took its rightful place. She leaned against the wall. It was an awkward space, difficult to get comfortable in since tails are not designed for long periods of standing. She showered as best she could, but got wedged a few times in the process. This wasn't making her feel better. She turned off the water and watched it swirl down the drain.

She dried her tail with a towel and as soon as the last droplet had evaporated, her legs reappeared. It was nice to know that she could bring her tail back whenever she wanted. She was grateful to Coral for that glitch in the spell. But still she felt anxious. With all her heart, she wanted to swim. Spending day after day not swimming was like asking a seagull to stop flying. Maybe she could find a way to swim without anyone seeing?

After changing into her new pajamas, she sat on her bed, opened her MirrorPad, and searched for a campus map. Then she perused the map, looking for large bodies of water. There was Mirror Beach, near the boat dock, but that was too exposed. There was the unicorn fountain, where the swans swam, but that was smack in the middle of the quad. There was a swimming pool in the Grimmnasium, but someone might see her there. She was about to give up when she noticed a small lake at the far edge of campus. Enchanted Lake. That sounded perfect! According to the map, she could easily walk there.

Farrah came back. She brought a late-night snack of toast and fairyberry jam, which she shared. Then she went to change into her pajamas. When she emerged from the bathroom she asked, "How did your day go?"

"Pretty good," Meeshell said.

"I'm glad to hear that." Then Farrah's gaze fell upon a fat hextbook. "Ugh, I have to study for a test tomorrow in Magicology. It's about the history of evil witches, my least favorite topic." She lugged the hextbook onto

her desk with a big thud. Then she sat and, using her wand as a highlighting pen, began to study.

Just then, Meeshell's MirrorPad chimed.

StoryTeller2: Hi.

Seashell: Hi.

StoryTeller2: How did Club Day go? Did you join anything?

Seashell: No. I didn't find anything that seemed right for me.

StoryTeller2: Yeah, I get that. When I first came to school, I couldn't find the right club, either, so I started my own.

Seashell: Really? You can do that?

StoryTeller2: Sure.

Seashell: Which club did you start?

Long pause.

StoryTeller2: Well, I gotta go. I need to do something. Talk to you later. Bye.

Seashell: Bye.

Every time she tried to find out any details about the mysterious StoryTeller2, he or she stopped chatting. Why?

As the chat box closed, the Ever After High campus map reappeared on the MirrorPad screen. StoryTeller2 wasn't the only one who needed to do something. Meeshell looked out the window.

She needed to swim!

Enchanted Lake

fter changing into her new bathing suit, then covering up with a coat, Meeshell told Farrah that she was going to take a walk. As she made her way down the hall, she stepped over a hedgehog who was waddling along at a leisurely pace. The Common Room was empty, except for a girl sitting in front of the fireplace, a book nestled on her lap. The girl looked up at her. "Did anyone tell you about curfew?" she asked.

Meeshell halted. "Curfew?"

The girl set a bookmark in place, then closed the book. She had lovely dark hair and matching dark eyes. Her dress was black and purple with silver lacework at the edges. "If you leave campus, you need to be back by midnight or you won't be able to pass through the wall of thorns. It's a magical wall that Headmaster Grimm uses to protect the school." She glanced up at the wall clock. "You have an hour."

"Okay, thanks for the warning."

"Don't worry, I'm not going to ask what you're doing," she said, which was a huge relief to Meeshell. "By the way, I'm Raven Queen, daughter of the Evil Queen," she added with a wry smile.

Meeshell's shoulders stiffened. Daughter of the *Evil Queen?* Wow! Of course she'd heard about Raven. *Everyone* had heard about Raven. She was as famous as Apple.

Raven waited patiently for Meeshell to introduce herself. "I'm Meeshell. Daughter of…" She paused.

Raven raised an eyebrow. When no answer came, Raven sat back in her chair. "You don't have to tell me. I get it. Sometimes it's nice if people just know us for ourselves and not for our families." She picked up her book and started reading again. "Good luck with whatever after you're doing."

"Thank you." Meeshell hurried down the stairs. Just from that short encounter, she got the feeling that Raven was much nicer than her family's reputation.

She only had an hour to swim and get back. Would that be enough time? She didn't want to get into trouble; that was not the best way to start her first week. Behind her, the dormitory windows shone brightly against the twilight sky. Most students were studying or getting ready for bed. Was she the only student out and about? She hesitated, but the need to swim was stronger than her fear of getting caught. She gripped her bag. She'd stuffed a towel inside. And onward she went.

She crossed the quad, then a footbridge, passing a sign that read:

THIS WAY TO THE EVER AFTER HIGH SWAMP

She hadn't noticed that on the map. Swimming in a swamp didn't sound like much fun, but she'd keep it in mind as a last resort. Soon she came to another sign:

THIS WAY TO ENCHANTED LAKE

The path was narrow but well groomed, with broom marks in the wood chips. Ashlynn's Forest Club did a lovely job. The path was also well lit, thanks to the full moon. Even though Meeshell wasn't breaking any rules, she felt nervous as she walked. *I'm not doing anything wrong*, she told herself. *This is my nature. I need to swim.*

An unsettling thought popped into her head. Once she became a permanent land-dweller, would she lose her craving for the water? How odd that would be.

After a few twists and turns, the path opened onto a clearing. Tall willow trees grew around the perimeter and in the center was a small lake with water so blue, it had to be enchanted. The moon reflected on the lake's surface. The only movement came from a pair of golden cranes who stood in the shallows, between large lily pads. They turned and nodded at Meeshell, not seeming upset by her arrival. She knelt and touched the water. It was perfect: not too warm, not too cool. Her toes wiggled excitedly, as if they were really looking forward to turning into a tail. She tossed her coat aside, adjusted her bathing suit straps, and dived in.

Water! How glorious! She kicked once, twice, and her legs became a tail. Joy flowed through her as she swam beneath the surface. Then she leaped from the water, flipping into a forward roll. She leaped again, this time soaring through the air in a backward arc. Oh, the freedom! She swam the entire circumference of the lagoon, around and around until she was breathless. The cranes watched with curiosity. Then she floated on her back, looking up at the twilight sky, the water cradling her. All was still. All was good.

The cranes made a sudden screeching sound. They twisted their long necks, staring warily at the path. Footsteps. Someone was coming! Meeshell sank until her shoulders were under the water, then she slipped into a shadowy place beneath the boughs of a weeping willow.

A person appeared around the corner. It was Humphrey. What was he doing out here? He wore a pair of checkered swim shorts and little flotation devices around his arms. Meeshell had seen kids wearing those on beaches. He stood at the edge of the lagoon, staring at the water. "You can do this," he said to himself. He put one foot in. Then the other. Ever so slowly, he waded up to his ankles. His brow furrowed. Was he scared of the water? He waded up to his knees. Then up to his waist. "You can do this," he said again. Meeshell didn't really know Humphrey, but she wanted to encourage him. *Go ahead*, she thought. *It'll be okay. The water will hold you up. Well, at least it does for mermaids.*

As if hearing her thoughts, he tossed the floaties onto the shore. And that's when everything went royally wrong.

Humphrey disappeared under the water.

Little bubbles appeared at the surface, but Humphrey didn't come back up. Meeshell waited. How long could a land-dweller hold his breath? She wasn't quite sure. Even the cranes watched nervously. And then the bubbles stopped.

Uh-oh.

Meeshell dived, swimming as fast as she could. She found him, struggling at the bottom of the lake. His back was to her, so she put her arms around his waist and pulled him to the surface. He took a huge gasp of air. Once she was certain he was breathing, she gave a strong push with her tail, sending him onto the shore. Then she swam into the depths so he wouldn't be able to see her tail. "You okay?" she asked.

He sat up and coughed a few times. Then he wiped his mouth with the back of his hand. "Yeah, I'm okay." He looked at her. "You…you saved me. Thank you."

"You're welcome." She swam a bit deeper, worried the full moon would give her away.

Humphrey coughed again. "I didn't know anyone was here. I…I thought I was alone." He was still struggling a bit to catch his breath.

"Maybe you should take some swim lessons," she said. She was trying to be helpful, but he looked insulted.

"Swim lessons?" He scrambled to his feet. Water dripped down his legs. "I don't need lessons. I can swim. I'm not afraid of water. What gave you that idea? I…I swim all the time."

"Uh, okay, I didn't mean to—"

"I came here to get some exercise, because I'm *not* afraid of the water. And because I *can* swim. But

then I got a cramp. In my leg. That's why I sank to the bottom."

He wasn't going to admit that he couldn't swim. As if he was ashamed of that fact. She wanted to tell him it was no big deal, that everyone has something they can't do, and that she of all people knew how embarrassing it was to have people think you're afraid of something most other people aren't afraid of...but she felt too shy to tell him something so personal. Plus, she knew he was trying to teach himself, and she'd been a witness to something he'd wanted to keep secret.

A chime sounded. Humphrey looked at his watch. "Curfew. We'd better go."

She couldn't get out of the water and let him see her tail. "Um, could you turn around? I need to change."

"Of course," he said, turning his back. She pulled herself out, grabbed the towel, and dried quickly. Her legs returned and she slipped her coat back on. Then together, they hurried down the path. He didn't say anything else, nor did she. But as he headed toward the boys' dormitory, with his floaties in hand, she realized something.

She'd saved a prince from drowning, just like her mother before her. Did this mean that Humphrey was her destined prince? No way. She and Humphrey seemed to have nothing in common. Except for the fact that they were both shy. And everyone knows that two extremely shy people could *never* work together.

Could they?

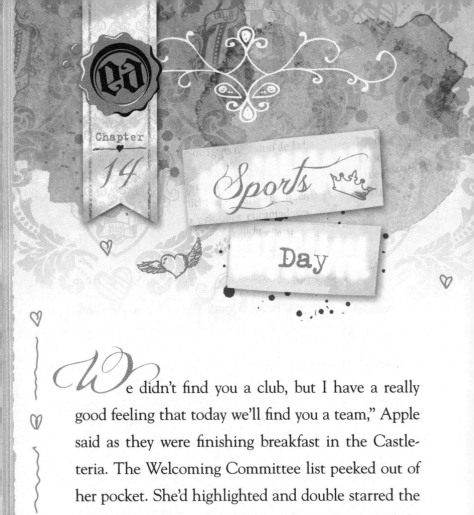

Sports

Day

e didn't find you a club, but I have a really good feeling that today we'll find you a team," Apple said as they were finishing breakfast in the Castleteria. The Welcoming Committee list peeked out of her pocket. She'd highlighted and double starred the last remaining item on the checklist. "We won't fail," she told Meeshell. "Determination is one of my best attributes. And I am determined to make this happen." Apple clearly wanted to add the Welcoming Committee to her high school resume, and so she needed Meeshell to join something. Meeshell also wanted to find something—she really wanted to have a full experience at Ever After High, like her father had—but Apple's list was adding pressure to the situation. Meeshell didn't want to disappoint anyone, especially Apple, who'd been so nice to her.

Sports Day was similar to Club Day, except that it was set up on the athletic field. All the teams were represented, with athletes present to answer questions, and coaches ready to hold tryouts.

"Ashlynn mentioned cheerhexing. Would you like to give that a try?"

At that moment, a pair of fairies flew past, the gust from their wings nearly knocking Meeshell over. The fairies laughed wickedly. They wore matching shimmering skirts, T-shirts with the letters *EAH*, and carried red pom-poms. They landed next to other students who were dressed in the same outfits. Ashlynn was among them. She called out Meeshell's name and waved.

"I...I guess I'll give it a try," Meeshell said.

But as they approached the squad, Meeshell realized she was about to make a huge mistake. The cheerhexing squad was no longer standing still. They'd erupted into a frenzy of movement, flinging themselves around, leaping, twirling, flipping, then landing on their feet with precision. Meeshell had leaped out of the water many times, and she'd done her fair share of flips, but those moves had been propelled by the power of her tail. She didn't know how to use her legs to do such things.

Then the squad performed a cheer.

"Spell!
Say what? Say what?
Spell!
That's what we do!
We spell,
We spell for you!"

Meeshell cringed. Those moves were way too complicated!

"What do you think?" Ashlynn asked Meeshell when the cheer was over. "You think you want to join? It's really fun."

"Uh…" There was no chance to opt out because a tall, scowling fairy was flying straight toward Meeshell. A thick turquoise streak ran through the fairy's shimmering blond hair. Her wings were iridescent and caught the sun's rays like a prism.

Ashlynn looked nervously at the fairy, then hurried back to the squad. "Good luck!" she called to Meeshell over her shoulder.

The fairy hovered in front of Meeshell. "Don't tell me *you're* going to try out," the fairy said in a snippy way. Meeshell recognized her. This was the same fairy who had made fun of her dress on the first day.

Faybelle didn't wait for Meeshell to answer. Instead she turned to Apple. "Why are *you* here?"

"I'm here because I've been assigned to help Meeshell. I'm her Welcoming Committee representative." Apple leaned close to Faybelle and frowned.

"Be nice to her, Faybelle. She's new and that means she's not used to your...*wickedness*."

Faybelle's mouth turned up, ever so slightly, and ever so wickedly. "Oh, I'll *be nice* to her."

"Good. I appreciate that." Apple beamed. Hadn't she heard the sarcasm in Faybelle's voice? Apple patted Meeshell's shoulder. "I'll wait over there while you try out." Then she grabbed Meeshell's bag and MirrorPad, and sat on a nearby bench.

Faybelle, still hovering, crossed her arms and gave Meeshell a very long, very intense look. "So?" she asked. "What can you do? Front flips? Backflips? Somersaults? Cartwheels? Handstands?"

At this point in time, Meeshell was grateful that she could *stand* without falling over. But obviously that wouldn't be enough.

"I'm not sure what I can do," she answered. "I've never been a cheerhexer before."

Faybelle rolled her eyes. "Oh, that's just spelltacular news." Her wings folded and she landed on the soft grass. Then she did a forward roll and sprang back to her feet. She pushed a strand of hair from her forehead. "Let me see you do that."

Apple gave Meeshell two enthusiastic thumbs-up. Ashlynn beamed an encouraging smile.

That didn't look so difficult, Meeshell thought. In fact, it reminded her of the kind of roll she did all the time when she was swimming and wanted to change directions. She decided that she might as well give it a try. How else would she know what she was capable of if she didn't try? So, with a deep steadying breath, she stepped onto the field and attempted a forward roll.

Graceful was not a word to describe what happened next. Nor was *skillful* or *coordinated*. Meeshell wasn't sure how she ended up sideways. She'd closed her eyes, she'd leaned forward with the intent to roll, but somehow she went wonky.

"How embarrassing for you," Faybelle said with a snort once Meeshell sat up. Then Faybelle rose into the air again, her wings beating with annoyance. "Newsflash, new girl, I don't have time to train amateurs." Then she flew over to another hopeful candidate.

"Okay, so cheerhexing's not your thing," Apple said as Meeshell picked blades of grass out of her hair. "It's not for everyone—mostly just for fairies, in fact! But there are many more tryouts going on. Follow me." With a tug on Meeshell's hand, Apple exuberantly pulled her down the field, her determination steadfast. As much as Meeshell liked Apple, she wished she could make that Welcoming Committee list disappear. Maybe Farrah could grant that wish for her?

Apple led Meeshell right up to an odd little man. His neck, arms, and legs were equally thick and blocky. His shirt was tucked into his gym shorts and he wore a pair of kneesocks with his tennis shoes. A whistle hung around his neck. While he looked kinda funny, he smelled *delicious*, like something that had been baked in an oven. "Coach Ginger-breadman, this is Meeshell, our newest student. Can she try out for the team?"

"You want to try out for Track and Shield?" Coach Gingerbreadman asked. "What are you interested in doing?"

Meeshell remembered that her father had been on the Track and Shield team when he went to Ever After High. "What choices do I have?" she asked.

"Well, we've already got a long-jump champion." He pointed to a boy who was jumping across a sand-pit. It was the same prince she'd seen earlier, the one who'd turned into a frog. Wow, could he jump! "And we've got plenty of students for the shield toss." He pointed to a bunch of students who were flinging shields at a target. "But you know, I could use some more sprinters. Can you run, run, run as fast as you can?"

Both Apple and Coach Gingerbreadman looked expectantly at Meeshell, who gulped. She hadn't yet tried to run, let alone as fast as she could. How did that work, exactly? "I have a good feeling about this," Apple said. "I'll just sit over here." Once again, she sat on a nearby bench.

"Start on this line," Coach Gingerbreadman said. "And run to that line." He pointed down the track. "I'll time you." Waddling on his thick legs, he made his way to the finish line. Then he turned and hollered at her. "Take your mark!"

She stood on the start line.

"Get set!"

What was she supposed to do? She looked down at her legs.

"Run, run, run!" He blew his whistle.

Fast was not a word to describe what happened next. Nor was *swift* or *speedy*. She told her legs to move. And they did. But her knees came up real high at first, as if she were a prancing horse. Then, once she'd gotten the knees to settle down, she couldn't keep a straight line. She'd veered to the left, then to the right. By the time she'd reached the

finish line, completely out of breath, Coach Ginger-breadman was standing with his mouth hanging open, aghast at what he'd just witnessed.

"What was that?" he asked.

"That was…" She took a huge breath. "That was running."

"Not in my playbook!" He shook his head. "If I didn't know better, I'd guess you'd never used your legs before."

Meeshell didn't disagree with him.

Apple was beginning to look a little desperate. "You want to keep trying? What about Grimmnastics? Oh no, that won't work since you'd probably have to do somersaults. What about Sorcerer's Soccer? Oh drat, that requires running. What about swim team? Oops, that won't work either, since you're afraid of water." She frowned. "I'm not sure what to do."

"It's okay," Meeshell said. She could tell how disappointed Apple was, and she felt badly. Especially knowing she'd be a perfect fit for the swim team…

if only she could tell Apple the truth about who she really was.

While other students walked past, wearing their new uniforms and carrying banners for their new teams, Meeshell had nothing.

The Secret Prince

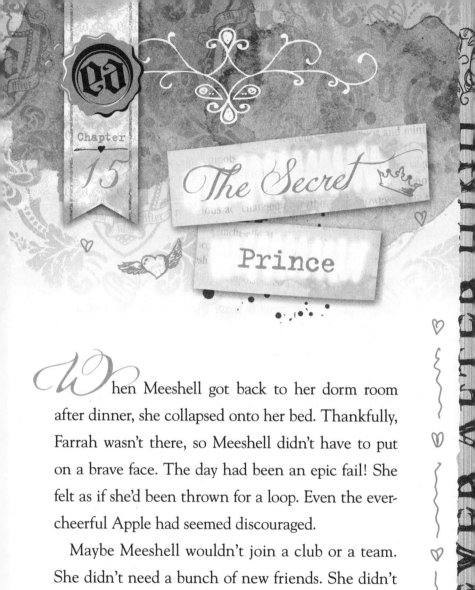

When Meeshell got back to her dorm room after dinner, she collapsed onto her bed. Thankfully, Farrah wasn't there, so Meeshell didn't have to put on a brave face. The day had been an epic fail! She felt as if she'd been thrown for a loop. Even the ever-cheerful Apple had seemed discouraged.

Maybe Meeshell wouldn't join a club or a team. She didn't need a bunch of new friends. She didn't need to be popular. But from what Apple had said, being in a club was part of the Ever After High

experience, and experiencing normal life on land was Meeshell's goal.

She checked her messages. The first was from Professor Baba Yaga, reminding her to check in if anything was wrong. The second message was from Hagatha, alerting students that there would be no green bean hash next week, due to a union dispute with the giants. And the third message was from Mrs. Her Majesty the White Queen with the throne-work assignment for Princessology.

MirrorPad in hand, Meeshell sat on the balcony, her legs curled beneath her. Where was a seagull when she needed one? She really wanted to send a message home. She really wanted to talk to her Merfriends. To someone who'd understand.

StoryTeller2: Hi. How are you doing?

The MirrorPad lit up, startling Meeshell. It was as if StoryTeller2 could read her mind, knowing she needed someone to talk to!

Seashell: Not so good.

StoryTeller2: How come?

Seashell: I tried out for cheerhexing and Track and Shield today, and I was a total disaster.

StoryTeller2: Yeah, I heard.

Seashell: You heard?

StoryTeller2: Word gets around. Blondie Lockes showed some highlights on her *Just Right* show. You can't keep any secrets at Ever After High.

She sure hoped that last statement wasn't true.

StoryTeller2: Don't feel too bad. I'm not good at sports, either. Why are athletes always popular? I don't get it. When will intelligence and artistic creativity get as much attention as sports?

Seashell: Thanks for trying to make me feel better. But it was hextremely embarrassing.

StoryTeller2: Believe me, I know embarrassing. And what I saw wasn't all that bad. At least you didn't fall flat on your face. I do that all the time.

Seashell: You do?

StoryTeller2: Yep. A bit of a klutz.

She felt better knowing that she wasn't the only klutz on campus.

Seashell: So, you obviously know who I am but I don't know who you are. Who are you?

As usual, a long pause followed.

Seashell: Hello?

Another long pause with no response.

Seashell: You still there?

Whoever was conversing with Meeshell clearly didn't want to reveal his or her true identity. But why? It seemed strange to her. Yet how could she feel annoyed, when she was also hiding her true identity?

> **Seashell**: Okay, you don't have to tell me who you are. But can you tell me just one thing about yourself? Just a little hint?
>
> **StoryTeller2**: Just one thing?
>
> **Seashell**: Yes. One thing and I'll stop asking.
>
> **StoryTeller2**: I'm a prince.

A prince? Her heart flitted for a moment. Not only did this mysterious person seem nice *and* sensitive, but he was also a prince? She'd promised to ask only one thing, but now a stream of questions flooded her mind. And one question in particular lingered.

Are you my prince?

Mirror Beach

The next morning Apple was back to her usual cheerful self. "We're going to Mirror Beach," she said. "Will you join us?"

"But Meeshell's afraid of the water," Ashlynn reminded her. The girls were dressed in bathing suits, with bright cover-ups and flip-flops.

"Oh hex, that's right." Apple carried a large beach bag stuffed with towels, swimming goggles, and sunscreen. "If you sit in the sand, and don't go near the water, will you come with us?"

Meeshell glanced at the thronework waiting on her desk. Yes, it needed to get done, but hanging out on the beach would be lovely. She missed the salty spray. The sound of gulls. The rhythm of the waves. As long as she stayed away from the water and kept her legs perfectly dry, she'd be fine. "I'd love to come with you."

"Spelltacular!"

Mirror Beach was a short walk from the dock where the *Narwhal* had delivered Meeshell. The sand was white, with tiny ground-up seashells that made it sparkle. A tall wooden chair had been built in the center of the beach. Perched at the top was a boy she hadn't yet met. He wore sunglasses and striped swim trunks. A sign hanging on the back of the chair read:

LIFEGUARD ON DUTY

When he saw them approaching, he waved. The girls waved back. "That's Ashlynn's boyfriend," Apple explained. "His name is Hunter."

Hunter scrambled down from the chair and planted a big smooch on Ashlynn's cheek. "Hi, Apple. Hi, Meeshell. It's great to finally meet you. Welcome to Mirror Beach."

"Thanks." Meeshell took a deep breath, the salt air filling her lungs. It felt so good to be near the sea! She couldn't take her eyes off the water. It was calling to her, as if it had a voice. She felt twitchy again. Her legs began to ache, wanting to be turned into a tail.

The girls quickly set up a large umbrella and some beach chairs as Hunter returned to his station. Ashlynn had packed snacks in a basket. She passed them each a bottle of Ice Queen Glacier Water. Meeshell settled into a chair. Apple handed out the sunblock, explaining its importance in keeping her the "fairest in the land." Then they nibbled on mini throne-cakes. The crumbs attracted a pair of gulls. Meeshell smiled at them. This was her chance to get a message home!

While Apple and Ashlynn busily applied some

sunblock, Meeshell leaned close to one of the gulls and spoke in his language. "Can you get a message to the king and queen of the Merpeople" The gull nodded. The gull, of course, knew Meeshell's true identity, for all creatures of the sea know a mermaid when they see one. "Please tell them that I am fine and that I miss them." The gull nodded again. She rewarded him with a corner of thronecake. He ate it, then flew off to deliver the message.

"I don't mean to pry, but were you speaking Gull to that seagull?" Ashlynn asked, her eyes lighting up. "I thought I was the only one who could talk to birds. Where did you learn?"

Meeshell hesitated for a moment. She didn't want to tell another lie. But Ashlynn had clearly caught her speaking Gull. "We have to take many languages at school in my kingdom," she explained. "I learned Gull at school. I know quite a few animal languages, actually."

Ashlynn's face lit up. "Oh, me too, I know all sorts. Maybe we can tutor each other. I don't know a word of Gull, but I know Owl really well. And Phoenix."

Meeshell was relieved that Ashlynn hadn't understood her conversation with the gull. But learning new languages sounded like a lovely idea, and she was about to say so when a voice nearby hollered, "Catch a wave!"

A bunch of students, each carrying a surfboard, ran past. Daring Charming was in the lead, his family crest plastered across his swim trunks. He turned and smiled, and this time Meeshell remembered to close her eyes until the brilliance had faded. Apple waved to him, as did Ashlynn. Following behind the pack was Humphrey. He stumbled under the weight of his surfboard, then plunked it into the water. He wasn't wearing his arm floaties this time, which seemed a bit dangerous to Meeshell since she suspected he couldn't swim. Daring and his crew headed straight into the water, then paddled out toward a wave as it began to crest. She'd seen land-dwellers surf before. But back home, she and her Merfriends didn't need special equipment to surf. Their tails were better than boards. And surfing was always good because Meeshell and her Merfriends all had the magical ability to make water ebb and flow at their will.

Meeshell watched with envy as Daring jumped onto his board, riding the wave with ease and grace. As his hair billowed, a few of his groupies stood on shore taking photos of him.

"That's another club," Apple explained. "The Surf Club. But with your fear of water, obviously not a good choice."

"You're right," Meeshell said. "It's not for me."

Humphrey hadn't caught the wave. He sat on his board, floating close to shore. Unlike the others, he was frowning and nervously looking around.

"I...I'm just going to stretch my legs," Meeshell told the other two. Then she walked slowly down the beach toward Humphrey. But as she walked and tried to ignore the urge to throw herself into the water, she overheard Apple confiding in Ashlynn.

"I'm disappointed in myself," Apple said. "I had a simple assignment for the Welcoming Committee and I've failed."

"It's not your fault that Meeshell's having trouble fitting in," Ashlynn said kindly.

"It *is* my fault. There's a place for everybody. I just have to think harder." Apple paused to think. "It's odd. I'm usually such a good judge of character. But for some reason, I can't figure Meeshell out. I'm not sure why."

Meeshell hated that Apple felt so much pressure to help her. It would be so easy to find a club or team if she stopped pretending to be someone she wasn't. But that would interfere with her plan.

Meeshell walked closer to the water's edge. She passed Daring's groupies. "Poor Daring," one of them said. "Where did the waves go?"

True enough, Daring and his fellow Surf Club members sat on their boards, floating, with no waves in sight. The sea had suddenly turned calm and now all the surfers were wearing frowns.

"Humphrey," Meeshell called. Her voice startled him so much, he almost fell off his board.

"Uh…uh…h-hi," he stammered.

She stood at the water's edge, making sure her feet didn't touch the water. "You don't have your floaties."

"Huh?" His face turned bright red and he laughed in a nervous way. "I don't know what you're talking about. I don't need floaties. I love surfing. I surf all the time." And with that, he leaned forward and began paddling with his arms until he reached Daring and the others in the deeper water.

Well, maybe she'd been wrong. Maybe he had gotten a leg cramp at the lake, and maybe he was a good swimmer after all. There was no reason for him to lie to her.

"Where are the waves?" one of the surfers shouted.

"Waves, waves, waves!" they all began to chant, even Humphrey.

They clearly wanted to surf. And she could help. Coral's spell had transformed Meeshell's tail into

two legs, but it hadn't transformed her magic touch. She'd been able to conjure that little wave that had pushed the *Narwhal* across the ocean. Could she risk using magic now to help create waves for the surfers?

She glanced over her shoulder. Apple and Ashlynn had walked to the Snack Shack to order shaved ice. Their backs were turned to her. Careful to keep her feet dry, she quickly reached out and touched the water. That's all it took. Her hand retreated quickly. No one noticed.

The wave came right away. The surfers cheered. Meeshell smiled proudly. She stepped backward, moving up the beach to avoid the wave, but keeping her eyes focused on the surfers. She didn't want to miss a moment of the hexcitment as they rode the magic wave. But something was wrong. The wave grew bigger and bigger. Oh no, what had she done? The surfers shrieked and paddled toward shore as fast as they could. Then they leaped from the water as the wave reached for the sky, roiling and foaming.

The lifeguard whistle blew. "Run!" Hunter cried. Meeshell ran, along with everyone else until they'd made it safely up the path. Then they turned and watched with horror as the wave crashed onto the beach, splitting the lifeguard chair in two. Luckily, Hunter had leaped away in time.

"Where's Humphrey?" Daring asked.

Meeshell looked around. Humphrey had disappeared!

Rescue

Repeat

*P*anic welled in Meeshell's chest. She frantically looked around. Apple, Ashlynn, and Hunter were standing next to her. The students who ran the Snack Shack were also there, along with a group who'd been playing beach volleyball. Daring and the members of the Surf Club were also safe. It appeared that everyone had avoided the rogue wave.

Except for one person.

"There he is!" Meeshell cried, pointing down the

beach where a shape lay in the sand. A mangled surfboard lay a few feet away.

What had she done? She had no idea how she got her legs to move as quickly as they did, but she flew down the beach and threw herself next to him. He lay on his back, his arms and legs splayed, his eyes closed. A crab skittered across his chest. While the others ran to catch up, she put her ear to Humphrey's chest. "He's breathing," she announced as Hunter and Daring knelt beside her. She almost burst into tears of relief.

"He's stunned," Hunter said. He and Daring helped Humphrey sit upright. Humphrey took a huge breath, then opened his eyes. "You okay?" Hunter asked.

After a few minutes of coughing, Humphrey reached up and felt his head. "No cracks. I'm okay. But that wave really tossed me around. I thought I was going to be crushed." He picked a piece of seaweed off his face.

"Sounds like the time in Hero Training when I got caught in the middle of a griffin stampede," Daring said. "But we survived. Good job, Dumpty." Then he slapped Humphrey on the back, bringing about another coughing fit. A pair of nurse fairies appeared. They flitted around Humphrey's head, then gave two thumbs-up and flew away.

Hunter helped Humphrey to his feet. All the other students had gathered 'round. Humphrey glanced at Meeshell, looking more embarrassed than ever.

"I'm sorry," she told him.

"Why are you sorry?" Hunter asked. "You were the first to reach him. You practically saved him." Hunter was congratulating her? That wasn't fair. She'd almost squashed Humphrey with the giant wave she'd created! "You've got good eyes. Would you like to join the lifeguard crew?"

"But Meeshell's afraid of water," Ashlynn said before Meeshell could reply.

"Afraid of the water?" Hunter asked. "That's too bad. We really need more help."

It was definitely too bad, because of all the students at Ever After High, Meeshell knew she'd be a superb lifeguard. She'd be able to conduct rescues underwater, and reach swimming speeds that no land-dweller could reach. If she admitted, right then and there, the truth about being a mermaid, then she could help Hunter save lives!

If she spoke up and told everyone she was a mermaid, and explained that she wasn't really afraid of water, her new friends would see that she was brave and fun-loving, just like they were. All of the things that must have seemed so odd about her, that they had been so kind and accepting of, would suddenly make sense. Sure, she was a little shy, but she wasn't yet used to life on land.

But admitting she was a mermaid would mean being treated differently. And that would mean losing a chance at having the authentic experience as a land-dweller. But the urge to tell the truth was overwhelming.

"I…I need to go," she blurted. As Meeshell hurried away, Hunter blew on his whistle.

"Okay, everyone," he called. "The rogue wave is gone. You can go back into the water!"

Once again, when she got back to the dormitory, Meeshell collapsed onto her bed. What a total disaster the week had been. Trying to be a land-dweller was really hard. She hadn't found a club, she'd failed at two team tryouts, and now she'd almost drowned everyone! She reached out to the one person who seemed to understand her.

> **Seashell**: I feel like a total loser.
>
> **StoryTeller2**: How come?
>
> **Seashell**: Every time I try to do something, it doesn't work.

StoryTeller2: Yeah, been there, done that. I feel that way a lot.

Seashell: Do you ever wish you were some-one else?

StoryTeller2: All the time.

Seashell: Really? Why?

StoryTeller2: Because I don't fit in. I never know what to say.

Seashell: I never knew what it felt like to not-fit in, but now I do.

StoryTeller2: Like a fish out of water.

Seashell: You have no idea how true that is.

She really wanted to meet her mysterious friend—this prince who wanted to hide his identity. Then it occurred to her that maybe he wasn't a prince after all. He could be a troll for all she knew. It didn't matter either way because she didn't care about his royal status. Or two-footed status. She felt as if she could tell him anything. And that he'd understand and be sympathetic.

Seashell: Will you please tell me who you are?

StoryTeller2: Believe me, you won't be impressed.

Seashell: Why do I need to be impressed? You're my friend.

Long pause.

StoryTeller2: I gotta go do something. Bye.

She'd scared him off again.

"Meeshell, can we talk?" Apple had poked her head into the room. Her voice was more serious than usual.

"Sure," Meeshell said. She set aside the Mirror-Pad, then pushed a pile of pillows off the bed so Apple could sit next to her.

"As you ran from the beach, I realized something." Apple took the Welcoming Committee list from her pocket. "When I offered to be your Welcoming

Committee representative, I wasn't thinking about you. I was thinking about myself."

"That's not true."

"Yes, it is. It's always been very important to me that I do things right, you know? That I meet my goals and succeed. I really wanted to be a part of this committee with Briar because she's one of my best friends forever after, and because it would look good on my records. But the truth is, it doesn't matter if I'm on another committee. What matters is that you're happy. And I think I've been putting too much pressure on you. You don't have to join a club or be on a team to fit in here at Ever After High. You don't have to belong to anything if you don't want to. That's perfectly okay." She crumpled the list in her hand, then tossed it into the recycling bin. "So from this moment on, I'm going to stop putting pressure on you. You do what makes you happy, Meeshell." She gave her a hug. "And I hope we can be BFFAs."

Meeshell smiled gratefully at Apple. She really was one of the sweetest people Meeshell had ever met. "Of course. Thank you, Apple."

After Apple left, Meeshell walked onto the balcony and gazed out over the school grounds. Ashlynn and a few other cheerhexers, dressed in their uniforms, were walking together across the quad. Some Track and Shield runners were sitting at the edge of the track, laughing about something. A couple of guys from the Tech Club were at a table, trying to untangle a huge pile of cords. At that moment, Meeshell felt very alone. Apple had said that Meeshell didn't need to join a club or team to fit in. But finding other students who shared the same interests or talents would definitely help.

A figure floated in front of her. Meeshell gasped. "Oh, Professor Yaga, you startled me."

The elderly woman sat crossed-legged on her pillow, hovering in front of the balcony. "I need your assistance," she explained. "Come with me."

Out of Hiding

Meeshell had to walk quickly to keep up with Professor Yaga's floating pillow. The professor led her away from the main campus, down a path, to a modern building built on a bluff above the sea.

"We have an extensive Beastology program of study here at Ever After High. There is a stable for the hoofed creatures, an aviary for the winged beasts. But this is the Creature Care Center, where injured or sick creatures are treated." Professor Yaga opened the door and ushered Meeshell into the building. "They receive the best possible care, of course, and we in turn learn a lot from them. And this room is where we treat creatures of the sea."

Meeshell squealed with delight. She stood facing an aquarium so vast that it spanned the length of the building and reached all the way to the ceiling. She pressed her face against the glass. Inside, eels peered out from rocky burrows, sea horses stampeded across bright coral, peacock fish fanned their tails. A thick kelp forest grew on one side of the tank. It reminded her of home. "This is a class?" Meeshell asked.

"Beast Care and Magicment is a specialty class," the professor confirmed. "Most of these creatures are here to enrich the curriculum. When their injuries or illnesses heal, they will be released back into the wild. But a few are pets." She pointed to a strange little fish in the corner that looked to be made out of candy. "Ginger Breadhouse insists on bringing her gummy fish here for playdates." The fish waved at Meeshell. Meeshell waved back.

Professor Yaga got off her pillow, then led Meeshell to a section of the aquarium where a small cave was set in a coral reef. "Yesterday, one of the students found an octopus on the beach," she told Meeshell. "The creature appeared disoriented and had suffered some trauma. We set her into this tank, and we were going to conduct our examination today, but she seems to have disappeared."

"You think she escaped?" Meeshell asked. She noticed that the aquarium didn't have a cover, so it was open.

"That is doubtful. I placed a magical spell on this aquarium that doesn't allow the injured creatures to escape. We want to keep them here, at least until they are well again." The professor peered through the glass. "No one has seen her since last night."

Meeshell looked carefully. She had an idea as to what was going on. "She is probably using her powers of camouflage to avoid us. Octopuses are very shy creatures. I can try to go in and communicate with her, to let her know we only want to help her, but I can't guarantee success."

"I understand. But we must try. If she doesn't get help, she might perish."

Professor Yaga and Meeshell pushed a stepladder across the floor, then rested it against the tank. Meeshell climbed the steps until she reached the top of the aquarium. She looked down at the professor. "We're alone, right? No one will see me?"

"Correct."

Meeshell climbed into the tank. Just as she began to tread water, her legs twitched, then turned into a tail. She swam directly to the cave, then stuck her head into its opening. It was empty. She swam around the tank, her eyes peeled for signs of tentacles, but Meeshell knew that if the octopus wanted to stay hidden, no one would be able to find her. So, once she reached the center of the tank, she began to speak in the language of all cephalopods. Using the tip of her tail, she tapped against a rock. It was a complicated language, but one she'd recently mastered. *Do not worry,* she tapped. *These land-dwellers are not going to eat you. They want to help you.*

The octopus did not appear. Was it possible that she had escaped, despite the magic spell? It wouldn't surprise Meeshell, for octopuses were among the most intelligent creatures in the sea.

She swam to another section, where the coral reef ended and the kelp reef began. The feel of the kelp against her skin was lovely. Homesickness washed over her. She found another rock and began tapping again. *The land-dwellers want to help you. You've been hurt and they can help make you better. Please come out of hiding.* She waited, her gaze still searching, looking for any shape that seemed unusual.

A tapping sound followed. *Do you promise they won't eat me?*

She tapped back. *Yes, I promise.*

What had looked like a gray rock, resting in the sand, slowly turned orange. The octopus stretched out her seven tentacles. The eighth, however, she held close. It appeared to have suffered a gash.

Meeshell swam up to the octopus. She was larger than most, which meant she was advanced in years. Meeshell tapped again. *How are you feeling?*

My tentacle got caught in a net. It is damaged.

Meeshell gently reached out and examined the injured tentacle. The gash was deep. She looked over at the glass, where Professor Yaga stood. The professor pointed upward, to an examination station that was built at the top of the aquarium.

We must go to the surface so your injury can be treated. Do you need my help? Meeshell tapped.

Yes.

Meeshell stretched out her tail. The octopus climbed on and held tightly as Meeshell slowly swam to the surface. Professor Yaga, thanks to her unique mode of pillow travel, met them and helped transfer the octopus onto a smooth platform. The creature quivered. Meeshell held one of her uninjured tentacles. *Do not be afraid,* she tapped. *This land-dweller will help you.*

Meeshell watched while the professor mixed a potion and applied it to the injury. "Is that magic?" Meeshell asked.

"It is not magic," the professor explained. "It is an ointment that will help keep the infection from spreading."

"Does it contain powdered urchin shell?"

Professor Yaga raised her gray eyebrows. "No, it doesn't."

Meeshell wasn't trying to tell the professor what to do, but she thought she should share this important information. "In the Merkingdom, we use powdered urchin shells to thicken our ointments so they will better adhere to the wound."

"That is most ingenious." The professor floated to a cabinet, searched around until she found a small vial, then brought the vial back to the examination platform. "Perhaps you would like to instruct me?"

Meeshell mixed the powder into the ointment, then applied it to the wound. Then she took a clear, waterproof bandage and wrapped the tentacle. The octopus held perfectly still, watching with her big, watery eyes. *Does it hurt?* Meeshell tapped.

No, the octopus replied. *It feels much better!*

Then Meeshell eased the creature back into the water. "Please tell her that she will need to stay here for a few more days to recover," Professor Yaga said.

Meeshell told the octopus. The creature thanked her, then glided back to the cave.

Meeshell took one more swim, then sat on the platform. Professor Yaga mumbled a magic spell and Meeshell's tail and clothing instantly dried. Two-footed once again, she climbed down the ladder. She looked back into the aquarium. The octopus peeked out of her cave and waved.

As they left the aquarium, Professor Yaga floating on her pillow, Meeshell walking alongside, the professor asked Meeshell how she was doing. Meeshell took a long breath. "Not very well," she admitted.

"Everyone has been really nice to me, but…but I'm not sure what to do with myself. I mean, everyone seems to have found a place where they belong. But I haven't found that yet. I don't know what else to do."

Professor Yaga pressed her fingertips together. "Perhaps the best way to solve your dilemma is to think about the octopus."

"How so?"

"Camouflage helps the octopus hide and survive predators. But when she takes on the color of a rock, she doesn't pretend to be a rock. When she takes on the color of an electric eel, she doesn't pretend to be an eel. She is always herself. Do you see what I'm getting at?" Meeshell shook her head. The professor spun around on her pillow so she was facing Meeshell. "You are having trouble fitting in because you are trying to be what you are not."

"But if I pretend to be a land-dweller, then people will treat me like one. And then I'll have a *real*, land-dwelling experience."

The professor smiled knowingly. "The only *real* experience, my dear, is the experience in which you are your *real* self." Then she turned back around.

As Meeshell and the professor made their way back to campus, Meeshell realized that she had a lot to think about.

The True

Tale

After leaving the professor, Meeshell stood in the center of the quad. The other students were inside the Castleteria, eating dinner. The sky had not yet darkened, so the twinkling above her head was not from stars but from a procession of cleaning fairies who were leaving the school grounds, heading to their forest homes. As Meeshell wiped specks of fairy dust from her face, she thought about the professor's words.

The only real *experience is the experience in which* you are your *real self.*

Was that true?

She felt fidgety again. She couldn't think clearly. Was her confusion a side effect of all the air she'd been exposed to? Even though she'd just had a lovely swim in the aquarium, she wanted more time in the water. Time to be herself and think.

She ran down the narrow path, all the way to the lake. When she got there, she jumped straight in. The golden cranes made room for her as she swam. As her tail beat a rhythm, her doubts washed away. She stopped worrying about wanting to fit in. She felt great—so great that she stuck her head above the surface and sang. How good it felt to sing! How she'd missed it. Then, when she reached a high note, she leaped out of the water.

And that's when she noticed Apple, Maddie, Ashlynn, and Briar all standing on the bank, watching her with mouths wide open. The girls were stunned silent. For a long, tense moment, Meeshell waited to hear what her friends would say.

"Meeshell! You're a mermaid!" Ashlynn blurted out. The girls laughed, and just like that, all the tension was gone.

"Yes, I am a mermaid. So I'm not really afraid of water. I'm so sorry I lied to you. My legs turn back into my tail when I touch water. That's why I acted so strangely."

"I knew it," Maddie said. "How could anybody not like my hat?"

"Why were you pretending to be someone else?" Briar asked.

"Because..." Meeshell looked down at her tail. "I'm just not very confident around people when I'm on land. I'd never really been around people before coming to Ever After High."

"I think you're doing a wonderlandiful job of being around people on land," Maddie replied. Meeshell smiled appreciatively.

"You all have made it so easy for me. But I also hid who I was because my future is living on land, without my tail, and without my singing voice. I wanted to see what that would be like. To see if I could make it work."

Apple sat next to her, a look of absolute understanding on her face. "Meeshell, we each have futures waiting for us. But what I've learned is this— that we can't control them. Yes, there are things that we're supposed to do. Things that are expected and foretold. When I first got to Ever After High, I tried to live for my future life. I tried to convince Raven that she had to be someone other than who she really is, just to fit this future life. But what I've figured out is that we can't live for the future. We have to be our true selves right now. In this moment."

Briar, Maddie, and Ashlynn all nodded. The little mouse peeked out of Maddie's hat, and he nodded, too.

Then Apple put an arm around Meeshell. "The Little Mermaid is my favorite fairytale ever after.

Now it makes sense. I couldn't help you find a club because I didn't know the *real* you. You would be a spelltacular fit for the Happily-Glees!" She stopped smiling and withdrew her arm. "But of course, only if *you* want."

Meeshell laughed. "Yes, I'd really like to join the Happily-Glees! I've wanted to join since I first saw them in the quad."

"Since you're a mermaid, I think you should also join Hunter's lifeguard squad," Ashlynn said. "You'd be the best lifeguard Ever After High has ever seen!"

"And what about the swim team?" Briar asked. "A mermaid would set some records for sure."

"I think you should join the Teapot Club," Maddie said. They all looked at her quizzically.

"I don't get it," Briar said. "What do mermaids and teapots have in common?"

"Oh, a riddle!" Maddie said, clapping her hands. "I don't know. What *do* mermaids and teapots have in common?"

Briar peered over her crownglasses. "Uh, I was asking you."

"Well, how am I supposed to know the answer? It's not *my* riddle, you silly." Then Maddie took a crumpet from her teapot hat and began feeding the golden cranes.

Meeshell couldn't believe how relieved she felt. Yes, they all knew she was a mermaid. Yes, they were treating her differently. But that was okay. Because right now, this was who she was—a Mergirl going to Ever After High. She hadn't yet given up her voice. She hadn't yet given up her tail. That was in the future. And when that time came, she'd be that girl. She couldn't live trying to be her future self. That didn't make sense. In the end it didn't matter what anyone thought of her, it only mattered what she thought of herself. She had to be her true self to be happy.

Just as Meeshell's tail dried and her legs reappeared, a nearby mirror lit up. Blondie Lockes's face appeared. "Listen up, my fellow fairytales, have I got a very hexciting scoop for you. It turns out that our newest student, Meeshell, is actually a mermaid!"

Wow, that girl was good.

The

Happily-Glees

$\mathscr{M}$eeshell and her fellow Happily-Glees stood in the wing of the Charmitorium's stage, waiting to be announced. The air around them sizzled with nervous energy and excitement. It was the night of the annual Ever After High Talent Show. The Happily-Glees were one of dozens of acts scheduled to perform in front of the entire student body. Duchess Swan and her pet swan, Pirouette, were waiting to dance a *pas de deux* in matching tutus. Ginger Breadhouse had prepared a magic trick with singing sprinkles and flying moonpies. And Sparrow Hood and the Merry Men were currently on stage, playing the school's anthem to warm up the crowd.

Meeshell went over her lyrics in her head. The choir had practiced all weekend. Meeshell had learned the solo part, while the rest of the choir had learned the harmony. With Meeshell's voice taking the lead, the other singers grew more confident, and the whole choir began to sound better. Melody decided to cut back on the choreography, instead focusing entirely on the music. The transition in her choir was amazing. "I'm so proud of each of you," she whispered as they huddled together. "Let's go out there and give them a performance they'll never forget." Then she paused, probably remembering the last performance, which had yet to be forgotten. "I meant that in a *good* way." They all chuckled.

Meeshell peeked past the stage's curtain. There were no empty seats in the Charmitorium. Even the balcony was full. Tech Club members busily worked the lights, the sound system, and cameras. Humphrey stood behind one of the cameras. He glanced at Meeshell. She waved at him, but he didn't wave back. He quickly looked away. Why was he acting shier than usual?

She hadn't heard from StoryTeller2 in a few days. Was he sitting in the audience? Her gaze flew across the gilded seats, looking for boys wearing crowns. She found Daring and his brother, Dexter. Hopper was seated in the third row. Another crown caught her eye, but then the curtains closed, blocking her view. Someone tapped on her arm. She turned around. It was Melody. "Okay, it's our turn. We have a surprise for you."

What did Melody mean? But before Meeshell could ask, a rumbling sound arose. Two giants pushed an enormous aquarium onto the stage. Meeshell looked at Melody with confusion. "It's for you," Melody said with a laugh. "So you can be your true self." Then she turned to her choir. "Follow me. And everyone, break a leg. Or a tail."

The Happily-Glees followed their director onto the stage. Meeshell wasn't sure what to do, but then one of the giants offered her his enormous hand. She stepped into it and was lifted to the water's surface. She dived in, instantly changing into her mermaid self. Most of the students hadn't yet seen her in this form. Even though she was in the water, the one place where she felt most at home, her heart pounded with nervousness. Would this go okay? "Everyone ready?" Melody asked. The choir nodded. The curtains opened and the audience gasped in unison at the vision that greeted them.

Floating with her head above water, Meeshell began to sing. Very few in attendance had ever heard mermaid singing, and once heard, they would never forget. So lovely was the sound, so enchanting, if asked later, no one would truly be able to find words to describe it.

She sang, *"This feeling inside is coming alive. No more waiting now..."* And then, with a kick of her tail, she sailed into the air, did a graceful flip, and landed on two feet. She was wearing her favorite dress, the one with the scalloped coral top and teal skirt, the ruffles moving as gracefully as waves. Beneath the stage lights, her princess mermaid bracelet glittered on her arm, and her white pearlized shoes sparkled. Everyone went wild, cheering and clapping for the performance. Meeshell joined her fellow Happily-Glees in the chorus.

"See the fire in our eyes, it's burning
brighter.
Let go of the fear and fly, higher and
higher.
Rise up, the sky's the limit now, at
Ever After High.
Oh oh oh oh oh oh oh!
Power princess shining bright!"

"They loved you," Melody told Meeshell as loud applause filled the Charmitorium.

"They loved *us*," Meeshell said.

"That was wonderlicious!" Maddie hurried onto the stage. "I guess it's my turn now. Damsels and gentlemen, prepare to be spellbound and behold, as I turn this aquarium into the biggest cup of tea ever after!"

As Maddie worked her magic trick, Headmaster Grimm greeted the choir backstage. "Ms. Piper." He spoke in his usual serious tone.

"Yes, Headmaster?"

"I wanted to inform you that I was delighted by the performance. I didn't feel the need to plug my ears this time."

"Thanks," Melody said.

"And it is nice to see that you are no longer living incognito," he told Meeshell. "Mrs. Trollworth won't be happy with the additional paperwork required to make the change to your name, but the truth is, trolls are rarely happy."

Meeshell made a mental note to take Mrs. Trollworth a bouquet of flowers. Or perhaps, something more troll-worthy, like a jar of bugs.

Apple and Briar were weaving their way through the crowd. "Ms. Beauty!" Headmaster Grimm called. Briar and Apple squeezed between some students who were congratulating Melody.

"Yes, Headmaster Grimm," Briar said.

"A new student will arrive tomorrow morning, from Wonderland. As the head of the Welcoming Committee, I will need you to meet that student at the wishing well portal."

Briar pulled out her MirrorPad and checked her calendar. "I'd be happy to do that, Headmaster, but I have a Party Planning Committee meeting first thing in the morning. However…" Following a long yawn, she tucked the MirrorPad into her bag, then pulled a small badge from her pocket. "I happen to have a new member on the Welcoming Committee who will handle the welcome duties spelltacularly." She pinned the Welcoming Committee badge to Apple's dress. Apple beamed.

A while later, after most of the students had congratulated Melody and her choir, Meeshell, Apple,

Briar, Ashlynn, and Maddie all decided to walk to the village to get mocha lattes. For the first time since getting two legs, there was a lightness to Meeshell's step, a buoyancy to her stride as if she were bobbing on water. She felt authentically happy.

"Now that we know you're not afraid of water, how about going to Mirror Beach this weekend?" Apple asked.

"Yes, you can teach us all how to surf," Briar said.

"That would be fun," Meeshell told them. As they sat at a table beneath a giant oak, waiting for their lattes, Meeshell wanted to send StoryTeller2 a note. Maybe he'd meet her at the beach? But when she pulled out her MirrorPad, she found an urgent message. And it wasn't from StoryTeller2.

Urgent message from Professor Yaga.
We have another injured creature and I could use your help.

Swimming Lessons

$\mathscr{M}$eeshell and her friends hurried toward the Creature Care Center, but then Meeshell spotted the colorful shape of someone sitting on the beach. It was Professor Yaga. As they grew closer, Meeshell could see that Hunter was there as well. The tide was low, and a series of tide pools had formed. Professor Yaga motioned from the largest tide pool. The girls gathered 'round.

"What's that?" Briar asked, pointing to a black shape lying on the bottom of the pool.

"It's a manta ray," Meeshell explained. She recognized the creature as one of the mantas that she'd ridden many times back home. She knelt on a rock to get a closer look. The manta was listless, his eyes closed.

"This creature is obviously suffering," Professor Yaga said as sunlight bounced off her hoop earrings. "Hunter called me and I got down here as fast as I could, but I cannot figure out how to help him. Can you speak to him?"

"Yes," Meeshell said. "Manta Ray was one of the first languages I learned."

"Oh, can I listen?" Ashlynn said, joining Meeshell. "I'd love to hear what Manta Ray sounds like."

"Sure." Meeshell stuck her head in the water and, to her surprise, Ashlynn stuck hers in as well. Then, with delicate precision, Meeshell blew some bubbles, their sequence spelling out words. The manta opened his eyes and bubbled back. After a few lines of conversation, Meeshell and Ashlynn both sat up and took deep breaths.

"He can't swim," Meeshell reported. "He collided with a shark."

Professor Yaga stuck a gnarled finger into the tide pool and gently stroked the manta ray's back. "If he can't swim, how did he get here?"

"Coral brought him," Meeshell explained.

"Who's Coral?" Apple asked.

"She's the daughter of the Sea Witch," Professor Yaga said. She looked out at the ocean. "Is she still here? It would be helpful to speak with her."

Meeshell expected to hear gasps of surprise at the mention of the Sea Witch, but none of the girls even batted a lash. Hunter looked unfazed as well. Guess they were used to witches of all sorts.

Meeshell pushed her wet hair from her face, then walked from the tide pool to the water's edge. "Coral!" she called, cupping her hands around her mouth. "It's okay. You can show yourself. We want to talk to you!"

Some ripples appeared at the surface. Then a

blue face popped out of the water. "Hello," Coral said to Meeshell.

"Hi," Meeshell said. "Everyone, this is Coral." She introduced the professor and her friends. Apple was the most delighted to meet someone new.

"You're almost old enough to come to Ever After High," Apple said. "Briar and I will make sure you get a warm welcome." She pointed to her Welcoming Committee badge.

"Thanks," Coral told her, smiling shyly.

"What can you tell us about the manta ray?" Professor Yaga asked.

Coral pushed her blue-black hair behind her shoulders and swam closer. "He and a shark got into an argument. I'm not exactly sure what it was about, but you know how opinionated sharks are. Anyway, he ended up getting hurt and he's having trouble swimming. I don't have all my magical powers yet, so I can't magically fix him. I thought someone here could help."

With the professor's guidance, Meeshell, Hunter, and Ashlynn put the manta ray into a tub. Then the girls and Hunter carried the heavy creature over to the Creature Care Center, leaving Coral and Meeshell alone on the beach.

"How are things going?" Coral asked. "I see your legs didn't fall off."

"Yeah, they've been pretty good legs. Thank you for that."

Coral pulled herself onto the beach. She stretched her red tail. "Do you think you'll be okay with living on land? With losing your singing voice?"

Meeshell sat next to her, cross-legged. "I was worried about what I'd do with myself on land, you know, if I couldn't sing and if I couldn't have a tail. But I think I figured it out." She looked up at the care center building. "I will never lose my connection to the sea because I'm going to focus on my studies in Beast Care and Magicment. I'm going to dedicate my life to taking care of sea creatures."

Coral smiled. "Whoa, that's amazing, because I've decided to do the same thing."

"Really?"

"Yeah. When Mom leaves to become a famous singer, I'm going to use my powers as the Sea Witch to take care of creatures, too. So we can work together!" They both laughed. Who could have imagined such a twist to their stories?

"I brought you a surprise." Coral reached into the water and pulled out...

"Finbert!" Meeshell cried. Her little narwhal stuck his happy face out of the water.

"I've been working on a new spell. It's a way for Finbert to stay with you at school. Watch." With a flick of her abalone wand, a little protective bubble formed around Finbert and he floated into the air. With his tail acting like a propeller, he floated straight into Meeshell's outstretched arms.

"This is so amazing," Meeshell said with a laugh. "Thank you!"

After they said good-bye, Coral swam out of the harbor, smacking her red tail one last time before she disappeared beneath the waves. "I'm so glad you're here," Meeshell told her beloved pet. "Wait until you meet my friends. They're going to love you!" She was about to walk up to the Creature Care Center when some splashing sounds drew her attention. It wasn't ordinary splashing, like a fish enjoying some sunbeams, or a seagull diving for a treat. The splashing was urgent and frantic. "Uh-oh," she said to Finbert. "Let's go!"

She ran past the tide pools, around the bluff, and onto Mirror Beach. The beach was empty. An OFF DUTY sign hung from the lifeguard chair. But there, in the water, arms flailed. Someone was trying desperately to stay afloat. Meeshell caught a glimpse of a gold crown and realized instantly who it was.

Then he disappeared under the water.

She was at his side in a heartbeat, pulling him onto shore. He broke into a coughing fit, but she wasn't worried. She knew he'd be fine. He'd only gone under for a moment. "Humphrey, I don't mind saving you, but what if I hadn't come by? Trying to teach yourself to swim with no lifeguard on duty, and no one around to look out for you just isn't a good idea," she told him. She reached out and grabbed his crown before it floated away.

"I can..." He puffed out his chest. "I can..." Then he deflated. "Yeah, you're right. I can't swim."

His floaties lay up the beach, next to a log where he'd left them. She shook her head. "That's not such a big deal! I'm sure a lot of land-dwellers can't swim. Why do you keep risking your life like this?"

"I..." He swallowed hard and looked away. "I thought I needed to swim, so you'd like me."

"Huh?"

Humphrey pulled his legs close and wrapped his arms around them. "I thought you'd only like me if I could swim. You know, because you're a mermaid. I knew you were a mermaid from the first moment I met you." He continued to look away.

"Really?" She was very surprised. "But how could you know that?"

He dug his toes into the sand. "Well, I knew you'd arrived by boat, so that was the first clue. Then I heard you tell Hagatha that you wouldn't eat fish. Second clue. And I saw you jump back from the spilled tea and I realized that you were avoiding water. It all made sense."

Wow, he was as smart as everyone said. "But if you knew I was a mermaid..." He still wouldn't look directly at her. What was he hiding? She knew his big secret, that he couldn't swim, but was there something else? The gleam from his golden crown drew her attention. "Barnacles! Are you Story-Teller2?"

He nodded, and finally looked into her eyes. She couldn't believe it. The secret prince who'd meant so much to her during this first week at school, the prince who'd understood all her doubts and fears and her longing to fit in, had been right in front of her the whole time. "You've been risking your life for me?"

"Well, yes. I wanted you to like me, but I've never been able to swim. How can a guy like me even hope to get a date with you without being able to swim?"

"Humphrey, you don't need to change yourself for me. Or for anyone. If I'm going to like you, then I have to like you for who you truly are." She stuck his crown on his head. "Besides, I can give you swimming lessons anytime you want."

He suddenly looked terrified.

"Or not," she said. "It's not necessary. Really. It's your choice."

He let out a sigh of relief. "Then…then maybe we can go see a movie at the multihex sometime?"

"Sure," she said happily. "That sounds like fun. But not a shark movie! Those are way too scary!" They both laughed. Then Finbert swam around Humphrey's head, startling him.

"Whoa! A miniature floating narwhal. You don't see that every day."

As soon as her tail had dried, Meeshell and Humphrey headed to the aquarium to join the others. "I meant to tell you...your performance in the Happily-Glees was astounding. I'm glad you found a club."

"Thanks. And I meant to tell you...Thank you for being there, when I needed someone to talk to." She leaned close and gave him a quick peck on his cheek. His entire face turned as red as Coral's tail.

A pair of gulls flew overhead, swooping in lazy circles. A seal barked in the distance, singing its own song. A tiny narwhal swam through the air. Meeshell inhaled the salty scent and smiled. Her heart was full. For she knew, without a doubt, that being her true self was the right thing to be.

And she put one foot in front of the other, taking the steps toward her next adventure.

Acknowledgments

*O*nce again, I am indebted to an amazing team of creative people, without whom this book would simply not be. In Gotham City, you will find my editor Kara Sargent, who guides and protects me, my brilliant copyeditor Christine Ma, publicist extraordinaire Kristina Pisciotta, and many more people, all an important part of the effort, listed here in no particular order: Mara Lander, Véronique Lefèvre Sweet, Lindsay Walter-Greaney, Christina Quintero, Ronnie Ambrose, Dani Valladares, and Victoria Stapleton.

And on the other coast, in La La Land, you will find the other half of the team, the geniuses behind the Ever After High brand, who provide me with fun new characters and the freedom to play around in their hilarious universe. Thank you to Ryan Ferguson, Debra Mostow Zakarin, Nicole Corse, Charnita Belcher, Stuart Smith, Sammie Suchland, Karen Painter, Kristine Lombardi, Robert Rudman, Talia Rodgers, Eric Vexelman, Lara Dalian, Audu Paden, Gary Leynes, and Izzy Garr.

Michael Bourret, I hope to continue this writing journey together forever after. And to Isabelle, Walker, and Bob, you are the wind beneath my fairy wings.

About the Author

*S*uzanne Selfors feels like a Royal on some days and a Rebel on others. She's written many books for kids, including the Smells Like Dog series and the Imaginary Veterinary series.

She has two charming children and lives in a magical island kingdom, where she hopes it is her destiny to write stories forever after.

Can't get enough Ever After High?
Keep reading about your
best friends forever after in
The School Story collection
by Suzanne Selfors:

On Guard

A History of the Detroit Free Press

Frank Angelo

The Detroit Free Press
1981

Published by the Detroit Free Press
         321 W. Lafayette
         Detroit, Michigan 48231

Copyright © by Frank Angelo   1981

Manufactured in the United States of America

Library of Congress Cataloging in Publication Data

Angelo, Frank.
  On guard, a history of the Detroit free press.

  Bibliography: p. 279
  Includes index.
  1. Detroit free press.   I. Title.
PN4899.D55D42   071'.7434   81-1719
ISBN 0-9605692-0-0   AACR2
ISBN 0-9605692-1-9 (pbk.)

Contents

Preface

This is the story of people and an institution — the Detroit Free Press — that they built for other people who themselves were dedicated to building a great community . . . Detroit.

It is written by a person who has observed and shared at first hand almost 40 of the 150 years of the paper's history, and it is written from the perspective of an enthusiast rather than of an impersonal historian. It is also presented, it is hoped, with a sensitivity to fairness and objectivity that is the hallmark of a journalist who believes that the severest critic often can be the most sensitive admirer.

There are no pretensions here of great scholarship, for this is a story that depends heavily on what many others have done, on personal stories of some of the participants, and of course on what has appeared in the Free Press itself. And the latter is studied with the full knowledge that a newspaper as printed often reveals only minutely what really went into its creation.

Obviously one does not complete an effort of this magnitude without considerable support. For that I am profoundly thankful first to the hundreds of men and women who have made the Free Press flourish.

More particularly, I am grateful for the thoughtful counseling of Philip P. Mason, director of the Archives of Labor and Urban Affairs, Walter Reuther Library at Wayne State University; for the production skills of Free Press Associate Editor Scott McGehee; for the contribution of background and stories by Managing Editor Neal Shine, and for the skillful composition of the jacket by Dick Mayer, Free Press art director. The staffs of the Detroit Free Press library and the Burton Historical Collections of the Detroit Library, whose assistance was absolutely essential, also deserve thanks.

A special word of thanks to Dr. James Stanford Bradshaw of the Central Michigan University for making available articles on the

London edition of the Free Press and on women in Detroit journalism, and to CMU's Clarke Library and the Jackson Citizen Patriot for use of pictures.

And finally there are some personal words of appreciation to Lee Hills for tapping me for still another exciting job, to David Lawrence for his intense interest in the project, and to Betty for her patience and tolerance while I lived for several months in the exciting world of printer's ink and editorial words. That patience and tolerance were absolutely essential for my well-being.

Frank Angelo

Detroit, Mich.
January 1981

Other books by Frank Angelo:
- **Yesterday's Detroit**
- **Yesterday's Michigan**
- **To Educate the People, with Otto Feinstein**

With the demise of the Detroit Times in 1960, only the Free Press and the News were left, and they engaged in "a circulation war of splendid dimensions."

Chapter One

Then There Were Two

Chapter 1

It was almost midnight when what had been an off-and-on, all-day meeting in Lee Hills' office broke up. Within minutes after the last person had departed, the publisher of the Detroit Free Press was stretched out, resting on a sofa. It had been a tiring, hectic Sunday, but now he could relax because everything was in place to begin publication of a new Free Press edition. An historic step in Detroit journalism awaited only a phone call.

The call came a few hours later, at about 3:15 a.m. Monday, Nov. 7, 1960. A stunned friend was telling Frank Angelo, the Free Press managing editor, that he had just received a telegram saying his newspaper, the Detroit Times, would no longer need his services. Although the telegram didn't make it clear, the Times was going out of business, and the Detroit News was buying, for $10 million, it developed later, the Times building and presses, its trucks and other equipment — and most importantly, its circulation lists — but not its staff.

What had been a lively rumor for several days had become a reality — and suddenly so had a new Detroit Free Press afternoon paper called the Family Edition. Following that phone call, Free Press editors, reporters, printers, truck drivers and supervisors were rousted out of bed to begin what was to become a classic newspaper struggle.

For the Free Press, which had been founded in 1831 as a weekly and had survived fires, numerous changes in ownership and several strikes, it was an unusual opportunity, and the paper was moving quickly and effectively to take away as much as it could of the circulation the News thought it was buying. It was a daring effort that made it absolutely clear to a fascinated reading and business community that the Free Press, no matter what advantage the News might build, was determined to insure Detroit would remain a highly competitive two-newspaper town.

3

Here, then, was a classic example of what had been a driving force in American journalism since the first newspapers appeared in the 17th century: competition for the minds of readers and for the dollars that make it possible to reach them and survive. It was a battle that would be fought at two levels. One was the struggle to be the dominant news medium in town. The other — at the business level — was to win the fight for advertising linage and circulation numbers.

It was a battle that would be fought with imagination and innovation. It came at a moment when the world was excitedly watching the coming to power of a bright, young John F. Kennedy; when Detroit was beginning to pull out of the late '50s recession and soon would have a new, young mayor, Jerome P. Cavanagh, about whom inevitable comparisons to Kennedy would be made; when stories like the civil rights movement, the emerging African nations and the Castro-ization of Cuba were presenting challenges to newspapers, and when the State of Michigan was about to launch an all-out restructuring of its constitution, with new political leaders — George Romney, William Milliken and Coleman Young among others — moving into the spotlight.

A showdown between the Free Press and the News had become inevitable with the arrival at the Free Press in December 1951 of Lee Hills, an energetic, single-minded newspaperman who was impatient with the Free Press' being anything less than the leader and who had the knack for inspiring others to reach for that goal with him.

The showdown that developed on that frosty November day had been triggered a few months earlier when circulation figures showed a stunning Free Press success. For the first time since the twice yearly Audit Bureau of Circulations (ABC) figures began to be recorded in 1916, the Free Press, on March 31, 1960, had achieved a year-long circulation lead over the News. It had led on Sept. 30, 1959, and, buoyed by its March success, passed 500,000 for the first time Sept. 30, 1960.

That development jolted News officials. Aside from injured pride, the News stood to lose the millions of dollars in advertising revenue that tend to go to the circulation leader. Over the years, the News had controlled about 50 percent of newspaper advertising dollars in the Detroit market by maintaining its first-place circulation position. In the late 1950s, the Free Press not only had moved up in circulation but also had boosted its advertising share from 23 percent to 29 percent, all at the expense of the Times. The News management urgently sought a dramatic halt to the Free Press challenge. They decided to buy the Hearst-owned Detroit Times.

Now on this November Monday in 1960, it had come down to a head-to-head battle. The Free Press, led by the indefatigable Hills, was ready with a surprise. Simply put, the Free Press plan was to hire the Times' circulation staff and immediately provide readers with an afternoon paper similar to the Times in look and content, on whatever day the sale of the Times might be announced. Thus the name Family Edition, which the Times had established in a last-ditch effort to eliminate its sensational Hearstian image and stop its circulation slide. The Free

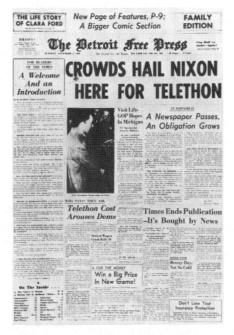

Front page of the Free Press
Family Edition, Nov. 7, 1960

Press even placed green (the Times color) boxes at the top of Page One and painted the Family Edition newspaper vending racks green to attract former Times readers.

Free Press planning had developed very quietly and at the same time the secret talks were going on between H. G. Kern, general manager of the Hearst Corp., and News officials. They were so secret even William Randolph Hearst Jr. was unaware of them. Only two Times officials would know of the negotiations. One was told a week before the deal was completed, the other only hours before the public announcement.

Shortly after noon on Monday, Nov. 7, the first Free Press Family Edition, with a press run of 250,000, appeared, and the bulk of the Times' circulation employees were standing by to deliver it.

The Free Press never intended to stay in the afternoon field, and seven months later the Family Edition was suspended. But the bold move accomplished what the Free Press had hoped for. It had surprised the News and slowed the gains it hoped to make by retaining Times sub-scribers. And it had impressed the public in general and advertisers in particular with the Free Press' competitive vigor. The News counted gains of only 248,000 from the Times daily circulation of 375,000, while the Free Press picked up 73,000. Time magazine correspondent Nick Thimmesch compared the News' situation to that of the determined fisherman in the Ernest Hemingway story of "The Old Man and the Sea." The News, Thimmesch's report to his New York office said, had landed a magnificent fish, but by the time the prize was finally reeled in, the sharks hadn't left much of it to enjoy.

When Hills arrived in Detroit on Dec. 1, 1951, he had been associated with John S. Knight, publisher of the Free Press, for nearly a decade. He had helped make Knight's Miami Herald one of the finest papers in the country. Knight had purchased the Free Press in 1940, had stayed closely involved with it as it began its circulation surge during the war years, but had lost some touch after 1944 when his attention was claimed by a new acquisition, the Chicago Daily News.

In the late 1940s, operations at the Free Press were guided by Henry C. Weidler, then the business manager; Malcolm S. Bingay, the editorial director, and Dale Stafford, the managing editor. Circulation gains continued, but the paper also was plagued with serious problems in building up its news staff and operating with an antiquated printing plant. Stafford's decision to leave the Free Press to buy his own newspaper, the Greenville (Mich.) Daily News, turned Knight's atten-tion once again to his Detroit paper.

The measure of his concern was his decision to move Hills from Miami to the Free Press, ostensibly to serve as executive editor but actually to be responsible for the total news and business operation. Within hours of his arrival, Hills, who never winced at working very long days, plunged into a massive examination of the paper. Within weeks, he was familiar with every part of the building, with nearly every person on the business and news staffs, with every cent of income and expenditure. His voluminous notes provided some startling information.

"I was stunned to learn that the Free Press actually was a late afternoon paper . . . it had only 33,000 home-delivered customers for its final Metro edition. It struck me that it would be a great time to launch a real morning paper in Detroit," he would say later with a chuckle.

Of the Free Press' 447,688 daily circulation (ABC, September 1951), about 217,000 was in the city edition that was printed beginning at 7 p.m. and was being home-delivered as early as 9:30 p.m. At the time, the Free Press trailed the News by 12,120 daily and led the Times by 8,549 in a hot three-way battle. Hills moved swiftly. He pushed for a series of news improvements, including the start of a Second Front Page for greater emphasis on local news. He also recommended Knight buy new presses and other production facilities. The next step was mounting a major circulation effort which helped to accomplish a massive shift of readers to morning delivery.

In the years that followed, the intensified efforts by the Free Press and News, decisions by Hearst that affected the functioning of the Times, and a series of strikes all played a part in gradually shifting the circulation balance until what was a magic moment for the Free Press at the end of March 1960.

The Free Press had taken the lead over the News in September 1959. It held it, 482,850 to 480,673, for the first time ever in the March ABC statement. That was an historic point, for while the Free Press had edged the News at least five times ('46, '47, '54, '57 and '59) in the September ABC reporting period, its growth in ABC's October-through-March period always had been slowed by the onset of winter when snow and ice made it difficult to distribute papers at 6 a.m.

The News indeed had cause for concern. It held a 91 percent lead over the Free Press in 1917, absorbed the old Detroit Tribune in 1919 and the Detroit Journal in 1922, then watched its margin steadily evaporate. The following table demonstrates the trend:

	News	Free Press	News Lead	% of lead
March 31, 1917	211,687	111,016	100,671	91%
March 31, 1927	320,970	201,861	119,109	59%
March 31, 1937	329,944	249,057	80,887	32%
March 31, 1947	421,999	401,140	20,859	5%
March 31, 1957	469,389	461,167	8,222	2%
March 31, 1960	480,673	482,850	-2,177	—

● The News absorbed the morning Detroit Tribune Feb. 1, 1919; approximate circulation 44,000.

● The News absorbed the evening Detroit Journal July 21, 1922; approximate circulation 120,000.

In the early 1950s, it was apparent the Times was struggling. A price increase in 1952 started a downward spiral that was abetted by the Times' failure to recover from further heavy losses after a 47-day strike in 1955-56. Not surprisingly, that also led to a shift in advertising linage that dropped the Times to third place in linage behind the Free Press while the News held its almost 50 percent share of the market.

The signs of impending change were evident. As early as 1957, Hills began to prepare for any eventuality. One study he prepared focused on what had happened in Cleveland, Cincinnati, St. Louis, San Francisco and Pittsburgh when two newspapers merged. Another analysis considered the possibility of the Free Press buying the Times. Production and promotion goals, particularly, were spelled out in internal memos. But Free Press executives decided against bidding for the Times.

The Times suffered still another jolt when the News on Nov. 2, 1959, introduced into its Sunday paper a TV Guide-sized book of television listings that brought it a fast 75,000 increase at the expense of the Times. The Free Press had studied, then discarded because of the high cost, the idea of using a TV Guide-sized book of its own. It opted instead for a less satisfactory quarterfold TV Channels section that it started before the News venture. "It was a major mistake," Hills would admit years later. (The Free Press introduced a TV Guide-like listings directory in 1973.)

The circulation shifts led Tade Walsh, an aggressive, effective circulation director who had spearheaded the Free Press' spurt in the early '50s, to develop a plan he thought would help both the Free Press and Times gain on the News. He got a positive response when he discussed it with Walter Aranoff, the long-time circulation boss at the Times.

The focus was on Macomb County where the News, which had been the most successful in following suburban growth, had made particularly solid inroads. Walsh suggested to Aranoff that they crisscross the circulation of the two papers, with Times readers receiving the Free Press in the morning and Free Press readers receiving the Times in the afternoon, at a reduced rate. News readers would be offered the two papers for the same price they were paying for the News alone.

The concept was unique and exciting — with enormous complexities. William Mills, Times general manager, was enthusiastic, seeing it as an important step toward rebuilding, but the Hearst general management delayed action. In discussing the plan, top personnel at the Times and the Free Press became well-acquainted. Although the crisscross circulation offer was never made to Macomb subscribers, Free Pressers had laid some solid groundwork for the new plan that evolved. When Warren Booth, publisher of the News, heard of the Free Press' dealings with the Times, he was reportedly furious and decided then to pay whatever was needed to buy the Times.

In the newsrooms of both the Free Press and the Times, a less official but nonetheless effective program of cooperation was emerging. Free Press reporters and Times reporters, who had come to consider the News a common enemy, often pooled information and sources on breaking stories to beat the News. Ed Breslin, one of the Times' top reporters and now a General Motors public relations executive, recalled those days: "There was always a more common bond between the Free Press reporters and the Times reporters than between either of us and the News. We both chased the same kind of stories, and whenever we got a chance to gang up on the News, we did it. The Free Press and the Times were on different time cycles, so we didn't compete head-to-head. We figured since we were both interested in beating the News, we could do a better job by cooperating on some stories."

So, with increasing indications of the News' intentions, Hills zeroed in on the expected new challenge. A closely knit management team that included Angelo, who had been named managing editor in 1955; Walsh, circulation director; Weidler, general manager; Dave Henes, promotion director; Bill Coddington, production manager; Cle Althaus, personnel director, and Robert Wheeler, advertising director, began meeting with Hills and their own aides to make contingency plans against the day the News' move would be made. Allen Neuharth, who became assistant executive editor on Nov. 1, was immediately involved.

The Free Press already had demonstrated its ability to move quickly in similar situations. In early 1959, it had moved into Grand Rapids and dramatized its dedication to imaginative, competitive innovations by establishing a morning edition, opening a news bureau and taking over the Grand Rapids Herald's circulation department when that paper was absorbed by the Grand Rapids Press. The Free Press started its own home delivery to former subscribers of the morning Herald and built a sizable Grand Rapids circulation with the effort. It made a breakthrough in western Michigan which had been dominated previously by Chicago papers.

Now it was time for another project, only this time closer to home with much more in the balance. Details were being worked out to expand the space for news and features. Lists of names of Times personnel whom the Free Press would want to hire were prepared. (One of them

was Ed Breslin, who was eventually hired.) Arrangements were made
quietly for the purchase of several new comics and columns and for the
United Press wire (regulations precluded use between 7 a.m. and 7 p.m.
of Associated Press material intended for morning newspapers). Henes
and his promotion people prepared radio and TV spots and other ads.
But the key action took place Sunday, Nov. 6, when the rumor of the sale
of the Times gained credence. It involved the circulation department,
critical to all else in the plan.

It had been hinted the News would not hire anyone from the Times.
Instead, it was reported, the News, which had an outstanding circulation department of its own, was planning to combine the Times'
circulation files with its own district lists and simply deliver the News to
all Times customers, counting on a high rate of retention. Saturday
evening, Nov. 5, circulation department executives of the Free Press and
the Times met to discuss the situation.

The next day, scores of Times men came to the Free Press Building to
sign up for jobs on a contingency basis. They were guaranteed papers at
their usual pickup spots if, as now seemed evident, announcement of the
sale came in the next few hours. Nineteen of 20 supervisors and 80 of 89
Times circulation station managers were hired that Sunday on that
basis.

Timesman Bob Cullinan, who later became Free Press circulation
manager, said, "The situation . . . involved hiring, testing, setting up
galleys (lists) for the number of papers each district manager would
need, arranging physicals and settling pay scales, which in the end
followed very closely those in the existing Free Press contract, with a bonus plan thrown in for those showing increases. It was chaotic . . . but it
worked."

First public word of the impending sale came mid-afternoon Sunday
in a broadcast by a WXYZ newscaster who reported the Times was
about to "be absorbed by the News." The Free Press ran the story in its
first edition with a "no comment" from the News. Others had also begun
to take the rumor seriously. Jim Jones, the capable, longtime Newsweek
correspondent in Detroit, sent a Nov. 4 report to his office in which he
said, "Detroit continues red-hot with rumors that Detroit Times has had
it. As usual, reporters are the last to get word of story involving their own
operations, but I can't verify single rumor . . . Times morale is shot.
Some editorial and business office people have asked management to
run a statement clearing the air, but no statement forthcoming. Hottest
line today is that the Detroit News is buying the Times, effective Nov. 13

or 14. Another weird report is that only the Times' Sunday edition will be sold. If News takes it over, it doubtless will throw Times away, including all but selected few people. Free Press source continues to maintain that Knight has no plans involving the Times. He, too, is unable to verify other reports."

On Sunday, however, Newsweek got a tip that the Times would be sold the next morning, and Jones headed downtown to settle himself in the News lobby where he finally intercepted Martin Hayden, that paper's editor. Hayden confirmed that the deal was complete, that it would be announced on Monday and that the Times would be discontinued. Hayden figured, Jones said later, that there would be no problem since Newsweek did not hit the streets in Detroit until Tuesday, the day after the News itself would have announced the sale.

From the lobby of the News building, Jones phoned New York with his story, then headed for a local bar where he met some Times people who obviously were not aware of what was about to happen. He "was jolted" as he drove home to hear a radio newscaster say the Free Press had a story saying Newsweek was reporting the sale of the Times to the News. Jones quickly headed back downtown. A visit to the Free Press revealed how the newspaper had gotten the story. Hills had called his longtime friend, John Denson, at that time editor of Newsweek, to ask whether Newsweek was using any stories about the newspaper situation in Detroit. Denson said it was, read what Newsweek was using and, as Jones put it, "That was that."

The Free Press final edition carried an eight-column headline saying, "Report News Buys the Times," and the story, quoting Newsweek, said that Hearst had made a deal for $10 million.

The sale triggered what one observer called "a circulation war of splendid dimensions." Newsweek headlined it: "The Battle of Detroit."

It was hardly that, of course, for the Times staffers who had unceremoniously lost their jobs. The Times, founded in 1900 by James Schemerhorn, had built up a reputation for local coverage and boasted some fine reporters, writers and photographers. But in the end, it had been caught in the crossfire between one powerful newspaper and another determined competitor.

On the morning the fateful telegrams went out, the Times had 1,400 people on its payroll. The message they got from Mills, the general manager, was simply stated:

"It is with deep regret that the management of the Detroit Times must inform you of termination of your services as of the opening of business on Nov. 7, 1960. It is not necessary for you to report for further duty. Your paycheck will be available on your usual pay day in the Detroit Times lobby. The chief accountant has been instructed to mail you a check as soon as possible for any monies that may be due you under the collective bargaining agreement reached between the Detroit Times and the Guild (or whatever other union might be involved)."

The terse message, delivered in most cases by Western Union messengers in the middle of the night, with no reason given for the

Front page of the last Detroit
Times, Nov. 6, 1960

terminations, caused scores of Times staff members each to believe intitially only he or she was being fired. The late Bob Maher, a renowned Times reporter (who was also later hired by the Free Press), often spoke of his reaction to the midnight telegram. "I remember sitting there in my underwear reading the telegram by the light of the streetlight coming through the window and wondering why in hell I had been fired. After about 30 minutes, I came up with about three good reasons. When I called another reporter to tell him I'd been fired, he said he'd been fired, too. A half-dozen phone calls later, it became pretty clear that we just didn't have a newspaper any more."

Officials later would insist that the apparent callous tone of the telegrams was because technically there was no News-Times merger. For the News to be able to buy just the assets, the Times management first had to kill the paper by firing everyone. The deal had been completed Monday, Oct. 30, in a meeting between Kern and J.D. Gortatowsky of the Hearst Corp. and Booth, Roy Merrill, Arthur Weis and Hayden of the News. An announcement was delayed to assure a clear understanding of what assets were involved. Mills, the Times general manager, who had been with the paper 24 years and was informed of the talks on Oct. 24, was stunned and bitter. Jack Manning, the editor, was told Friday, Nov. 4. Both were pledged to secrecy until the last minute. Phil de Beaubien, who had been publisher of the paper three years and who was vacationing in North Carolina, also was kept in the dark. And it was only because a friend at the News felt "it would be cruel" not to let the longtime and popular editor know that Manning finally was informed.

Those Times staffers who were at work at 3 a.m. putting out the Monday paper suddenly were faced with private policemen who had been assigned to the Times building by Weis, the News' general manager, "as normal procedure." As other staffers began to arrive to clean out their desks, they were escorted by a guard.

One Times reporter, Ray Girardin, later to become police commissioner, said bitterly a few days later, "I don't think any of us have any beefs. When the cops came up to throw out the nightside guys, they didn't use their clubs. When the telegrams came, they weren't collect. When we went to pick up our personal belongings in our desks, nobody hit us in the teeth." Ken McCormick, a Free Press reporter and president of the Detroit Press Club, ordered the bar to serve free drinks to Times people all day. In the meantime, the Free Press sent word to newspapers in 10 states, calling attention to scores of job applicants it was not itself able to hire.

On Tuesday, the day that Jack Kennedy was elected president, the dimensions of the Free Press effort became clear. Prominently displayed on Page One of the new Family Edition was an editorial signed by Hills and headlined, "A Newspaper Passes, An Obligation Grows." Hills joined Times readers "in mourning the loss of the Detroit Times" but added that the demise was "no reflection on the men and women who worked to bring distinction to their profession." Rather, the editorial continued, "it was a reflection of modern newspaper economics."

The editorial spoke of "heavy losses" (reported as $10 million over the previous five years). Then, emphasizing that the Free Press and News "are fiercely competitive," it added the competition "would mean an increase in services to readers." Hills concluded, "In the long run the public will judge the Free Press and the News on the manner in which they fulfill their responsibilities to report the news with honesty and enterprise and (on how they meet) their obligation to provide a forum for facts and conflicting viewpoints. The Free Press accepts this greater challenge and responsibility."

On the same page was a story detailing some of the additions to the Free Press, ranging from a new full feature page and added space for news, business and women's sections to an enlarged comics section. In addition, on that day, the Free Press ran a full-page advertisement headlined, "Special Notice to Insurance Policyholders of the Detroit Times." Then, in 36-point type, it added: "The Times has been sold! Don't lose your valuable insurance protection! By subscribing to the Free Press, you can have exactly the same protection you enjoyed through the Times. You will pay exactly the same premium, receive benefits that are identical! This protection, underwritten by Washington National Insurance Company, will be put in force immediately. Just fill out and mail the coupon below. Act Now! Don't take chances with your family's security. Mail the coupon today!"

This ad was especially significant because in that first hectic week of the battle, it became apparent to the Free Press that much of the Times' circulation (51 percent, a later survey would show) was tied into the accident insurance plan it had been promoting for many years. Readers paid a small weekly premium for the accident-protection policy. In some districts, 70 to 80 percent of Times subscribers had this insurance. The Free Press, which had used the accident insurance policy promotion sparingly over the years, had visions of being able to switch Times readers to its plan quickly so it would wind up with much of that circulation.

When the News sensed what a devastating impact the insurance switch might have, it had the Old Line Life Insurance Co., holder of the account, send letters to the Times' insured subscribers, informing them that unless they took the News, they could not receive accumulated benefits. Although the Free Press insurer, Washington National, also promised to pay those accumulated benefits, the Free Press was stymied. It found people reluctant to exchange the policies they held for new ones. And to fulfill state insurance laws, the Free Press could not provide actual policies on such short notice.

The Free Press' determination not to concede any part of this venture to the News without a fight was demonstrated at every level. For instance, the Times' single most popular syndicated feature was a medical advice column, "To Your Good Health." It was ghost-written by Times medical reporter Jack Pickering under the byline of Dr. Joseph G. Molner, who was also health commissioner for Detroit and Wayne County. The Free Press sent reporter Tom Craig to Dr. Molner's office with a notebook full of medical questions from Free Press "readers" which Craig insisted that Molner, in his role as a public health official, answer for publication in the Free Press. After some strong initial resistance and some equally strong reminders from Craig of the doctor's community responsibility as a public official, Molner reluctantly agreed to answer the questions. Thus the Free Press, with its own Dr. Molner column, quickly neutralized any advantage the News would have gained through exclusive rights to the column.

These efforts were just part of the total approach. In its initial sampling, the Free Press produced and distributed 250,000 papers free to former Times readers, and Times district managers signed up about 3,000 of their carriers for new Free Press routes. Soon the News began to call the same carriers to deliver its paper. Some skirmishes occurred among carriers over who was going to deliver what paper to whom, and Walsh charged that Free Press carriers delivering papers to former Times subscribers "have been intimidated, coerced and threatened." The News, meanwhile, said that former Times substations, which it was now operating, had been looted. The result was a conference at which Police Commissioner Herbert W. Hart and Superintendent Louis Berg pledged "that policemen will protect the right" of Free Press carriers to deliver the paper.

Hart added, "We are happy about the fine cooperation from the Free Press and News officials on this matter, which has been minor in scope up to the present," thus taking note of the fact that the News also had complained of carrier intimidation.

Meanwhile, the promotion and advertising departments also were pulling out all stops. Wheeler, the advertising director, quickly sent telegrams to advertisers: "We suggest you immediately consider switching any advertising now scheduled in the Times into the responsive morning Free Press. We are launching an intensive circulation drive to assure you a more productive coverage of the market than ever before."

The promotion department prepared special brochures. For one series, Henes, the promotion director, used the talents of reporter Louis Cook as writer and art director Verne Minge for illustrations. In another, he called attention to 12 major national advertisers who had quickly switched their linage to the Free Press and eight retailers who had boosted schedules. In addition, a "4-for-the-money" contest was announced based on the use of Social Security, license plate, telephone and dollar bill numbers for the payoff, and the Free Press was able to boast that in three days more than 11,000 entries had been received. The contest was comparable to one that had run in the Times.

But major emphasis was placed on promoting the content of the Free Press, with ads calling attention to new features including columns by Joe Falls, former Times sports writer, and Manning, the former Times editor. The Free Press had hired a number of other former Times staffers, including Tom Kleene, Jack Saylor, Harvey Taylor and Bob Wood, as well as Breslin and Maher.

The intensity of the promotional push was spotlighted in midweek when the Free Press printed a letter written by a former Times carrier on Page One. The actual letter was reproduced in two-column width. It read:

> "To the staff of the Detroit Free Press, Dear Sirs, I know that all of you are busier now than ever & will probably be from now on. I would appreciate it though if you would take a little of your precious time to read this note and find out just how much I appreciate what all of you are doing to help the former Detroit Times carriers and their station managers to get jobs.
>
> "I and all of my customers know that the Detroit Free Press did not have to give jobs to the former Detroit Times employees but out of the kindness of your hearts you did give them jobs and I want you to know that I & many other former Detroit Times carriers and customers are behind you 100%.
>
> "I just hope when I grow up that I will be half as nice as any one of the Detroit Free Press staff.
>
> Yours truly,
> A former Detroit Times Carrier
> Charles Morin, Branch B-2"

Hills followed the letter with a note expressing pleasure that Charles and his friends "are happily back to work delivering the hundreds of thousands of extra copies of the Free Press." A brief account explained that Charles was 16 and an honor student at St. Anthony's High School.

The News, of course, was making its own promotional effort, and the depth of its feeling surfaced in its continual complaints to the Associated Press about any AP copy that happened to slip into the Family Edition.

In its promotion efforts, the Free Press called attention to the many news services it used besides the AP, such as the New York Times, Chicago Daily News and Chicago Tribune wires, and it spotlighted Judd Arnett, Louis Cook, Jean Sharley, sports columnist Lyall Smith and Washington Bureau columnist Ed Lahey among others as representative "of special talents on the Free Press staff." Beyond that, it explained to Times readers, it also had "to-the-point editorials, crisp writing, financial stories, top television commentary, sparkling society and women's news, amusing features and all the rest, including the finest in pictures, taken by a prize-winning photographic staff." It also took cognizance in one of its promotions of the fact that "the Free Press will seem a bit 'different' to you for a while," but it suggested that given a fair trial, "you'll find, as the months and years go on, that the Free Press is your best bet for enjoyable reading."

The Free Press staff was thoroughly enjoying the spirited competition and working diligently to produce an additional afternoon paper in a morning-paper atmosphere. One new skill that proved tricky for them in the early days of that transition was the writing of "overnight leads." That is the process of rewriting the first paragraph or two of stories that had appeared in the morning edition of the Free Press so they could be carried over into the new afternoon Family Edition. Writers on p.m. dailies did this as a matter of routine. The Free Press writers found it difficult to adapt to the style. One reporter, after struggling to write an overnight lead for a traffic accident story, had this facetious lead rejected by his editor: "Still dead Friday was John Smith who was killed Thursday when his car hit a tree near Bay City."

Finally, in mid-December, a series of departmental meetings was held. In the city room, with all staffers gathered, Hills stood on a desk to deliver his review and pep talk in which he said, "Things are shaking down into a stiff, tough, wonderful long-term fight, and we're headed in the right direction." Hills also expressed pleasure with the news staff's performance, especially the follow-up coverage on the election.

The Free Press continued to introduce a steady stream of special features, and, more importantly, to provide intense coverage of major local stories that would have a long range impact on Detroit — the fight over union-exhibitor relations at Cobo Hall, the battle over whether to tear down old City Hall and the need for more hotel space to help save convention business for the city, particularly after the American Legion announced it was cancelling its appearance.

Most dramatic of all was coverage of a series of unrelated murders that led to a police crackdown which had profound political impact in the months that followed. The police action included widespread arrests and street searches, mostly of blacks. The resulting disaffection by blacks — and a number of whites — laid the groundwork for the surprise defeat of Mayor Louis C. Miriani by an unknown challenger, Jerry Cavanagh.

Big Page One news was announcement of a new building downtown for First Federal Savings, and another spate of stories told of troubles at Chrysler, with columnist Mark Beltaire coming up with an exclusive interview (used on Page One) with Chrysler President William C. Newberg, center of that particular controversy.

The paper's Washington correspondent, Jim Haswell; Hub George, the political writer; Jim Robinson, the Lansing bureau chief, and his assistant Owen Deatrick produced a heavy flow of copy about President-elect Kennedy's pre-inauguration efforts, focusing on former Gov. Soapy Williams' appointment as assistant secretary of state for African affairs. And with help from the Miami Herald, the Free Press was well on top of the Cuba story.

Editorially, the Free Press was prodding Mayor Miriani on the Cobo Hall situation but supported his position on tearing down the 90-year-old City Hall. An editorial Nov. 16 said: "Mayor Miriani says he's tired of reading about troubles between exhibitors and the unions and that he wants to find out just what the problems are. We are too and hope he succeeds."

A few days later an editorial reacted to the City Hall controversy under this headline, "Old City Hall's Fate . . . Facts Dictate the Answer." It said: "It is hard to part with something which has long been familiar and which served a useful purpose.

"But if all landmarks were to be preserved just because they are landmarks, we would find ourselves living in a museum-like atmosphere in which progress would be impossible . . . Age alone does not make a building an historic structure and while the old City Hall had its moment, there is no great aura of history surrounding it . . . Considering Detroit's needs for the present and future, there is no other choice but to align ourselves on the side of progress, even though the decision is hard and regretfully made."

The appointment of Bob Scheffing to manage the Tigers kept the sports pages lively. And a poignant note was struck on Nov. 17 when Free Press music and drama critic J. Dorsey Callaghan retired and was honored by the Detroit Symphony Orchestra. Callaghan had joined the Free Press in 1935 — after running a dime store in Mt. Clemens and herding camels in Africa — because Malcolm Bingay was impressed with some poetry he submitted under the pen name "The O'Callaghan." He started as a reporter, soon was covering music, and in 1947 become the paper's drama critic.

The promotion department was conducting weekly surveys to monitor the Free Press' progress. Not unexpectedly, the News was picking up a major portion of the exclusive Times readers, particularly in the suburbs where its home-delivery system was better organized. Sadly, the survey also indicated that a shocking 60 percent of Times readers were "indifferent" to its demise, with only two percent "angry" and the remainder "sorry" to see it go.

But the Free Press effort paid off. On the one hand, its intensity forced the News to make major changes in its plans for the future, but on the other, much more of the Times' circulation was converted to the Free Press than might have been expected.

Such intense competition attracted national attention, but more important from the Free Press standpoint was the favorable reaction of Detroiters to this all-out combat. That, plus a solid circulation gain, made the effort connected with the afternoon Family Edition worth every cent of the cost by the time it was discontinued June 9, 1961. The Free Press, a solid seven-figure profit-maker in 1959, equalled that performance in 1962 after a slight dip in 1960 and 1961, but it also moved into position to take almost 40 percent of the advertising market.

In the last ABC period before the Times ceased publication, September 1960, the Free Press led the News, 501,115 to 482,384. By March 31, 1961, the first post-Times ABC report period, the News had a 160,310 lead, 733,583 to the Free Press' 573,273.

This did not reflect the full benefit which the News got from its purchase because the Free Press was publishing its afternoon Family Edition during most of that period. On March 31, 1962, about 10 months after the Free Press dropped its afternoon edition, the News had a 211,000 lead.

The News was not able to hold that spread. In fact, its circulation pattern has been declining ever since, while the Free Press has continued a steady upward climb to within 4,000 of the News in 1976. Again, the

News retaliated in the face of a threat to its lead, this time by introducing a morning edition that restored its lead to 15,000 to 25,000. But the battle goes on unabated.

The Free Press has been a spirited competitor for 150 years. Since its founding, extraordinary people have provided the words that inspired and enraged, prodded and uplifted, informed and entertained a community. And its foundation, rooted in the pioneer days of the early 1800s, has become stronger. It is a colorful history, and it began on a simple flatbed press with hand-set type on a Wednesday, May 5, 1831.

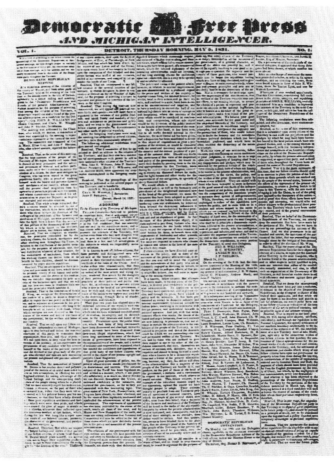

The Democratic
Free Press and
Michigan
Intelligencer, born
May 5, 1831.

Chapter Two

The Beginnings

Chapter 2

I t was a time when one could walk into the wilderness that surrounded the village on the banks of the Detroit River and "bag a deer or several partridges in a morning's tramp."

Jefferson and Woodward avenues were quagmires in wet weather, dusty in dry, and people "talked about hogs being stuck in the mud on Jefferson . . . and sinking gradually out of sight." The city's boundaries (within which 2,222 persons were counted in the 1830 census) were what are now Brush Street on the east, Cass on the west. The principal streets were Woodbridge and Jefferson, and the settled part did not extend up Woodward as far as what is now Kennedy Square.

It was a time when men of ambition and optimism attacked the wilderness to build homesteads and great cities and states. They vigorously expressed opinions on how all this should be done by creating political parties — and newspapers to serve them. Even then, "the plain people" were pitting their visions against those of the "city aristocracy," and that gave impetus to development of the populist movement which catapulted Andrew Jackson into the presidency in 1828. Both sides, as one historian put it, were "amply fortified with the loyalties, animosities and prejudices of political partisanship."

Detroit, founded in 1701, survivor of wars, fires and cholera epidemics, had established a foundation that grew out of its French, British and American heritage, and it now stood as "one of the bastions of the frontier." Physically, its limited area and its wooden buildings constituted little more than a frontier settlement. Its people, reflecting a spirit that would continue for many years, were described by a correspondent for an Eastern newspaper in 1831 this way: "The society of Detroit is kind, hospitable, and excellent. A strong sense of equality and independence prevails in it. A citizen whose conduct is . . . decorous is respected by all and associates with all . . . A genuine friendliness and cordiality are evident ... Recently domiciled here, we can speak feelingly upon this subject."

Just a few months earlier, on Aug. 21, 1830, a large crowd had gathered near the riverfront to see the first water pouring into three-inch wooden pipes from a new 21,870-gallon water reservoir, and territorial Gov. Lewis Cass was moved to exclaim, "Fellow citizens, what an age of progress" ... a cry that would be raised many times in future eras.

Michigan, with a population of 32,000, was moving closer to statehood. A newspaper, the Democratic Free Press and Michigan Intelligencer, was created to serve the needs of some who would be leaders in the growth of the city and state — and to serve the needs of a political party.

In truth, that first Free Press was little more than a political sheet, filled with bits and pieces of information about the world beyond but mostly with fervent opinion about the prospects of the Democratic Party closer to home. It first appeared May 5, 1831, and a Free Press has been published in Detroit uninterruptedly except for those days when fires and strikes have intervened.

That first edition, four pages, each five columns wide, printed on a "smaller sheet than was intended" because of an error in ordering paper, contained four-week-old Washington correspondence, foreign news (some of which was three months old), the text of resolutions just adopted by the Democratic Republican Party, three local items and a few advertisements, one of which announced the ferry between Detroit and Windsor would be available every half hour during the day.

Paul Leake, in his "History of Detroit," reports 38,000 copies were printed in the first year. It began as a weekly and grew with the city, which found itself the center for a "tide of immigration." The Free Press proudly reported that fact from the start. On May 19, 1831, for example, an item called attention to the arrival in the past week of several steamboats bringing a total of "more than 2,000 and all in the prime of life; mostly heads of families who have come for the purpose of purchasing land and settling in Michigan." That, it emphasized, did not include those who recently had come to Detroit by land.

In 1835 — when the Free Press became a semi-weekly in June and then, on Sept. 28, the first daily published in the Michigan Territory — the city had grown to more than 5,000 people, and Michigan was the focus of the nation's land craze. Sale of public lands totaled 37,865 acres in 1818 when the first land office was opened in the territory. Sales soared to 147,062 acres in 1830; 498,423 acres in 1834; 1,817,248 acres in

1835, and, just before the boom burst, 4,189,823 acres in 1836. The 1836 total exceeded sales in any other state or territory that year.

Against this backdrop, strong-willed men produced that first Free Press edition, and they have been followed by others of the same mold — John Bagg, Wilbur Storey, Henry Walker, William Quinby, E.D. Stair, John S. Knight and Lee Hills, to name only a few of the prime movers in shaping this powerful institution.

First, however, there was John Pitts Sheldon. Among Michigan journalists, Sheldon is a pioneer of major proportions. It was Sheldon who in 1817 produced Michigan's first regularly published newspaper, the Detroit Gazette; who fought the first freedom-of-information battle from a jail cell in 1829, and who was editor of the Free Press in 1831.

Like so many Easterners, he came to Detroit seeking new opportunity. He began his journalism career in a print shop in Ogdensburg, N.Y., where he was born in 1792. He had served in the War of 1812 and had started a paper in Rochester, N.Y., before heading west at age 25. Fortuitously, while awaiting a ship on the Buffalo waterfront, he met Ebenezer Reed, who had served as a printer's apprentice in Utica, N.Y., and who at 21 also sought new fields. They became partners. Sheldon traveled to Detroit where, "at the suggestion and under the patronage of Governor Cass," he prepared to publish a Democratic newspaper while Reed was completing arrangements to buy a press and type on credit. Their efforts came together Friday, July 25, 1817 (within a day of the city's 116th birthday), when the first copy of the Gazette appeared. It sold for $4 a year to city subscribers.

Within a year, it offered to establish what amounted to a 19th century version of the latter-day Action Line. On Sept. 11, 1818, Sheldon, after warning readers about a person who had defrauded the paper, wrote: "Citizens who have been wronged by scoundrels have only to send a notice of the wrongs and the name of the scoundrel to this office in order to put the public on their guard. Such notices will be published gratis."

Other problems — as well as the scope of the paper's circulation — are suggested in an excerpt from the edition of July 14, 1820: "We have in the City of Detroit 82 subscribers, at River Raisin 17, and in other parts of the territory 19; total, 118 subscribers in Michigan Territory; two subscribers in Upper Canada, and 32 in different parts of the union. Total subscribers, 152. Not one of the advertisements have been paid for

John P. Sheldon   John S. Bagg

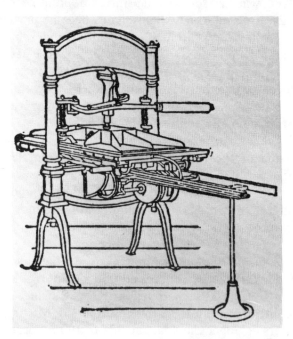

A Washington press like the one first used to print the Free Press

and only 90 subscribers have paid for the papers."

It was not an unusual circumstance. Scores of other printer-editors would make the same sort of plea to subscribers. Somehow the newspapers survived. Political parties provided support, and income came from publication of state and city notices. In addition, there was revenue from job printing and, in the case of Sheldon and Reed, a book and stationery business. Many a printer was happy to be paid in bushels of wheat. Printers also often were able to get the job of postmaster through political patronage — a tradition rooted in the days of Benjamin Franklin, that well-known printer-postmaster. It was a time when a newspaper was considered "the heavy artillery of party politics."

The well-established Federalist Whig group, led by William B. Woodbridge, Henry S. Chipman and Maj. Thomas Rowland, among others, had induced George L. Whitney, a New Yorker, to come to Detroit to publish the Northwestern Journal. It appeared Nov. 20, 1829. One year later, it became the Detroit Journal and Michigan Advertiser.

About that time, too, the Detroit Courier was launched, developing into the voice of the politically important anti-Masonic movement. The two papers were merged into the Detroit Journal and Courier in 1835. The Journal, meanwhile, maintained a separate tri-weekly that was converted to the Detroit Daily Advertiser in 1836, about a year after the Free Press itself had become a daily.

As Royce Howes, editor of the Free Press in the 1950s, wrote: "It was a publishing condition expected and accepted by the reader. Political passions burned fiercely. Doctrinaire dogmatism hopelessly outran sweet reason. What the reader wanted was reiteration of his own partisan sentiments with no space wasted on anyone in disagreement unless it was employed for cantankerous chastisement. A subscription, in fact, was often considered to be virtually a contribution to the party; a duty to support its voice."

However, it is important to emphasize that newspapermen of that period were, like Sheldon, people of strong convictions, with great confidence in their own political views. They could expound them with vigor — and venom. Sheldon strongly supported Andrew Jackson and violently attacked John Quincy Adams, who had won the presidency by defeating Jackson in an election decided in the House of Representatives in 1824.

Sheldon was characterized by opposition papers as "a fretful and malicious little man" and as "a literary dagger man of Detroit." He was a "slender man physically (about 5 feet 8) with a haggard, melancholy face ... But he was sharp and gutty and had bright, black eyes that looked at the bottom of things," wrote George Catlin, a Detroit News writer and historian. He added that "while earning the enmity of public officials and malefactors by his criticisms, he usually managed to please the people at large."

How well he pleased them was abundantly indicated in 1829 when Sheldon was jailed for contempt of the Michigan Supreme Court (the judges were Whig appointees) after a series of critical articles in the Gazette about one of that august body's actions. The incident also dramatized Sheldon's commitment to "the majesty of the press."

It started when a man named John Reed, who had been convicted of larceny, was granted a new trial on the grounds that he had been wrongfully forced "to use one of his statutory rights of peremptory challenge in order to get rid of (an) objectionable juror." Sheldon was critical because the person to whom Reed had objected did not serve on the jury, and in any case, Reed had other peremptory challenges available to him.

On Jan. 8, 1829, Sheldon wrote, under a headline, "Progress to Perfection of Reason in Michigan," that "as usual (during the court's most recent session) there was but little business done, and a portion of that little, we are led to believe, was poorly done." He proceeded to criticize the award of a new trial to Reed. It was the first of several articles on the topic. On March 5 he was arrested for contempt and fined $100. Friends offered to pay the fine, but he refused to allow that and went to jail instead.

That evening a public meeting was held at the Mansion House, a noted hotel on Jefferson near Cass. The group resolved to raise the money for the fine "in sums of not more than 12½ cents from each person" and made plans for a big public dinner. Two days later, for the first and only time in Michigan's history, a prisoner was honored with a public dinner inside a jail. Nearly 300 attended, an impressive turnout considering that Detroit's population was slightly more than 2,000. Silas Farmer, a noted Detroit historian, described the dinner as "both sober and hilarious. Songs, toasts and speeches were the order of the day and the old jail rang and rang again with cheers of the gathered throng."

During the nine days Sheldon was in jail, he continued to write for his paper. Finally on March 14, a committee, accompanied by another crowd, paid his fine from the money raised publicly and sent him home in a carriage. It should be noted that, during all these festivities, Thomas Carlton Sheldon, John's brother, was the sheriff in charge of the jail. A

Whig commentator, meanwhile, expressed this view: "Never before had the Wayne County Jail contained 300 Democrats at one time. For the good of the community, the whole bunch should have been detained for 90 days."

Sheldon stepped down as the Gazette's editor shortly thereafter, at least partially for reasons of health, and his nephew, Sheldon McKnight, whom he had introduced to "the art and mysteries" of the business, took over. By October, he was repeating the often-heard complaint. "Michigan (subscribers) pay or never pay," McKnight wrote, "as it may chance to suit their fancy. Sometimes we get a pig or a load of pumpkins from them, and once in a great while there is a man of mettle who pays cash for his paper."

The Gazette printed what proved to be its final edition on April 22, 1830. That day's paper announced a temporary halt in publication and included a notice by McKnight: "Some light-fingered gentleman entered our office and took from there a double-cased silver watch with a steel chain and two gold seals and a key. The man who would steal from a printer ought to be compelled to drive a snail through the Black Swamp (an area in northern Ohio) to Boston in the dog days, and suck a dry sponge for nourishment."

Four days later, a man named Ulysses G. Smith, who had been a printer at the Gazette, was accused of stealing the watch. After Smith was served with a warrant, he "declared his purpose of being revenged on McKnight and armed himself with a pistol which he loaded and primed in the evening," according to an account in the Journal. He also set a fire in the paper's loft that left only some old type to be salvaged. As the Journal story explained: "On the evening of Monday he was in the printing office; the lad belonging to the office he sent to inquire for a letter at the post office. On the return of the lad, Smith was in the street in front of the building. He passed back and forth, twice looking up at the building. Within two or three minutes the fire broke out in the loft, in where were kept loose paper and old files. But little fire had been kept in the office during the day; and the mechanic who built the chimney testified that work was so constructed that a spark could not have escaped from it. Smith was apprehended soon after the fire was discovered." The watch was recovered — by McKnight, who found it where he himself had misplaced it. Smith went to jail for the fire.

And the demise of the Gazette made the way clear for the founding of the Free Press.

Some shed no tears. Judge B. F. H. Witherell wrote to a friend, "The

Gazette people saved their type, I think, for which I am not glad nor anyone else. A sword in the hands of a madman is a dangerous weapon no
matter how he uses it."

The elements for launching a new venture in 1831 were all in place.
Party leaders urgently needed a voice for the Democratic Republicans
and for one of their leaders, John R. Williams, who sought major
political office. Williams, the first elected mayor of Detroit, and his
uncle, Joseph Campau, Michigan's wealthiest man and a leader of the
Democrats, learned from Sheldon that printing equipment was available.

Sheldon had moved to Oakland County, just north of Detroit, in the
mid-1820s and had become acquainted with Thomas Simpson, editor of
a newspaper established in 1830 to help promote a land boom. The
venture proved unprofitable, and Simpson was prepared to sell the
equipment needed for the project in Detroit. First word came in the
Journal of April 27, 1831, which told its readers: "The Oakland
Chronicle — This paper which has been conducted in Pontiac by Mr.
Thomas Simpson for nearly a year, has been discontinued, and the
printing establishment transferred to the Joseph Campau & Co. of this
city. We are informed that a paper will soon make its appearance from
this press under the name of 'The Democratic Free Press and Michigan
Intelligencer.'" The printing equipment included a Washington press
which could produce about 250 pages an hour, hand-operated by two
men. It was installed, after being hauled in a wagon over rough roads, in
a building at Bates and Woodbridge streets and turned out a four-pager,
14 by 20 inches in size, with five columns of type.

McKnight was publisher of the newspaper. Sheldon became the
editor, and Campau and Williams headed a group providing the money.
It was a cast of characters worthy of a pioneer drama — which is just
what it became. A test of wills soon developed between McKnight and
Williams, who made a desperate but futile effort to seize control.

Campau's forebears had come to Detroit with its founder, Antoine de
La Mothe Cadillac, in 1701. By 1831, Joseph Campau was thought to be
the largest landowner in Michigan. He was a six-footer, described as "of
spare frame, wrinkled, clean-shaven, white-haired and dark complex-
ioned, with sharp, twinkling bright eyes, and a clerical appearance to
which his ruffled shirt . . . and black clothing contributed." A great
friend and counselor of the Indians who dealt with him at his store on
their visits to Detroit, Campau was a man of firm convictions. That
became apparent in his relationship with the revered Father Gabriel

Richard, pastor of St. Anne's, Detroit's first Catholic church, after Richard became involved in a political race against Williams in 1823.

Williams was born in Detroit in 1782, the son of Campau's sister, Cecile, and her husband, Thomas Williams, and he became Detroit's first elected mayor April 4, 1825, with 102 votes to a total of seven for the other candidates. He is described as a man "of spirit, an erect figure, a noble brow, a beak of a nose, bold eyes and humorous mouth, the very picture of a public man." He also liked to write letters to the editor. In 1823 he made a bid to be elected the Michigan Territory's congressional delegate and wound up fourth in a four-man race when Father Richard, supported by the French community, decided to run at the last minute and became the only priest to be elected to Congress until Father Robert Drinan of Massachusetts in 1970. Richard's election so infuriated Williams, who was a marguiller (or warden) at St. Anne's, and Campau that they left the church. Both became Episcopalians, and Campau, until his death, was a constant and severe critic of Catholic priests in general and Richard in particular.

Williams had been defeated again in 1829 and now, in 1831, was trying a third time to become the territorial delegate.

McKnight, born in Herkimer County, N.Y., was 10 years old when he came to Detroit in 1820 to join his two uncles, Thomas and John Sheldon. In an 1885 biographical sketch in the Free Press, McKnight is described as a "man of great mental acuity, somewhat quick, but generous and warm-hearted, and while he was belligerent and plain spoken in his political expression and not backward on occasion in reasonable pugnacity, he was much liked by those who knew him, whether allies or opponents."

Williams and McKnight shared characteristically quick tempers that later were to bring each man afoul of the law. Williams was once arrested and held several days for shooting a man with whom he had argued. When it became apparent the wounds were not fatal, Williams was released. McKnight, for his part, was charged with manslaughter after the death of a man he had struck in a saloon fight. He was tried and acquitted. Two such volatile tempers were destined to collide.

These, then, were the key people in the effort that produced the first issue of the Democratic Free Press and Michigan Intelligencer May 5, 1831. That first front page was given over entirely to reports on public meetings of the Democratic Republicans, later called the Democrats, which is what the supporters of Andrew Jackson were calling themselves. Also included was word that John R. Williams would be the Democratic Republican candidate for territorial delegate in the July election.

On Page Two McKnight spelled out his paper's philosophy:

> The democratic citizens of this territory having found the two newspapers (the Journal and the Courier) already established in Detroit completely under the control of the city aristocracy have been compelled to set up an independent press. Forming as they do a large majority of the electors of the Territory, they have found no medium with which to communicate to the public.
>
> This dilemma was presented to them, either tamely to suffer a knot of politicians, in whose patriotism they have no confidence ... or to establish a press which should be guided by the wishes of the majority. They have adopted the latter alternative, and fearlessly appeal to their fellow citizens to sustain an establishment intended to support principles rather than men.
>
> Our appeal is made to the people of the outer counties, and by their verdict we "sink or swim." We know the opposition we must encounter here in Detroit, and have made our calculations accordingly. We depend entirely on the country influence.
>
> We shall endeavor to merit the favor of our fellow citizens of the interior, by giving them a newspaper conducted on true democratic principles, and with such industry and judgment in the selection and arrangement of foreign and domestic news and the usual variety of miscellaneous matter, as we can command. We hope to be able to present them weekly, with an agreeable and instructive sheet.

In the beginning the youthful McKnight served as publisher and editor. On June 2, Sheldon, whose health was fragile, revealed in a brief editorial that he had been "employed to superintend its editorial department" and added that "should circumstances induce him to relinquish the important duties ... note of such relinquishment will be given." McKnight, while denying that the Free Press was beholden to any person, unmercifully flayed Williams' opposition, Austin E. Wing, the Whig, and Samuel W. Dexter, the anti-Masonic party candidate.

News coverage, of course, was in no way comparable to today's efforts. It was not until 1847 that the first telegraph line was opened, and then only to Ypsilanti. A year later, the connection was extended to New York. Before then, communication was painfully slow. The Free Press and other newspapers were filled with material clipped from weeklies from around the country, as well as long letters and official reports of meetings and legislative actions, most of which had taken place weeks ago.

Interspersed were the editors' comments, and Sheldon and McKnight made it clear their support lay with Andrew Jackson and the election of Williams. His campaign, according to a bill the Free Press company sent Williams, included such expenditures as "printing 100 handbills, $4; address to the public, 1,000 copies, $15; memorials to Congress, three editions, $9; address in French, $10; 200 addresses to the St. Joseph's convention, $5." The total bill was $138.75. In addition, Williams bought $55 worth of extra copies of the Free Press to distribute during the campaign. Despite these efforts and the partisan support of the newspaper, he lost again.

Typical of the reporting of the day is this July 21 article, two weeks after the election, in which the Free Press said: "Sickness has prevented the editor from collecting the returns from several counties. All the counties have not yet been heard from. The anti-Democratic candidate (Wing, the Whig) will no doubt be elected by a majority of two or three hundred over either the Democratic (Williams) or anti-Masonic (Dexter) candidate. Some remarks upon the late election and other subjects are omitted this week to make room for the important public notice relative to the supplies for the military posts, which was not received until yesterday."

And three columns were filled with a listing of the food and other supplies the federal government was interested in buying for its army posts. Subscribers to the Democratic Free Press may have found the list of supplies good reading, but McKnight and Sheldon were willing to forego "some remarks" to make room for the public notice because it was an important source of revenue. The news might have been more urgent, too, if their man had won.

Finally, on July 28, three weeks after the election, the Free Press in a long commentary at the bottom of Page Two noted that Williams had indeed lost the election (by a margin of almost 2-1) and went on to say:

"The Democratic Republicans can draw abundant consolation from the circumstances attending the campaign; from the certainty that they have effected an organization, and that they will hereafter be prepared at all times to meet the enemy and beat them."

Politically, McKnight was trying to make the best of it, but he faced another battle, this one also fought in full public view. He and Williams were struggling for control of the newspaper.

A portent of such a fight can be read in McKnight's editorial in the May 23 edition. He attacked those who were saying that the Free Press "was established for 'local purposes' or for the advancement of 'individual interests.'" It continued: "To those who have read the paper so far, we presume it will not require our assertion to stamp that insinuation with the mark of falsehood. The Democratic Free Press was established for the purpose of giving one portion of the citizens of this Territory an opportunity of making their sentiments known. It was established because a combination . . . refused to give publicity to the proceedings of those citizens who did not see fit to follow in the wake of their selfish, aspiring aristocracy . . . The editor of the Journal says he refused because he believed their proceedings 'were at war with the interests of Michigan.' Who, we would ask, gave the right to the editor of the Journal to decide what is, or what is not at war with the interests of the Territory?"

McKnight saw the Free Press as something more than an organ to promote Williams. In August he again assumed the editorship when Sheldon, because of his "continued indisposition," stepped aside. McKnight made it clear he would "be responsible for all original articles which may appear in the Free Press, unaccompanied by the name of the writer." In October, Charles Whipple, among the group of 11 men who put up the money to start the Free Press, was appointed to represent them. By December, Williams was identifying himself as primary owner and wanted all debts to the paper paid to him.

Then, in a night raid on the premises, Williams tried to take possession of the paper physically. It was unsuccessful, and McKnight followed it by publishing a threat to close the paper:

> All persons having accounts against the Democratic Free Press, or who are indebted to said Free Press, are requested to present their accounts immediately, the notice of "John R. Williams Chairman" to the contrary notwithstanding. The late proceedings of this Notorious General render it necessary that the concern should be closed.
>
> *S. McKnight,*
> *Publisher of the Democratic Free Press and*
> *Michigan Intelligencer*
> *Detroit, Dec. 22, 1831.*

McKnight showed the depth of his feelings about Williams when he added, in another announcement, "Circumstances not within our control have, within the week, so disarranged our business as to deny us opportunity to bestow our usual attention to the editorial department of the newspaper. It is needless for us to comment on the recent transactions of persons who attempted to take possession of our office on Sunday night last. The public will reward them with their punishment."

The paper remained open and McKnight remained as publisher, but in an apparent compromise, on Jan. 2, 1832, the Free Press had a new editor — Charles Cleland, a lawyer who had "the looks and ways of an educated Southern gentleman" and "a penchant for journalism." He was a Virginian, about 5 feet 10, 140 pounds, of "florid complexion and dark brown hair and bright, forceful gray eyes." Considered one of Detroit's leading lawyers, Cleland was closely associated with Franklin Sawyer Jr., who happened to be one of the owners of the rival Courier. So the prognosis for the success of his relationship with the Free Press was not bright.

The Cleland tenure points up the volatility of the newspaper business at the time. Quick changes in personnel were commonplace among Detroit's earliest publications. Cleland was a writer of great circumlocution. His first editorial began: "The editorial department of the Free Press has passed into new hands and in entering upon his duties, whatever diffidence we may entertain in our ability to accomplish a faithful and acceptable discharge of them, we are sustained and encouraged by the assurance that our efforts will be directed to the happiness around us, the advancement of our country's good, and the support of those principles which constitute the only safe reliance for the administration of political affairs. We are aware of the responsibilities of an editor, and how much the happiness of society may depend on the judicious directions of his exertions ... in politics, we profess no neutrality — our colors hang out — and we frankly avow ourselves the decided friends of the present National Administration."

Cleland's style of editing, it became quickly apparent, was in sharp contrast to McKnight's. Articles on temperance and some heavy with religious overtones began to appear. Finally Cleland did something unheard of in those violently politicized days. He reported a dinner given to honor William Woodbridge, Henry Chipman, Solomon Sibley and R.J. Doty, who were retiring as Supreme Court judges. They were not only Whigs but also leaders of what the Democrats — and the Democratic Free Press — viewed as a notorious junto. In a Feb. 9 editorial, boding ill for Cleland continuing as editor, McKnight announced:

The interest and concern recently held in the printing apparatus of the Free Press office, by Gen. John R. Williams and Mr. Joseph Campau, has been transferred to other hands; and the embarrassments under which this establishment has labored for several months past, now cease to exist. It will in future be printed by Subscriber, who is duly and legally authorized to manage the "fiscal concerns" of same.

SHELDON McKNIGHT

Feb. 9, 1832.

McKnight had gotten financial help from his uncle Thomas Sheldon, John's younger brother, and from Andrew Mack, owner of the Mansion House, one of the city's major hotels. That enabled him "to buy outright the materials and equipment from Williams." On May 3, Cleland announced he would "discontinue his labors as Editor of this paper, after the present number . . . He feels confident that, in the political cause which he has attempted to aid, no one will attribute to him that virulence of party which some so erroneously think essential to a manly and fearless support of honest opinions."

However, in 1832, moderation in the service of a newspaper was not necessarily a virtue. "If charged with lukewarmness," Cleland continued, writing of himself, "he would reply that more zeal than he has shown, though it might have accorded better with the views of many, would still have been inconsistent with his own, believing as he does that a bad cause cannot be helped by violent measures, and that a good one does not need them. He professes his confidence in the unwavering integrity of the national executive, and believes that its true friends will not think the less of his attachment because he does not consider it infallible."

Cleland, not surprisingly, became editor of the opposition Journal on June 21, 1832, then joined with Sawyer to buy the Courier in August. In July 1833, Cleland became sole owner of the Courier and also had the city's printing account. But he soon tired of the business and, after merging the Courier with the Journal in 1835, returned to the fulltime practice of law.

The Free Press showed little sympathy for its departed editor. Early in 1834, an article said, "We feel called upon to notice one Mr. Cleland's assertion, viz: That he was urged to continue his editorial labors for the Free Press until his successor arrived. This is a positive falsehood. On the contrary he was rather unceremoniously desired to retire, and that, too, for his *base* and *treacherous* conduct." Another time the Free Press chided

Cleland for speaking "of the solemnity of oaths as though he would or could make the public believe he regarded them in any other light than things to be broken, as easy as made."

John Sheldon returned as editor in June 1832, remaining into early 1833 when once again he departed, this time to take one of those patronage jobs which so often went to editors. He became superintendent of federal lead mines west of the Mississippi. Prior to his departure, the paper had been moved to new headquarters on the third floor of a building owned by Thomas Sheldon on the corner of Jefferson and Wayne. It was known as the Sheldon Block.

It was Thomas Sheldon who persuaded McKnight to drop "and Michigan Intelligencer" from the paper's name. On the day that change occurred, Nov. 28, 1832, the paper was expanded to six columns wide with bigger type, and the Democratic Free Press left no doubt about its stance in support of Andrew Jackson, who had just been re-elected:

"Another lesson has been taught those selfish politicians who love themselves better than their country; who adhere in these contests to the rule that 'the end justifies the means'; and who have always considered themselves able to build up a strong party out of the credulity and confidence of the people; which to them means the same things as the ignorance of the people."

The Free Press, of course, had solidly supported Jackson when early in 1832, to the amazement of Nicholas Biddle, head of the Second Bank of the United States, Jackson had vetoed a re-chartering effort. Biddle reflected some attitudes of the times when he referred to the Democrats as a party made up of "men with no property to assess and no character to lose."

After the election, a line under the masthead announced that Sheldon McKnight was "Publisher of the Laws of the United States and of the Territory of Michigan." The paper's well-being — and that of the Democrats — is reflected in the Free Press' contracts for Detroit's printing in 1832, 1837 and 1840, in its work for the territorial Legislature in 1834, 1835 and 1836, including lists of tax delinquents, and in contracts in 1837, 1838 and 1839 when the new owner, John S. Bagg, was named the State Printer. His income from that source was $15,002.96 that last year.

Given the problems with collecting from subscribers (who were charged $2 per year in advance or $2.50 at the end of the year) and advertisers (who were charged $1.25 per square — one column by 12 agate lines — for three weeks), such government support directly affected growth of the paper. The Free Press said as much in an editorial the day it expanded to six columns:

> After much exertion and considerable expense we are enabled to fulfill the promise which we made to the public, some time since, to present the Democratic Free Press in an enlarged form. Aware that the distribution of that patronage upon which printers mainly depend, among the five presses now in the Territory, would hardly warrant the additional expense which we have just incurred, we have been urged to the measure by the solicitations of our friends ...

McKnight then spelled out some of his goals for the Free Press — "to make the paper useful, to make its columns the medium of correct political principles, and the support of sound constitutional doctrine," to treat "political subjects with that truth, candor and fearlessness, which the simplicity and liberal character of our free institution demands from all their sincere supporters."

Aside from politics, McKnight also said the Free Press would "not lessen our solicitude for the advancement of other interests of a less general nature; and the farmer, the merchant and mechanic (worker) will often find our columns containing valuable selections and essays intended to promote the welfare of their several callings."

There was one thing, however, on which the Free Press said it would not focus: religion. "Entertaining the most sincere wishes for progress of pure and undefiled religion, still we cannot promise to make it the subject of discussion in our columns, except when called on by imperious necessity, to defend it from abuse and pollution," said the editorial. "A journal devoted to the holy cause should be exclusively so. Our columns, however, will be open to notices of its progress and the success of the heralds of the gospel."

On April 7, 1833, goaded by the opposition Detroit Journal, which had raised questions about the ownership of the Free Press, McKnight ran an editorial that explained how the Free Press had come to be. He chided the Journal for "intermeddling with our private affairs," then said:

> At the commencement of the campaign in the election of 1831, the friends of the administration found themselves without a paper in this city, to rebut the weekly attacks made in the other two papers then published here. Messrs. John R. Williams, Joseph Campau, Andrew Mack, Thomas C. Sheldon, John P. Sheldon, James Abbott, H.B. Brevoort, Garry

Spencer, N.B. Carpenter, A.D. Frazer and Charles Whipple purchased the establishment of the Oakland Chronicle, and we were induced to commence the publication of the "Free Press" on our own account, and with the express understanding that, when the establishment was cleared of its debts, it should be absolutely ours.

Subsequently, some disagreement arose between the publisher and a few of those who had advanced money for the purchase of the materials and the rights of all the others were purchased by Thomas C. Sheldon and Col. Mack and the publisher. Were we blamable in this proceeding — in availing ourselves of the liberality of two individuals, one a relative and the other a friend?

Since that time, we have added greatly to the materials of the establishment and enlarged our paper; the consequence is that it has become a valuable establishment and when we are enabled to collect our outstanding debts and pay over the money advanced and the liabilities incurred for us by the two gentlemen last referred to, the whole concern will be absolutely ours. Until that time, we consider that those who originally purchased the materials have an equitable lien upon the establishment.

Some of our readers will recollect that after the destruction of the Detroit Gazette by fire, the publisher of this paper was out of business, and it was as much owing to his solicitations as to any other cause that some of the gentlemen we have named took an interest in the establishment of the Democratic Free Press.

We might retort by asking some questions of the Journal as to its first establishment, but we are desirous only to defend ourselves from its charges and insinuations.

John P. Sheldon having retired from the editorial department of this paper, the subscriber will be responsible for the contents of its columns until some other arrangements are made, of which due notice will be given. The very liberal patronage which the Democratic Free Press has received warrants the belief that the course pursued by the late editor has been acceptable to the Democratic party, and it shall be our aim to sustain for the paper the character it has acquired.

S. McKNIGHT
Detroit, April 14, 1833

Since the above was in type, we have seen the Journal of yesterday, which has corrected itself in an honorable manner. We trust that if we must hereafter differ with our neighbors, we shall be enabled to do it in good faith and good temper.

This statement making clear McKnight's commitment might be considered a symbolic cornerstone for the Free Press. The paper would undergo many more changes in ownership in the years ahead, but it would endure and grow with the community it served.

In those early years, while the emphasis had been on politics and vitriolic exchanges with rival newspapers, the Free Press also managed to reflect a concern for its community. On July 7, 1831, it raised questions about conditions of the streets and the city's meat market: "The health of the city requires that the common council, and all of its offices, should at this time devote much more attention to clearing the streets and seeking out and abating nuisances.

"We would also direct the particular attention of the common council to the market. Beef and other meat has recently been offered for sale . . . which from its leanness, we should suppose, could not have been from a healthy animal.

"There should be some measure taken to supply the market with better and fatter meats than are usually offered for sale; these measures must emanate from the citizens generally to be effective, and there must be concert of action."

It was not until 1853 that the council approved selling meat elsewhere than at the central market.

The Free Press pressed its concern about sidewalks. In November 1831, it demanded something be done about the fact that, for the greatest part of the summer, "the sidewalks have been encumbered by boxes, building materials, etc., and at times safe, open passage has not been preserved."

On July 14, 1831, the Free Press covered the death of James Monroe with a brief story at the head of its editorial column which said, "James Monroe, ex-President of the United States, The Patriot, The Soldier, and The Statesman, is no more. It has pleased an All-Wise God to call from this earth another of our greatest and most favored citizens on the anniversary of that Independence which his labor and blood assisted in achieving."

On the same day, the paper reported "the wheat crops along the Detroit River will be light and much of the wheat will be foul. The crops in the interior, upon the rolling openings, will be good — those upon level, heavy timbered lands have a good deal of chess, owing to the wetness of the season."

But the most prominent item that day was headlined, "Horrible," and related the story of a teenage girl being ravished and murdered near

Painesville, Ohio. It ended with this commentary: "It would seem from this, either that the citizens of Painesville and those living in its vicinity, lacked vigilance and activity, or that their neighborhood was infested by a band of bold desperadoes whose secrecy and cunning enabled them to set the ordinary means of detection at defiance."

Those early Free Press editors kept the public informed of internal problems, too. For example, Sheldon once reported, "We have been favored with a file of late English papers from which we may make extracts hereafter — at present we have not had time to look them over."

And on Jan. 30, 1833, the Free Press reported, "English papers to the 4th Dec. have been received in N. York — their contents are not important."

On another occasion when most of the paper for several weeks had been filled with the text of federal and Michigan laws (for which the Free Press was paid), it said, "We trust our readers, for some weeks past, have found the laws 'interesting' — if they have not, we certainly owe them many thanks for their forbearance; for we have not yet heard a word of complaint on account of our exertions to complete their publication as soon as possible. They are now finished; and the space in our columns which they have occupied will be filled, in part, with more diverse and agreeable, if not more useful, matter."

Printing laws in newspapers was one way the government could let people know what was going on. A Congressional act of 1814 required that all federal laws be printed in two (later three) newspapers in each state or territory. The income from such public notices, later including council minutes, probate notices and the like, made possible the spread of newspapers in the country. Their number grew from 376 in 1810 to about 900 weeklies at the time of Jackson's election. Government printing also helped keep costs of papers down for subscribers.

The candor in explaining delays in printing news also pointed up a practice basic to the operation of U.S. newspapers for many years — the use of materials from other publications. Simply lifting news from other papers was generally accepted, serving as sort of a forerunner of modern cooperative efforts like the Associated Press. Editors anticipated their material would be used by others.

Detroit had just begun to get daily mail service (Jan. 9, 1831) from the East, and the Free Press reported it received "intelligence in seven days from Philadelphia and New York and in a little more than three days from Pittsburgh and Buffalo," but mail from Washington still took 11 days.

One topic which got early attention in the Free Press was the dispensation of justice. Commentary on Jan. 29, 1832, provides some insight into conditions at that time. After noting that some justices of the peace had neglected their "duties in attending to the call of poor debtors who were confined to jail," the editor said: "A justice who would forget or neglect the call of a debtor in a dungeon, should himself have a taste of the comforts of a bed of straw, four bare walls, and a grated window. At any rate, they should be removed from office.

"We have a communication, saying in substance that Mr. Goodell, the jailor, drew up a certain paper for a debtor in confinement (who had not the means to pay an attorney) which required the signature of a justice — that he took it to a justice to sign, and informed him of the poverty of the debtor, and that he (the jailor) had drawn up the paper without fee, and from motives of charity. The justice, however, insisted on being paid 25 cents; and the demand not being complied with, he tore off his name and handed the paper back, with the intimation that his signature should not go without a fee. Is this so?" Typical of the news reporting style of the day, no followup told what, if any, action was taken.

McKnight quickly took the lead in an important issue — statehood for Michigan. On Sept. 8, 1831, pointing out that immigration to Detroit was "beginning to revive," he said, "the people of Michigan should direct their attention to the subject of forming a state constitution for their government." McKnight urged a calm discussion of the principles of government, spelling out what he thought they were: "a pure republican system, based upon sound democratic principles" in which citizens would be careful of how much power they would cede to authorities. And, McKnight said, the state constitution should provide for "universal suffrage, a system of universal education; the unrestricted liberty of speech and of the press; an enlightened and independent judiciary . . . and a distinctly defined separation and definition of powers of the different branches of government."

The Free Press was stunned when, in October 1832, Michigan citizens voted against taking the first step toward statehood — calling a constitutional convention. McKnight wrote, a bit sarcastically, that it would "be charitable to conclude that the many who did not vote were kept at home by 'inclemency of the weather.'"

An October 11 editorial conceded that "the fear that an enjoyment of institutions more consonant with republicanism would be attended with increased taxation, operated on a large majority of those who voted in the negative. This fact, as we have stated before, is groundless." But

McKnight suggested the territory's legislators should understand people felt they already were taxed too heavily, concluding, "No people should be so severely taxed (in the shape of town, county, poor and highway taxes) as to be unwilling to give a little of their means in exchange for political privileges."

Probably the Free Press' most dramatic story in its early years was the cholera epidemic that hit Detroit in July 1832. Its coverage — for those times — was excellent.

A June 18 story, under a headline "The Cholera," said: "As this pestilence has at length passed the Atlantic and fixed upon our continent as the field of its ravages, we shall devote an article to the history of its progress, from week to week, until the disease ceases to cause alarm." The paper thus reported cholera had hit Quebec on the 9th, with two deaths in Montreal on the 11th and 114 on the 14th, and the cholera had also spread along a route from Montreal to Albany.

On the same page, a long article explained what the local board of health advised. The text of a proclamation by Mayor Lev Cook outlined the steps being taken by officials, including regulations forbidding any ships to get closer than 100 yards or to land anyone until a health officer had boarded. The board of health recommended "all streets, alleys and houses requiring it, be forthwith thoroughly cleaned, and the walls of the houses white-washed; that communication with infected districts or places be prohibited to diminish the chances of extending the infected atmosphere, and that the poor and indigent be furnished with provisions and clothing suitable for the preservation of health."

The health board also outlined some preventive measures: "Avoid all chances of being chilled, and keep the body warm, particularly the stomach, bowels and feet. Avoid placing feet on the cold floors, abstain from sleeping with the windows open, and return home at an early hour, in order to avoid the cold and damp of the night air." The next week, the Free Press reported it had "just learned that a soldier died on board the Henry Clay (a ship just arrived in Detroit) last night of cholera." The Henry Clay pulled out the next day. Eventually 77 men on the ship died. The following week, the Free Press was "obliged to announce to our readers that the Spasmodic Cholera has made its appearance in this city. As might be expected, the prevalence of such a malignant disease among us has produced very general alarm among our citizens.

"The first case occurred . . . among the troops on board the Henry Clay. The subject, who was a soldier of intemperate habits, expired after an illness of seven hours. Others were soon after taken ill, and all of them exhibited the usual symptoms . . . The vessel was ordered to leave the port and she proceeded to Hog Island (now Belle Isle) where she was furnished with supplies from this city for her voyage to Chicago."

By July 19, the Free Press was reporting 58 cases since July 5, with 28 deaths. Sheldon wrote a story about what he called the "ridiculous" and "censurable" action of people in other cities against anyone who had been in Detroit. "At Ypsilanti such were the fears of the people from the supposed contagious nature of the cholera . . . that the mail stage was fired upon because the driver insisted on doing his duty. A fine horse was killed, and the driver himself narrowly escaped."

At Rochester, travelers from Detroit were forced out of public houses, "their baggage thrown after them," and bridges were ripped out. In Pontiac, armed men patrolled highways leading to the village. Sheldon concluded, "It is to be hoped that the considerate and calm portion of the inhabitants in every settlement will exercise their influence and activity in arresting the unmanly and un-Christian terror which exists."

By Aug. 2, the Free Press was reporting, "We have heard of no case of the cholera as having occurred in this city since our last. Some of the symptoms, however, are still prevalent." Ninety-six cholera deaths had been recorded by Aug. 15 when the epidemic abated.

The editor then managed a light touch with a bit of promotion for the paper: "Cure for Anger — It is allowed on all hands that anger may bring an attack of the cholera if the system is predisposed. A preventive of anger, therefore, is a preventive of cholera. We have an infallible preventive, which we recommend, gratis. When you find yourself getting into a passion (no matter for what cause), immediately open this number of the Democratic Free Press and commence the perusal of the act to establish certain Post Roads, etc., which begins on the first page. Read until you find yourself perfectly cool." The reference was to a report on legislative approval for building many new roads in the territory, considered a major necessity and a great sign of progress.

A second cholera epidemic hit the city in August 1834 with 122 deaths, and there were others in 1849 and 1854.

Despite the epidemics, Detroit was growing, with newcomers pouring in. By 1835 the city boasted its first four-story building and a new City Hall. Plans were underway for major expansion of the railroads.

And on Sept. 28, 1835, the Detroit Daily Free Press was introduced to the thriving city. It was Michigan's first daily newspaper.

McKnight wrote: "Our city is now full of prosperity; her population, her business, her wealth and corresponding advancements in public improvements, present the most encouraging and animating considerations for the employment of individual effort and exertion to promote the general welfare. We would not in our humble department remain behind the spirit of the enterprise of the day . . . "

The daily newspaper, four pages about the size of a modern large magazine and selling for $8 a year, reflected the boom in the city's business. Its first page was solid advertising, as were two other pages. Only one local news item, a few lines about a "shocking steamboat disaster," the explosion of the Commodore Perry, was included. McKnight continued to produce the weekly Democratic Free Press,

The first daily Free Press, Sept. 28, 1835

which had much more news and commentary than advertising and was geared for mailing to farmers and other newspapers around the country. During the state constitutional convention in 1835, he also added a special semi-weekly. That edition contained the full minutes of the convention.

On Feb. 1, 1836, McKnight sold the Free Press to John S. Bagg and L. LeGrand Morse. Perhaps politics pulled him away from publishing; a few months later, on June 18, he took over the Detroit postmaster's job, a patronage plum. But more likely it was the jolt of his manslaughter indictment that caused him to give up the Free Press.

As historian George Catlin describes the incident, one H. K. Avery, a bank cashier who had imbibed too heartily, tried to pick a fight with McKnight in the Bull & Beard's saloon. Avery was a slender man, McKnight "massive and powerful." McKnight pushed Avery away, according to Catlin, but he kept coming back until "McKnight struck him on the side of the head with his hand. Avery hit the floor with such force that his skull was broken."

McKnight was charged with manslaughter, tried and, on Jan. 23, 1836, acquitted. Nine days later, he sold the Free Press. McKnight, according to Catlin, was filled with remorse and "made such a reputation as he could by assisting Mrs. Avery and befriending his son Charles, who was given a position with the Bank of Michigan."

McKnight held the postmaster's job until the early 1840s when the Democrats lost the presidency. Even without the voice of his newspaper, McKnight remained a power among Democrats. In 1845, the federal government established "an office expressly for (his) benefit."

Lucius Lyon, Michigan's first U. S. senator, wrote McKnight on March 18, 1845, after Democrat James K. Polk had been elected president: "As there seems to be very little prospect of your getting the appointment as postmaster of Detroit, Gen. (Lewis) Cass set himself to work to make an office expressly for your benefit. He has informed you that you will be appointed by the Secretary of War (as) Assistant Superintendent of United States Mines with a salary of $1,200 per annum, and be stationed at Sault Ste. Marie to take accurate account of ores that may be smelted there or carried through the place down the lake. I have been with the General of the War Department today and got the office established."

Cass, of course, was one of Michigan's foremost leaders and Democrats. He helped, as noted earlier, to establish Detroit's first newspaper and served as territorial governor and in President Jackson's cabinet as Secretary of War. He was a U.S. senator in 1845 — Michigan had become the 26th state Jan. 26, 1837 — and would be the Democrats' unsuccessful candidate for president in 1848. In 1857, he became Secretary of State under President Buchanan.

McKnight was already in Sault Ste. Marie. After serving as Detroit's postmaster from 1836 to 1842, he had headed for the Soo about the time ore was discovered in the Upper Peninsula. He established a transportation company that carried goods from Lake Superior around the St. Mary's River rapids until 1855, when the Soo Canal was opened.

While the man who helped launch the Free Press was comfortably into other pursuits, the paper itself was in the throes of a series of changes, dramatized by two fires that might have been fatal to a less hardy institution.

The period from February 1836 to February 1853, when a dynamic new publisher and editor, Wilbur F. Storey, would appear on the scene, was dominated by John S. Bagg. He had become the sole owner by buying out L. LeGrand Morse in July 1836. Like so many prominent Detroiters, Bagg was an Easterner, a native of Massachusetts. He had come to the city in 1835 from Watertown, N.Y., where he had been editor of the Watertown Standard. He was 27 years old when he took over the Free Press.

In a biographical sketch appearing in the Detroit News in 1894, Bagg is described as "a tall man, with sandy complexion, dignified, formal manner, rather quiet and not very approachable." He was considered "a keen and sarcastic writer and edited the Free Press with great ability, although the criticism of political opponents sometimes degenerated into abuse."

Bagg carried the union of publishing and politics even further than Sheldon and McKnight. His association with the paper was interrupted a number of times because of his political activities, and a measure of his stature was his appointment as postmaster of Detroit in 1845 (when McKnight was passed over and given the job at the Soo). Bagg also chaired the Democratic State Central Committee twice and became U.S. marshal in President Buchanan's administration. It is no surprise then that he thanked the "members of the Senate and House of Representatives for the 'flattering distinction' in electing him (Bagg) State printer by an unanimous vote." His election came just before the Free Press plant was destroyed by fire, and only a fortuitous set of circumstances enabled him quickly to resume printing and save that contract.

In a one-sheet Democratic Free Press-Extra with a three-word headline, "To the Public," Bagg told of the fire on the morning of Jan. 4, 1837, that wiped out the Sheldon Block, including the Free Press plant, despite the efforts of three fire engine companies. In large type, the Extra said:

It becomes my unpleasant duty to announce to my patrons and friends that the office of the Democratic Free Press was last

night utterly consumed by fire. Not a particle of the whole
establishment was saved. This disastrous event will place it
entirely out of my power to continue the usual issues of the
Daily and Weekly Free Press until the opening of navigation
when it is my intention to resume their regular publication ...
In the meantime, I shall issue only a weekly Free Press of the
largest type for which I can find paper in the state ...

John S. Bagg
Detroit, Jan. 4, 1837.

The misfortune that winter of another would-be publisher, however,
allowed him to resume publication of the Free Press sooner than
expected. The weather was uncommonly severe, and the cargo —
including a printing press — of an icebound ship was stored in a
warehouse on Atwater Street instead of being on its way to the west
coast of Michigan.

The printing press belonged to Henry Barns, a Britisher and "a
bustling little man with a head full of enough schemes to make fortunes
for a half-dozen men." He would not sell the equipment to Bagg because
he planned to start his own newspaper in Niles. By Feb. 1, however, he
had completed a deal that gave him a one-third interest in the Free
Press, and John Bagg gave another third to his brother, Silas. A new
firm of Bagg, Barns and Co. was now publishing the paper, and regular
publication of the weekly resumed Feb. 22. It wasn't until June 5, after
new type arrived by steamer, that a daily Free Press reappeared.

Later, James E. Scripps, founder of the rival Detroit News in 1873,
would point out that this edition was tagged Vol. 1, No. 1. But Bagg's
continuing involvement and his declared intention to resume publication dispels any notion of a break in the historical continuity of the Free
Press. Further, Bagg himself stated in the June 5 edition: "We are
gratified in being able to inform our readers that we have resumed the
publication of the Daily Free Press, the first number of a new series of
which we lay before them today." Bagg went on to extol the wonders of
his new plant and his ability to handle fine job printing, and added, "We
would here take the liberty of calling the attention of merchants and
business generally to the importance of advertising through the medium
of our columns ...

"We trust that we shall be excused for stating that the Free Press has
a much larger circulation in the interior than any other paper issued
from this city. There is scarcely a post office in Michigan or Wisconsin

at which there are not from one to thirty numbers of the Free Press taken."

A year later, Barns left the company "upon the most friendly terms" to publish the Niles Gazette. He became something of a major entrepreneur — the owner of the only telegraph line between Detroit and Chicago at one point. In 1851 he returned to Detroit to become part owner of a new paper, the Tribune.

A description of the Free Press office in those days, typical of other early newspapers, is found in a thesis by Winston March Hamper at Wayne State University. All departments — news, composing, printing, circulation — were on one floor "without so much as a partition or screen to separate them... Toward the front... a small space fenced off from the rest of the room by two rows of type cases, were the quarters of the editor ... Here, at a scarred and ink-stained table, John S. Bagg would sit by the hour, reading exchanges and clipping items of interest from such leading political journals as the Washington Globe and National Intelligencer, the Richmond Enquirer, the Albany Argus and the Louisville Courier... The long room, lighted by lard oil lamps hung from the ceiling, was heated during the winter months by a large, cast-iron, box stove."

Thus did a newsroom of one editor-writer, a production department of seven or eight compositors and a couple of boys in the mailing and circulation department get out the paper. In its issue of Jan. 1, 1839, the Advertiser reported an aggregate daily circulation of about 7,000 for three Detroit papers (the Morning Post was the third).

The Free Press was going through a succession of changes. A third Bagg brother, Asahel, who had become a printer's apprentice in Pontiac at age 13, took over sole ownership in 1840. While Asahel was proprietor, the Free Press was victim of another fire. This one swept Detroit Jan. 1, 1842, destroying 25 buildings in a square block bounded by Woodward, Jefferson, Woodbridge and Griswold streets.

The Free Press had moved into the old Museum Building on the southeast corner of Jefferson and Griswold only four months earlier. It was destroyed along with the plant of the Advertiser, its chief rival.

Asahel Bagg moved quickly to get back into business. For financial help, he formed a partnership with his foreman, John M. Harmon, an Ohioan who had come to Detroit in 1838 after becoming a journeyman printer in his father's shop. Bagg was able to rent equipment from the Port Huron Observer and Macomb County Republican. Ten days after the fire, Asahel Bagg calmly stated in an editorial, "This is the second time the establishment has been (closed) by fire within five years; and we are getting used to it."

Business was good for the Free Press until near the end of the decade. Detroit's population was still soaring, growing from 2,222 in 1830 to 9,102 in 1840, and 21,019 in 1850. The city had established its first public school system, and the Free Press was impressed and supportive. An editorial in June 1848 said: "We were highly gratified in a visit paid the public schools . . . There are now upwards of 500 children in three schools, and we deem it but justice to say that we never saw schools better conducted . . . If any citizen hesitates to pay the small tax necessary to support these schools, let such a one visit one, or all of them, and we believe that he will pay most cheerfully, regarding it as a noble and sacred object." Such visits, the editorial concluded, might end "the prejudices existing in the minds of many, against the system."

Trains had begun to run twice daily between Detroit and Ypsilanti ($1.50 each way). The railroad reached Chicago in 1852. Telegraph lines reached Ypsilanti in 1847, and on Nov. 30 the Free Press was able to report, "The Lightning Flashes — the First in Michigan . . . It is in excellent working order, and our citizens have an opportunity to hold 'talk' with our neighbors of that thriving village . . . "

Later, as additional lines were opened to New York, Chicago and Milwaukee, a Free Press reporter described Detroit as being "surrounded with flashes." But the modern technology quickly was taken for granted. Just as they had in the days when they counted solely on mail, editors began complaining when wires broke down. The Free Press, on June 25, 1850, reported, "We are again compelled to go to press without any news by telegraph. We do all we can toward furnishing our readers with the latest news — expending a heavy sum monthly for the transmission of news and salaries of reporters in the East for furnishing news — but when news is not sent of course it cannot be published. We live in hope of better times." Those times would come.

The development of mining in the Upper Peninsula and of lumbering in the Lower began to draw large numbers of people to Michigan. By the end of 1847, Michigan had moved its capitol from Detroit to Lansing and the University of Michigan from Detroit to Ann Arbor.

Through the 1840s, the Free Press published weekly, daily and tri-weekly newspapers, with varying page sizes. The Free Press even became an afternoon paper for a time, apparently to accommodate its printing commitment to the state, a major source of income. It held the state printing contract for seven years (1842-49) and shared in printing contracts from Wayne County, the federal government and the City of Detroit for which it printed official proceedings and other reports in 1840, 1842 and 1847.

In 1847, the Free Press attempted printing a paper in Lansing to handle state business, calling that weekly the Democratic Free Press while changing, on Jan. 4, 1848, the daily paper's name simply to the Free Press. The Lansing venture was short-lived, finally being taken over by a couple of Detroit printers who turned it into the State Journal, which still survives.

The Free Press moved several times in the '40s, first to the building on Jefferson near Griswold that burned, then in 1845 to the corner of Woodward and Congress, and in 1849 to a new building, built by John Bagg, on the northeast corner of Griswold and Jefferson.

Another indicator of Free Press prosperity was the fact that in 1846 Asahel Bagg and Harmon installed the first power-driven press west of Buffalo. The single-cylinder press, built by the Hoe Co., was steam-driven but soon had to be hand-driven because, as historian Silas Farmer explained, "the boiler and engines were defective and the floor not strong enough" to support the heavy equipment. The new press could run off about 400 four-page papers in an hour, a major improvement in production.

It would not be until 1851 that steam was used, and then, as Farmer confirms, it was "singular indeed" that "an important event, an event marking an era in the West, should have gone unnoticed" so that no precise date is available. Finally, on March 2, 1852, the paper did take occasion to speak proudly of its machinery. An item in the local column proclaimed: "By Steam . . . the neatest, fastest and prettiest engine in the West, is the one we have 'hitched' on to our big power press, to help matters along a little. The accomplished machinist and engineer, Mr. Johnson, who built it for us, may well be proud of his job as one in every way creditable to any mechanic in the country. Steam is the fashion in these days (and) as the lady once remarked, 'One may as well be out of the world as out of fashion.' So we go by steam!"

William Quinby, who became owner of the paper in the latter half of the century, recalled that press fondly: "I remember well the single-cylinder press, the first that ever came west of Buffalo, in the Free Press, propelled by two sturdy Germans," he wrote. "Old Peggy Ann, as the press was named, later ran by steam and after many years of service left the newspaper and joined the ranks of the job room."

Innovations in news gathering came at this period, too. They were sparked by the interest in the Mexican War, for which Michigan provided part of an impressive mounted company, made up of men at least six feet tall. On April 24, 1847, after the company left for Vera Cruz, a parade and torchlight procession celebrated victories reported by the Free Press. The paper provided the news "by the Windsor Stage," which it claimed beat mail service by three days. The Free Press had arranged to get news from Hamilton, Ont., the terminus of the eastern telegraph circuit. From there, news was rushed to Windsor by stagecoach where it was picked up by a courier who came across the river by boat and delivered it to the Free Press.

This era saw no lessening of the paper's allegiance to the Democratic Party nor any softening of the expression of political opinions, though some ambivalence on the issue of slavery was apparent. The Free Press excoriated the Advertiser for supporting "arguments for disenfranchising foreigners" and for opposing the appointment of other than native Michiganians to state office, and also attacked that paper for being "in favor of abolitionism and giving the emancipated black equal rights and privileges with native American citizens."

Consistent with Democratic Party policy as the city, state and nation debated the question of abolition, the Free Press was not in favor of freedom for slaves but did support emphatically the right of any state to have or not to have slavery within its borders. That position would be dramatically expounded later, particularly when Wilbur Storey was editor and proprietor.

The Free Press bowed to no one in its concern for the community. During the financial panic of 1837 when, taking note of reports in Eastern papers "that in consequence of the embarrassment of the time (an interesting euphemism for what would be called a depression today) large numbers of mechanics (workers) are thrown out of employment in that quarter," the Free Press suggested they seek work in Michigan. "There is no part of the country that is in so much need of industrious classes as the West." It admitted that the cost of living was high, explaining "there are not enough farmers and laborers to raise the necessary articles of consumption." It went on to say that "in Michigan every town and village are in want of mechanics" and that a major attraction was the "liberality of the state in regard to public schools," funds for which "are so ample that the fountain of education and learning in Michigan will be emphatically *free* schools." It also minimized the cost of coming from the East to Detroit, pointing out that "it would not exceed $10 from Albany to Detroit and the cost of deck passage aboard steamboats, from Buffalo to this city, will not exceed $4."

When the Free Press raised its price, the announcement was in the style of the 1840s but the message sounds remarkably current: "We have made an advance of one dollar in the terms of the paper. The measure has been adopted after a most careful calculation of the receipts and expenditures of our establishment, the latter of which have most fearfully increased. Our rents, the wages of labor, the cost of the stock to carry our business, and the price of everything we eat, drink and wear have long been increasing and are now enormously high."

Among the decade's newspaper innovations was one in advertising. As historian Clarence M. Burton, who later donated his extensive collection to the Detroit Public Library, explained in a 1910 Free Press article about this period, advertising notices (comparable to today's classified ads) would be inserted and "remain unchanged sometimes for months. A notice of the reception of new goods . . . the last lot to arrive before the close of navigation . . . would remain standing until it was necessary to announce the arrival of new goods in the spring." Illustrations in advertisements were unknown until the Free Press of June 5, 1849, ran the first "real illustration made for the purpose of advertising" in Detroit. It was for the Boston Shoe Store, on Woodward between Jefferson and Larned. The illustration was made from a daguerreotype of the building. Another such illustration appeared in the Advertiser late in 1849, about the time of the appearance of the Daily Tribune and the Commercial Bulletin.

The Advertiser, which had become a daily in 1836 and passed through several hands thereafter, was merged with the Tribune in 1862, and the Tribune eventually was merged with the Detroit News in 1915. The Commercial Bulletin merged with the Free Press within a few months of its introduction.

The impact of politics on newspaper ownership continued when, in 1848, Democrat Lewis Cass was defeated for the presidency by the Whig Zachary Taylor. Within a short time, John Bagg was out of the postmaster's job and bought back his interest in the Free Press from his brother, Asahel. In June 1850, John Bagg sold his share to Thornton F. Brodhead, a distinguished soldier.

A quick succession of partnerships ensued, with politics always in the background. Harmon set up a firm with Brodhead as editor and with Jacob Barns as another partner. Then Harmon sold his share to Simeon M. Johnson of Grand Rapids. Johnson became editor when Brodhead also stepped aside and left the paper in the hands of Johnson and Barns.

Harmon became mayor of Detroit in 1852. Brodhead was active in the election campaign of Franklin Pierce and was rewarded with the job of postmaster of Detroit from 1853 to 1857. In 1859 he was a state senator.

The many changes in ownership and a Whig presidency may explain why, by the time Wilbur Storey was tapped to take over the Free Press in February 1853, with the Democrats coming back into power, the paper had become "a limp sheet that showed every sign of early expiration. It . . . was short of circulation, short of cash, and . . . short of capable editorial direction."

The era when a newspaper could survive purely on its political connections was coming to an end. Competition was increasing with improvements in the means of collecting and distributing news and the continuing population growth. The concept of the penny press, inaugurated in New York in 1833 with the birth of the New York Sun and the development of James Gordon Bennett's Herald and Horace Greeley's Tribune, was sweeping West.

Detroit was ready to accept an unusual person dedicated "to print the news and raise hell" . . . and it got him in the person of Wilbur Fisk Storey.

Wilbur Fisk Storey

(Courtesy of the Jackson Citizen Patriot)

"His most lasting achievement was the impulse he gave to journalism in Detroit during (his years at) the Free Press."

James E. Scripps,
Founder of the
Detroit News

Chapter Three

The Storey Era

Chapter 3

The adjectives describing Wilbur Fisk Storey range from "fanatical" to "brilliant," from "vicious" to "obsessed." Those adjectives suggest, of course, the complexity of his personality and the variety of opinions about him, but friends and critics do agree on one point.

It was Storey who turned the Detroit Free Press from a journal that could be called "a dull, spiritless montage of scissors and paste enterprise" into a vigorous, readable "news" paper. Others would build on that foundation, while he himself would die perhaps best remembered as "the original Jekyll and Hyde of American journalism."

It remained for a competitor, James E. Scripps, founder of the Detroit News, to capture the essence of the man when, after Storey's death in 1884, he said: "It is sad to look back over the utter fruitlessness of so earnest a life as Storey's. He left no children, made a fortune and lived to see it vanish, and built up a great newspaper (the Chicago Times) which ceased as soon as his master hand was withdrawn. His most lasting achievement was the impulse he gave to journalism in Detroit during the short period of eight years which he managed the fortunes of the Free Press."

Now, almost a century after Storey's death, his successors at the Free Press and Scripps' heirs at the News remain locked in one of the most intense competitive battles among newspapers anywhere. But it is hardly as colorful or vitriolic as the one Storey himself launched when he landed in Detroit on Feb. 2, 1853, to take over the Free Press.

Storey was a man of undoubted skills — as a writer, as an editor and as a spokeman for the Democratic Party's point of view in those pre-Civil War days. But he was also a man, said friendly biographer Justin Walsh, deeply troubled, whose "personality defects, so graphically reflected in both his personal life and his newspaper, clearly indicated alternating delusions of persecution and omnipotence."

"In no other way . . . can both the man and the newspaper of this period (1853 to 1861) be explained," wrote Walsh.

When Jacob Barns & Co. turned over the paper to Storey, Editor Simeon M. Johnson wrote that the paper was "in condition of great prosperity," a statement others have challenged. Still, it was well-established, the longest-lived of the five papers competing for public favor in Detroit.

Storey, as publisher and editor, put together a skilled team and had the imagination to know how to use it. Again, Scripps confirmed Storey's contributions when he wrote the Free Press staff was "as remarkable a combination of journalistic ability as perhaps ever existed on any American newspaper."

Storey's professional stature is further explained by Walsh: "Storey was instrumental in revolutionizing the American newspaper — departmentalizing it with experts, perfecting the editorial and its headline, establishing the first foreign press bureau in the Midwest, and pioneering in reporting of religious news . . . His technical innovativeness and professionalism paved the way for later journalistic expression by such greats as Pulitzer, Hearst and Macfadden." Despite Walsh's enthusiastic assessment, however, Storey remains something of a footnote in U.S. newspaper history, remembered more for the seeming irrationality of his editorial voice than for his technical contributions which bore their first — and lasting — fruit at the Free Press.

Within weeks of his arrival in Detroit, he was involved in two libel suits. And his attacks on abolitionists, his denunciation of Negroes, and his eventual excoriation of Abraham Lincoln — particularly, in the Chicago Times, after the Emancipation Proclamation — were so bitter that his legacy is a cruel caricature of editorial responsibility.

His first effort at the Free Press, an essay on "What Is Expected of an Editor," was deceptively mild and delightful:

> Has it ever occurred to you that an editor is expected to know everything and all at one time, too? It is his duty to be thoughtful, vigilant, watchful and withal judgmatical; but we deny that anyone has a right to regard him as infinite. He is brought within the sweep of almost every variety of subject and upon most of them is expected to say something . . . If a street is neglected, he is abused soundly for not knowing it and calling upon the marshal to do his duty. He is expected to be everywhere, know everything, and never be out of town . . . He is

a mark for everybody; and that's right for he expects to be abused, ought to be abused, and always is abused ... We see but one way in which to please anybody, and that is to be sure to please our humble selves; and even that is pretty hard work ... We want you to understand that our business is conducted very much like yours — except that we are more industrious and painstaking than you. We work more hours and more intently. We try hard to do well. We are in a situation to be talked about, abused and criticised — you are not. Think of this difference between your position and ours.

Much more characteristic was an early statement of his political position: "In politics the Free Press will be radically and thoroughly democratic," he wrote, "and not in name merely, but in the advocacy of those principles of popular liberty which have always been the cardinal doctrines of the republican (state's rights) party in this country, and which are supporting pillars of the Union."

Later, when he left Detroit and took over the Chicago Times, he gave an even more succinct summary of his views when he said, "It's a newspaper's duty to print the news and raise hell." He did both at the Free Press.

Immediately after taking over, Storey increased the size of the Free Press from seven columns to eight, began to brighten it typographically, and most importantly established what is still the heart of any newspaper — an emphasis on local news. The Free Press for the first time began to run verbatim reports of court testimony and decisions. He changed the paper's deadlines, from 7 p.m. to midnight, to make possible inclusion of later news in the next morning's paper. Within months, on Oct. 2, 1853, Storey published the first Michigan newspaper distributed on Sunday morning. It began as a substitute for the Monday edition and was the prototype of what is now a strong journalistic tradition.

Storey's announcement of this historic break was matter of fact. It ran under a simple headline, "Our Sunday Paper," and read: "As we have before announced, the Free Press will hereafter be issued on Sunday mornings instead of Monday mornings. The object of the change is to avoid Sunday labor ... the only Sunday labor will be performed by the city carriers, and this before the rising of the sun."

This change, cloaked in righteousness and unchallenged by another paper in Michigan for eight years, also eliminated the need to produce a paper on the week's dullest news day.

While Joseph Pulitzer is credited with being the first to develop a Sunday newspaper (in his New York World in 1883), Walsh insists that because of Storey's "exploration of the possibilities of the Sunday paper . . . he deserves important consideration in the history of American journalism."

At the same time, Storey announced he would publish a semi-weekly instead of a tri-weekly, in addition to a daily and a weekly. It was usual for publishers to package material used in the daily for less frequent rural and national distribution. While the daily was carrier-delivered and sold on street corners, the weekly and semi-weekly were mailed.

On Oct. 2, 1853, the Free Press introduced the first Sunday newspaper.

Free Press compositors were not very impressed with Storey's innovations, and he soon faced a strike. The printers were demanding better pay for night work. Characteristically, he told them "to go to hell or something like that." But failing to round up some tramp printers, he settled with his own crew. In March 1852 about a dozen printers had organized a union which got a charter from the national organization in New York to become the Detroit Typographical Union.

Storey's route to Detroit was circuitous. He was born Dec. 19, 1819, on a farm just outside Salisbury, Vt., a descendant of New England pioneers. Biographer Franc B. Wilkie wrote that as a child, "Storey exhibited no marked peculiarities, save that he was somewhat more grave and less frolicsome than his companions," and yet was neither a reader nor studious. Years later, when someone told Storey that the education of a friend of his had been limited to reading the Bible, Rollin's Ancient History, Shakespeare and some American history, Storey responded, "What else can a vigorous mind require?"

When Storey was 10, the family moved to Middlebury, Vt., and two years later he was "bound out" as a printer at the Middlebury Free Press. At 17, with $27 in his pocket ($10 of which was a gift from his mother) and the blessings of his parents (whom he would never see again), he headed for New York to work at the Journal of Commerce. There, under the tutelage of David Hale, "a man of great moral worth," according to Storey, he was exposed to the anti-abolition sentiments he himself later would expound with vigor. He also could observe the New York penny press, Ben Day's Sun and James Gordon Bennett's Herald, with their emphasis on sex, crime and scandal that was the hallmark of papers designed "for people to read."

In 1838, with $200 in savings and an invitation from a sister, Storey headed west to Indiana. In South Bend, he joined Martha, whose husband, a Whig and Presbyterian, was unlikely to develop a pleasant relationship with his Jacksonian brother-in-law. Soon after, Storey departed for LaPorte, where he formed the LaPorte Herald in partnership with Edward Hannegan, sometime later described "as the cussinest and drunkenest Indianan" in Washington.

The Herald was dedicated to re-electing Hannegan to Congress. He had been defeated after serving two terms in the House. In the 1840 election, Hannegan lost again and left the paper. Storey stuck with it, however, forming a partnership with one Joseph Lomax.

How he, at age 21, handled Lomax says something for Storey's toughness. After weeks of bickering, Storey got wind that Lomax had made a deal to move the Herald to Mishawaka, 25 miles away, for $500. One night in March 1841, Storey piled the Herald's equipment — press, type and all — into a wagon, headed for Mishawaka himself and made a deal to publish the paper without pay, undercutting Lomax.

Thus was launched in April 1841 the Mishawaka Tocsin. It got mixed greetings from opposition editors who wondered whether Storey's "unusual noise and heavings" would produce "a mountain or a mouse," but who also admitted he was reported to be "gentlemanly and honorable." The cordiality did not last. The first Tocsin appeared just a couple of weeks before a special congressional election. Two days before the vote, Storey announced the death of the Whig candidate. There was nothing to do but elect the Democrat, he suggested. An extra edition put out by the opposition paper revealed that Henry S. Lane, the Whig in question, was very much alive — and subsequently was elected. Undaunted, Storey in his next issue admitted his report was "without foundation" but attacked the opposition editor for attacking him.

Not surprisingly, in less than a year, he had to close the Tocsin. He sold his equipment and headed for Jackson, Mich., where for almost nine years he honed his skills as a newsman, intensified his commitment to the Democratic Party, and for a brief period found love and serenity.

His sister, Mary Elizabeth, and her husband, Fairchild Farrand, an ardent Democrat, had moved there a couple of years earlier, just as the city was on the verge of a boom. In this more congenial atmosphere, Storey began to study law. In 1844, when the Democrats needed a local newspaper to be the voice of the party, he launched the Jackson Patriot in partnership with Reuben Chaney and with financial help from Farrand. James K. Polk was running for president; Lewis Cass, a man whom Storey much admired, was running for the U. S. Senate. After Polk was inaugurated, Storey was named Jackson's postmaster. He maintained his newspaper connection, contributing some delightful essays including one entitled, "No Time to Read":

> How often do you hear men excuse themselves from sub-scribing to a paper or periodical by saying they have "no time to read." When we hear a man thus excuse himself, we conclude he has never found time to confer any substantial advantage either upon his family, his country, or himself. To hear a free man thus express himself, is truly humiliating; and we can form no other opinion than that such a man is of little importance to society. They have time to hunt, to fish, to fiddle, to drink, to "do nothing," but no time to read. Such men generally have uneducated children, unimproved farms and unhappy firesides. They have no energy, no spirit of improvement, no love of knowledge; they live "unknowing and unknown," and often die unwept and unregretted.

In 1846, Storey met Maria P. Isham, a "petite, slender woman, with a sweet face, great sensitiveness, and an amiable disposition." They were married in 1847, "a mating of the hawk and the dove," as biographer Wilkie put it. In April 1848, Maria gave birth to a daughter who lived only three days and, according to Walsh, "the effect of her death on the editor and his marriage seemed to be for the worse."

The relationship between Storey and his wife and her family, headed by her anti-slavery father, the Rev. Warren Isham, began to cool. Storey, who had been active in the Congregational Church for the period after he met Maria, soon found himself in a battle with his father-in-law.

Storey had established a drug store and bookshop while he was postmaster, and it was his family's major source of income when he was stripped of the postmaster's job after Polk lost in 1848. Despite his father-in-law's strenuous objections, Storey insisted on selling liquor at the shop. Their disagreement led to his alienation from the Rev. Isham, withdrawal from the church (shades of Campau and Williams) and a decision "never after (to be) identified with a religious body," according to Wilkie. After they had moved to Chicago years later, Maria got a divorce on the grounds of incompatibility. Storey would marry twice again.

Meanwhile, Storey was building a political base in Jackson. Some measure of his position as a Democratic leader was evident by his defeating Austin Blair, later to become governor, for the right to represent his district at the state constitutional convention of 1850.

Politics led him to Detroit in 1853, when the Democrats prevailed on him to take over the ailing Free Press. Storey got a half interest in the Free Press, and Chaney, his partner at the Patriot, became Jackson postmaster as soon as Franklin Pierce, the new Democratic president, took office. William Hale, a prominent Detroit Democrat, held the other half-interest in the Free Press until July, when Storey bought him out for $3,000. From that time, Storey retained full control, and his newspaper began to grow rapidly.

By September 1856, he reported his circulation at 2,420 daily, 1,008 semi-weekly and 14,672 weekly, a total of 18,100. His major competitors, the Advertiser and the Tribune, admitted he sold about 500 to 600 copies daily more than either of them. Detroit's population almost doubled, from 21,019 to 40,127, between 1850 and 1854 and reached 45,619 by 1860, and newspapers blossomed, and died, aplenty during this period. Among them were the Free Democrat, a Free Soil paper (Free Soilers wanted to stop the spread of slavery into new states and territories); the Peninsular Freeman, also a Free Soil paper; the Daily Enquirer, which leaned to the Whigs; the Daily Express, a Whig paper; the Daily Times and the Daily News, in addition to several papers espousing temperance, a cause much on people's minds in those days.

A German-language press was flourishing in Detroit too, including the Allegemeine Zeitung, the Michigan Volksblatt and the Detroit Abend Post, the last still being published in the 1980s. Large numbers of Germans first had arrived in the 1830s, and the German revolution of 1848 triggered a new influx of immigrants to Detroit. A move to have common council proceedings published in the German newspapers was denied, as was an effort to have the proceedings published in both German and English in the official organ of the city, which at the moment was the Free Press.

Storey, who worked up to 16 hours a day, six days a week, was a stickler in writing headlines and ordering the type for them. He "would go frequently to the pressroom and oil up the machinery and help get it in good running order." His presence in the composing room each night had a ritual aspect. He always arrived at 11 p.m. to supervise makeup of the editorial page in silence, simply pointing out from proofs what story he wanted and where he wanted it placed. Then he "put on his hat, turned off the gas, and went home, usually at between 12 and 1 o'clock."

Up to 1858, the Free Press staff, in addition to Storey, included Harry M. Scovel, "a good-natured, plodding individual, with no interest outside the office;" Storey's brother-in-law, Warren P. Isham, who began his career at 19 in Jackson; Thomas B. Cook, and Moses M. Ham, who later became a publisher of the Dubuque (Iowa) Herald and who provided some of the best insights into Storey's personality. Scovel, the only Free Press employee Storey retained when he took over, handled the exchanges and the telegraph news and became Storey's chief assistant. They worked together for a quarter century.

Although, according to historian Silas Farmer, "little attention was paid to local items, or else there was a remarkable dearth of events worth noting," Detroit News founder James Scripps took a more admiring view of "the polished and genial" Isham, who served as a sort of city editor, and the "bold and reckless" Cook, his assistant. Scripps wrote that they sat at "the first table as one entered the editorial room from Griswold street," and neither lacked for inventiveness. Isham would jot down some likely headlines, then he and Cook would start writing. Their stories the following morning fascinated readers — and left the opposition a bit helpless. "In contrast the old Advertiser, with only a single reporter and confining itself strictly to facts, scarcely had an item," said Scripps, who had joined that paper in 1859. "So everybody took the Free Press because it was the best paper in town."

James H. Tiller, a Free Press compositor who had filled in as a reporter for a time before Isham and Cook were hired, wrote: "I freely admit that Mr. Isham, particularly, had a gift (if gift it is) largely developed, invention, while I did not think it right to manufacture an article out of whole cloth . . . (but) Messrs. Cook and Isham were able and frequently fascinating writers."

Tiller recalled an item about "A Child Eaten by a Bear in Hamtramck." "It was so well written," he said, "that, so far as I know, it has up to this time been accepted as fact, although the child supposedly was eating berries off a bush at the time and it is not likely that there would be any bears in Hamtramck."

Tiller, in defining his own assignment, reveals the kind of coverage Storey sought. "My duties," he said, "were to get every local item possible . . . also to patrol the docks from Brush Street to Third Street for marine items, and the two depots for commercial items and the total receipts of livestock, dressed hogs, wool, wheat, corn, oats, etc."

Tiller also recalled, after the opening session of Congress, being called in by Storey, handed a "liberal amount of money" and told to find the conductor of a Great Western Railway train because he had a copy of newly elected President James Buchanan's message. Tiller was to pay, if necessary, to get it. Unfortunately, he never found the conductor.

The president's message always was a major story, and newspapers competed to get it first. Eastern papers were given an advance copy of the speech so they could set it in type and be printing it as the president spoke. Storey once arranged to have someone meet the train from the east in Ontario and buy up all the papers on board. That ploy gave him an exclusive and forced the opposition to delay press starts until they could get a copy of the speech.

Ham, the fifth member of the news staff and a graduate of Hillsdale College, handled the commercial news. He described his boss' routine thusly: Storey came to the paper at 9 a.m., checked with the business office, then headed for his desk at the back of the building from which he could keep an eye on everything. He worked until about 4 p.m., then went for "a ride behind a little white horse that he used to drive." About 9 p.m., he returned to the office to wind up the day with his ritual visit to the composing room.

"Writing was always hard for Mr. Storey," Ham said. "He might work as much as an hour on a short article. Among other things, he also insisted that the Republican Party was always to be referred to as 'Black Republican' Party." Storey also "demanded that his copy (be set in type) exactly as written" and once threatened to discharge a compositor who "ventured to change a comma."

"I have seen him go for weeks without addressing a word to one of his assistants, although working for hours each day in the same room," Ham wrote. "When he died, his mind was entirely gone and he became in fact a mere gibbering imbecile," Ham said. "I have often thought the seeds of the disease were with him as far back as those days (in Detroit) and would account for many of the queer things he did."

Storey, who could say "meaner things in fewer words than any person," edited with "such meticulous care . . . every facet of his Free Press domain that from Feb. 15, 1853 (the day he first actually edited the paper), until June 4, 1861, there was only one occasion on which the newspaper published a completely favorable comment on any abolitionist." (It was a notice about noted orator and reformer Wendell Phillips delivering a lecture to the Detroit Young Men's Society.) And biographer Walsh noted that "judged by the evidence of obituaries printed in the Free Press (during the Storey era) not one prominent Detroiter of Whig or Republican affiliation died."

Never forgetting his own political purposes, Storey also had committed "to spare no pains or expense" in making the Free Press "a sheet . . . which shall be not only in name, but in fact, a newspaper." Slowly, he added local news, establishing a City Intelligence column that, by the early 1860s, filled almost a page and contained reports from council meetings and the police blotter. In the Sunday paper, he introduced a column of Commercial Intelligence, the beginnings of financial news coverage.

He was alert to developments in Lansing, pushed for establishment of a public health department after another cholera epidemic in 1854, and supported the reforms in mental institutions being urged by Dorothea Dix.

In 1854, he helped promote a great civic celebration for the arrival of the first Great Western Railway train from Niagara Falls and then covered it in a long story which, biographer Walsh wrote, "was a job that would have done credit to any newspaper . . . " It was hand-written, edited, hand-set, and appeared on the street 15 hours after the train arrived.

Storey's enthusiasm for the city and its progress is evident in his comments on how the coming of the Great Western would affect the area. "The same causes that will conspire to make Detroit a great city will make Michigan a great state," he wrote on June 21, 1854.

"Railroads do not benefit town more than country . . . The Sault Ste. Marie Canal will in another year open the whole Upper Peninsula to the commercial and manufacturing enterprise of the lake cities. Detroit may, or she may not, as her activity or supineness elects, outdistance all competitors in securing the benefits to be derived (but) if the same policy hitherto pursued should be allowed to prevail, we fear our rivals will carry off the cream of the Lake Superior trade." Storey urged the "prompt erection of copper and iron mills in our midst and the establishment of such relations as will bind the upper country to us by ties of commercial, manufacturing and monetary interest."

Characteristically, Storey called for careful spending of the public's money. In the panic of 1857, he urged help to "the hungry and ill-clad," but from private charity. He denounced the doctrine that "it is the duty of government to furnish land to the landless . . . bread to the hungry, clothes to the destitute, and labor to the idle." That, he wrote, is "the most demoralizing and pernicious doctrine of any age. We know of no surer way of vagabonding individuals and communities."

In his concern for government spending, Storey opposed plans for a greatly expanded police force, even in 1858 when the Free Press reported gangs of young people were knocking down people "for fun." Said the Free Press: "There is no city in the country where so much liberty is given to those lawless street-brawlers and bacchanalian revelers as ours. It would undoubtedly be bad policy to attempt to organize a night watch in the present state of financial affairs, but could not such a disposition of our present police force be made as to reach this evil?"

On Aug. 17, 1858, coinciding with the announced completion of a transatlantic telegraphic connection, Storey changed the look and the content of the Free Press. A year earlier, an underwater telegraph had been completed between Detroit and Windsor, eliminating the need for "the slow progress of the messenger boy's canoe" in carrying news across the river in "this fast age."

Storey saw the Atlantic connection (which would not be successfully completed until the mid-1860s) as very significant, bringing news of the world to Detroit instantly. He immediately increased the width of the paper by one column, began to use bigger type for headlines (though still no wider than one column) with interesting typographical displays, and increased the size of the body type.

The transatlantic telegraph also caught the fancy of the citizenry.

Under a headline that read, "The Triumph Complete — The Atlantic Telegraph Successful — The Queen's Dispatch Received," the Free Press reported: "As we write, a thousand people are assembled before our office, to whom our principal citizens are delivering addresses; bonfires are burning and bells are ringing."

And the next day, the Free Press reported that even firemen "caught the contagion" and set bonfires. "No event within our recollection has ever taken the city so by storm . . . There was no end of jollity, much rejoicing, excitement and firelight, and the small hours of the morning were far gone before the embers died out, the quiet citizens went to bed and revelers stilled their boisterous voices . . . Over zeal in a good cause gives light offense."

The paper was operating at that time out of a four-story building, with two presses in the basement, a double-cylinder one that produced 2,500 impressions per hour and a single-cylinder one capable of about 1,250 an hour. The mail room and news offices were on the first floor; the composing room, with two foremen, 11 compositors and two apprentices, on the second floor, and the job shop on the top floor.

On May 11, 1860, the Free Press moved from this building to a newer one on the northwest corner of Griswold and Woodbridge, where it would remain for almost a quarter century. About this time, too, Storey hired William Quinby to become the first court correspondent for a Michigan newspaper. (Quinby later would own the paper.)

A special Free Press style was developing from Storey's efforts to publish a newspaper "for people to read." It provided a steady and vivid diet of stories on murders, rapes and assorted other crimes, presented under headlines that read "Shocking Depravity," "Horrors of an Opium Den," "Saved by His Wife's Corpse." On July 8, 1858, for example, the City Intelligence column was led by an item which noted: "Our usual amount of local matter failed us yesterday; there were no accidents, incidents, rows, or assaults — Fourth of July must have acted as a powerful soporific, for there certainly never existed a more sleepy state of affairs. Every court in the city was empty and two or three of them closed. We only hope it won't last."

The style of the day — at the Free Press and other newspapers — permitted the injection of editorial comment in a news item. To a story about one Charley Lawrence, who had been convicted of keeping a disorderly house and had skipped out, the Free Press added, "He will probably not return to fill the sentence but, if it has the good effect to keep him away, a most desirable end will have been attained. He has always kept the worst house in the city."

In a story reporting that two women were cleared of a charge of murdering a man during a robbery, the Free Press added, "After having heard the testimony throughout, we became convinced that the death was the result of natural causes, and that the women, though innocent of the deed, were well pleased to have the job taken off their hands. Having secured his property, they became anxious to get rid of him by any means and were gratified by the interposition of Providence to that end. He died of the combined effects of liquor and heat, we have no doubt."

On May 11, 1860, the Free Press moved to this building at the corner of Griswold and Woodbridge, where it would remain for a quarter of a century.

In his first issue as editor, Storey said he wanted to "cultivate relations of the utmost courtesy" with other editors and added that while they might disagree, "they should not for a moment . . . forget . . . that they are, or at least ought to be, gentlemen."

Within weeks, however, he was involved in the first in a series of libel cases with Joseph Warren, editor of the Whig-oriented Tribune. Warren had a major role in setting up on July 24, 1854, in Jackson the first convention of the Republican Party. As another editor, William

Stocking, wrote: "Formation of the Republican Party was largely a newspaper movement" and Warren was the most "conspicuous in it." He was described as "a sedate, gentle, kind-hearted man personally, but one who wrote with a pen dipped in gall. When engaged in controversy, nothing was too bitter for him to say."

The first battle with Storey was triggered by Warren's anti-Catholic views expressed in the Tribune and Storey's defense on behalf of his Irish Catholic readers. Their conflict deteriorated to pure name-calling, with Warren tagging Storey "an impotent man whose deficiencies led him to seek gratification as a denizen of dens of debauchery." Storey responded by charging that Warren was a fugitive from a New York penitentiary. When Warren sued for libel, Storey retorted that "we have yet to learn that it is possible to libel a wretch who is the living personification of falsehood . . . a living, moving gangrene in the eyes of the community — a stench to the nostrils of decency."

Before it was over, Warren had filed two libel suits against Storey and Storey had responded with one against Warren. Awards of $50 in one case and of six cents in another were made in favor of Warren, a measure "of the value of Warren's character," Storey suggested. But Storey was additionally gratified when in June 1855 a Wayne County Circuit Court jury found Warren guilty of criminal libel. Warren was sentenced to six months in jail, but a gubernatorial pardon saved him from serving time.

While editors throughout the state viewed with disgust this battle between Warren and Storey, Rufus Hosmer, who was "radically Republican" and was associated with the Advertiser and the Enquirer, also took up cudgels against Storey. Hosmer was considered one of Detroit's most noted wits. For example, he classified the Free Press publisher as the Democratic chieftain's "dog" who "is kept chained up . . . is regularly aired, and led to his meals." Storey, replying in kind, took advantage of Hosmer's obesity to remark that it would be difficult to say Hosmer "wears his wits in his belly and his guts in his head" because that would mean that Hosmer's "wit would be inexhaustible."

These personal diatribes were no more intense than Storey's broader editorial positions. It was a time when anti-Catholic and anti-immigrant attitudes crystallized in the formation of the Native American and Know-Nothing movement. Storey, on one hand relentlessly criticizing the Negro, still found it unconscionable that the Native American movement "proscribed men for the accident of their birth and denied the rights of conscience." He pointed out that "Catholics were among the first settlers of American soil, and among the sternest and purest patriots of the American revolution."

Storey worked hard to block passage of prohibition laws in the state. Although he conceded that liquor could "blunt the moral sensibilities, benumb the social affections and make of a man a beast," he insisted that a coercive law was no cure for such evil. "Man's appetites," he said, "cannot be controlled by legal instruments; and it is an inherent desire in the human heart to seek that which is forbidden — a never to be forgotten example of which is to be remembered in the fall of our first great Mother."

Storey insisted those who thought laws could deprive men of drinking "were irresponsible and worthless, bankrupt in reputation as they are in purse, for the most part reformed drunkards, who have been drawn from the mire only to relapse deeper into the gutter — men depraved and debauched in their instincts as they are lazy and indolent in their habits."

Incidentally, Storey himself was a man who, according to biographer Wilkie, "was often the victim of intoxication." But he was unsparing when it came to an employee's habits. "I don't care how much or how often any of my people get drunk, if they don't slight my business," he said. "They may be drunk at all other times, if they like, but when they are at work for me, they must keep sober or get out."

When prohibition was approved, Storey granted the law "must be obeyed" in line with his position as a strict constitutionalist. But he pointed out the difficulty of enforcement by featuring a stream of stories about drunkenness and debauchery.

Storey's editorial attacks sometimes seemed to be "governed by an insatiable appetite for sensation and meanness." One such blast came on a Christmas Eve against Dr. Henry P. Tappan, president of the University of Michigan. Tappan was berated, among other reasons, for taking the title of chancellor instead of president. For weeks thereafter, Storey kept picking at all sorts of developments at the university, finally making peace in January 1855 when he reported that Tappan had "dropped the title of 'Chancellor', a fact which augurs returning sense, indicates respect for public opinion, excites in us symptoms of esteem."

When the Board of Regents proposed in 1858 that women be admitted to the university, however, Storey resumed his attack, editorializing, "The proposition, in our view, might better have come from the (university's) enemies than its friends, for in that event there would be less danger from it." He went on: "If the purpose were to unsex one sex or the other, and abolish the distinction which was created between the two, it would be eminently the thing to proceed upon this hypothesis." He did grant that "it is perhaps a defect in our state educational system that no high school, or seminary, or college — or whatever else it might be called — for girls has been provided. If so, let the defect be remedied." Storey considered the feminist movement of those days as "part of the abolitionist-socialist madness," and when the regents denied admission to women, Storey saw the action as preserving the school "from degeneracy . . . if not, in fact, from total destruction."

Storey supported an expansionist policy, even going so far as to suggest annexation of Mexico and Cuba. Yet in 1854, in a strange, apparently unprovoked editorial, Storey viciously attacked "Hispanic-Americans," saying: "Devoid of the slightest spark of moral principle, devoted to the worst debaucheries, and utterly destitute of industry and enterprise, they answer no purpose but to cumber the earth and to render worthless the territory upon which they have existence."

His vitriol was unequaled, however, when he turned his attention to the Republicans and the abolitionist movement. He called the Republican Party "this monster of frightful mien — this party made up of white abolitionists, black abolitionists, and fugitives from slavery — this rabble of discord and destruction." It was only the beginning of a steady stream of invective against "Black Republicans."

As Walsh, a sympathetic biographer, explained, at the heart of Storey's every political stand were "two tenets, racism and state rights, which he tenaciously held and constantly expounded." Walsh insisted that while Storey never left any doubt that he "did not consider the Negro even remotely worthy of consideration for freedom" and was totally convinced of the "certitude that the Anglo-Saxon race was ordained by the Almighty to spread the blessings of American liberty to all in the Western Hemisphere except Negroes," he was not pro-slavery.

According to Walsh, Storey saw slavery as neither good nor evil and doomed to ultimate extinction, but until it "died of 'natural causes' it was the business of each state to settle the slavery issue." As a strict constructionist, he thought the federal government had no authority to intervene.

Storey believed freedom was intrinsically tied to self-government at the local level and that abolitionists were merely promoting the expansion of central control, but he was as opposed to states seceding from the union as he was to Abraham Lincoln emancipating the slaves.

His views on the race issue bordered on obsession. He published many items in the guise of news stories designed to heap ridicule on blacks, and from the day he arrived at the Free Press until his departure, Storey's editorial columns were filled with comment on the question of abolition.

In May 1860, after Lincoln was nominated by the Republicans, Storey commented: "Lincoln is not a statesman; he has not been a soldier; he is not an orator; he has performed no distinguished service of any sort; he has never betrayed any administrative abilities — the nomination of this description of a man for the presidency is never fit to be made."

On Jan. 1, 1861, the eve of the start of the Civil War, Storey wrote:

> Revolution is now a fact ... We have done all in our power to prevent it ... We are now as we always have been, opposed to secession. There is no necessity for it — no good in it — and so far as the leaders are concerned, no excuse for it ... The Union cannot fall without a great struggle; the ruins of the constitution will crush the prosperity it was designed to cherish.
>
> The question is — should the Union be destroyed? Will the people plunge into a future the end of which no man can foretell? We wish to arouse them — to induce them to discussion — to a survey of the causes of difficulty — to action — peaceful, manly, patriotic actions for the preservation of their own property and happiness, and of the integrity of their native land.

And two days later, under the headline "The Disunion Movement," Storey summarized his position: "Mr. Lincoln can never be president of the Union unless the party shall, before the 4th of March (inauguration day) consider a plan of adjustment which will satisfy the conservative slave states. We do not ask them to conciliate South Carolina, nor the disunion leaders of other States. We only ask them to satisfy the good men, the Union men of the South."

Storey achieved national prominence in February when he wrote his "Fire in the Rear" editorial that attacked the radical Republicans who fought compromise and sought a "bloody termination" to the problem. As a warning to Republicans at all levels, he wrote:

> ... If the refusal to repeal the personal liberty laws shall be persisted in, and if there shall not be a change in the present seeming purpose to yield to no accommodation of the national difficulties, and if the troops shall be raised in the North to march against the people in the South, a fire in the rear will be opened upon such troops which will either stop their march altogether or wonderfully accelerate it ... We warn it (the

The fall of Fort Sumter (misspelled "Sumpter"), reported April 14, 1861.

Lee's surrender, reported April 10, 1865.

Lincoln administration) that the conflict which it is precipitating will not be with the South, but with the tens of thousands of people in the North. When civil war shall come, it will be a war here in Michigan and here in Detroit, and in every Northern state.

He said abolitionists would "wince" at the "apparition of an army of Northern men, forbidding an anti-slavery war," yet, he continued, while it "is not a pleasant sight . . . nevertheless it is a sight that they may be compelled to look upon."

Storey's news sense was sharp enough to produce a "wonderful stroke of enterprise" by having Warren Isham in Montgomery, Ala., to

The Detroit Free Press.

VOLUME XXVIII · DETROIT, MICHIGAN, SATURDAY MORNING, APRIL 15, 1865. NUMBER 205

THE LATEST

BY TELEGRAPH.

THE PRESIDENT AS-
SASSINATED.

He Is Shot at the
Theatre.

Escape of the Assas-
sin.

Lincoln's assassination, reported April 15, 1865, in columns lined
with black rules as a sign of mourning.

cover the convention at which the Confederacy was organized.

War was at hand, of course, and on April 13, under a one-column headline which read, "The National Crisis — The Blow at Last Fallen — War! War! War!" the Free Press reported the attack on Fort Sumter (misspelled "Sumpter"). Two days later, the lead story said: "We have to announce this morning the painful intelligence of the fall of Fort Sumpter. Major Anderson defended until to defend further was to involve himself and his devoted garrison to common destruction . . . The excitement throughout the day and evening in this city yesterday was most intense. We need not add that there was no divided sympathy among our people. All prayers were for Major Anderson."

The next day Page One was given over almost entirely to reports on the war, and Storey wrote an editorial spelling out his deep sense of frustration. Under the heading, "They Will Not Forget," he said: "Democrats and all conservative men will do their duty in the present dreadful emergency, but they will not for a moment forget though the war be of 10 years' duration, that it was the result of courses which they have steadfastly, persistently and untiringly protested.

"Let nobody suppose that while as journalists and citizens we support the government in 'the exercise of all its constitutional functions to preserve the Union, maintain the government and defend the federal capital,' we shall cease to hold up to the scorn and detestation of mankind those party leaders who have purposely and maliciously conspired for the shedding of blood. Nor can those party leaders turn the public eye from their crimes by boisterous exhibitions of spurious patriotism now or hereafter. The mark of Cain is upon them, and they can no more erase it than the leopard can change spots."

On April 19 the Free Press reported "no cessation of the war spirit that has raged so furiously for the past few days in this community." It also announced it would raise over its building the Star Spangled Banner. "Every individual connected with the (Free Press) office is a contributor to the purchase of the colors . . . Once given to the breeze the flag will remain there, and the force employed in the office will remain by it and protect it, for better or for worse, forever." The story added that two staff members, John Galloway and Timothy Finn, had already enlisted. "There are no more patriotic men in the city than those employed in the Free Press establishment," the article concluded.

Storey's stay in Detroit was coming to an end at this climactic moment in U.S. history, and his famed "Fire in the Rear" editorial played a part in his departure. It brought him to the attention of the owners of the Chicago Times, who were in deep financial trouble. They offered him the paper at a very attractive price.

Storey left behind in Detroit an extraordinary journalistic heritage, and a daily circulation of about 3,000. But it was overshadowed by his exploits in Chicago. From his arrival at the Times on June 12, 1861, until his death in 1884, he created one sensation after another. His attacks on Lincoln after the Emancipation Proclamation became so violent that a Union army general became incensed enough one day to move in with troops to shut down the paper. Lincoln ordered him to halt that effort at censorship.

Storey's notoriety was not altogether political. He once was beaten on the street by a burlesque troupe, and scrapes with his wives and other ladies of Chicago kept him in the public eye. He also attracted attention with such headlines as this one on the story of a hanging: "Jerked to Jesus."

Without question, he left the Free Press far stronger than he had found it. From the standpoint of his own pocketbook, he showed a 10-fold increase, selling it for $30,000 after having paid $3,000 to take control in 1853.

Biographer Walsh's words perhaps best summarize Storey's impact on Detroit journalism:

> A man who realized the futility of looking at things "as we would have them, instead of as they are," he still proceeded to ignore completely the very real fact that a significant number of Northerners believed the enslavement of human beings because

of an accident of color to be an intolerable evil. A man who preached the necessity of an appeal to the intellect if men were to be won over to the truth, he nonetheless strove incessantly to produce a newspaper that specialized in the gratification of the baser instincts of the mob who built his city circulation to the highest in Detroit ...

Had he been a man of more moderate temperament, had he stopped to follow the good advice he so frequently doled out in his editorial columns, had no "bigotry," no intolerance, no bitter words, no imprecations upon opponents, really been guiding principles of his editorial policy, he might have enjoyed posterity's recognition that he was the greatest journalist in Michigan in the decade before the Civil War. But then he would not have been Wilbur F. Storey.

William Emory Quinby

"He possesses . . . rigid views of the mission of journalism as a public educator."

Chapter Four

The Quinby Era

Chapter 4

The words were predictable.

Wilbur Fisk Storey expressed "sincere regrets" that he was leaving and gratitude for "a thousand evidences of public confidence."

For his part, Henry N. Walker made a promise. His name replaced Storey's as editor and proprietor of the Detroit Free Press on Page One that June 5, 1861, day, and he pledged to "sustain the high character and position (the Free Press) had acquired under its former able editor." He also made it emphatically clear that he, too, would keep the paper's "political character . . . thoroughly democratic."

Yet in the midst of this pro forma exchange was a hint of a major shift with the change in leadership. Walker said the Free Press would, of course, cover the news and "discuss all questions . . . with the utmost freedom." But he stipulated: " . . . without pandering to the vulgar appetite for abuse and scandal or violating the strictest propriety."

Thus was signaled the transition of the Free Press from the hands of Storey, who has been called by biographer Justin Walsh "a specialist in pandering to the baser instincts of mankind in order to build circulation," to the quieter combination of Walker, a lawyer, political leader and railroad promoter, and William Emory Quinby, a scholarly journalist.

Quinby, who would be intimately involved as editor and owner until 1905, served as the connecting link between the hand-set and linotype eras, but in 1861 it was Walker who was crucial to the paper's survival.

If Sheldon McKnight and his colleagues can be credited with the birth of the Free Press and Storey with nurturing it into vigorous adolescence, then Walker and Quinby must be credited with carrying it to maturity and forging a link with the 20th Century journalism of muckraking, explosive circulation growth and incredible technological expansion.

Walker was a man of some means, involved in the chartering, financing, building and running of various railroads that made Detroit a major transportation center. His connection with Storey dated to 1845, when the legislature gave the attorney general — Walker — power to dispense the state's printing dollars. In Jackson, Storey and his partner, Reuben S. Chaney, heard of the opportunity and rushed to Ingham County to start a newspaper. Walker awarded them the state contract. And he may well have had a hand in 1853 in bringing Storey to Detroit.

Walker earned the reputation of being a "copious and forcible writer," but it was Quinby, then only 25, who provided the newspaper skills when they took over the Free Press. Most of Storey's staff went with him to Chicago, so Quinby's know-how was important for the continuity of the operation.

As a journalist, Quinby was as different from Storey as the Free Press of 1861 was from the paper Storey bought in 1853. Storey had learned his trade in a printing shop and in the rough-and-tumble of politics. Quinby, a recent graduate of the University of Michigan, had his first exposure to publishing through his father's literary magazine. He was as quiet and reserved and consistent as Storey was raucous, rebellious and unpredictable. But Quinby had acquired a touch of newspaper savvy under the demanding Storey, and until 1872 when he himself would become the proprietor, he worked closely with Walker.

While Walker and Quinby played dominant editorial roles, ownership became more diffused. By August 1861, F. L. Seitz was a partner, and in December a new firm was organized, with Walker holding three-eighths of the stock, Charles L. Taylor another three-eighths, and Jacob Barns two-eighths. Quinby purchased a one-eighth interest from Taylor and became managing editor in 1863. In 1866, after the Detroit Free Press Stock Co. was set up, Quinby held a quarter share, as did Col. Freeman Norvell, Walker's brother-in-law, who became the editor. Walker held 50 percent of the stock. (Walker was married to Emily Virginia Norvell, whose father, John, was a U.S. senator from Michigan in 1840-45.)

Beyond that, the transfer of ownership from Storey came at a critical time. On June 4, the day Storey announced his departure, his final editorial was a eulogy to Stephen A. Douglas, the man on whom the national Democratic Party had leaned on so heavily in the previous decade.

The major story the next day was the departure of Michigan's Second Regiment for the Civil War front.

Detroit's population had soared to 45,619 and would be 79,577 in 1870. The city was becoming a business and industrial center, a leader in the manufacture of drugs, railroad cars, stoves and tobacco products. A copper smelting plant, the largest in the United States, and steel mills were built. Wood and metal working industries flourished.

The city had bought its first steam fire engines, had recently been visited by the Prince of Wales, and had almost daily been involved in wartime displays of patriotic fervor, with flag-raisings and singing of "The Star-Spangled Banner."

Storey's handling of the prince's visit, incidentally, was just the sort of approach not likely to be taken under Walker and Quinby. The prince came to town with a duke as chaperone. After his guardian had retired for the night, a Free Press reporter had, according to James E. Scripps, "taken him on a midnight frolic in the gilded palaces of those days." The next day, Scripps said, the Free Press had "the effrontery" to run a complete report of the prince's escapade.

"The staid old Advertiser, the other morning newspaper, could muster no such enterprise and fell behind in the (circulation) race," added Scripps. But not for long. An important competitive change was in the making.

Scripps joined the Advertiser in 1859 as commercial editor at $10 per week (Joseph Warren, the editor, was making $16). He became a part owner and, by 1862, assumed editorial management. Then the Advertiser and Tribune merged. For the remainder of the Civil War period, the Free Press and Tribune would be the only competing papers.

But because the Tribune lost some of its Republican zest, another paper, the Post, was started in 1866. Later, Scripps decided to go it alone and launched the Detroit News in 1873. The Free Press and the News are the modern survivors — and still staunch competitors.

The Free Press maintained the broad coverage inaugurated by Storey, but its presentation was more muted, its writing less strident, and its reports of crimes and other vices matter of fact. Where earlier articles had a leering quality, now the tone was compassionate. An example: "Bound To Keep Him Sober — A young man named Thomas Quinn, for whose reformation various measures have been heretofore tried without success, was sentenced to the House of Correction for six months yesterday for drunkenness." And while Walker was a strong Democrat and increased the emphasis on party matters, his comments lacked the viciousness so often apparent under Storey.

Walker was a man of varied business and community interests. He was named to a committee of the Detroit Young Men's Temperance Society "to distribute a Temperance Almanac to every family in the city" the same year he was appointed a general agent of the Protection Insurance Company. He was named to the honorary post of city historiographer in 1843, served as a Master in Chancery in federal court, was a vice president of the Detroit Savings Bank (later to become Detroit Bank & Trust) when it was founded in 1849, and was president of the Detroit, Grand Haven and Milwaukee Railroad Co. He served as state attorney general and Detroit postmaster and was a candidate for the U.S. Senate.

In a review of his career that appeared in an anniversary number of the Free Press in 1891 (for which Quinby probably was responsible), Walker was described as "a copious and forcible editorial writer, his production showing excellent literary powers combined with breadth, grasp and discrimination . . . He was very loyal in his friendships, and with his subordinates he was much admired and liked."

Perhaps Walker's most lasting contribution to American newspapers was his role in the formation of the Associated Press as it is today.

In 1848, at a time when newspaper competition was heightened by the rapid development of new printing and telegraphic techniques, New York City publishers formed a private news-gathering corporation called the Associated Press. As newspapers flourished in the West, they were organized loosely into the Western Press Association. But they found themselves having to buy news from the New York group (the Free Press had signed up in 1854) at what they considered prices out of all proportion to the services they were receiving.

Walker also found some troubling selectivity in the Civil War news the New Yorkers were putting on the wire. He expressed those doubts in an editorial on Nov. 21, 1862 when he bemoaned the poor service and continued:

"We believe the Western press will take means to place themselves on an equal footing with the New York papers. It can do it, and it is undoubtedly for their interest, at least, to remove the evils which we have mentioned, and which are of such serious character as to call for speedy and effective remedy."

At an organizational meeting in Detroit in 1864, Walker was charged with getting a charter for the group from the Michigan Legislature, which passed "an act to provide for the incorporation of associations engaged in the publication of newspapers" on March 21, 1865. Thirty newspapers in 11 cities were in this first organization, "including Joseph Medill of the Chicago Tribune, 'Deacon' Richards of the Cincinnati Gazette, John Knapp of the St. Louis Republican, Murat Halstead of the Cincinnati Commercial, W. W. Brigham of the Pittsburgh Commercial, and H. C. Baker of the Detroit Tribune."

In 1864, the Western association paid the New York group $4,000 a month for about 2,000 words a day. The amount was split among the 11 member cities, with the Free Press and the Tribune in Detroit dividing a $364 cost.

Two years later, at another meeting in Detroit in which representatives of papers from Chicago, Milwaukee, Pittsburgh, Indianapolis, Cincinnati, Wheeling, Cleveland and Toledo participated, "the whole question of the cost and quality of news (provided by the easterners) . . . was discussed at considerable length." The upshot was formation of a committee, led by Walker, to negotiate with the New Yorkers.

Walker, Medill and Richard Smith of the Cincinnati Gazette went to New York, and, on Jan. 11, 1867, an agreement was reached between the two warring associations, with Walker signing for the west and William Cowper Prime of the New York Journal of Commerce for the east. The result was a daily report to papers in the Western association averaging 6,000 words, but control still rested with the New Yorkers until September 1900, when the Associated Press was formally born "as the world's only non-profit, co-operative news-gathering organization" it is today. Under the AP charter, member papers make available their local news coverage to the association for worldwide distribution, and papers share the cost of gathering all other news. A board elected from among the membership operates the service. In contrast, commercial wire services (United Press International, for one) gather and sell news with profit as a major goal.

During those war years, Detroit was just beginning to shift from a commercial to a manufacturing center. Streets were cobbled, if paved at all, and the horse-drawn streetcar had just come into vogue. There was no organized police or fire department. The city's limits were roughly defined by the toll gates located at Jefferson and Joseph Campau, Woodward and Baltimore, Grand River and Trumbull and Michigan and 21st Street. Beyond were great open spaces. In the early 1860s, the Free Press had three newsboys delivering papers on the east side and four on the west side. The number had increased to 13 by 1867.

A news summary became a fairly regular feature on Page One, as did a column of "Sayings and Doings" which would include such items as: "An Englishman 92 years old is visiting friends on Macomb Street" . . . "Hot apple pies are a success at the City Hall market" . . . "A third drinking fountain was erected yesterday at the corner of Woodward and Fort Street" . . . and "The alley on the north side of the post office building is being paved with wood."

Another column called "Gossipy Paragraphs" provided these sorts of tidbits from a broader front: "The largest hog thus far brought to market kicks up to 700 pounds," and "At a fox hunt, recently held in Vermont, the fox ate up two dogs and frightened the rest away."

The Free Press began to present more poetry and book reviews. An expansion of the paper emphasized society and general features about a wide variety of subjects, including travel and fashion.

One theme, though, had changed little since the Storey era, apparent in a story headlined "Another Amalgamation Case." It reported on the elopement of "a white girl with a negro" and their subsequent arrest. The Free Press reporter added this observation: "The girl is forever lost to decency and respect. Even should her separation from her negro paramour be eternal, the finger of scorn will be pointed to her, to her dying day, as the white woman who disgraced her sex and common decency by consenting to become the wife of a black, ugly looking, disgusting negro."

Such bias was even more evident in its coverage of the case of one William Faulkner, a black man who was charged with raping a 10-year-old white girl. The Feb. 27, 1863, headline on Page One read, "Horrible Outrage . . . A negro entraps a little girl into his room and commits a fiendish crime upon her person . . . Full history of the shocking event." The story told by the white girl's mother detailed, without qualification, how Faulkner and a Negro woman collaborator had lured the child into the back room of his saloon. Faulkner was arrested, and on the day of the examination, the Free Press story concluded, "The evidence of the negro's guilt is overwhelming and cannot be controverted." Faulkner's trial a week later ended when the jury, after being out four minutes, returned a verdict of guilty. He was sentenced to life in prison. The Free Press added, "An outraged community finds that no more than justice has been done."

On the same page, the Free Press documented the "outrage." A long story said, "Yesterday was the bloodiest day that ever dawned upon Detroit" and went on to tell of a riot in which 35 buildings, belonging primarily to blacks, had been burned. When police fired on the crowd to disperse it, one person was killed and two later died from their injuries. A large police force was put together to "guard the city" but only the appearance of a contingent of federal troops ended the violence.

Although Free Press coverage of the Faulkner case could be said to have inflamed the community, the paper editorialized righteously: "Our city (has been) the scene of the most lamentable and disgraceful riot we have ever been called on to record ... Flames burst forth from two tenements occupied by this unfortunate class ... We hope that all citizens ... will rally as one man to support their city authorities in putting down all attempts to disobey the law. Let those who are guilty in bringing this disgrace upon the city be arrested and punished."

Faulkner was released from prison in 1870 when his accusers recanted. The Free Press failed to report this development. According to the historian Silas Farmer, "A number of gentlemen contributed a sum of money, and he was installed at a stand in the market," where he worked until his death a short time later from an illness his doctor attributed to the harsh treatment he received in prison.

Greatest editorial attention, of course, was directed toward the Civil War and the move toward emancipation. Walker made his position clear on June 8, 1862, when he wrote: "As the Constitution is the only bond of allegience, as it is the only bargain the people have made, they believe in respecting the Constitution ... They made one horrible mistake ... They expected that the appalling danger of the country would hush the voices of faction, would kindle the flames of patriotism in the hearts of northern radicals. We say that that was a mistake and the results prove it ... It is as wicked to countenance abolitionism as secessionism."

When Abraham Lincoln issued his Emancipation Proclamation in September 1863, the Free Press ran the text of the proclamation, rather routinely, on Page One. The next day, Sept. 25, Walker wrote this commentary:

"The Proclamation of the President threatening upon the first day of January next to emancipate and free all the slaves in the states where the rebellion should then have the ascendancy, is an act which marks an era not only in America but in the history of the world. It is the beginning of a revolution which, if carried into full effect, will be second to none recorded in the pages of history. (It) must, we regret to say, be considered as a triumph of the radicals in the counsels of the administration."

Walker said the proclamation "would color" conduct of the war, turning it into a fight about slavery rather than one to save the Union. "We have protested against this; and while we have opposed showing any favors to slave owners, and slave property, we have earnestly wished that the Constitution should be preserved and its mandates obeyed . . . but all this is in the past — the proclamation has been issued. It is now a fact and must be treated as such"

He went on to worry about the impact it would have on bringing the border states into the battle, the possibility of a "slave insurrection," whether France and England might become involved because of the effect freedom for the Negro might have on world trade. Then he added:

"What will become of the slaves? Are they to remain in the South when emancipated? Who believes it? Are they to come into the North to take the bread from white labor? Who will endure it? Are they to be admitted to citizenship? Who will submit to it? Are they to occupy as colonists the states from which their masters have been exterminated? Who will fight for such a result? . . . Truly, Mr. Lincoln has taken an important step. We hope that it may not be the beginning of the success instead of the defeat of the rebellion, but we fear that it will be barren of consequences against the rebels because it is impracticable, unconstitutional, and beyond the power of the government to enforce . . . But above all, we have no idea that it will receive the co-operation of the slaves."

A few days later, after Lincoln had also issued a proclamation suspending the right of habeas corpus "for all persons arrested for disloyal acts," Walker, in an editorial that better stands the test of time, begged, beseeched, appealed to Lincoln, "by that liberty we believe he loves, not to leave a precedent which a less honest ruler may use to oppress the nation . . . We implore him not to suspend the constitution and the law . . . To abandon the precious liberty embodied in that clause (the First Amendment) is to betray freedom, to commit suicide upon our liberties, to give carte blanche to usurpation and enslavement."

As the war developed, inflation became a major problem, and Walker didn't hesitate to charge the Republicans with causing the problem. "From one end of the country to the other, working people are demanding an advance in the price of their toil and, not withstanding the grave homilies and the officious advice of the radical (Republican) press and politicians, seem determined to insist upon their demand," Walker wrote Dec. 2, 1862.

Only a few days later, the Free Press found it "absolutely necessary" to raise its price, explaining that the price of paper had doubled in two months and that labor was up 25 to 50 percent. Interestingly, the announcement was jointly signed with the Advertiser and Tribune. Both newspapers went to $8 a year and 16 cents a week, delivered in the city. Another indication of the times came Dec. 24, when the Free Press announced in the future it would ask for payment in advance.

The heavy Free Press war coverage was highly personalized. One of the paper's correspondents was Sullivan Dexter Green, who had come to Detroit from New Hampshire, had put out a Temperance paper for a brief period, then enlisted in the 24th Regiment Michigan Infantry. Green's attitudes which colored his reporting were reflected in a letter he wrote to his parents in September 1862: "How time is passing and death gathering us to his numbers. As for myself I am ready and willing to go at any time. Only I would like to see you and my friends first . . . . Should it be your lot never to see us, remember and be comforted with the thought that we tried to live like men to do our duty. If we fall in this rebellion, it will be . . . because of ambitious, wicked demagogues and unprincipled politicians but, dear Father, what else can we do now than to fight it out! I do firmly believe that the Union will be restored, but not till the people take the matter in hand and demand that this war be conducted as wars should always be conducted. It has been drawn out and dragged out to please such men as Sen. (Zachariah) Chandler of Michigan and others like him. But we cannot stop now to talk . . . ."

On June 21, 1865, Green was one of the 24th Regiment greeted on their return home. The Free Press story that day noted:

> Our citizens felt a peculiar gratification and pleasure yesterday afternoon in welcoming to their homes the gallant 24th Regiment. It is the special pet and pride of our city and county, being raised almost exclusively here. The Free Press was largely represented in the regiment, having many of its best employes and attaches who were numbered among the best fighters, among others Capt. O'Donnell who was killed at Gettysburg, as brave an officer as ever dealt with "leaded matter" or held a shooting "stick." His manly form sleeps the sleep of the brave who
>
> > *" . . . sink to rest*
> > *By all their country's wishes blest."*
>
> With his blood be sealed and "justified" the cause in which he fought and fell.

The Regiment had rendezvoused in Detroit Aug. 9, 1862, headed for Washington with 1,027 men. Only 150 of the original group survived.

A June 21, 1865, editorial best summarized the Free Press' political position during this period:

"An article abundantly weak and silly appears in the Advertiser and Tribune of yesterday morning, in which an attempt is made to show inconsistency in the democracy, and that it is now 'adopting the confirmed policy of the republican administration . . .'

"A constitutional, and legal emancipation by the states which properly owned the institution (of slavery) has always been regarded by the democracy generally as desirable. But they do *not* insist that slavery *must* be abandoned by the rebels, or that negroes that were set free *must not* be permitted to vote. They regard the whole matter as one for the states to decide for themselves, and they deprecate and oppose any impertinent outside interference with it. They do not regard the negro fitted for the electoral franchise, but they do not presume to demand that North Carolina should adopt their view . . .

"The republican party could have no policy. It was made up of abolitionists, miscegenationists, renegade democrats, radical black republicans and free soil or moderate republicans. Poor Lincoln was pulled and hauled by the various factions, 'controlled by events,' as he called it, until it was a mystery that he didn't escape Booth by being torn to pieces by faction.

"Occasionally he took temporarily a stand on his own judgment and independent of his party when he received the commendation of the democracy; and his successor, who has thus far indicated a democratic and conservative tendency, will receive the same, so long as he deserves it."

The editorial expresses generally the same stance Storey had taken on states' rights. That would remain Free Press policy throughout Reconstruction.

With the end of the war, the Free Press began a period of growth and innovation that brought the newspaper an international reputation. It updated its production facilities, gathered a group of writers who attracted national attention, and introduced two ambitious additions — a London weekly, which was the first overseas edition published by an American newspaper, and a four-page supplement for women readers, also the first of its kind.

And it remained a strong voice for the democracy and fought corruption and vice with equal fervor. At one point, for example, when the police raided several brothels in one evening, the Free Press coverage the next day on Page One included the names of all the men and women involved — and expressed the hope that by doing so, it might discourage such activity in the future.

Growth at the Free Press included doubling the size of the paper — from four to eight pages. There was a regular flow of foreign, Washington and Lansing news, but the paper also stayed atop such local developments as the city's first concrete sidewalks. A serious problem of that day — rampaging gangs of youths — was noted in a letter to the editor suggesting a drive to build a youth home. "There are several hundred boys in this city who have little or no means of support," the letter writer said, "and no opportunity for moral or mental improvement. Some of them sell papers, black boots and pick rags part of the day, and are running loose the rest of the day and evening. . . . With suitable efforts and a due degree of liberality, a large number of now neglected boys might be made useful again instead of training them up as expensive criminals. . ."

And there was other editorial comment of the 1860s that strikes a chord more than a century later. A Dec. 10, 1869, editorial suggested the best way to reduce taxation would be to cut expenses. The national debt, said the editorial, "weighs heavily upon every individual in the whole nation. The taxes necessary . . . sap a material part of the vital force of the country." That editorial criticized congressmen who were being paid $5,000 annually so they could "have a grand time" at taxpayer expense.

The Free Press, like other newspapers of the era, had its origins in a political party. It aimed at readers who shared its political views. And politics was seen as a man's concern. Women were barely, if at all, considered as potential readers until the Free Press, in 1878 when it improved production facilities, introduced "The Household." It was a weekly compendium of information on subjects as diverse as elocution and needlework, as predictable as recipes and child-rearing, as farsighted as personal advice and women's rights.

The London edition, which was published first in 1881 and at its height sold nearly 200,000 copies a week to European readers, also owed its existence to the paper's new technology and to its collection of provocative writers.

Quinby, who bought the controlling interest in the Free Press in 1872, was at the center of these developments, but the public was much more aware of such featured writers as C.B. Lewis, known as M. Quad;

London office of the
Free Press.

The Detroit Free Press, London
edition, Jan. 2, 1892 (courtesy
of the Clarke Historical Library, Central Michigan University).

The Detroit Free Press advertised on the back of a carriage in London's
Fleet Street, 1880s.

Robert Barr, known as Luke Sharp, and George Goodale, who became one of the nation's leading drama critics.

Barr and Lewis were part of what has been called "the decade of the humorists" in American journalism. Mortimer Thompson of the Detroit Advertiser was writing satire under the pseudonym "Doesticks." Charles Browne was writing for the Cleveland Plain Dealer as Artemus Ward, and Robert Henry Nevell wrote comic political articles as Orpheus C. Kerr (Office Seeker).

Lewis, born in Ohio in 1842, was raised in Lansing where he began learning the printing trade at age 14. After serving in the Civil War as a private, he was en route by boat to Jonesboro, Tenn., to run a newspaper there when he was badly hurt in a boiler explosion. The accident brought him $12,000 from the steamship company and journalistic fame from the article he wrote and hand set himself for the Pontiac Jacksonian: "How It Feels To Be Blown Up." He used M. Quad as his signature, a bit of printer's jargon which means a space the width of the letter "m."

Lewis joined the Free Press staff in 1869 as a legislative reporter. Edward G. Holden, who was a longtime Free Press editorial writer, later described Lewis as a "reporter with so little skill and talent that Quinby was constantly urging him to better work."

One day, according to Holden, Lewis "suddenly handed a few sheets (to Quinby) with the remark, 'Maybe that will suit you.' Quinby saw its value as a 'feature' . . . it was the first of a 20-year series known as the Lime Kiln Club."

Holden claimed the club, an imaginary organization Lewis introduced in 1877, "was his only gift . . . His speech lacked humor. He was not a joker or a storyteller." Nevertheless, the humorous column was a hit; it enabled Lewis to earn $10,000 a year, a fabulous salary for that day. According to Holden, Lewis enjoyed "twitting fellows on the Free Press on the smallness of their salaries compared to his."

Lewis achieved great notoriety personally, and his writing about the Lime Kiln Club helped the Free Press earn a reputation as a paper more quoted from than any in America, according to Kenneth O'Reilly of Marquette University, who extensively studied Lewis' work.

Lewis' column featured a philosophic and pretentious Negro named "Brother Gardner" as presiding officer through whom, reports O'Reilly, Lewis spewed his "rapacious wit . . . homespun philosophy and common sense interpretation of the average man's life in America."

His Lime Kiln Club sketches were presented in a purported Negro dialect and, O'Reilly suggests, while they appear "crude and insensitive

to present day readers, one must keep in mind that Lewis was . . . a reflection of his age."

Thus when Lewis introduced such characters as "Giveadam Jones,"
"Waydown Bebee" and "Trustee Pullback," who formed committees to
study such things as the watermelon, the wisdom of buying a snow
shovel in August, or whether man had progressed "to dat pint where he
will almoas' give up his seat in a New York street-kyar to a woman," he
was reflecting — and helping to reinforce — stereotypes of Negroes.

The bit about the watermelon committee, which appeared Aug. 4,
1889, illustrates the flavor of Lewis' work:

> Giveadam Jones said he arose in the interests of the 6 million
> colored people of the United States. He had culled from the
> newspapers during the last two weeks no less than seven
> instances where watermelon had exploded and wrought more or
> less havoc, and in each instance they were in the hands of
> colored men. Had the time come when the watermelon had an
> element of danger to life and limb? Was it to descend into
> history along with the kerosene can and the Washington pie? If
> the time had come when a colored man walking homeward with
> a watermelon under his arm was liable to be driven through the
> sidewalk by an explosion or a family group saw the risk of being
> blown through the roof of their cabin, then life had no further
> charms for him. He would move that a committee be appointed
> to investigate and report.
>
> "I will appint as sich committee," replied the president
> (Brother Gardner), "Bruders Jones, Bebee an' Watkins, an' I
> will gin it as my personal opinyon dat in de meantime we had
> better take all risks an' keep right on devourin' de melyons."

In 1870, the black population of Detroit was 2,235 (three percent of
the total). Almost all were crowded into a near east side area known as
"Kentucky." Lewis quoted the imaginary Brother Gardner as saying,
black men "have got al de rights the white man has and dar's no
occashun for crowdin' in whar' we am not wanted."

Lewis' biases were clear in his writing. As O'Reilly pointed out,
Lewis believed education, hard work, sacrifice and self-help represented
the only road to social and political equality, "and he had Brother
Gardner saying, 'We'se been niggers long 'nuff, 'n now we'se going to
hab all de rights ob white folks, or else white folks won't hab no rights
left.'" But, O'Reilly concluded, "Lewis failed to recognize the connection between the two (work and basic rights) since political and civil
discrimination limited employment opportunities."

Newspaper critics of the period, according to Marquette's O'Reilly, recognized the Free Press "as a humorous newspaper and Lewis as its foremost comic writer," but they condemned this trend and singled out the Free Press as "the single most extraordinary example of this kind of journalism." In fact, there were those who viewed the paper as simply a vehicle "for the feeble blathering of Mr. Lewis." That he had popular appeal, however, is apparent in the paper's circulation growth, particularly of the Free Press' weekly. In 1871, circulation of the weekly was 6,100; in 1881, it was 23,000, and by 1891, it had reached 120,700 and was mailed to all U. S. states and territories. After Lewis left the paper in 1891 (to go to the New York World, where he became one of the highest paid syndicated writers of his time), the circulation growth leveled off.

George Pomeroy Goodale, another of the Free Press stars of the era, was a far different type than Lewis. He was known especially for his drama criticism and his fine writing. And few could match him for longevity of service. He joined the Free Press Oct. 16, 1865, and died on May 7, 1919, a few hours after he had written still another "Kaleidoscope" column for that Sunday's Free Press — a span of 54 distinguished years.

Goodale, who was born in Olean, N.Y., in 1843, learned the printer's trade in Geneva and Elmira, N.Y. In the early 1860s, he worked for the New York World. After service in the Civil War, he headed for Detroit and the Free Press to serve as a reporter, city editor, critic and columnist.

Holden said Goodale also served as an effective "procurer of the theatrical printing of several New York managers for the Free Press job room." According to Holden, Goodale made annual spring trips to that city where his "unusually pleasant, merry, hearty persuasive personality" meant "considerable cash for the Free Press, of which he received a fair percentage as reward."

In Free Press stories about his career, he is described as "first and last a journalist, not of the pedantic type but a man whose every printed thought or impression was recorded with a facile pen in the purest of English, with never so brief a lapse from the dignified standard he maintained from the outset."

Another account added, "His writings (were) tempered with kindness . . . ever alert to detect and commend sincere endeavor . . . to lend a helping hand rather than tear down needlessly, yet . . . unsparing in his criticisms when such course seemed warranted."

Apparently it was warranted the time an actor's agent popped into

From 1884 to 1894, this five-story building on the corner of West Larned and Shelby was the home of the Free Press.

In 1894, the Free Press moved to the Abstract Building on Lafayette.

George Pomeroy Goodale, who joined the Free Press in 1865 and had a distinguished career, principally as a drama critic, until his death in 1919.

Goodale's office to excoriate him for a review of his client's show. Goodale responded by asking the agent if he would "like to know just exactly . . . my personal opinion of your show" and when the agent replied in the affirmative, "like a thunderbolt from a clear sky there followed a flow of language that sizzled and scorched and seared, every word driven home with the incisiveness in which Mr. Goodale was a past master.

"The agent fled."

Affectionately called "G.P.G." by his colleagues, he was honored by being the only non-professional admitted to the Lambs, the famed New York club for theater folk.

At the time of his death, the newspaper said simply, "The Free Press is stricken."

In contrast to Lewis and Goodale, Robert Barr's association with the Free Press was relatively brief — but brilliant. He was a fine writer, and his humor, according to Holden, was marked by "exaggeration, extravagant contrasts, unexpected turns and twists of phrase and subject, and sudden changes from apparent seriousness to absurd conclusions." He wrote under the pseudonym of Luke Sharp.

His role in Free Press history is enlarged by his participation in one of the paper's most dramatic efforts, the London edition. Weekly editions continued to be published for mail distribution in addition to the daily paper circulated in the city. The weekly Free Press was read from New York to San Francisco. When nationwide circulation had reached 120,700 in 1891, only 37,720 copies were being sold in Michigan. As part of Quinby's effort to gain even wider attention for the Free Press, he sent Barr to London in 1881 to establish the new edition.

The project was possible because of the introduction of the rotary press and its stereotype matrix. Previously, the printing process involved setting type — placing by hand the individual metal letters into lines of a certain width — then arranging the columns of type into a page held tightly together in a metal frame called a "chase." A printer slid the chase onto a flat press, and the printed impression was made directly from the handset type. To print a page on a faster rotary press, a curved printing plate was needed. The stereotype matrix — generally called a mat — was the intermediate step. It was cardboard-like papier mache, thick enough to take the impression of the type. A mat was pressed against the page of type, then put in a rounded mold. Molten lead was poured into the mold with the mat, and when it had hardened, it was a curved metal printing plate, ready to go on the rotary press.

Setting type by hand was a slow, highly skilled job. With mats, publishers could reuse material without having to have it reset. The Free Press weekly, for example, which contained mostly feature articles rather than more quickly outdated news, recycled stories that had appeared in the Sunday edition. The relatively lightweight mats could be shipped to London in about four weeks' time.

Barr, who with Quinby owned the London edition, moved to England

Hoe Drum Cylinder Press, 1851.

to write stories to supplement the material being shipped from Detroit. The Free Press first appeared in London July 16, 1881. Its eight pages contained stories about life in the United States, a serialized novel, some contributions from M. Quad, a short story by Barr, and a collection of material aimed at women readers.

The Free Press announced in Detroit that an office had "been established at 325 Strand, London" and that "visitors will at all times be made welcome, and are invited to make themselves 'at home' there while in London."

The Free Press London edition had a major impact on British journalism, according to James Stanford Bradshaw, a journalism professor at Central Michigan University who studied the London edition extensively. Besides providing Britons with "unique insights into American life and culture," it also helped to dramatize to British publishers the appeal of typical "penny press" material and the value "of tested American journalistic techniques for capturing popular interest and circulation." The Free Press appeared in London at a time when British papers, although selling for a penny, were aimed at "an elite and (were) of comparatively low circulation." It was also a time when, after the British Education Act of 1870, the level of literacy was rising.

Bullock Press, 1878.

On the London edition's first anniversary, Barr explained its success in these words: "When the proprietors resolved to print and publish their paper in England, they pinned their faith to two things; First, they knew they had a good and readable journal on which they spent and continue to spend a great deal of money; second, they believe that the people of England and Scotland know a good article when they see it. They expected that if in three or four years the circulation went to about 10,000 a week, the venture would be considered a success. The result has far exceeded their expectations. The smallest quantity printed was the first number. That amount was 16,848. The number printed each week after that ran 17,180, 18,688, 20,644, 22,696, 25,000, 25,440, 28,300, 29,665, 31,800, 42,035, 33,145, and so on to the present, the weekly increase averaging about one thousand copies." At its peak, the paper reportedly achieved a circulation of close to 200,000.

Barr was crucial to the operation and its success. He was a Scotsman, born in Glasgow, who said jokingly he "was emigrated against my will" by parents who moved to Canada. Barr worked on his father's farm at St. Thomas, Ont., and was educated there and in Toronto. As a child, he is reported to have produced a miniature newspaper with his brothers, using the fly leaf pages of a church song book. By 1876, he was a school teacher in Windsor. He sold a story to the Free Press about an open boat trip he made with a companion from Windsor to Buffalo. This effort, headlined "A Dangerous Journey" and signed "Luke Sharp," impressed Quinby enough that he hired Barr to work at the Free Press.

By 1881, when he left for London, he had handled the "Personal," "Etchings" and "Various Topics" columns and had served as news editor. His brand of humor is characterized as "bordering on the quaint, the bizarre and the fantastic in life." He wrote novels and essays as well as newspaper articles, and he was an admirer and friend of Samuel Clemens (Mark Twain). Barr had been one of the youngest members admitted to the journalists' guild in Detroit, and he was a charter member of an informal Detroit club called "Wittenagemotte," or "meetings of the wise."

James Barr, Robert's brother, who also worked at the Free Press, wrote, "My brother had an active brain and brilliant imagination. He would see an accident and ten minutes later would have added several features to the situation. Fifteen minutes later there would be a more elaborate description of the accident's events, and half an hour afterward the original happening was so changed and improved by him as to be scarcely recognized."

Robert Barr used satire to jibe at politicians and their peccadilloes and pretensions. One example is his commentary on the battle to establish a civil service system. In a "Looking Forward" column in August 1884, a takeoff on a novel of the time entitled "Looking Backward," Barr pictured a young man who had just graduated from a business school as a clerk. Instead of looking backward, he wrote that the young man, Mr. Smith, had fallen asleep, had awakened 100 years later, and had gone to apply for a job. The potential employer, a Mr. Brown, explained matters to the young man this way:

> The great discovery of the 20th century has been the investigation in the sciences of the mind. Now there is a committee of mind readers which a person like you, for instance, goes before. They hold an examination and then they

tell at once what business you are suited for.

No man is allowed to go into business until he has passed the civil service mind-reading committee, when he gets a ticket showing just exactly what business he is adapted to. Naturally, he takes to the best business he is suited for, and it has been discovered by statisticians that the law of nature provides just as many people for an occupation as is necessary. If we had only known this years before it would have saved all the trouble and worry of competition and failure and disaster that has been so characteristic of the nineteenth century and those that preceded it. In the 20th century every man takes that business that he is suited for, and every man therefore is prosperous. Nobody asks for a situation because we put in our application for one to the committee, and they send us all the help that is needed. And with this, Mr. Brown of the 20th century gave Mr. Smith of the 19th the address of the local committee, the Civil Service Mind Reading Association.

Examination showed that Mr. Smith was not intended to be a clerk, but for a digger of sewers to which occupation he then turned himself because he was not allowed to go into any other, and strangely enough found himself happy and contented and successful.

The London edition continued to be published until 1899. By that time, scores of other British publications had adopted something of its personal style, and the Free Press was beginning to have troubles at home. Barr, who had left Detroit in 1881, remained in England, where he became a noted author and publisher of a magazine called "The Idler."

In that first London edition, a commentary was included from one Bronson Howard, a native of Detroit who then lived in England. It gives some insight into the kind of paper Quinby was producing in Detroit. Howard wrote: "I have known the paper all my life . . . I know that it is edited at home with the most sincere purpose to have nothing in its columns that can give offense or do harm within the sacred precincts of home; and to have only such matter as will tend to make its readers more cheerful and happy in their daily lives."

While attention centered on his star writers, Quinby himself became a much respected newsman. The New York Graphic said in an 1880 article: "Since it (the Free Press) has been under Mr. Quinby's exclusive management, its influence and usefulness have increased and the sphere of its circulation widened, until it has attained a national and even European reputation . . . His literary taste is of a high order; he possesses a very ready judgment of values in news and holds rigid views of the mission of journalism as a public educator."

Those sentiments were corroborated, by implication, in the words of James Scripps who, having hailed Storey for the impulse he provided, wrote in the Detroit News in 1890: "I think any competent judge of a newspaper to whom the question might be referred would, off hand, declare the journalism of Detroit to be head and shoulders above that of any other city of its size in the United States. For more than 40 years Detroit has held that high rank . . . "

William Quinby was born Dec. 14, 1835, in Brewer, Me., and came to Detroit with his family when he was 14 years old. He attended Capitol High School on Griswold street, John M. Gregory's Preparatory School and the University of Michigan, where he earned a bachelor's degree in 1858. He entered a Detroit law office after graduation and, by 1859, was admitted to the bar after an examination by the full bench of the state Supreme Court.

His father, Daniel Franklin Quinby, with a partner, J. K. Wellman, in 1850 had founded a journal called "Wellman's Literary Miscellany." Young William, as a schoolboy, got his first taste of publishing by working in the magazine office. Perhaps it was that early experience that caused him to leave a legal career; he soon went to work for Storey at the Free Press as the town's first fulltime court reporter. By 1872, he had taken full control of the newspaper.

True to the heritage of the Free Press, the change in ownership hinged on a political position strongly held. In the early 1870s, the administration of President Ulysses S. Grant was under attack for inadequacy and corruption by frustrated Democrats who had been out of power since Lincoln's election in 1860, as well as some members of Grant's own party. As the 1872 campaign geared up, a major power struggle was developing, with liberal Republicans seeking to dislodge Grant. In May 1872, they held a rump convention and selected Horace Greeley, the New York publisher, as their presidential candidate.

Hints were in the air of a coalition between the liberal Republicans and some Democrats who began to push for their party also to nominate Greeley. The Free Press suggested, "These falsifiers will be shown largely to consist of copperheads and soreheads — more or less repudiated by the Democracy . . . whose cry of 'anything to beat Grant' means 'anything to get a little governmental pap.'" The Free Press continued its attacks on Greeley and those who supported him — until a few days after the Democrats at their June convention also nominated Greeley.

Quinby's partners, Henry Walker and Col. Freeman Norvell, who between them held the controlling stock, thought the election of Greeley would be a disaster. Quinby argued that not to support the Democratic nominee "was unthinkable" for the "thoroughly Democratic Free Press." It came to a showdown, with Quinby finally convincing Walker that failure to support the Democratic ticket would be disastrous to the Free Press. Walker agreed to turn management of the paper over to Quinby if he would buy out Norvell's quarter interest, valued at $25,000.

For Quinby, it was a bittersweet moment. "He recalled the toil, the ardor and hope that had made him part owner of a valuable property," wrote Edward Holden, a Free Press editorial writer, "and now he found himself facing the prospect of its being swept away from his grasp in a few days" unless he could find the money to buy out Norvell. His one hope was that a friend, Alfred G. Boynton, who had expressed an interest in editorial writing, would join him. Within hours, Boynton, a lawyer and police court judge, had agreed to help Quinby buy out Norvell, and a few weeks later Boynton bought half of Walker's stock, too. Quinby took over the remainder of Walker's stock in 1875 and, when Boynton died, bought the remaining shares.

Norvell wrote a departing editorial to explain that because of "the difference of opinion between the partners who have purchased the controlling interest . . . and myself . . . I desire to say to the Democratic readers of this paper that I took the anti-convention side in the controversy from a profound, deliberate and firm conviction that it is an honest, Democratic and rightful one, and that I retire from the editorship of the Free Press, which I have held for several years, rather than endorse or advocate . . . the transfer of the Democratic Party to . . . one of the avowed life-long enemies of the party."

Another statement in the same paper presented the Quinby point of view: "As the foregoing explanation by Col. Norvell indicates, the proprietorship of the Free Press has passed into the hands of those who believe it to be the duty of the Democracy and Democratic organs to support the nominations made by the Democratic Convention at Baltimore. Col. Norvell voluntarily retires rather than compromise his convictions.

"The views of the present owners are that the only hope of the country is the defeat of the Republican party . . . that the convention determined . . . the standard-bearers . . . (that) it is the duty of the whole body of the Democracy and of all Democratic organs to give those candidates a hearty and loyal support.

"Henceforth, the views of the Free Press will be in accord with the views of its proprietors and (will render) wholehearted and faithful service to the cause of conservative principles and the Democratic faith . . . thereby to put an end in the country to radicalism, centralization, personal government and corruption."

Free Press support for Greeley did not go unnoticed by opposition papers. One of them delighted in quoting some of Greeley's most violent anti-Democratic rhetoric — "Not every Democrat is a horse thief, but every horse thief is a Democrat" — followed by an excerpt from the July 21, 1872, Free Press: "No estimate of Horace Greeley would be complete which did not mention his life-long devotion to truth."

Quinby stayed the course, giving mild support to Greeley but hitting hard at Grant and his administration. On election day, he wrote: "A vote more or less in Michigan for the national or state reform ticket may not be of immense benefit to the candidates on those tickets, but to the voter himself it will be of incalculable value, for it will identify him with the course of right which, whether it fall or not today, must ultimately triumph." Greeley was badly beaten and triumph postponed. On Nov. 7, Quinby wrote that the result of the election was "not entirely unlooked for . . . but it is sufficient to treat the re-election of President Grant as a fair expression, in the constitutional way, of the will of the majority."

The Free Press already had stiff competition from the Post and Tribune when James Scripps, on Aug. 23, 1873, began publishing the Evening News. The competitive effect at least partially was alleviated for a few months while Scripps paid the Free Press to print the News in its plant. But Scripps convinced his brother to sell his Illinois farm and invest $15,000 in the new paper so he could arrange for his own plant. In 1872, the Free Press led the field with circulation reported at 8,321 daily, compared to the Tribune's 8,000 and the Post's 6,300. By the mid-1880s, the News had taken the lead in daily circulation.

The 1870s continued as a period of innovation for the Free Press, with only an occasional setback. On April 29, 1878, a fire gutted the plant at Griswold and Woodbridge. The Free Press not only did not miss an edition but published a dramatic account of its own fire hours after it had happened. Goodale wrote the April 30 story, which was topped by a

"Fire! The Free Press Establishment in Ruins" reported the edition of April 30, 1878, demonstrating the ability to continue to publish despite the fire.

one-word headline — "Fire!" — followed by a series of subheads in descending sizes of type: "The Free Press Establishment in Ruins ... A gas explosion in the basement the cause ... Several employes severely bruised and burned ... Fearfully rapid progress of the flames ... The loss estimated at almost $50,000 ... The materials, etc., insured for $42,000 ... Insurance on building $20,000 ... No interruption ... Words of sympathy and encouragement" ... and finally, just before the story began, "Call at No. 51 Griswold and see us."

The story included such details as the names of the companies with which the Free Press was insured and for how much. It pinpointed the gas explosion at 5:40 a.m. and explained how John Connors, chief pressman, had taken forms off the press and gotten them to the Post's plant in time for the press run. The Free Press managed to save its subscription lists and, according to the story, "Everything in the safe and the counting room was saved," too.

That very day, coincidentally, the Free Press had finished laying the foundations for a new press. It was able to move into a modernized plant early in June and print "from stereo plates taken entirely from new type" on a new Bullock Perfecting Press, which had a capacity of 7,000 eight-page papers per hour. A new stereo plant, which had been put in place Jan. 20, made the Free Press "the first establishment employing the papier mache process (those aforementioned "mats") in Michigan ... (and) marked the commencement of a new era in the history of

printing in the state." The new technology allowed Quinby to expand his
weekly operation and made possible, three years later, the introduction
of the London edition. The Free Press used the new press for the first
time June 1.

Another 1878 innovation was "The Household," the first newspaper
supplement for women. It was four pages, magazine-sized, edited by
Eva Best. One of her successors as women's editor, Mary Humphrey,
years later wrote: "The diversity of interests touched upon in those four
pages of handset type — entirely without illustration — is amazing.
Music, art, elocution, fancy work, science, recipes, travel, fiction,
occupations for women, women's rights, child guidance, and even diet
and a column-family of correspondents that would surely hold our own
Ruth Alden (one of Detroit's first advice columnists) fascinated."

Articles were signed with such bylines as Home Spun, Wych Hazel,
Innocencia, Skeeter and one Deacon Dusenberry, who wrote: "I am one
of the bungling, awkward, lumbering creatures called man and most
meekly do I beseech you to adopt me into your family. Now I am going to
say something that I fear you will not accept in the same spirit that it is
rendered. I think woman should not mix in politics. Not that she is not
insufficiently educated to do so, not that she is not equal to man nor that
we men are so immensely wise that she cannot comprehend our
workings, but that it will produce no good . . . There are corrupt women
as well as men, and these would flock into politics by the thousands and
this would promote evil, inasmuch as it is a peculiar quality of human nature that it can be more easily influenced for evil than for good."

The Household was a popular feature, appearing every Thursday. A
Free Press promotion soon after it was introduced said: "Ladies who are
interested in this much-admired feature . . . will find a charming variety
of original letters treating diverse branches of the general subject in a vivacious and instructive manner. The recipes are practical, fresh and
numerous; the notes and queries full and the information precisely of
that nature that the ladies will cherish. Thursday's Free Press will be for
that reason a good number to buy, to preserve, to send to friends. If desired, papers of that issue may be had in wrappers ready to mail."

In response to its popularity and usefulness, the Free Press by 1881
had printed and sold three editions of a 664-page book also called "The
Household" which was dedicated "to the Women of 'The Household' as

the outcome of their zeal and cheerful co-operation in the work that has produced these pages." Subjects ranged from how to construct Aeolian harps to bread-making to taxidermy. The book did not reprint any of the delightful letters published in the weekly supplement in which more personal affairs of the heart were discussed.

Soon after the start of "The Household," the Free Press had its first woman staff member (Mrs. Best apparently worked out of her home) — Jennie O. Starkey, who for more than 40 years was society editor. The cream of society considered it a privilege to have Miss Starkey, "a walking Blue Book," ask them for news of their social doings, according to Mary Humphrey. About this time, Margaret Eytinge was editing the Young People's Department, and Martha Louise Rayne, who had worked on the Chicago Tribune, was a special writer and a novelist.

In her book "What Can a Woman Do; or Her Position in the Business and Literary World," Mrs. Rayne devoted a perceptive chapter to journalism as a career. She noted that "30 years ago a woman who wrote for the papers was looked upon as a great curiosity," but that "some did manage to add respectable sums to their otherwise meagre purses . . . by writing." She explained that journalism "not only requires special talent of a high order, but the greatest amount of technical discipline, general adaptability, quickness of diction, and fertility of resources. With all this it requires, too, what is almost a sixth sense, the mental habit of keen analysis and swift combination. While these qualifications are in their perfection the result of experience, they must also be natural gifts. The journalist, even as the poet, is born, not made." Mrs. Rayne resigned her job at the Free Press to open a journalism school.

Trying to pass judgment on newspapers from a distance is difficult. But, by chance, the Detroit newspaper scene in the mid-1870s was well reviewed in the Allegan (Mich.) Journal in a series of articles beginning in January 1878. The reporter called William Stocking, editor of the Post and Tribune (which had merged in 1877), "an accomplished literateur, thoroughly versed in national and state politics," and described Stocking's paper as "a bold and outspoken champion of unadulterated Michigan Republicanism." The paper was reported as doing well financially.

The observations about the Free Press were full of praise: "What shall we say of Michigan's peerless newspaper — the Free Press? Why that it is a non-pariel in Western journalism, a sheet of unequalled excellence. It is not the thick-and-thin partisan organ it was a few years ago, but a moderate, conservative Democratic sheet.

"It is the only paper in Detroit that employs the stereotype process in printing of its immense editions — daily, tri-weekly and weekly. One of the editions of the Free Press weekly is printed for foreign circulation and gives little or no state news. This edition publishes the more salient of the Free Press editorials, correspondence (foreign and domestic) together with novels, tales, poems and inimitable sketches and pungent paragraphs of M. Quad (C. B. Lewis) whose humorous writings are household words wherever the English language is spoken . . .

"The chief editor of the Free Press is a born journalist . . .. Mr. Quinby is an amiable and affable gentleman whose motto in journalism is 'excelsior.' The animating spirit with him and his wide-awake coadjutors is to give the Free Press a national and world-wide reputation. Therefore no expense is spared to employ the most talented contributors to grace the columns of this vivacious newspaper."

The News, founded only five years earlier in 1873, was seen as "newsy, spicy, pungent and irrepressible . . . which dares to do right regardless of libel suits and all species of bulldozing and intimidation, come they from public officials, politicians or bullies."

The reporter's closing comments noted, "There are several lady attaches at the Detroit daily press but the masculine editors-in-chief of the dailies most ungallantly neglected to introduce us to any of them. So we can say nothing of their merits and capacities as journalists."

For many readers and onlookers, nothing is more interesting than a newspaper "feud." That sort of competitive zeal keeps the juices flowing and tends to go on non-stop. Quinby told the story of how one ended between the Free Press and the Post which then was led by James F. Joy, "a sturdy, able, forceful man."

When Quinby picked up a phone in the Free Press office, the voice at the other end said, "I am Mr. Joy. I wish to speak to Mr. Quinby."

"He is here," said Quinby.

"Don't you think, sir, that the wrangle between the Free Press and the Post is disgraceful?"

"I do, sir."

"Will you stop it in the Free Press if I will stop it in the Post?"

"I will, sir."

"All right, sir."

"Good day, sir."

And thus ended the feud.

Years later, John S. Knight would tell how he, too, settled one in Chicago after he bought the Chicago Daily News which had a running feud with the Chicago Tribune. JSK simply met with Col. Robert McCormick, the Tribune owner, and told him that he thought it was about time to stop such foolishness.

And that was that.

But now the year was 1884, and the Free Press moved into a new building on the northeast corner of Shelby and Larned that boasted electric lights and telephones. It also provided more press capacity, and the Free Press celebrated the occasion by publishing what it hailed as "An Amazing Paper" — a 36-page edition, one whole page of which was devoted to a minute description of its five-story quarters. The paper's circulation at the time was a daily average of 15,759. It was selling for three cents daily or 15 cents a week. The Free Press offered free want ads on Sunday for job seekers and employers (it had about two pages worth).

Bragging about its 36-pager the previous Sunday, the June 10, 1884, Free Press said: "None have reached the magnitude of last Sunday's issue (which) left an amazing impression on readers and was a source of wonderment how it could be done." It went on to provide such details as these: The paper used would have stretched 108 miles, from Detroit to Marshall; piled on top of one another, the total circulation would have been higher than the Washington Monument; there were 148 men in the composing, stereo and press room, with 35 editors, reporters and regular contributors and 42 correspondents providing editorial material, besides the Associated Press. The writer concluded:

"With all its merits, probably no reader would scarcely care to have so mammoth a sheet furnished them very often. It is only once in a while that one can spare the time to 'note, read and inwardly digest' such a feast of good things as subscribers to the Free Press had laid before them in that number of the paper. For our part, though, the experience was neither disagreeable nor unprofitable . . . we do not especially hanker to repeat it. It won't do, with the present capacity of American paper mills, to educate our patrons to the point of (their wanting) such extraordinary newspapers as last Sunday's Detroit Free Press."

The excitement about so large a newspaper was justified. The standard at the time was eight pages. Because all the type was handset, 50 compositors were needed to set type for one eight-page edition. In August 1892, the Free Press became the first paper in Michigan to install linotype machines, which had been invented in 1885. The typesetter used a keyboard at the machine to cast lines of type automatically from molten lead. When the Free Press installed its first four linotype machines, it could print 10- and 12-page papers during the week and 20- and 24-page papers on Sunday.

It was in 1884 also that the Free Press delighted in the election of Grover Cleveland as president and the return to power of the Democrats. (It had suggested Cleveland's opponent, James G. Blaine, "was most acceptable to those human beings who prefer acting like lunatics rather than rational creatures . . . Blaine evidently is the crazy man's candidate.") But Cleveland was beaten four years later, and a year after that, the Free Press expressed bitter disappointment with the local political scene when, in 1889, "the strongest ticket ever put together by the Democrats" was beaten by Hazen S. Pingree, a Republican, in the Detroit mayoralty race.

The day after Pingree was nominated, the Free Press conceded the Republican ticket was a fairly good one because "Mr. Pingree, prominent and highly respected, belongs to a class (businessmen) that is represented less frequently in our municipal politics than it should be." Yet two days later, the Free Press endorsed incumbent Democrat John Pridgeon because "a good Democrat makes a better public servant than any Republican — good, bad or indifferent."

The Free Press barely mentioned the approaching municipal election until about two weeks beforehand, when both the Democrats and Republicans, on successive nights, held their conventions and nominated candidates. The two-week campaign ended Nov. 6, and the Free Press ran the story of Pingree's victory by 2,002 votes on Page Three; a major story on Page One detailed the triumphs of Democrats in off-year elections around the country.

The Free Press editorial used the occasion of Pridgeon's loss to take a few swings at its rival, the News. Claiming that Pridgeon had been "in a state of constant obeisance" to the News, the editorial argued that Pridgeon had "no real faith in the cobra newspaper of Detroit, but its glittering puffs and its basilisk-eyed editorial approval fascinated him. He surrendered his independence and followed the destructive course of the Evening News on public improvements. He antagonized supporters of the boulevard, he fought the rapid transit lines, he opposed franchises for competing street railroads. John Pridgeon was honest. He thought he was a valuable servant of the people when he was merely a slave to his deceiver's every bidding."

In the next decade, with Pingree leading the same progressive political movement that grew out of his battles with utilities and his handling of a depression in the mid-1890s, the Free Press conceded Pingree's "sterling integrity" but still opposed many of his policies. In 1891, the Free Press opposed Pingree's re-election. By 1894 the Free Press was suggesting that "Mayor Pingree has done the public excellent service in some things, notably in the matter of the Citizens Street Railway," which was the focus of a major franchise fight. Still Pingree came under heavy fire from the Free Press for his tendency "to arrogate to himself all the wisdom and virtue there is in Detroit." In later months, the Free Press thought Detroit had gotten "the reputation of turning the cold shoulder to propositions which add to the building up of the city; and there are too many who feel . . . that an enterprise which promises profit to its managers should be viewed with suspicion." That editorial said most Detroiters "resent and denounce old fogeyism which wants to fence the city and check its growth."

When Pingree finally left public life Jan. 1, 1901 after serving two terms as governor, the Free Press headlined its editorial "The Shattered Idol," and concluded: "He (Pingree) aroused the state from its political lethargy; he re-created old ideals of public responsibility; he awakened the civic conscience of the people; he again impressed upon their minds by his volcanic force the old lessons that eternal vigilance is the price of liberty, and some good that he has done will live after him. For his own sake and for the sake of the Commonwealth, we may venture to hope that the evil will be interred with his political bones."

There were other battles to be fought, other elections to come. In 1892, when Grover Cleveland was returned to office, Free Press stories and editorials pushed for federal appointments of Michigan people, a typical stance in those days when patronage was a major factor in political life. Unlike other politically oriented publishers, however, Quinby had taken the position that neither he nor any of his staff would go into politics or accept political appointments because he wanted to remain free to criticize. Suddenly, though, Quinby was faced with a minor embarrassment.

On May 26, 1893, it was announced that he had been chosen as envoy to The Netherlands. An editorial on the day of the announcement stated, "That it was entirely unsolicited need not be said," and added, "There is no reason why the Free Press should not say that it is a distinguished honor, and appreciated as such by Mr. Quinby's associates on the paper, as it will be by all his fellow citizens." That was emphasized when the paper ran three columns of congratulatory telegrams Quinby had received.

Quinby accepted the appointment and served until 1897, leaving his

The Spanish-American War had begun, according to the multi-column headline of the April 23, 1898, Free Press.

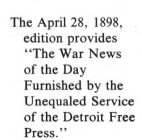

The April 28, 1898, edition provides "The War News of the Day Furnished by the Unequaled Service of the Detroit Free Press."

two sons in charge at the Free Press. Theodore handled news and editorial matters and Henry was business manager. Ironically, Quinby's political appointment came at a time when he was about to shift the Free Press from its strongly Democratic position into a more independent role. The change occurred in 1896 when Quinby refused to support William Jennings Bryan, who had swept the Democratic convention after his famous "You cannot crucify mankind upon a cross of gold" speech.

The key issue of the campaign was monetary policy, with the hard money (gold) people lined up against the free coinage (silver) people. For weeks prior to the Democratic convention in early July, Free Press editorials had cautioned against any platform or candidate that supported the free coinage position which it saw as "nothing but the most vicious kind of protection for a plutocracy more powerful than any other trust or monopoly in the country."

When the Republican convention had nominated Wiliam McKinley, the Free Press said it was "a gathering utterly lacking in dramatic interest or sentiments and scenes that make the heart leap. Mark Hanna's suzerainty over the Republican party, which made the convention the past week mere formality, was manifested in the selection of the ticket . . . (which saw) men vastly superior to McKinley in intellect passed over."

But on July 12, after Bryan's nomination, Quinby wrote: "The Free Press will stand by its convictions and will not endorse the Chicago platform (supporting free coinage of silver at a 16 to 1 ratio with gold) or candidates," and then he added, "(We) hereby declare our independence of all party organizations. It is the true attitude, we are convinced, for all newspapers, and it will certainly be the future attitude of the Free Press.

"We abandon no Democratic principles; for it is not democratic for a majority to force upon the minority a policy which is utterly at variance with the party creed and all party precedent. We shall support in the future as we have tried to support in the past what we believe to be soundly Democratic in the platform."

As the United States moved closer to war with Spain over the issue of independence for Cuba, the newfound political independence of the Free Press became more evident. The paper was supportive of President McKinley, agreeing with his cautious approach to the problem. Before the sinking of the Maine in February 1898, the Free Press repeatedly urged whatever was reasonable to avoid war, and in a Feb. 22 editorial, it decried the "False Journalism" of Hearst and company for its reaction to that tragedy:

"Fortunately for the cause of peace the mad antics of the yellow journals are not being taken seriously by the country. These travesties upon journalism, from the big concerns of New York with millions of capital and unlimited resources at their command to the smaller papers of the country that take their cue from the metropolitan sheets, have not ceased day and night since the sad news of the loss of the Maine . . . These journalism freaks . . . deserve only contempt."

However, after reports that the Maine's sinking was not an accident and that Spain remained firm in its position, McKinley and the Congress moved gradually toward declaration of war; the Free Press moved with them. On April 23, a Page One headline read, "War Is Now A Fact . . . From This Time Forward the United States and Spain Are Enemies on Shore and at Sea." Editorially it added: "The United States has begun the stern task of freeing the Western Hemisphere of Spanish dominion. Spain must abandon her hold upon a long-suffering people, and the last gun will not be fired until Cuba is freed from the Spanish grasp forever . . . We have hoped to avoid this war. But now that the alternative of the sword is the only one left to us, let the war be prosecuted with such vigor that the last gun of the strife shall follow the first."

In the weeks that followed, its intensive war coverage had a heavily patriotic flavor, reflecting the attitude of the community, and the Free Press had new graphic devices to shout its message. One-column headlines gave way to multi-column headlines, and vast stretches of gray type were broken with the first use of drawings. The first — that of a woman — appeared on the cover of Part Four of the Sunday, Feb. 20, 1898, paper. But it wasn't until Jan. 14, 1900, that a drawing (depicting a Boer War battle scene) was used on Page One. Two weeks later, the Free Press used its first photograph on the front page (a picture of Britain's Windsor boys). Photoengravings became commonplace thereafter.

Even the war coverage did not displace advertisements from Page One. An ad on April 28 in the top lefthand quarter of Page One ran this headline: "War News vs. Store News." It went on to say, "Side by side with thrilling war news you will find stirring news from this store (C. A. Shafer Company)." But at the moment ads on Page One had more to do with the financial condition of the Free Press than the judgment of the editor. It was a condition that led Quinby finally to sell the paper.

The paper's financial health had slipped badly after Quinby left to accept his ministerial appointment. His sons, according to historian

By 1898 the Free Press was using halftone photographs, left, as well as line drawings to illustrate stories. And illustrated advertisements, below, were becoming more elaborate.

Clarence Burton, "were . . . unfaithful in their duties and nearly ruined the paper and Mr. Quinby." Plagued by debt, Quinby in 1905 entered negotiations with James Scripps, who had built the News into the dominant paper in the city but who was regarded as something of a political maverick in business circles. A deal for the merger was nearly completed when Scripps was angered by a demand for payment of $3,000 from Ralph Booth for his services in helping to arrange the deal.

Scripps refused to proceed. In the meantime, Col. Frank J. Hecker, a leading businessman, had heard of Quinby's moves. Hecker, upset and determined to stop a sale that would give Scripps a virtual monopoly in the city, got in touch with Quinby. After getting agreement of support from William McMillan, Charles L. Freer and Truman Newberry, among others, all prominent businessmen, Hecker and McMillan arranged to buy controlling interest from Quinby. As part of the arrangement, Hecker insisted that "under no circumstances should the paper be used for personal political advancement by any of the partners." It was a significant agreement that would figure later in bringing E. D. Stair to the Free Press.

William Quinby, who had marveled at his privilege of being an editor in a period when "the telegraph, the web press, the typesetting machine, stereotyping, the halftone, the long distance telephone and the typewriter first appeared," gave this vision of his profession in a speech to members of the Michigan Press Association:

> The noblest profession on earth is that of the editor. Affording the opportunity for noble deeds, for beneficence, for aiding all good works, it carries with it also great responsibility. No man should have or does have a greater sense of this responsibility than does the conscientious editor. So believing, I take to myself also that which I say to you, as St. Paul said to Timothy: "Oh, Timothy, keep that which is committed to thy trust . . ." It is, indeed, my friends of the press, a goodly heritage that we have, a sacred trust.

Quinby sold the last of his stock in 1908 and shortly afterward, on June 7, he died of shock following an operation. Friends insisted he had been ailing since the death of his wife, Adeline, in 1905. A Free Press editorial summed up his life:

> The people of Detroit were his friends and neighbors and fellow workers. He grew up with them; he labored with them to advance the fair fame of the city and the commonwealth of his love.
>
> His home was a center of intellectual refinement and a model of hospitality in which was no taint of ostentation. He was a teacher, patriarch, friend and playfellow in one.
>
> No man of his time had keener relish of wit or greater rejoicing in humor; and few could apply those gifts to every day intercourse with the pungency, the timeliness and the appositeness that marked Mr. Quinby's facile mastery of them.
>
> His life was rounded, symmetrical and complete.

Edward Douglas Stair

"The name E. D. Stair was synonymous with rugged individualism."

Chapter Five

Steady with Stair

Chapter 5

A
s the 20th century began, both Detroit and the Free Press were on the verge of new beginnings. A new industry would transform the city, and a new owner would reshape the Free Press. For both there was the promise of exciting growth.

Detroit, which was founded when 100 men landed with Antoine de La Mothe Cadillac in 1701, started its third century with a population of 285,704. Tree-lined streets, many beautiful homes and a variety of industries made it a buoyant city, reflected in its motto: "Detroit, Where Life Is Worth Living." In the latter half of the 19th century, the city had become a center for steel production, the manufacture of railroad cars and car wheels, refrigerated cars, tobacco products and shoes. A heavy influx of foreign born (more than one-third of the population in 1900) helped provide a solid source of dependable labor. As the century turned, the first signs of a new product were appearing, one that would change not only the face of Detroit but also the way the world lives: the automobile.

The Free Press, although recognized as a force in American journalism, needed strong financial management to establish itself as a firm competitor with the News, the Journal, the Tribune and the Times, which was founded Oct. 1, 1900, by James Schemerhorn. And it got that ingredient when Edward Douglas Stair, who owned the afternoon Journal, was prevailed upon in 1906 to buy an interest in the Free Press. From that day, it would be a financially well-managed newspaper.

Stair had a penchant for work and success that started when, as a youngster in Morenci, Mich., he and his brother, Orin, who was two years older, set up an amateur printing outfit in the family's attic and published "Boys and Girls." They sold the paper for 25 cents a year, and it broke even. To get spending money, he also took odd jobs, including one with the local printer. At 14, he dropped out of school and joined his brother to start the Morenci Weekly Review, where he learned "accuracy is the most important thing to impress on a newspaperman" and where it became clear to him that "there is usually precious little difference between achievement and failure. Most men who do fail do so by just a little. They give almost, but not quite, enough. Another ounce of steam and they'd have turned the trick."

It was on that philosophical base that Stair, in the next 28 years, started and sold several newspapers, established a theatrical business that gave him control of 158 theaters, launched the careers of innumerable stage stars and began to build an interest in Detroit real estate that made him at one time the largest individual real estate taxpayer in the city.

He bought his first Detroit paper, the Journal, in 1901. At that time, Stair saw the theater business becoming too "salacious" for his taste, and he was "just a little homesick for the old newspaper life." When he bought the Journal, it had a circulation of 25,000 but was losing money. Stair quickly raised the price from one to two cents and "added a little to the value we were giving the reader." By the third year under his management, it was breaking even. By the fourth, it was profitable. In 1922 when the Journal had achieved a circulation of 120,000, he sold it to the Detroit News.

Stair's efforts caught the eye of Col. Frank Hecker, one of the group of powerful Detroit businessmen who had bought the Free Press in 1905. Another political disagreement among Free Press owners had created the need for a fresh start.

William C. McMillan, who had joined Hecker in the purchase of the Free Press from Quinby, apparently imbibed a bit too freely one day in 1906, called in a reporter and issued a long statement declaring his candidacy for the U. S. Senate. The resulting story infuriated Hecker, who had insisted on a ban on political activity among the principals of the Free Press. A month later, Stair was offered an interest in the paper, and Phillip H. McMillan, William's brother, took control of the McMillan shares. At the time, there were 11 stockholders, but by 1917, Stair had bought out all but a portion of the McMillan stock and had firm control.

By 1925, the paper had moved twice to successively larger buildings commissioned by Stair. When Stair arrived at the Free Press, the newspaper was housed in relatively dingy quarters in the former Abstract and Post Building on Lafayette just off the corner of Griswold. He moved the paper first, in 1913, to an impressive 10-story structure at

131 West Lafayette that later was called the Transportation Building (now the Grand Trunk Canadian National Building). In 1925, the Free Press moved to a $6 million, 14-story, Albert Kahn-designed plant and office building at Lafayette and Cass. Considered the finest of its kind when it opened, it remains home of the news and business staffs after production facilities were moved in 1979 to a new plant on the riverfront.

Malcolm S. Bingay, who became editorial director of the Free Press in the early 1930s, regarded Stair as "a pioneer son of Michigan, soil of

In 1913, the Free Press moved into a new building on Lafayette.

this soil." That, as much as anything, serves to explain the kind of newspaper Stair would publish — one with a strongly patriotic tone and, reflecting his own personal and business interests, one concerned with and involved in Detroit's development.

In every real sense, the Free Press thoroughly reflected Stair's personality, even after 1930 when he hired the flamboyant Bingay to edit the 100th anniversary edition (May 5, 1931) and to remain as the boss of the news staff. Bingay, who in the coming years became probably the paper's most identifiable personality, provided a bit more spice in the newsroom, but the editorial page remained pure Stair.

John S. Knight, who bought the paper in 1940, probably caught the essence of Stair's character better than anyone else in his eulogy on Stair's death in May 1951. Said Knight:

> E.D.'s life span covered 92 fruitful years ranging from humble beginnings as the editor of a small town weekly to great achievements in the business, theatrical, banking and publishing world.

In 1925, the newspaper moved again, into this Albert Kahn-designed building on Lafayette, between Washington and Cass, where Free Press business and news offices remain.

> The name E.D. Stair was synonymous with rugged individualism. He came up the hard way and had little tolerance for "carrying people around on a pillow."
> E.D. was a man of tremendous mental and physical vigor. Although he had the reputation of being a "tough negotiator," I

found that in my own dealings with him, he was ever kindly, understanding and sympathetic.

E.D. Stair was one of Detroit's foremost citizens. Through all of the tumultuous '30s, he stood strong and erect when all around him weaker men broke under the strain of business and financial reverses . . . No one could bluff, bulldoze or back down E.D. Stair. There are few such uncompromising men left . . . He was a symbol of his times . . . when strong, self-reliant, adventurous men grasped their opportunities and helped America prosper . . . (He was) one of the last sturdy warriors to fight to the end against social, economic and political philosophies he held in utter contempt.

The ingredients for that philosophy grew out of his early experiences. Stair was born March 29, 1859, in Morenci. A year after he and his brother, at ages 14 and 16, had begun their first weekly newspaper, they struck out on a new venture. They loaded "the old job press, type, dictionary and other incidentals onto the lumber wagon we had hired . . . My brother and I trekked along with that lumber wagon. The trip took four days." They had traveled 125 miles to Maple City, Mich., just outside Midland, then a small lumbering town. They called their new weekly the Dispatch, and when they realized that, working 12 hours a day, they were only breaking even, Stair said they applied "a little more steam." By working 14 to 16 hours a day, they made a profit.

When Stair learned the Midland newspaper was failing, he bought it, leaving his brother behind in Maple City with the Dispatch. "Under the previous owner, I discovered the paper had been absolutely neutral in everything," Stair recalled. " . . . He figured that the community was so small that he couldn't afford to offend anybody. But by this policy he took all the life and go out of the paper. He drew off all the steam." Stair boasted, "Within two months I had a lively crop of enemies — not personal enemies, but opponents to the paper's policies. But they were enjoying the fight! They read the paper. Furthermore, they advertised in it because they knew other folks were reading it, too. Between the friends the paper made, and the enemies it made, losses . . . became profits . . . I've yet to see a strictly neutral paper that was a success, or a strictly neutral man who was a success. I've always tried to have something to fight for in my newspapers."

After selling the Midland paper, Stair headed west looking for new opportunities. Finding none in Kansas, he went next to Chicago, where he landed a job with the Times and an assignment to travel to Seattle with former President Grant. In 1881, he was working for the Fargo,

(N.D.) Argus. A story he wrote about a plot to keep the county seat in Hope, N.D., by using unqualified voters in an election brought threats against his life. At the first opportunity, he walked down the main street of Hope accompanied by a six-foot-tall friend; each had a six-shooter strapped to his belt. They were not molested.

A new town was being settled 40 miles away, and Stair later told an interviewer how he "got some equipment for a (printing) shop, hired a sled, and started overland for the new village . . . There were no roads. The ground was deep with snow, the temperature was 10 to 20 degrees below zero . . . He found less than 50 people settled there (but) started his weekly, the Cooperstown Courier." He led the fight to make Cooperstown the new county seat — and won.

By 1884, he had an interest in several other North Dakota and Iowa papers, but because he "was homesick for trees," he returned to Michigan and with his brother bought the Livingston County Republican in Howell. The paper was founded by Kingsley S. Bingham, who became the first governor of any state elected as a Republican after the new party was organized in 1854. The Stair brothers owned the paper until 1889 when E. D.'s career took a strange turn. He got into the theater business.

A new opera house had been opened in Howell shortly before the arrival of the Stair brothers. By September 1885, E. D. was involved in managing it. Stair was stuck for a printing and advertising bill when a show flopped. He went to Detroit to collect his bill from the woman who owned the mortgage on the opera house. In a short time, she foreclosed on the mortgage and installed Stair as manager. He admitted he knew nothing about the theater business, but he figured the same principles that applied to producing a successful newspaper would bring a profit to the opera house. He established a new policy of theatrical standards which provided that "it will not only be the aim of the management to give patrons of the opera house first class amusement, but also to protect them from 'snide' and unworthy shows."

In March 1886, Jessie Bonstelle arrived in Howell to star in a play called "Gypsy's Prophecy" with Fred Crittenden. She played a number of parts and also danced. She made an impression on Stair, who rewrote the play, called it "Trixie, the Romp Heiress," and arranged to take it on the road the following year. It played from Philadelphia to San Francisco.

In 1892, at 33, he came to Detroit to work at the Whitney theater for $20 a week. He eventually teamed up with John H. Havlin of Cincinnati, who owned a group of midwestern theaters. Nine years later, the Stair-Havlin circuit had 158 theaters from coast to coast, and he controlled "the American popular-priced theatrical business — plays, actors, programmes, houses, billboards, theater tickets; yes, even soda water and peanut privileges in the lobby."

As John Herbert Greusel wrote in the Free Press, "He has inculcated (in the theater business) lessons of economy, sobriety and diligence where formerly there were discord, drunkenness and follies." Greusel added that when Stair came to Detroit, he was worth $10,000. By 1905, at 46, he reportedly had accumulated $10 million. Stair built the Majestic Theater in New York and had a hand in the careers of well known actresses Eva Tanguay, Mary Boland, Katharine Cornell and Ann Harding.

Stair was described as a man "with penetrating bluish-gray eyes, clean-shaven oval face, a firm mouth, strong jaws and a stocky form" who viewed life "like a banker," and was "secretive and self-contained" except with his own small circle of friends with whom he enjoyed playing golf and poker. Perhaps a reason that Stair was described as "clean-shaven" had something to do with the fact that he had his own barber shop on the sixth floor of the Free Press building, and every morning a barber came in and shaved him.

Greusel wrote that Stair had great confidence in the people he hired to run his theaters (and his papers, it might be added) and kept track of them by getting a penny postcard each day from the manager of each theater listing the receipts and other pertinent information. Greusel added: "E. D. Stair, the man, is nothing if not strictly business. He is bigger than anyone in Detroit has thus far ever dreamed. Some day, E. D. Stair's mastery will be recognized as little short of genius. I make the prediction that E. D. Stair will yet be known as one of the greatest Michigan businessmen of his day and generation."

Stair also helped organize the Paige-Detroit Motor Car Co., was one of the founders of the Detroit Creamery Co. and served as a director for years of the Detroit Savings Bank (now Detroit Bank & Trust). In 1932 he became president of the Detroit Bankers' Co., a holding organization that had brought together several small banking institutions. He was on a vacation trip to the West in 1933 when the bank holiday was declared. He headed back to Detroit immediately and insisted the holding company was sound and would pay depositors 100 cents on the dollar. It did.

When Stair came to the Free Press, circulation was 40,000 daily,

45,000 Sunday. The daily paper sold for a penny, and the Sunday for a nickel. By 1926, daily circulation was almost 200,000 and Sunday, 275,000. The daily paper cost three cents, the Sunday paper a dime. Operating expenses had jumped from $45,000 a month to $500,000. He continued to promote his idea that a little extra effort — or a "little more steam," as he was fond of saying — made all the difference in quality. "Here is an editorial," he explained one day. "It is fairly well written. It presents a novel viewpoint. Structurally it is all it should be. But the effect it leaves is flat. It has no kick. Therefore, as it stands, it is a failure. But cut a word out of its title. Replace a long word here and there with a vigorous, more pointed short one. Cut that long, tiresome sentence in half — and what happens? You have a strong, telling presentation of the case. The failure is a success. Yet all you have done is add a little ginger, put on an ounce more steam!"

One staff member assigned to editorial writing for a couple of years in the early 1930s recalled he would go up each morning to Stair's office on the 13th floor to join fellow editorial writers Hamilton Butler and Carl Shier to review what had been written, or would be written. Walking into Stair's offices, he would see office clerk Walter Jordan sitting on a high stool at a standup desk just outside.

That editorial writer also recalled, "Mr. Stair wasn't bashful about the fact that his reporters at City Hall (Cliff Prevost) or at Lansing (Jimmy Powers) spoke for him and were partisans and participants in local politics on behalf of his interests." A regular editorial page feature, reflecting Stair's other business interests, was theatrical reviews. And it was no accident that the Free Press opposed zoning laws, since Stair firmly believed zoning laws took away a property owner's freedom to use his property as he wished. But Stair was a fair man, the editorial writer insisted, always as good as his word. During the depth of the Depression, when the banks closed and Stair could only pay half-wages in cash, he promised to pay the balance later, and he made good.

On two notable occasions, Stair, a rather private person, spelled out his philosophy publicly — once in 1919, shortly after he had become principal owner, and again in 1935, in the midst of what Stair saw as the Roosevelt Administration's efforts to pack the Supreme Court.

The earlier exposition came as part of the statement the Free Press sent to the Audit Bureau of Circulations (ABC) with its figures for the 1919 April-September period (150,947). In a space left for additional comments, Stair wrote: "The Free Press is the only morning newspaper in Detroit, a city of more than a million population. It circulates thoroughly in the city and the prosperous territory within a radius of one hundred miles. With nearly a century of meritorious newspaperdom behind it, it represents permanence and worth of the highest sort.

"Politically, it is independent, with Republican leanings to national affairs. In civic matters, it has essayed to interpret the public spirit and direct it into those channels which lead to good judgment, sanity and betterment. It has persistently refused to attempt to lead thought in any cause until the issue has been carefully studied, with the result that its editorial policy has been accepted as fitly interpretive among those best qualified to judge."

The statement was blatantly promotional, but the ABC reports did end up in the hands of advertising agencies and other potential advertisers, a circumstance that apparently did not escape Stair's attention. The comments concluded with a plug for the paper's rotogravure section (first published in 1916), an eight-page, full-sized production which Stair called "a distinctive medium for advertising" because of its high standards. The report also emphasized Free Press circulation "embraces homes which form the genuine 'buying power' in the community." Even in 1919, the appeal to advertisers of upscale readers was not being overlooked.

Stair used a full page on Oct. 31, 1935, to make his own position clear in one of the most comprehensive editorial policy statements ever published in an American newspaper. Probably written by Bingay, it was headlined "Americanism, a Statement by The Detroit Free Press," and started with an historical review, from the paper's founding in 1831 "to fight the battles of the people, to defend their rights and to maintain the principles laid down by the Founders of our Republic . . . "

> The first candidate for President the Free Press supported was Andrew Jackson. The last Democratic candidate for President the Free Press felt it could give its wholehearted support to was Grover Cleveland. (It would be 1976, when the Free Press endorsed Jimmy Carter, before the paper supported another Democrat for president). Under the brilliant editorship of William E. Quinby, the Free Press departed from its historic position in 1896.
>
> The reason was plain and obvious at the time. The Free Press did not depart from its fundamental principle of popular representative government. But the Free Press could not support the crackpot theories of the radical wing of the Democratic Party, known as the Populists and headed by William Jennings Bryan.

The Free Press city room, election night, 1929.

Phil J. Reid, managing editor when Stair took over the Free Press.

Harold Mitchell, who became managing editor when Reid retired.

The Free Press stood with Grover Cleveland for sound money against printing press money, for constitutional government against wild-eyed vagaries.

The Free Press at that time did not become a Republican newspaper, it became an independent newspaper. Realizing that both old parties outlived the issues which gave them their birth, the Free Press has ever remained an independent newspaper ...

The Free Press is against the New Deal, or as it has been more aptly called, the New Ordeal. The Free Press opposed Franklin D. Roosevelt as President and feels that his record in office, as a breaker of promises, has justified its judgment.

There is a fundamental principle at stake and the Free Press places principles above personalities.

For 104 years the Free Press has been on guard, fighting for the rights of the people of Detroit, the State of Michigan and the United States of America ... regardless of circulation and its attendant advertising, it has ... never deviated ... because of the clamor of the hour ...

The Detroit Free Press fights today for the same rugged American individualism that first brought it from the old handpress in the days of Andrew Jackson — a clarion voice in the wilderness of the Northwest Territory.

It still stands for American individualism, American courage, American initiative, American thrift and American industry.

And we pray to God that it will carry on through the generations to come against the forces that would Stalinize, Hitlerize or Mussolinize our people — that this historic institution of journalism will never deviate in its war to safeguard our Democratic-Republican heritage of government, of and by and for the people.

It was with this dramatic statement that the Free Press emphasized the change of its motto from "More Than a Century of Service" to "On Guard for Over a Century." That first appeared on Page One, under the masthead, on Monday, June 9, 1933, and it has been a statement of the paper's philosophy ever since.

When Stair took over the Free Press, Phil J. Reid, noted as a scholar and developer of writing talent, was managing editor. When Reid retired in 1926, Harold Mitchell became managing editor. Stair soon had also put together a team that would serve and grow old with him in the decades until 1940 when he sold the paper to John S. Knight. Among

Celebrating the 100th anniversary of the
Free Press in 1931, E. D. Stair passes
out birthday cake to the staff.

E. Roy Hatton, who
went to work for
the Free Press as
a carrier in 1896,
served more than
half a century as
its circulation
director.

these men were William Lowe, the managing director; William H. Pettibone, general manager; Otis Morse, advertising manager; E. Roy Hatton, circulation manager, and E.A. Meiser, secretary.

One of Reid's oldest friends, and another distinguished Detroit editor of the 1920s, Harry Nimmo, of the slick-paper weekly Detroit Saturday Night, described Reid as an "old school newspaperman of the highest type." Nimmo added, "He possessed a full knowledge and appreciation of the ethics of the profession."

Reid, a New Englander, was graduated in law from Brown University in 1887 but became a sports writer for the Providence Journal in 1890. He worked briefly for the Detroit Tribune, then joined the Free Press and in 1893 became an assistant city editor to the well known John C. Lodge, who retired to enter politics in 1896 and later became mayor of Detroit. Reid became city editor, then managing editor in 1904. Years later, Malcolm Bingay told how Reid helped name the Detroit Tigers.

"My first memory of the Rube (Waddell, one of baseball's greatest pitchers) was when (G.A.) VanDerbeck, of Toledo, owned the Detroit team. That was in the days before the beginning of the American League — in 1898," Bingay wrote in 1945, in one of his celebrated stories of Iffy the Dopester, an imaginary sports prognosticator. "VanDerbeck, with a flair for fancy dress, had his ball players wearing striped stockings of orange and black. The late Phil Reid, managing editor of the Free Press, took one look at them and dubbed them 'Tigers.' That's what they've been called ever since."

Reid is credited with helping develop scores of fine newspaper people, among them sports writer Joe Jackson, founder of the Baseball Writers Association of America. It grew out of a meeting he called at the old Pontchartrain Hotel during the 1908 World Series to discuss the sorry plight of press box facilities.

Jackson is also the central figure in one of those legendary newspaper stories that focus on the drinking capabilities of reporters. There was no doubt of Jackson's capacity. One day, during a World Series game in Chicago, he fought the cold breezes with many nips. Finally he suggested that his colleagues take him to the Western Union office, prop him at a typewriter and leave him to write his story. A short time later, the wire operator, responding to an insistent call from Detroit, found Jackson asleep with his head in his arms on the table next to the typewriter. In the machine was a sheet of paper with this story:

By Joe Jackson
Chicago, Ill., Oct. 10 — Pickup AP.

It was not the first time, nor would it be the last, that the wire service would bail out an errant reporter.

But the most famous of all Reid's proteges was Edgar A. Guest, the Poet of the Plain People, who spanned the Quinby, Stair and Knight eras before his death in 1959. Through all those years, Guest was a vital part of the Free Press, and it of him. He was fond of saying that he had only had two loves in his life — his wife and the Free Press — and he delighted in reminding people that he was simply a "reporter who happened to be writing verse." Critics said his efforts lacked literary merit — one of the most vitriolic was Louis Untermeyer who in 1922 decried the fact that the American people were so taken with Eddie's work — but as Roy Marshall, one of Guest's biographers, wrote:

"Eddie Guest makes no claim to profundity, assumes no lofty

attitude for the doubtful distinction of being different . . . His appeal is
to the great masses — the plain people who sit in front of base-burners,
who wear overalls and pay their grocery bills on Saturday nights and say
grace at meals and stick up for the under-dog and fish for trout in brooks
— and live and die The Great American Public . . . (Those who know
him) know of the well-springs of his wide sympathies, know that varied
experience tempers his judgment, know the understanding that makes

Two of the Free Press' best-known personalities, Malcolm Bingay, left,
and Edgar A. Guest, in 1947.

him able to bring cheer to the lonely, encouragment to the down-and-
out, hope to the hopeless."

Edgar Albert Guest was born in England in 1881, barely a month
after the Detroit Free Press introduced its London edition. He was the
son of an accountant who came to Detroit to "start a new life" in
America. Guest came in 1891 with his mother and four other children to
join his father and brother who had come ahead. Eddie first saw Detroit
from the deck of a ferry crossing the Detroit River from Windsor,
Ontario, and he rode with his family to their home in a horse-drawn

streetcar from the foot of Woodward. He was soon working small jobs, first making a few pennies holding the check-rein for drivers of carts when they watered their horses at a fountain on Clifford and Cass, and then, at 13, as a soda fountain clerk in the Doty drugstore on the corner of Sibley and Clifford. He made friends, one of them a rival drugstore owner who convinced him to work for him, and another, Charles Hoyt, an accountant at the Free Press. In the summer of 1895, Hoyt got Eddie a job at the Free Press "doing chores and helping on the ledgers and posting the baseball scores on a bulletin board in front of the Free Press building."

Guest wanted to be a reporter, and Lodge, the city editor, gave him a chance. Eddie's next assignment was to the exchange desk, for many years the heart of many newspaper operations. That job as described by Guest's biographer, Marshall, helps explain his function:

"The man at that desk, completely surrounded by wave upon wave of the printed sheets, from the Boston Transcript to the Wahoo Bugle, is the man who looks at the world through wide-angle lenses. Across the desk of the exchange editor sweeps the flood of the world's opinion, the sum total of the world's woe, the tinkling brooks of the world's joy. To him come the poet and the plunderer, musicians and murderers, jokesmiths and junkers, prophets and perjurers . . . and it is he who clipped and pasted many a printed column to be grabbed frantically and set up by the profane foreman of the composing room to plug a hole . . . when the town's foremost haberdasher failed to come through with promised advertising copy." It was during this period that Eddie began to write verse.

He slipped a poem to the Sunday editor, Arthur Mosley, who published it Dec. 11, 1898 — the first of more than 15,000 verses by Guest to appear in the Free Press, in books and in more than 100 newspapers around the world. He had his own radio show for eight years, was lured to Hollywood for a brief period, produced some one-reel movies, and worked in television briefly. There was tragedy in Guest's life, the death of his beloved wife, Nellie, in 1945 and of two children, but there was also the joy of his daughter, Janet, now Mrs. M. Henry Sobell Jr., and a son Edgar A. (Bud) Guest Jr., who also worked for the Free Press, then went into radio and became, as his father had been, one of the finest after-dinner speakers in America. The family connection continues with Eddie Guest's grandson-in-law, Mike Duffy, who is married to Bud Guest's daughter, Jane, and is the Free Press television critic.

The stories about Eddie Guest are legion, but one particularly deserves repeating because it involves the verse that triggered his fame and led to publication of his first book in 1909 (a run of 800 copies). As son Bud tells the story:

"He was walking up to the house from the streetcar one evening and stopped to visit with some men who were building a house next door to ours. 'What are you fellows up to?' Dad called out. One of the men recognized him and answered, 'Why, hello, Mr. Guest. We're building a home for a Dr. J.W. Smith ... He's going to be your next-door neighbor.' And there was this idea tailor-made for him. 'I don't think you're really doing what you said you are doing,' Dad replied.'' From that casual conversation came these lines:

HOME

It takes a heap o' livin' in a house t' make it home,
A heap o' sun an' shadder, an' ye sometimes have t' roam
Afore ye really 'preciate the things ye lef' behind,
An' hunger for 'em somehow, with 'em allus on your mind.
It don't make any difference how rich ye get t' be
How much yer chairs an' tables cost, how great yer luxury;
It ain't home t' ye, though it be the palace of a king
Until somehow yer soul is sort o' wrapped 'round everything.

Home ain't a place that gold can buy or get up in a minute;
Afore it's home there's got t' be a heap o' livin' in it;

Within the walls there's got t' be some babies born, and then
Right there ye've got t' bring 'em on up t' women good, n' men;
And gradjerly, as times goes by, ye find ye wouldn't part
With anything they ever used — they've grown into your
    heart;
The old high chairs, the play things, too; the little shoes they
    wore
The hoard; an' if ye could ye'd keep the thumbmarks on the
    door.

Eddie Guest had a profound sense of friendship — and a great love for golf. His home was on the 12th hole of the Detroit Golf Club, and there were few days when he was not there with friends, among them Mark Beltaire, the father of the Free Press' Town Crier of later years. And every Monday, the Eddie Guest Club, an amorphous group that included Free Press regulars Bill Coughlin, Morgan Oates, Helen

Bower, Jimmy Pooler, Dorsey Callaghan and whoever else was handy, would gather downtown at the Old Wayne Club for lunch and lots of laughs and talk. And on Saturdays, Eddie was likely to appear to take a hand in a long-running weekly crap game in the city room.

When he made a hole-in-one, he wrote a note to Bingay: "It is high time the lowdown was given on this hole-in-one business. For years I have been led to believe that such a feat is difficult to achieve, and when accomplished, was highly rewarded by merchants, manufacturers, self-advertisers and gift-bearing Greeks . . . I turned the trick three weeks ago . . . Since then I have remained at home waiting for the rewards. Not a van has been sighted on our street since the foreclosing of the last mortgage in February . . . As a matter of fact, I'm sorry (I made that hole-in-one) . . . it has robbed me of my favorite line: that only dubs get holes in one."

Eddie Guest had a deep feeling for Detroit. As Daniel Wells, a longtime Free Press staffer, wrote once: "No one told Detroit's story or sang her song as well as our beloved little troubador in his poem entitled 'They Earned the Right.'"

THEY EARNED THE RIGHT

I knew Ket and Knudsen, Keller, Zeder and Breer.
I knew Henry Ford back yonder as a lightplant engineer.
I'm a knew-em'-when companion who frequently recalls
That none of those big brothers were too proud for overalls.
All the Fishers, all the leaders, all the motor pioneers
Worked at molds or lathes or benches at the start of their
*   careers.*
Chrysler, Keller, Nash and others whom I could but now
*   won't name*
Had no high-falutin' notion ease and softness led to fame.
They had work to do and did it. Did it bravely, did it right,
Never thinking it important that their collars should be
*   white.*
Never counted hours of labor, never wished their tasks to
*   cease,*
And for years their two companions were those brothers, dirt
*   and grease.*
Boy, this verse is fact, not fiction. All the fellows I have
*   named*
Worked for years for wages and were never once ashamed.
Dirt and grease were their companions, better friends than
*   linen white;*

Better friends than ease and softness, golf or dancing every
*   night.*
Now in evening clothes you see them in the nation's banquet
*   halls.*
But they earned the right to be there, years ago, in overalls."

Guest was equally eloquent in recalling some of his colleagues in a story he wrote for the Free Press' centennial edition in 1931. He wrote of "Miss Jennie Starkey, who for more than 40 years recorded the social life of growing Detroit," and of marine writer Bob Wagstaff, and of George Hellwig and Baron Wielhoff who handled the "Sayings and Doings" column, for years a Free Press staple, and of "dear old David Carey, keen mind, sharp wit and lovable personality," who was one of the first to adapt to using a typewriter when that new fangled machine was introduced to the staff, and of C. Nick Stark, "the happiest heart that ever graced a newspaper" who finally gave up newspapering to go on the stage.

And, Guest continued, "There was Frank Codrington and Harry Christiancy, who knew everybody in the state, and dear old Col. C.C. Colbrath," who gave 45 years of active service to the paper, and Jim Leroy, who later went to the Philippines with William Howard Taft and "was sporting editor for a year or two." Arthur Mosley, the Sunday editor, "knew no night nor day, nor pleasure, nor pain, nor hobby that could keep him from the needs of his paper . . ." Bob Needham, Ed Granish, Hugo Gilmartin, Mason Jernegan, Everett Dunbar ". . . were of our frame and fibre . . . The city knew them and honored them and believed in them."

He recalled William Robinson and city editor Billy Bolles, who got into a contest over who "could eat the most oysters on a half shell at a cent a piece, the loser to pay for all." "There was a contest worth seeing," wrote Guest. "Bolles ate three dozen and stopped, but Robby kept on to the tune of 96, saying with every one that slipped down, 'There goes another cent of Billy Bolles' money.'"

It was a colorful company on hand when Stair took over, and it was an interesting time for the city. The Free Press, like other newspapers, saw the day's news events more clearly than history. It reported at the completion of a $422,000 fund-raising drive to build a YMCA: "a militant aggressive young Detroit is . . . going to build here a great city, and casting about later for an event to mark the epoch, this one will admirably serve the purpose," while it left the story of the auto industry mostly to the sports pages — where auto racing got considerable attention.

In January 1914, when Henry Ford announced what is now considered one of the most important developments in industry — the $5, eight-hour day — the Free Press played the story rather routinely, giving it secondary position on Page One. The story led with a quote from Henry Ford: "We believe in making 20,000 men prosperous and contented rather than follow the plan of making a few slave drivers in our establishment multi-millionaires."

It went on to say: "Because Henry Ford believes that the distribution of wealth between capital and labor is too uneven, the world's greatest profit sharing plan, by which all the employes of Ford Motor Company will receive a part of about $10 million added to their regular salaries this year, was announced Monday morning by the company." Readers had to go deep into the story to learn that, after Jan. 12, 1914, workers who had been making $2.34 a day would be assured of a minimum of $5 a day.

Editorially, the Free Press commented: "That unskilled laborers, engaged in even menial tasks that call for no prolonged training to master, should suddenly be transformed from recipients of a bare living wage into enjoyers of incomes that are comparatively rare among professional workers, will excite the admiration, perhaps, the jealousy, of their less lucky kind. To be a worker in the Ford factory will mean hereafter that the proud claimant of the honor is among the privileged of the earth . . . "

The next day, a Page One story reported hundreds of people were lined up for jobs at Ford. But the lead story that day was about the strike of copper miners in the Upper Peninsula. In a Christmas Eve tragedy in Calumet, 72 people, most of them children, had died. Hundreds of wives and children of miners had gathered in a hall for a Christmas party and someone shouted, "Fire!" Those who died were suffocated in the stampede for the door. Suspicion ran high among the miners that the tragedy was caused by company agents. Rumors were circulating that mining company detectives had barred the door at the bottom of the narrow staircase where most of the victims died. Despite a spate of investigations, the tragedy was never resolved, and the man who raised the fatal false alarm was never found.

In the Calumet case, the Free Press stated emphatically, amid talk of federal investigations, that "Michigan wants no interference" from the government. "The government has no concern whatever with this matter," and the manner in which the federal government was threatening to act was "offensive," the Free Press said.

Another sign of Free Press attitudes appeared in an editorial headlined "Quit Babbling and Go to Church." That editorial bemoaned "the sociological propaganda" that "has flooded the land with filthy discourse, literature and drama until the nation is sick almost to death from a surfeit of nauseating frankness." The editorial writer recommended people "go to church to think over their own sins rather than the sins of their neighbors."

In February 1914, the Free Press chided those "professional politicians" who had failed to support a new city charter, but also admitted the charter proposal "contained endless blunders." Four years later, with the Free Press more emphatically in support, a new city charter was approved.

While Europe was on the verge of war in July 1914, the Free Press was extolling growth and pushing the idea of a "City of Greater Detroit." It urged Royal Oak businessmen to advertise in the Free Press, noting that the newspaper was "reaching the suburban home with the same facility that it reaches the close-in city home." More important, said the Free Press, "a greater Detroit is coming with surprisingly rapid strides, every day bringing the suburban points closer to the bosom of the city of which they will someday form a corporate part . . .

"Detroit has within its corporate confines far more than 600,000 persons at this hour. Inside these limits an amazing growth has taken place within a decade and a still more striking growth is daily going on toward the million mark which when set a few years ago by a few faithful enthusiasts seemed to others so improbable that it was considered a subject for quip and jest — but now no longer matter for merriment."

The Free Press vision of a Greater Detroit went on: " . . . All the way to Pontiac, to Rochester, to Farmington, to Ann Arbor, to Mt. Clemens, landholdings are being cut into ever smaller parcels and peopled by the overflow from the big city. There are thousands of new homes, big and little, and shops and stores and factories even, going up yearly in a radius of 30 miles of the limits of Detroit city. All these are tributary to Detroit. Many thousands of these suburban dwellers rub elbows with city dwellers every day in shop, factory and office and really constitute in interests and aims one great and growing family.

"Some day, not so far away that prophetic vision cannot see the glimmers of its dawn, this family will hold a great reunion — and there will rise to greet the nation, more than a million strong, the city of Greater Detroit."

A few months after this editorial, Detroit achieved its million population. That growth led to traffic congestion so troublesome that in March 1917, Mayor Oscar Marx asked the city council's public utilities committee to "get subway plans underway as the only permanent solution to the transportation problem." A fund of $15,000 was created "for further investigation and preparation of subway plans," and the Free Press story on Page One mentioned, "another proposed solution is the construction of an elevated monorail system."

Financially secure again, the Free Press was able to show the kind of innovation to attract readers that had marked Quinby's era. A rotogravure section and a Sunday magazine were introduced. The sports section thrived on the Tigers during the exciting pennant-winning days of 1907, '08 and '09. While coverage of foreign news was, at best, sketchy, the coverage of local and state events was solid. In the tradition established by Quinby, the Free Press featured a strong women's section and emphasis on children with a page devoted to their writings and activitities. What had been a section of "Merry Times for Boys and Girls" in the 1880s and beyond was now the Sunbeam Club.

A distinguished group of women served on the Free Press staff during the period of Phil Reid's editorship, including Elizabeth Johnstone (who edited Household, wrote book reviews and editorials), Mary Humphrey, Leila Bracy, Maude Bush, Florence Buttolph, Harriett Culver, Grace Barber, Gertrude Bombenek, Helen Bower, Frances Givens, Edrie McFarland, Ella Mae Hawthorne McCormick, Charlotte Tarsney, Dorothy Williams, Lorraine Wendell, Mae Wagner and Jane A. Humphrey.

Mary Humphrey and Gertrude Bombenek played major roles in the Free Press Fresh Air Camp program, one of the paper's most productive promotional efforts. On June 24, 1906, Sunday Editor Arthur Mosley ran a box on the page devoted to "Our Boys and Girls" that read: "Wrap up a nickel in a piece of paper and send it to the Free Press to be used to send a poor crippled girl and a poor crippled boy to the country for a month's vacation."

Within days, enough money poured in to send eight children to the country. The money continued to pour in, posing a problem about what should be done. Mosley decided the Free Press should establish a camp. In August, having obtained a plot of land on Sylvan Lake, near Pontiac, he and two other Free Press men went out to get ready for the arrival of 24 boys. With the help of neighbors who volunteered, they managed to

put up a cook tent, a mess tent for which tables and benches had to be
made of rough lumber, a small tent for the cook and one for the director
and six tents for small boys. By the end of the summer, 84 boys had vaca-
tioned at Sylvan Lake, and Mosley and the Free Press were committed
to continuing the effort which Mosley saw "as an experiment in
philanthropy, founded on an ideal and developed by experience."

A story by Leila E. Bracy in the July 26, 1931, Free Press told how

Fresh Air Camps sponsored by the Free Press were a hit with the children
who attended. Often the first trip to camp was also the first auto
ride.

Mosley "gave year-round thought to the camp, planting trees in the
spring and fall, and after camp opened he could be seen daily, laden with
bundles and parcels, rushing to catch the late afternoon interurban.
Back at his desk at 1 or 2 o'clock in the morning, he declared that the trip
refreshed him mentally."

Camp life in its early days says something about the hardiness of
children and attitudes of the period. One camp director wrote: "The
meals were served in a big tent where the dining hall is now. In rainy

weather mud got so thick boards were put down for the children to walk on and even the benches got so dirty that the children couldn't sit on them. Flies were always thick. Dishwashing was done where the pump-house now is.

"The dishes were taken down in the same kind of carts we use to pick up papers with. The water was heated over bonfires in large washtubs. First the water had to be scooped up from the lake. Boards were laid on barrels to set the dishpans on. While children washed dishes, (a supervisor) sat back of them and brushed the mosquitoes away and painted their arms and legs with dope to keep them away. The dish towels were rinsed and laid on bushes to dry until the boys started wiping their faces on them and then they had to stop.

"Candy store was the reward for the harder jobs about camp and there were lots of them then, as digging and building the buildings we now use. The children were paid in camp money and then cashed their checks at the candy store."

Free Press employees from all departments pitched in when help was needed to fix up the cottages (which replaced the tents), to paint or build roads. For years Mary Humphrey and Gertrude Bombenek served as directors. They also worked on the annual Ruth Alden dress drive, another promotion sponsored by the Free Press to give a hand to the Old Newsboy Goodfellows, a charitable organization of former newspaper carriers. Each Christmas hundreds of dresses are collected to be included in the Christmas boxes the Old Newsboys distribute to poor children.

For years, the camp was supported entirely by contributions from readers. But in the 1940s, the Free Press took full financial responsibility for the camp and set up the Fresh Air Fund to support it. The following decade, the camp was turned over to the City of Sylvan Lake.

The Free Press gave little attention to the developing war in Europe until July 25, 1914, when a Page One headline declared: "War Is Likely to Involve Half of Europe." In the days that followed, the coverage intensified. "The outlook is so appalling," the Free Press said July 31, "it baffles the imagination. It sweeps to the wings all the things that for the last two years have engaged the center of the world stage and have been considered matters of prime importance.

"The Mexican situation, equal suffrage, the Panama Canal opening, even the Irish home rule, sink into comparative insignificance. Many

The war in Europe begins, reported in the Free Press Aug. 2, 1914.

The United States joins World War I, reported in the Free Press April 6, 1917.

projects which a week ago seemed to be of vital moment may forever be forgotten.

"Today there is one overshadowing fact before the world and to it everything else is subsidiary or subordinate. It is changing the whole aspect of life. It promises to readjust social and economic conditions the earth over.

"That one fact is — WAR."

Nevertheless, the Free Press continued to treat the war as a

European phenomenon until German submarines began to attack American shipping. Then, with the rest of the country, the Free Press moved steadily toward support of American involvement in the conflict. In April 1917, after President Woodrow Wilson called for a declaration of war by Congress, the Free Press said:

"President Wilson's address . . . means open war with Germany in substitution of the impossible situation hitherto existing, a situation which has given the government in Berlin a monopoly of positive actions . . . The president (calls) for a war of offense and defense, a fight to the finish, not, however, against the German people, only against the present outrageous and barbarous governmental regime of Berlin."

And in another editorial it said: "There can be and will be no question of loyalty. Here and there individuals and even bodies of men, moved by quite comprehensible and ineradicable motives of sympathy for the lands of their birth, may be guilty of regrettable spirit or action, but these will be negligible among a hundred million people devoted to the country of their birth or adoption with a passionate and self-sacrificing affection exceeded by the people of no other country the world over. To believe less than this is an act of gross insult to our institutions and our history, which alone are responsible for the spirit of our people."

Free Press support of the war effort was unquestionable in the months that followed, but after the war it was less enthusiastic about President Wilson's 14-point peace plan and the League of Nations.

Wilson's successor, Warren G. Harding, was enthusiastically supported by the Free Press. When he died, a Free Press editorial called Harding "a great man with a great soul and a great courage and steadfastness who did not suspect his own greatness, but in all humbleness undertook to do what his conscience, his best judgment and his country led him to do."

About this time, too, the Free Press led the unsuccessful fight against public ownership of the street railway system. A Free Press editorial in 1923 got a chance to say "We told you so" after fares were raised to six cents in an arbitrator's award. The editorial called the fare increase "a bitter pill" for the News "not because it is solicitous for the welfare of the car rider . . . but because the fare increase shows it up as a maker of false and impossible promises."

The '20s brought another fierce competitor into the Detroit newspaper scene. In 1921 William Randolph Hearst bought the Times. Within months, the Times — aided by its vigorous coverage of local events, and especially its sensational attention to murders, kidnappings and other lurid crimes of the era, aiming at "the common man" — moved into second place behind the News. Its circulation, like the city's population, was soaring, from 15,527 for the year ending March 31, 1923, to 261,911 by the end of March 1925. In the March 1928 one-year figures, the Times (330,313) trailed the News by less than 5,000. The Free Press was in third place at 222,484.

Detroit was in the midst of a great boom, moving from a population of 993,739 in 1920 to 1,535,964 in 1926 when the Penobscot (now the City National Bank Building) and the Maccabees (now the School Center) buildings were constructed. Two hundred movie houses were bulging and 2,000 industries were providing jobs. It was the era of Prohibition, and the Free Press, compared to the competition, was restrained in its handling of many related stories, ranging from blind pigs — illegal drinking spots — to the killings that accompanied the illegal gambling and liquor business. It did inveigh editorially against lawlessness, a safe and plentiful target for editorial attacks in the free-wheeling '20s.

Despite its third place in the circulation war, the Free Press continued to prosper. In 1924 ground was broken at Cass and Lafayette for its second new home in 12 years. A measure of its growth was the boost in advertising linage from 8,437,072 one-column lines in 1911 to 14,486,304 in 1923. Its circulation more than doubled in the same period.

On Nov. 22, 1925, the Free Press marked the opening of its new building with a 24-page rotogravure section giving readers a close-up look of the building's interior, and E.D. Stair took the occasion to share "A Word or Two With You:"

> It is the earnest desire of the men now in control of the Free Press to preserve and strengthen their legacy of truth, honor and high ideals; it is their earnest hope that the people of Michigan will regard with approval the past, the present and the future career of this newspaper, will have confidence in its sincerity, and will forgive its errors as mistakes of the head, not of the heart ...
>
> The Free Press fights for what it considers right or advisable and against what it considers unwise or evil. It is jealous of the liberty of the country and the free institutions of the nation. But its aim is to battle without animus. It steadfastly refuses to accumulate friends it must reward or foes which it desires to punish. For the newspaper that does either of these things betrays the trust its readers repose in it ...

While the Free Press exulted about its new home, the paper of Nov. 19 carried stories signaling problems to come. A bank president, one headline said, "sees no 'boom' in prosperity." The president of the University of Michigan, according to another headline, "urges limit put on poor families; fewer children would better chances of each, he asserts." Women's rights and Prohibition were topics of other stories. And a two-column headline said: "Race Psychology Told in Sweet's Testimony."

The latter referred to one of Detroit's most celebrated trials. On Sept. 8, 1925, Ossian Sweet, a black doctor, and his family had moved into a house on Garland at Charlevoix, an all-white neighborhood on Detroit's east side. A crowd of angry whites gathered that night and the following night. Stones were hurled at the house, and shots were fired from inside the house, killing one man in the crowd and injuring another. The 11 persons in the house, including Sweet, were arrested and charged with murder. The Free Press gave thorough, albeit discreet, news coverage to the story. Clarence Darrow's eloquent defense drew national attention. In court, Darrow did not deny the fatal shot came from the house. He built his case, instead, on the doctor's right to defend his family and his home.

At the conclusion of the second trial in the case (the jury had deadlocked in an earlier trial), the famed attorney summed up his defense: "I may not be true to my ideals, but I believe in the law of love, and I believe you can do nothing with hatred. I would like to see a time when man loves his fellow man and forgets his color or his creed. We will never become civilized until that time comes. This case is about to end, gentlemen. To them (Sweet and the other defendants) it is life . . . Their fate is in the hands of 12 whites. Their eyes are fixed on you, their hearts go out to you and their hopes hang on you . . . I ask you in the name of progress, and of the human race, to return a verdict of not guilty in this case." Three hours later the jury did as Darrow had asked.

The Sweet case put the spotlight not only on race relations in Detroit but also on a new judge on the Recorder's Court bench, Frank Murphy, who five years later was to become mayor. He was at that time the only Detroit judge willing to risk involving himself in a racial controversy by hearing the case. It was a time of growing bitterness between the races, as a swelling number of blacks migrated to the city in search of jobs in its booming economy. The Ku Klux Klan became increasingly active, and the Klan became the major issue in the 1925 mayoral race between the incumbent, John Smith, a Catholic, and his challenger, Charles Bowles

— but because of the Klan's religious bigotry, not its philosophy of racial hatred.

In a Page One editorial Oct. 30, the Free Press said: "Certain political elements are at present bitterly opposing the re-election of Mayor Smith. Among them is the would-be journalistic boss of the town (the News), and a few men who have been disappointed in their desire for positions which the mayor gave to better qualified people . . . the religious issue has been raised against Mr. Smith by local Ku Klux Klan officials, whose motives are apparent."

In another editorial, the Free Press said: "At his mass meeting in the armory, Charles Bowles denied that he is a member of the Ku Klux Klan. This he has done before. He also said that he disclaims sympathy with any faction or organization that would deny to any citizen the rights and liberties guaranteed by the constitution, that he has no patience with intolerance and would not deny to any man his inalienable right to adhere to the religion of his choice.

"This is pleasant to hear. It remains true nevertheless that last Fall the Ku Klux Klan leaders tried to put Mr. Bowles in the mayor's chair because they considered him 'satisfactory,' and that since then they have been constantly organizing and working in his behalf and are now doing their best to elect him. Mr. Bowles has known and consented to this all along. Under the circumstances his statement comes rather late to be impressive."

Smith was re-elected, and the Free Press hailed the fact in an editorial, saying, "Altogether Detroit has given the Klan a smashing blow." It also ran on Page One a statement by Mayor Smith which said, among other things, "I have a right to commend the Free Press on its fearless editorial exposition and its honest presentation of news. That attitude appears most striking in contrast with the attitude of the Detroit News which, sympathetic with the aspirations of the Ku Klux Klan, conducted a peculiarly cowardly campaign. Lacking the courage openly to espouse the cause of the Klan, the Detroit News covertly and by innuendo and insinuation conducted the Klan campaign in editorial and news columns alike."

Former Free Press City Editor John C. Lodge beat Smith two years later, then Smith lost to Bowles in 1929 when Lodge retired. Bowles was blamed for a violent crime wave sweeping the city, and an effort was mounted to recall him. The Free Press at first expressed some qualms about the recall but solidly backed it by the time the vote was held in July 1930. It was a wild campaign climaxed by the assassination of popular radio commentator Jerry Buckley, who had been an outspoken critic of Bowles, on the night the results were announced.

The new election was scheduled for early September. It turned into a major battle between the Times, supporting Frank Murphy, and the Free Press and News, which were backing businessman George Engel. It was a climactic point in the political battles that had been raging among the newspapers through the 1920s. The papers had disagreed over composition of the Recorder's Court bench and municipal owner-ship of the street railway system. Frank Murphy, whose fortunes were intertwined with those of the Times, had been a particular subject for dispute. Joseph Mulcahy, managing editor of the Times, gave vigorous support to Murphy. In 1930, Murphy actually had a hand in planning editorial and news strategy for the Times.

The intensity of the campaign for mayor is indicated by Free Press headlines on Page One beginning on the Sunday before the vote: "Vote to Crush Crime Reign, Engel Urges," "Emmons (Harold Emmons, a former police chief) Denounces Bowles, Backs Engel" and "Elect Engel or Recall Battle Fails, Lodge Says." On the morning of the election, the climactic headline read, "I Will Free Detroit of Gangs, Says Engel."

Murphy won easily. Engel finished third behind Bowles, and Smith was a distant fourth. It was an historic election because, while the Republicans scored their usual state sweep that November, the emer-gence of Murphy, a Democrat, at a time when the Depression was taking on political overtones as well as social and economic ones, was a portend of the Democratic landslide to come two years later.

The conservative-leaning Free Press was soon more than critical of Murphy's approach to handling welfare and other aspects of the Depression-plagued community. Its attitude was clear in a comment it made on "some remarks by Sen. (James) Couzens regarding the dole in particular and public charity in general as opposed to private charity." The June 15, 1931, editorial continued: "We are left with the impression that the senator is a little hazy in his conception of the function and pur-pose of free government in America. Apparently it is his idea that our government should act as a sort of general nurse, caretaker and disciplinarian of the public rather than be a simple modus vivendi, maintained by people who wish a convenient piece of machinery to help them live in an orderly, pleasant, secure manner while going about their business of earning their bread, bringing up their families and generally improving their opportunities as they think best and find convenient.

"Although the senator may not be conscious of the fact, his

conception of the function of government is more paternalistic and socialistic, and therefore potentially autocratic, than genuinely democratic." That editorial typified the Stair philosophy.

Although the Depression was taking its toll, the Free Press was able to take some civic pride in Detroit's continued growth. The 1930 census reported the city's population at 1,568,622. The Free Press was "pleased by the justification of our claims to progress and increase which the figures provide. . . . Detroit has definitely emerged from the mere big city stage and has become one of the recognized and established metropolitan centers of white civilization. And it is still only commencing to realize its possibilities for advance.

"But this in no sense means that Detroit's problems are solved . . . great public works remain to be undertaken . . . (with) wise constructive economy, which will frown upon every suggestion of extravagance just as it will discountenance parsimony . . .

"There also is evident in the community a desperate necessity pressing for more tolerance for the rights and opinions of others, more common honesty, more common courtesy, more ordinary respect for, and enforcement of, law. Lacking these things, our material growth and wealth will sooner or later become a mockery. It is just as important for Detroit to become great within itself as it is for it to become great to the eyes of the outside world."

Malcolm Bingay appeared on the Free Press scene in 1930 and in the next decade managed, with his brilliant pen and imaginative approach, to become the most talked of newspaperman in Detroit. He was a man people either loved or hated wholeheartedly, but in either case they did not want to miss reading him. Bingay's characterization of "Iffy the Dopester," an imaginary sports prognosticator with a white beard and a twinkle in his eye (the cartoon creation of artist Floyd S. Nixon) and his editorial page column, "Good Morning," made him the paper's most identifiable personality.

No other Detroit newspaperman during the first half of the 20th century came close to arousing the emotions of readers — and colleagues — as Bingay did. He was a big man, 6-foot-2, with an imperious presence and a voice that could boom, and he had a way of delivering a withering glance that left many shaken. He loved books, he loved his friends and he loved to drink, often to a fault.

His individualism was apparent early. "It was because I was interested only in the things that interested me and not what the teachers were interested in that I was such a complete flop as a student in the years that I attended grammar school," he wrote in his autobiography, "Of Me I Sing." "That is why I got kicked out of Central High School in Detroit two months after I started." He suggested it may have been "some sort of prenatal hunch" that caused him to want to become a newspaperman "rather than a policeman or fireman," and at 14, when

Iffy the Dopester, whose words were written by Bingay and whose all-knowing face was the work of Floyd Nixon, Free Press art director.

he was graduated from the Pitcher grammar school, he predicted that he would one day be editor of the New York World.

His first job was pasting labels on boxes at a food wholesaler's warehouse. After quitting another job as stockboy at a hardware store, he spotted a boy-wanted sign in the window of the publication Michigan Farmer. "Here was the thing of which I had dreamed," he wrote later. "Horace Greeley started as a printer's devil at the age of 14. Horace and I — we would show them. That was 50 years ago, and I have never done a day's work since."

His next job was as a copyboy at Detroit Today (which later became the Times). When, he said, he realized for him at Today "there was no tomorrow," he moved his copyboy skills to the Detroit News and began a meteoric rise at that paper — to sports writer, to city editor, to managing editor by the time he was 29. About the time he became city editor, he married his beloved Sarah Rose and they had a daughter, Sybil, before Sarah became an invalid after a spinal injury in a fall on the ice at Belle Isle. In 1928, Bingay wound up in London to write, study and rehabilitate himself. Friends finally convinced him to return to take a job with an advertising agency. That lasted a few months before he joined the Free Press in 1930. A short time later, "kindly Death at last ended the long years of suffering of . . . Sarah."

He was hired to work on a special edition of the Free Press marking its 100th anniversary May 5, 1931, with 14 rotogravure sections. The "Good Morning" column, which began as a collection of short paragraphs of commentary, appeared with no fanfare on May 21, 1930, on the editorial page. It became a fixture, and when Hal Mitchell retired as managing editor, Bingay also took on the job of running the staff.

Years later he wrote that "not until 1940, after 40 years in the business, did I arrive at a position where I did not have to fight with the office boys and reporters about their raises and their troubles. John S. Knight, in my book, the best of all publishers in the best of all worlds, had the God-given perspicacity to rescue me from all this and to let me roam in the Elysian Fields of typewriter pounding."

It might be added that the feeling was mutual as far as many office boys, reporters and other editors were concerned. While giving him high marks for his editorial skills, few found him sensitive in handling the people with whom he worked. One former employee recalls asking Bingay one day to "mark the two or three names in the telephone book who aren't on your son-of-a-bitch list."

Bingay inherited a colorful crew, among them Jack Weeks; Katy Lynch and her father, Bart; Andy Bernhard; Bud Sloan, who wrote a memorable story on a hanging in Windsor, and Mike Bullion, who had a penchant for abusing the English language in his sports writing. Bingay insisted that "anyone whose work does not conform with the code of ethics of American journalism will be fired," but he interpreted the code himself and had been known to fire a staff member out of hand. There were those who insisted he helped to speed the coming of a union, the Newspaper Guild, to the Free Press newsroom.

Bingay could write and he could edit. In many ways, during a period in which the paper and the city were hard hit by the Depression, when social and economic turmoil was the order of the day, when the UAW and industrial unionism began to flourish in what had been an open-shop town, when political traditions were being shattered, and when the paper found itself enmeshed in a battle with Father Charles Coughlin, the fiery radio priest of the '30s, as well as the Times on one hand and the News on the other, his trenchant typewriter proved vital to the Free Press' growth.

A clear indication of Detroit's plight can be found in auto production figures. The industry had reached a record production level of 5,337,087 cars in 1929, but was down to 1,331,860 units in 1932. Through it all, the Free Press focused on whatever positive news it could muster. While welfare rolls soared and the city faced the threat of bankruptcy, the Free Press waged a "War on Waste of the People's Money." On Oct. 15, 1932, its lead story was headlined, "Five Million Saved Taxpayers by Cut in All County Salaries," and its editorial page that day summarized the differences between the fiscal philosophies of the two papers:

> That our contemporary (the News) has a different view of things is, perhaps, not surprising. That paper never has been very much interested in keeping down public expense or in protecting the home owner from crushing taxes. Its enthusiasm always has been for projects involving large outlays of tax money. It was a great champion of a municipal ownership experiment (the DSR) that has cost the city quite a number of millions of dollars. It yearned intensely for an extravagant waterfront development that would have benefitted chiefly a few property owners with land for sale. Lately, it fought strenuously to get the county committed to an expansive port development.
>
> The Free Press has not been interested in these devices for throwing away funds on a big scale . . . It has believed in keeping taxation at the lowest possible figure; and so far as the dignity and the feelings of Circuit judges is concerned we think a good way to insure their preservation would be for the aforesaid judges to imitate the very sensible and public spirited action of the judges of the Wayne Probate Court, who have gone to the Board of Supervisors and have expressed their willingness to waive all legal technicalities and accept any salary cuts the board may consider proper and may decide to impose generally on county officials and employees.

The Free Press, no fan of Franklin Roosevelt's, editorialized the day after he defeated Herbert Hoover: "The sweep that has carried the

Democrats to victory throughout the nation and in almost every subdivision of it, could have been stopped no more than a tidal wave can be stopped. It was the result of deep-seated forces which would not be denied their way . . . (There was) a profound, nation-wide demand for change and new things that had little to do with the men, party records, party policies or party allegiances.

" . . . The vast majority of the people in this country have now gained what they have been talking about, and dreaming of. And the consciousness of their success ought to give them a new optimism and a new confidence in the future. . . . The belief among millions that the coming of a brighter day has been hastened by the political upheaval of Tuesday should itself help the sun to rise on that day."

But as far as the Free Press was concerned, the sun did not rise. The paper became increasingly strident in its opposition to Roosevelt, to the New Deal, to the development of unions, and to what it believed were FDR's maneuvers bringing the country closer to war. The late Joe Ryan, a long-time circulation department supervisor at the Free Press, remembered what it was like to deliver a newspaper with an anti-FDR stance in a town where Roosevelt had overwhelming popular support. He recalled trying to deliver the Free Press one day in the late 1930s when the paper contained a particularly scathing attack on the president: "When I pulled the truck to the first spot to drop the papers, a bunch of UAW guys were waiting for me. They punched me around a bit and then burned the papers I dropped off. At the next stop, another crowd of UAW guys were waiting and did the same thing. At the third stop I saw more of them waiting for me. So I got out of the truck and told them: 'Listen, your pals have already beat me up twice, and I think that's enough for one lousy editorial. So just take the papers and leave me alone.' They took the papers and let me go without any more rough stuff."

Michigan's eight-day bank closing in 1933 was a big story, and the Free Press scored a major beat on the behind-the-scene battle between Sen. James Couzens and Henry Ford, which helped precipitate the crisis. Throughout, both in its news pages and editorially, the Free Press emphasized that the bank holiday was "in no sense a disaster:"

> The eight-day bank holiday . . . is a precautionary measure, designed for the general protection of the state. It is in no sense a disaster . . . The situation is temporarily unpleasant but it is in expert hands. Inconvenience will be felt because of lack of funds

with which to transact daily business, but that is something to bear with patience.

The necessity of the bank holiday arose because of the appearance of a special situation at one institution (the Union Guardian Trust Co.) which could not be handled completely over the weekend. The problem can be taken care of most effectively and permanently if the financiers have an opportunity to proceed in quiet, unhampered by distracting pressures ... Meanwhile, the people of Michigan may find reason for confidence in the knowledge that the banking system of the state is, as a whole, one of the strongest the nation possesses.

Essentially, that editorial set the tone for Free Press coverage for months as all sorts of charges, counter-charges, hearings and examinations followed, with Father Charles Coughlin, the radio priest of Royal Oak's Shrine of the Little Flower, taking a leading role.

In his broadcast of Sunday, March 17, 1933, Father Coughlin first attacked Stair for his role as president of the Detroit Bankers Co. and publisher of the Free Press and suggested that the city's financial institutions were "hopelessly insolvent." Stair quickly sent a telegram to President Roosevelt asking that "to save our city from such inflammatory attacks, to still all false rumors, and to vindicate the dignity and decency of our community, I urgently request that you direct your Department of Justice to begin an immediate and thorough and complete investigation of the slanderous attack ... (that) has been made against myself and other citizens of this city in connection with the banking situation here by Father Charles E. Coughlin who presents himself from time to time as spokesman for your administration ... We are unafraid and eager to co-operate in every way to save our city from slanderous wreckers."

Two days later, the Free Press, depending on bank records probably made available through Stair's contacts, came up with a jolt of its own. It reported in a two-line, full-page-wide headline, "Father Coughlin's Gambling in Stocks with Charity Donations Is Revealed." The story charged that Father Coughlin had used Radio League of the Little Flower funds to speculate in stocks in 1929 and 1930, losing $7,000. Father Coughlin denied the charge, saying that "it was bought with my own money — all my own — and I got a $7,000 lesson."

On the following Sunday, in a much publicized answer to the Free Press story, Father Coughlin said, "The Free Press defames me for investing in productive Michigan industries, which I will do again." Then he launched into a new attack on Stair that included a charge that

Stair had "won his money from a cheap and vulgar and suggestive theater business . . . with one at least that became known to the police and public of Detroit as the Crime Academy."

On April 23, the Free Press ran a full page ad, which it said it had also run in cities throughout the country, answering Father Coughlin's charge of insolvency. The text went on to say Free Press average net paid circulation was 10,000 "in excess of what it was just prior to the start of the Bank Holiday," and suggested that the paper would be a fine place for advertisers to spend their money.

The relationship with Father Coughlin got no better as the years passed. In 1934, the Free Press made much of the fact that a Coughlin associate had been speculating in silver futures when Coughlin was promoting the free coinage of the metal on the air and was featured at a Silver Dinner, given by a self-styled "Committee of Patriots."

In 1938 Father Coughlin sued the Free Press for $2 million for charging in an article by Bingay that he was "congenitally unable to tell the truth" and that he made anti-Semitic remarks during a broadcast. Kenneth Murray, the Free Press lawyer, represented Stair and Bingay. "Father Coughlin correctly interpreted Bingay's statement to mean that he (Coughlin) was a born liar, so he sued," Murray recalled. "We filed a 125-page answer to the charges with a lot of help from the Anti-Defamation League (of B'nai B'rith) and Rabbi Leo Franklin, who was a beloved leader of the Detroit Jewish community at the time." The case finally got to court about two years later before Circuit Judge Ira W. Jayne. At the pre-trial hearing, Murray said, the judge looked at Prewitt Semmes, Father Coughlin's lawyer, and said: "I suppose you don't want any Masons on the jury. Or Jews." Semmes replied quietly that he probably did not. Turning to Murray, the judge said: "And I suppose, Mr. Murray, that you don't want any devout Catholics on the jury." Murray said he could think of a few Catholics he might not object to as jurors. The judge then set the stage for settlement of the suit by asking both lawyers: "I would like your proposals then, gentlemen, on how you expect to get a jury without any Catholics, Protestants or Jews."

"The case was dropped, and the Free Press wrote a small story about how both parties agreed to the dismissal since it would not be in the best interests of the community to continue the suit," Murray said. "But Mr. Stair wouldn't sign off until Father Coughlin agreed to pay court costs, which were $35. Father Coughlin paid, and Stair was so delighted that he framed the check and hung it on the wall behind his desk."

The Free Press continued its opposition to labor organizing, but its approach became more reasoned than strident, as illustrated in a Dec. 14, 1936, editorial which followed just after the elections of Franklin Roosevelt as president and Murphy as governor, and just before the start of the historic sitdown strike by the United Auto Workers against General Motors: "Workers the world over are more conscious of their dignity and power today than ever before. And those employers who are lagging behind in their effort to restore pre-Depression wages and working conditions, as rapidly as they can do so without destroying their business, are laying up trouble for themselves and for the public.

"Common sense and enlightened self-interest should restrain labor and its leaders from demanding more wages, which enter into the cost of products, than can be paid them without reducing sales and thereby curtailing employment . . .

"The short-sighted employers who expect all work and no pay will be forced in the end . . . to give their employees full justice and credit for their contributions to returning prosperity . . . and the sooner they wake up to that fact the better it will be for all concerned."

The theme continued in an editorial a few days later: "Although organized labor includes only a fraction of the country's workers, it has always been the spearhead of the movement for improving the conditions of all workers, and if the rank and file listen to enlightened leaders, there is every reason to believe that the influence of labor unions will increase rather than diminish. The intelligent employer already realizes that and bargains with his employees frankly and honestly. And the unintelligent employer will eventually be forced to."

Even though Stair himself carried a union card as a printer, when his own newsroom and business office employees plunged into organizing a chapter of the Newspaper Guild within a year after Roosevelt's election, he was so opposed to the union movement that he threatened "to board up the front door" if the Guild organizing drive succeeded.

More than 75 members of the staff of the three Detroit newspapers, including 40 from the Free Press, launched the effort at a meeting at the Statler Hotel Dec. 31, 1933. The move came in the aftermath of three pay cuts announced by Stair. The first negotiating session with the Free Press did not occur until Nov. 14, 1936. A committee led by Bill Fanning, an artist, met with Stair, who explained that while the paper's losses for "1932 and 1933 were very, very heavy, and while we have not restored those losses, the present year is good enough to help us materially to restore a good share of the losses suffered by our staffs" in the pay cuts.

In early December, a bonus, the first ever at the Free Press, was announced; in February 1937, further pay adjustments were made. Meanwhile, Stair made it clear he himself would not deal with the Guild because his primary responsibility was "the editorial end of the paper." He appointed a management committee which included Bingay. Contract talks did not begin in earnest until October 1939. It was not until March 1940, when Stair began winding up negotiations with Knight for the sale of the Free Press, that they moved toward a conclusion. A Guild contract was signed on April 30, 1940, the day Knight signed the purchase papers.

In a union organizing effort that had a far larger impact on Detroit, the Free Press characterized the fight between General Motors and the United Auto Workers as a case of "enlightened" management versus a union that threatened the economy and was seeking "to run the plants of General Motors." As the 44-day sitdown strike at GM's Flint plant was coming to a climax in early 1937, the Free Press editorialized: "The darkest cloud hanging over American business today is the labor unrest — and particularly in the automobile industry which so far had led the parade toward recovery (from the Depression), and which, for the most part, appears to have maintained an enlightened position with respect to its employees."

When the strike finally ended, the Free Press gave full credit to Frank Murphy, now governor, for his role in bringing about a settlement. A Feb. 12, 1937, editorial said: "The governor showed neither bias nor passion. He manifested a good understanding of the situation; and maintained a helpful attitude of impartiality . . . ."

While political, social and economic problems dominated the news in the Bingay years, he organized a team of reporters who, in 1932, won the Free Press' first Pulitzer Prize. The prize was for coverage of the American Legion parade during its national convention in Detroit in 1931. The story, which ran a full eight columns, was put together by five reporters — James S. Pooler, Frank D. Webb, William C. Richards, Douglas D. Martin and John N.W. Sloan. Years later, it stands as a brilliant example of writing and reporting, including detailed description of each group in the march and background on what many veterans had done during the war. The first group arrived at Jefferson and Woodward just after noon; the last marched by nine hours later, and the story ran

The team who won the first Pulitzer Prize
for the Free Press, in 1932, for the story
of an American Legion parade, from left,
James Pooler, Frank Webb, William
Richards, Douglas Martin and John
Sloan.

complete in that night's first edition. Richards, who had joined the paper
in 1916, and was associate editor, wrote the lead:

> The Legion marched.
> The Yanks came — thousands upon thousands of them who
> have been sung about always as coming. Pulses quickened.
> Tempo moved up. The pendulum flew faster. And those who
> thought they had laid away the World War in a cobwebby file
> felt again a familiar throbbing.
> The crowd that watched was estimated at a million. The
> number of marchers was put at 85,000 by National Command-
> er Ralph T. O'Neill. Other estimates, among them Maj. Gen.
> Guy Wilson's field marshal, were as high as 300,000.
> Still, that was nothing new. Men have marched so down the
> ages. They marched in Athens and Nineveh and Marathon,
> fighting their various Armageddons and, when these were over,

they marched behind their Hannibals and Alexanders and
Caesars before those they fought for.

It went on then — for 6,500 more words.

One Free Press reporter passed up a chance to share Pulitzer glory,
although he didn't know he was doing it at the time. Frederick O'Malley
Schultz was working the day of the parade and volunteered to staff the
emergency room of Receiving Hospital rather than work with the team
covering the parade. It turned out to be a decision he regretted. "While I
was sitting there counting the paraders and spectators being treated at
the hospital, history was passing me by," Schultz lamented in later
years.

Schultz was involved in another episode in the '30s that didn't make
news but made what newspaper people consider almost as important —
legend. He was covering a story in which the police were shooting it out
with a gunman barricaded in a Detroit house. During a lull in the firing,
Schultz tried to move to a better vantage point but slipped on wet trolley
tracks and fell on the street in the "no-man's land" between the police
and the gunman. As he fell, both sides started shooting again. The
diminutive reporter, caught in the middle, suddenly shouted: "Hold
your fire! It's Schultz, of the Free Press!" Miraculously, the shooting
stopped. Schultz stood up, wiped the mud from his pants, and walked to
safety behind a police car. As soon as he got behind the car, the police
and the gunman resumed the shooting. When the gunman was apprehended, Schultz realized that he had broken his pencil when he fell. He
borrowed a bullet from a policeman and used the soft lead point to take
his notes.

In April 1934, Martin approached Bingay with an idea that helped
greatly in bolstering Sunday circulation. He proposed that the Free
Press publish a tabloid Screen & Radio Weekly "to interest adult-
minded readers, with no salacious gossip and a bare minimum of press-
agent claptrap." It was successful enough for the Des Moines Register-
Tribune Syndicate to sell it to 20 other newspapers and build a
circulation for the magazine alone to 1.7 million within a year. It was replaced in the Free Press later by Parade Magazine. In 1939 Martin
became managing editor.

Jimmy Pooler, who had joined the paper in 1923 and was a movie
critic and feature writer at the time of the Legion story, became one of
the paper's more memorable personalities — "a gentle talent ... a
subdued zany, an artist whose every phrase was tailored to poetic

perfection." Jimmy arrived as a copyboy, stayed while he finished his work at the University of Detroit in 1928, and proved to be a solid reporter who could spur officials into action after a series on juvenile delinquency (as he did in 1943) or help to rid the citizenry of incompetent officials. But mostly "Si" (for Silas, his middle name) was remembered for his stories about people. His secret was that he understood — and liked — them.

"You know," he'd say, "there's something everybody should remember: The more things seem to change the more they really are the same because people keep being people." Pooler did a column, "Sunny Side," for eight years, and his writing frustrated some editors who felt that sentences must have verbs and subjects, and punctuation should be kept to commas and periods. Jimmy wrote many short stories that were published in anthologies, and he wrote some articles for the Free Press which became the sort of classics that readers wanted reprinted from time to time. One of them was "Santa Missed the Boat to Beaver Island." Another favorite of readers was "The Perfect Christmas Story":

About Christmas time we always think about the time "the perfect Christmas story" — from the newspaperman's view — came along. And nearly got spoiled.

It was long ago on a dull Christmas Day — so dull that the city editor chased out a good reporter, John Wagner, on just the bare report of a little, lost girl.

Then the pieces of the story started coming in.

The little girl had gone looking for Santa Claus because he hadn't come to her house on Christmas Eve.

When Wagner and the policemen took her home there sat a pack of little, shabby, forgotten kids. Their Christmas dinner — not to mention breakfast and lunch — was a well thinnned out cabbage soup.

Then the mother came home. She had tramped seven miles across Detroit — and seven miles back — to see if the Goodfellows had left a package where they used to live. She didn't even have carfare on Christmas.

Now you don't have to be told that on the most sentimental day of the year there were present, frankly, all the elements of a tear-jerker.

But the trouble was that it started jerking tears even before the story got to the public.

Maybe you remember reading the story. But, until now, no

one has ever been told of what happened between the writing and the publishing ...

In the Free Press sat those cynics with ulcers — the copyreaders — reading about the little girl who went looking for Santa Claus. The bleak, bare home where a little faith fluttered — and there was a noisy gulp from a copyreader.

Strange things happen — even to copyreaders — on Christmas. This one stood up, blew his nose and said, "What's the matter with you guys! Why haven't you started a collection for those kids?"

And this character — from whom you couldn't bum a dime if you gave him a mortgage on your home — came up with five bucks to start it off.

Before you could say "Merry Christmas" there was a hatful of bucks in the Free Press city room. Even the city editor chipped in!

When Wagner returned, trying to keep a quaver out of his voice, and saw that money, he turned into a cyclone of charity. The dial on his telephone spun like crazy.

And the next thing Tommy Long, who ran the saloon-restaurant around the corner, was downtown. He sniffed and great Irish tears plopped on the floor as Tommy muttered: "Them poor little kids with nothing but soup on Christmas."

Meanwhile, Tommy was ripping great holes in his restaurant stores. Cans of peas, peaches, corn and caviar. Two bushel-basketsful, each topped with a turkey. Take our money, indeed! Tommy threw in a ten of his own.

A fellow who managed a drug store came downtown and opened up his store. A family forgotten on Christmas, eh? He grabbed toys right and left off the shelves and out of the display window.

Take money with this fine chance to do something good on Christmas! Would somebody like a punch in the nose implying he was lacking in just decent, human instincts?

An odd thing as any came along when we asked John Beaton, then the Free Press mailing room boss, how about loaning us a truck?

A rough-hewn character drove it and helped Johnny load up. He wanted to know what it was all about.

"No Christmas tree — no nothing!" our truck driver said. The truck tore down some back streets and pulled up at a house. And a few minutes later the truck driver staggered out carrying a Christmas tree, complete with trimmings.

"My kids said to give it to them," he said, with a lot of pride in the way he said "my kids."

So they went out to the bleak home, set up the tree and a

room and small faces lit up. And there were presents to unwrap as Johnny explained that Santa Claus broke his leg falling down a chimney just a block away.

And a mother started cooking, basting a turkey with tears of gratitude.

Back in the Free Press reporters and copyreaders, even their ulcers in a mellow mood, sat round saying what a fine thing the spirit of Christmas is. People just aren't lucky enough every day to do like the Magi did — bring gifts to a poor child in a bare place.

Just then the city editor came in and screamed, "Do you characters know what you have done? With that hatful of money, food, Christmas trees and a brace of turkeys you have just ruined the perfect Christmas story."

But we hadn't. It was pointed out newspapermen never figure in the news — that we'd leave our modest part out of the story.

We were right about our part. It wasn't much compared to what the good people of Detroit came rushing in to do when they read about the little girl who had to go looking for Santa on Christmas.

That pixie quality was demonstrated in another Pooler ploy: The dividing line between day and night shifts was 6 p.m., and having been assigned to feature writing, Pooler discovered that the city desk was not sure to which shift he would be reporting. The result: Pooler introduced the two-hour day. He'd arrive at 5, busy himself until the day shift left at 6, and stayed at his desk until 7 when, at the urging of the night city editor who thought Pooler was a daysider working late, he'd depart for home — with the night editor wishing he had more men like Jimmy working for him, and the day city editor equally impressed with the young reporter on the night shift who came to work every day an hour early.

Bingay himself, of course, was an outstanding writer who made his mark on the community very early in his stay at the Free Press. His Christmas column in 1930 became a newspaper classic and was reprinted several times. He headlined it: "He Who Went About Doing Good," and based on the response, this story about Jesus Christ touched something in readers harassed by the Depression of the moment.

On this day is celebrated by people of many faiths, and by many of no faith, the birth of Him Whom the world calls Jesus of Nazareth.

What is His significance today?

He left no written record. He created no party, political or otherwise. He led no uprising. He elaborated no formal program. He was not an organizer. He had no panacea for this earth's ills. He advocated no revolution other than that for which He died on Calvary; the moral revolution of the inner life.

He moved quietly, serenely, peacefully, among the villages of Judea and Galilee, speaking to the people about God and life and duty. He preached a new doctrine of love and forgiveness. He mingled with the lowly and the outcasts and was scorned as their friend. Repulsive disease and anguished sin won His tender sympathy and aid. He knew not where to lay His head. He offered no rank, no earthly glory; only service, self-sacrifice and suffering. Yet He launched a movement that has transformed the world.

He "went about doing good."

On this there is no disagreement between the churchgoer and the non-church attendant, between Jew and Gentile, Mohammedan and Buddhist, Catholic and Protestant, atheist and agnostic. No matter what version of His life is given or how it is interpreted. His goodness of heart and His purity of purpose is universally admitted.

To those who see in Him the living Christ; to others who see in the story of His ministry only a beautiful symbolism of the age-old longing of groping mankind for a better way of life; even to those who deny Him, there is this agreement. No matter how low and how vile and how wretched a creature a man may be, once he has heard the story, he is forever haunted by a feeling that His words are true; that in some way He has sounded the profoundest depths of man's moral being.

His philosophy transcends all races and tongues, all creeds and forms. In nineteen hundred and thirty years, governments and civilizations have crumbled and passed away; the whole face of the earth has been transformed by a multiplicity of man-made laws and machines. But His lessons remain for us as pure and as undimmed as when He first gave them to His lowly followers.

And so it is on this day of all days when men's hearts are opened to one another by the impulses of the season we come a little closer to an understanding of His purpose. You who have brought joy and laughter to little children, who have kindled a light in the tired eyes of a struggling mother, who have placed a hand of loving comradeship on the shoulder of a broken brother, who have in any way helped make lighter the burdens of a fellow mortal, you have, to some degree — knowingly or not — fulfilled His command: "Thou shalt love they neighbor as thyself."

As the years roll on, the world grows less cruel; with enlightenment there comes understanding. Through corroding cynicism, pessimism, greed, love of luxury, crass materialism, His light of love still shines. Down in the heart of every mortal there is something noble and clean and fine; something that is made manifest to us on this, His day.

And this light which is permitted to shine more brightly this one time of the year is the only hope for our now troubletorn world which has forgotten, in the pursuit of material success, that man cannot live by bread alone; that there are spiritual values, intangible, imponderable, but more powerful than all the fortresses of finance.

Today men who have developed about themselves a crust of hardness in buffeting against the world, drop their acquired reserve and obey the finer impulses of their being; they act naturally, "as little children." They do generous deeds willingly, joyously, with no self-consciousness. When His dream of peace on earth comes true, it will not be for one day but for all days.

Those of you who have gone forth this Christmas in the joy of unselfish service, who have soothed the suffering, strengthened the weak and aided the needy now find your reward in your own hearts, for you have but followed in the footsteps of Him "Who went about doing good."

But the writing that won Bingay even greater acclaim was his "Iffy the Dopester" pieces which began to appear on Page One at the height of one of the most dramatic times in the city's history — the drive by the 1934 Detroit Tigers to their first pennant in 25 years.

The columns were a superb combination of nostalgia and cheerleading at a time when the city had been devastated by the Depression. They were written, of course, from the wealth of background Bingay had acquired as a sports writer during the heady days when the Tigers won three pennants — 1907, '08 and '09. There were wonderful stories of fiery Manager Hughie Jennings, and of Ty Cobb, and of Rube Waddell and other legendary figures in Detroit baseball history, and plenty of commentary on what was happening with Mickey Cochrane and Schoolboy Rowe and Tommy Bridges and Charlie Gehringer and Billy Rogell, et al. Even when the News and Times had joined in saturating the community with baseball stories, people couldn't get enough of old Iffy's tales. Longtime art director Floyd Nixon, himself a rather colorful personality, provided the right touch with a cartoon representation of Iffy. Although people soon learned who Iffy really was, they delighted in trying to maintain an air of mystery over the identity of the old codger. In mid-September, Bingay made a valiant effort to wind up his Iffy stint with a column in which he conceded the pennant to the Tigers, but he was soon back in the paper "by popular demand." That non-final column began:

> Iffy has worked himself out of a job. Yes, my hearties, the old man today joins the ranks of the unemployed.
>
> "Diamond me no diamonds," said Tennyson in his "Idylls of the King." And Fielding put it: "But me no buts." Ah, yes, yes. Shakespeare said, "Thank me no thanks, nor proud me no prouds." And so I say unto you who have stuck by me all through a long weary grind to the very finish, "If me no ifs."
>
> The die is cast ... Jacta est alea — and all that sort of rot. The American League pennant is won by the Detroit Tigers. The old iffin' machine has been placed back in the attic and covered with tarpaulins and will not be brought out again until the year of our Lord 1935. T'hell with mathematics. It's in the bag. And, ladies and gentlemen, what a ball club we'll have then after this year's trial spin! It's been just a workout.
>
> All we've got to do now is worry about the Word Series. Old Iffy has got to find a nice soft seat in the park and wait for the CWA or the PWA or the XYZ or some other organization to feed him through the long hard winter.
>
> Nobody needs any more iffing done.

The style of that September column was typical of the easy, fun-filled approach he took. Combining it with his authentic reminiscences of the good old baseball days, his Iffy columns had a very special touch and caught the fancy of Tiger fans like nothing else did in that wild era. The Tigers actually clinched the pennant one week after that column, by which time Iffy was back in the paper.

That Tiger revival was important to the paper in another way — building up its circulation base which had slipped from a peak of 245,898 in September 1929 to 188,408 by September 1933. Much of the decline was a measure of the ravages of the Depression which also affected sales of the News and Times and caused the death of the Detroit Mirror, a morning tabloid.

It was owned at the time of its closing by the McCormick-Patterson interests, proprietors of the Chicago Tribune and New York Daily News. In June 1931, they had announced the takeover of the lurid Illustrated Daily by making it clear that "the Detroit Mirror is not to be confused with any paper of the past! When the present owners took charge of the existing property, they established a brand-new morning newspaper, the Detroit Mirror, with an utterly different policy! Every bit of inheritance that conflicted with the publishing principles of the new owners was waived!"

When Depression economics had doomed the Mirror to failure, the Free Press made the announcement in a two-column reproduction of the Mirror's own obituary, which said, in part: "The management has been forced to the conclusion that there is not room in Detroit for two morning newspapers . . . The prospect of the paper making a profit still seems remote after more than a year of operating at a loss . . .

"A number of features which have ornamented the Detroit Mirror will be carried beginning next Monday, in the Detroit Free Press. Among these will be the concluding numbers of the crossword puzzle contest and the serial 'The Death of the Duchess . . . ' The other Mirror features which the Free Press will carry on are as follows: the daily comic strips, Harold Teen and Dick Tracy, Fred Bailey's series on current economic conditions throughout the country, and Bert Collyer's racing selections and comments.

"In saying goodbye, we want also to thank all those friends of ours for all the interest and good will they have shown us. Goodbye."

There followed a brief summary by the Free Press which included the statement that "the suspension of the Mirror does not mean that there has been a merger. The Free Press assumes no responsibilities and takes over none of the Mirror personnel or property. Rumor mongers have persistently spread the report in connection with the departure of the Mirror that the Free Press has been sold. These rumors are based on falsity and are born of pure viciousness. The Free Press has not been for sale, and is not for sale except at three cents per copy on the newsstands."

In fact, a deal was completed between Stair and the McCormick-Patterson interests, who had given Stair $75,000 in option money. After killing the Mirror, however, the Chicagoans, without explanation, decided not to follow through with the purchase and told Stair to keep the money. A few months later, on Oct. 28, 1932, still another report of the sale of the Free Press appeared in the local Legal Courier. It stated flatly in a headline: "Old F.P. Going; New F.P. Coming." The story went on to say that the transfer to the McCormick-Patterson families of Chicago was "scheduled for Nov. 13th or immediately after the current election" and that "several of the top notchers of the Free Press staff are already out looking for new jobs."

Bingay posted that story on the bulletin board with a note that said:

> Pure falsehood . . . we will all be here doing business at the same
> old stand. The paper has not been sold and there are no changes
> contemplated. Don't worry. Bet anybody who says the F.P. is
> sold and get some Xmas money.
>
> *M.W. Bingay.*

At that moment, Bingay was correct but negotiations for another sale had almost been completed, with a company headed by Sen. James Couzens who had recruited Jay G. Hayden, long-time Washington Bureau chief for the Detroit News, and Jack Manning, a nephew of Couzens and an editor of the Detroit Times, to join him in the takeover. The deal was all set, according to one insider, but fell through at the last minute because Stair insisted that the buyers, whom he may not have known since a broker was serving as go-between, had to take much of his downtown real estate holdings as part of the purchase. "Couzens didn't want to be in the real estate business" was the explanation for his refusal to go through with the deal. In any case, Couzens then tried to buy a Memphis paper, lost out again and stuck with politics. It was not until 1940 that Stair sold the Free Press, to John S. Knight.

E. Roy Hatton, the long-time circulation director of the Free Press, believed the Mirror's departure from morning competition helped the Free Press recover from Depression losses. The competitive newspaper scene of the 1920s had already had an effect. In 1921 the paper had boasted in its ABC statement that "it has not tried to increase circulation by questionable methods, but has depended upon its merit as a newspaper for popular appreciation and support. Its growth has been constant and sound."

By 1923, however, the Free Press was offering "needle sets free to new subscribers," and soon it was also giving away bread knives. By the April-September period, 1925, with the Times competing actively, the Free Press offered a $7,500 Accident Insurance Policy and by 1928 had 87,071 policy subscribers. It was the sort of inducement that not only helped gain new subscribers, but was effective in holding old ones.

Another factor that helped circulation was stability in the price structure. Selling at two cents in the early 1900s, the Free Press went to three cents daily on April 19, 1920, and remained there until 1943 when it went to four cents daily and 12 cents on Sunday. But while it stood pat on price, the Free Press by 1932 was offering cookbooks and dictionaries and $10,000 insurance policies as inducements to new subscribers.

But improvement began in 1934, with the Tigers' spurt and the continuing growth of Detroit, which had hit a population of 1,568,622 in 1930. The Free Press also found a rich market by shifting its edition pattern, again taking advantage of the surging interest in baseball and other sports which, at the time, were all played in the daytime. In 1930 the Free Press first edition began running at 8:07 p.m., and 100,000 of its 250,000 papers were printed before midnight. By 1935, the City Edition was starting at 7:22 p.m., and 164,000 copies in a press run of 280,000 were run off before midnight. That emphasis on the City Edition would continue until the early '50s when the shift moved once again to the morning edition with later news, especially the results of night sports competition. For years, the City Edition was home-delivered by 9:30 p.m. in the Detroit area, and the salutation of people heading home after a night on the town invariably was, "Well, I think I'll go to bed with my Free Press."

Hatton, the key man in the circulation department for the first half of the century, recalled another Free Press reference point for many Detroit residents. He and George Mulford, chief of the mailing room and a Free Press employee for 60 years, hired thousands of Detroiters to come to the Free Press plant on Saturday nights "to stuff" inserts by hand into the Sunday papers. Those Saturday night jobs helped put through college men who became leaders in many facets of Detroit's life, but what they could recall most fondly was the crap games they played between runs.

In 1939, when circulation was approaching the 300,000 mark, the Free Press took occasion in a March editorial to explain the gains: "The morning newspaper is coming back. The clock is not what it once was. The habits of the people have changed. The motor car, the movie and radio, shorter working hours, more leisure for all classes — all have worked toward restoring to the morning paper an acceptance it had before the rise of the so-called evening papers, which are now printed around noon.

"The housewife of today is no longer a drudge of the kitchen. Modern inventions and modern systems of merchandising have given her the leisure to read through the day. Before doing her shopping she has time to read the women's pages of her morning paper. In this development the Free Press has pioneered. The Free Press receives more letters in response to its women's pages than any other newspaper in the United States."

And to those who were critical of the paper's strong anti-New Deal stance, the writer went on to say, "We believe its steadily increasing popularity is due to the fact that the people like and respect a newspaper that says what it thinks, regardless of the clamor and the hysteria of the hour. The Free Press has never deviated from its policies or stepped lightly for fear of losing circulation."

The Stair era had a special patina about it, a quality portrayed in the words of Eddie Guest in 1931 on the occasion of the paper's 100th birthday:

> We have lived with an army of great spirits; we have known rare comradeships down through the years. Countless contributions of courage have been made to sustain through the century this great newspaper. Its splendor is not all of now; it is not all ours to boast. It has drawn its life from the lives of all who have gone before us. It was cherished and strengthened and comforted by a glorious company of devoted men and women. Many of them found no fame other than the fame of the Detroit Free Press.
>
> They handed the paper down to us. Had they failed at their task we should not now be celebrating this century of toil and service.

John S. Knight

"He's what the old town has needed for a long time," said Malcolm S. Bingay.

Chapter Six

Enter, Jack Knight

Chapter 6

Years later, John S. Knight was still shaking his head in wonderment over how he was able to buy the Detroit Free Press. When negotiations with E.D. Stair were completed and a price of $3.2 million was determined, Knight said, "Stair asked me how I planned to pay for it, and I told him I was going to get a loan from the Chemical Bank of New York, at which point Mr. Stair said, 'Why don't you let me lend it to you?' "

Thus, on April 30, 1940, were arrangements made for the transfer of one of America's great newspapers. Kenneth Murray, the attorney who represented Stair in the transaction, said the whole thing took about 20 minutes. "Mr. Knight handed us his check for $100,000 and signed promissory notes for another $3.1 million and that was it." Murray said it became clear quickly why the Knight interests chose May 1 for taking over operation of the paper. "Payment from advertisers came due on the first of the month and that morning John Barry (who handled all Knight's financial transactions) had people out collecting all the accounts from places like J.L. Hudson's, Kern's, Crowley's and all the shops on Washington Boulevard. By the end of the day they had collected more than enough to cover Mr. Knight's $100,000 check. I remember how impressed I was and thinking that this is the kind of outfit I'd like to work for." In fact, after the deal was closed, Barry called in Murray, who first began representing the Free Press in 1929, and asked him to remain "temporarily" as the Free Press counsel, at a retainer of $75 a month. After 51 years, Murray, along with his son, Brownson, who joined him in 1962, still represent the Free Press' legal interests.

Stair, who was 81 at the time of the sale, made it clear why he was selling to Knight. "We're all too old," he said, speaking of his top management people. In a sense, Stair's analysis confirmed public

John H. Barry, who handled John Knight's financial affairs.

Douglas D. Martin, managing editor.

feeling about the Free Press of 1940. Although the paper had demonstrated solid circulation strength, boasting in an ad two weeks before the sale that it had gained 100,000 readers in recent years, it still came across as a tired institution in its coverage and presentation of news, and in its editorial philosophy, as a paper out of step with its time. A Detroit Times circulation official called the Free Press then "an afternoon paper with a slight morning paper hangover." In any case, the time was right for aggressive new leadership, and John S. Knight provided it.

Knight, who had proved himself to be an intensely committed newspaperman in Akron and Miami, learned of the availability of the Free Press through Smith Davis, a representative of a Cleveland newspaper brokerage firm. Knight had known Davis only slightly when the big, self-confident salesman walked into his Akron office in March 1937 and told him about the availability of the Miami Herald. In October, after a series of negotiations with Herald owner Col. Frank B. Shutts, that deal was completed. Three years later Davis again was the middleman in Knight's purchase of the Free Press.

It was an ideal bit of matchmaking. In partnership were the Free Press, described by authors Kenneth Stewart and John Tebbel as "an ancient and honored paper which had bogged down," and Jack Knight a relatively young (45), energetic, tough-minded, modern publisher-editor.

Knight was raised in a newspaper family, and his own commitment, he said, "began in June 1914, when, as a boy, I worked in the composing room and learned to love the smell of printer's ink." His father, Charles Landon Knight, epitomized the best of the old-style, individualistic editors, even to the point of being involved in politics for a time as a congressman. C.L. developed quite a reputation as a vigorous, forthright writer of editorials as owner of the Beacon Journal in Akron, where he landed in 1900 after working as a writer, cowhand and teacher.

C.L., who wrote in pencil rather than with a typewriter, demonstrated to his son, John, the value of principle and the power of words. Those basics would serve as a foundation as he moved into a more modern, less impetuous era of journalism. But John was as free-spirited as his father.

On the occasion of his 50th anniversary in the newspaper business, John S. Knight explained how "our approach to endorsements is quite a departure from my father's day when newspapers carried a party label and always found the opposition sadly lacking in competence and ability ... When I was very young," he said, "I once asked my father which of the two candidates for sheriff would get our support. He gave me a wry grin and said, 'Why, the one who promises us the county printing, of course.' This was my first exposure to political and newspaper realities of that era" — an era which John Knight would have much to do with ending.

Knight expressed his tenets of newspaper proprietorship in a statement accompanying the announcement of his purchase: "Under the new ownership the Detroit Free Press will be politically independent in its editorial policy. It will always be operated in behalf of the general public, uncontrolled by any group, faction or selfish interest and dedicated solely to the public service . . . " On May 2, 1940, the slogan, "An Independent Newspaper," was added to the editorial page masthead, and it has remained.

When he arrived in Detroit, John S. Knight had already demonstrated the soundness of these principles and his dedication to make them come alive "with well-edited, vigorous newspapers" that were "tolerant, just, friendly and fair." Combined with a solid understanding of newspapers as business institutions, it proved to be an effective formula for success. In September 1945, five years after Knight bought the Free Press, the paper moved into the circulation lead in the three-newspaper city for the first time since official Audit Bureau of Circulations records were established in 1916. The paper had gained 79,075 readers daily and 108,131 Sunday since September 1940, and showed a solid increase in advertising linage.

John Shively Knight, born in Bluefield, Va., Oct. 26, 1894, attended Central High in Akron and the Tome Preparatory School in Maryland before enrolling at Cornell. A junior at Cornell when World War I started, young Knight quickly enlisted in the Army and served in Europe. His Army stint, in addition to military experience, exposed him to "other Americans of a kind with whom his lot had not been thrown before," said authors Stewart and Tebbel, and it gave him some insights into other things — crapshooting for one. As an example of the intensity with which he sought excellence, Knight claimed to have become the finest crapshooter in the world after being a loser early in his Army career. When someone later suggested that his pride in that achievement hardly befitted someone of his dignified journalistic standing, he responded forthrightly and typically: "But I *am* the best crapshooter in the world."

"I had $6,000 when I came home from the Army . . . made crapshooting . . . and I went to Santa Barbara (Calif.) to have a good time . . . playing golf, dancing and so on," he explained. "But there never was any doubt about my returning to work on my father's newspaper," he added, putting to rest stories that he had wanted to get into all sorts of other businesses.

When he returned from Santa Barbara in 1920, Knight explained, "Mother said Father thought I ought to get to work. I sat down with him and we made a deal. I would get into the business with the understanding that I would get bounced if I didn't work out or would walk out if I didn't like it. I stayed. I liked working with reporters as a managing editor, and my brother Jim and I said we would take no dividends until we paid off the paper's debt after Father died. We did."

Young Jack gradually took over, first becoming city editor and in 1925 managing editor. After his father's death in 1933, Knight became editor — and faced the task of keeping the paper solvent in those Depression days. In 1936 there came a moment when, during a protracted strike in the rubber industry, a friend and former Akron mayor organized a Law-and-Order League that wanted citizens and non-strikers to break through the picket lines. Knight's front-page editorial attacked the move as "deliberately provocative and inflammatory" and made clear "we need no vigilantes here." In a rare tribute, the Times-Press, the opposition newspaper, noted the editorial on its own front page. Shortly thereafter, Knight further demonstrated his independence. When management refused to negotiate with the strikers, he ran another editorial under the title, "We've Had a Bellyfull," in which he excoriated management. It was about this time, Dec. 1, 1936, that he launched his Editor's Notebook as a daily feature signed with his initials, J.S.K. Pressure on his time soon forced him to a once-a-week schedule.

Besides his forthright expressions of opinion, Knight developed two other basic concepts that contributed to his success in Detroit, and in other cities. First, he made it clear, as his group of papers grew, that each newspaper must stand on its own feet financially. He would drive home the point by quoting a friend who had said, "A penniless newspaper, like a penniless lady, is more susceptible to an immoral proposition than one well-heeled."

And, secondly, he gave local editors great freedom from central authority. With that freedom came great obligations of responsibility, of course. In later years, Knight's philosophy carried beyond local and state matters to national politics, with editors on each paper making their own decisions on presidential endorsements.

Knight brought to the Free Press more than general leadership and his philosophy that "a typewriter means more to a newspaper than an adding machine." One week after announcement of the sale, his first Editor's Notebook column appeared on the editorial page. It would become one of the most popular items in the Sunday Free Press. His approach in preparing the Notebook column also spoke to the sort of person he was. Every Thursday morning he walked into his fourth-floor office, pulled out his notes and, guarded from any intrusion in person or by telephone by his secretary, Margaret Harvey, he would not emerge until he completed his effort. The procedure occurred Thursdays, no matter where he happened to be.

"Average writing time, three hours," he wrote once, then added, "Being a bleeder, it comes hard . . . But I cling to the old-fashioned view that editors are supposed to have opinions. So I express them. You can fault the composition or style of the Editor's Notebook, but it doesn't muddle up the issues or leave the reader in doubt as to where the editor stands."

Knight started his Notebook in Akron because "newspapers were becoming as impersonal in those days as banks and corporations . . . Editors preferred ivory tower seclusion and the anonymity of the unsigned editorial. So why not, I thought, say what was on my mind and prepare to dodge the brickbats?"

In 1968, Knight won a Pulitzer Prize, the journalism profession's highest award, for a collection of 10 Notebook columns on the Vietnam war and the right to dissent. In the citation, the Columbia University trustees said:

> Mr. Knight was awarded for his distinguished editorial writing both in 1967 and for many years previously, his best work being done in a signed column, carried in the Knight Newspapers, called "The Editor's Notebook," in which he discusses the issues of the day.

His reportorial enthusiasm was demonstrated nationally in 1952 when he came up with the exclusive story revealing that Richard Nixon was Dwight Eisenhower's vice presidential choice.

In 1940, however, the more immediate concerns had to do with taking hold of a paper that had its share of problems and with establishing rapport with a community that was used to a heavy dose of hometown leadership, even on the Hearst-owned Detroit Times. And at the moment, the Free Press was third in circulation behind the locally owned Detroit News and the Times.

Knight acted quickly to get acquainted with the city's leadership. One of his first visits was with Oscar and Richard Webber, top men at the J.L. Hudson Co., the city's department store giant. Knight explained who he was, his background, what he wanted to accomplish. They listened, then went through a list of things they thought were wrong with the Free Press.

"I agreed with some, but when they said we gave too much coverage to horse racing, I pointed out that there had been 15,000 people at the race track and only 3,500 at the ball park that particular day." (Knight later became a successful race horse owner.) Another important introduction came when Malcolm Bingay, whose Good Morning column was one of the "must-read" items for Detroiters, wrote one which he headlined, "Meet John S. Knight." He outlined Knight's background in Akron and in the Army and provided some personal characteristics: "He is 45. Tall, slim, trim, athletic . . . Six times champion of his golf club . . . Crack football player, boxer, fisherman, swimmer . . . His modulated voice articulates his thoughts clearly and concisely. No nonsense. Says what he thinks and thinks what he says."

Then he wound up with an important message: "He is no New Dealer (Gott sie dank!) nor an Old Dealer. He's a square dealer by all the dope I have heard about him.

"He knows personally just about every one of our national celebrities and, in that quiet, easy way of his, finds friends wherever he goes. Takes every walk of life in his stride. With him it's never who you are but what you are.

"Detroit, I am sure, is going to like him tremendously. He'll be respected for his courage, common sense and fidelity to any program for civic advancement. He's what the old town has needed for a long time: The zest of youth with a wide vision for the awakening of community un-derstanding."

Even before he took over, Knight had insisted on solving one problem with the signing of the Free Press' first contract with the Newspaper Guild of Detroit, a union which eventually represented news, advertis-ing and some circulation employees. Knight made an effort to convince the Guild, in a statement he delivered himself at a negotiating session, that "the conscientious objector" to union membership should not be forced into the union. But a modified union shop clause was worked out. The Guild gave a no-strike pledge for the duration of the war.

Most Free Press staffers welcomed Knight's purchase. Bulletin board notes had popped up in April with reminders to colleagues not to give up hope because "the Knight is coming," and Knight himself reassured everyone at a staff meeting on the afternoon of the signing, saying, "I didn't buy a newspaper, I bought a staff." Charlie Haun, a longtime editor and picture man, recalled how, shortly after Knight's arrival, he was handling a story that was not very complimentary to the J.L. Hudson Co., a major advertiser. "I took this story to him and told him I didn't know what to do with it. He settled that quickly. 'You're the editor,' he told me, and I fired back, 'I'll run it.' "

Knight installed Barry, his longtime financial mentor, and Donald Walker, who became controller, in the business office. Knight's relationship with Barry was a special and profoundly personal one, dating from the time Knight took over the Akron Beacon Journal after his father's death. Barry had been C.L. Knight's financial man since 1911 and, as he had with the elder Knight, he struck a deal with John Knight: Knight would run the news side of the newspaper and Barry the business side.

The principle was tested soon after Knight bought the Free Press. The paper had run a full-page ad for a book company promoting what some readers considered "pornographic and irreverent" material. The ad caused a furor. Knight publicly repudiated it and demanded of Barry that the salesman who placed it be fired. Barry didn't defend the ad, but he made it clear that Knight couldn't fire anyone in the business office; the salesman stayed. Barry's and Knight's agreement was inviolable, and it set a precedent for the separation of business and news that continues at the Free Press.

One Free Press staff member who was close to him described Barry as a "helluva character who went to mass each morning . . . a man who put in 16-hour days (yet) liked 40-hour-a-week people . . . a master of handling details."

Knight kept Doug Martin as managing editor and brought in Ben Maidenburg from Akron with the title of Sunday editor to work closely with Martin in handling the news staff. Maidenburg, a big, hearty man, added to the camaraderie in the newsroom and helped shift the paper to the Knight style. His stay was relatively brief. He enlisted in the Army in 1942, serving with distinction in the South Pacific. After the war, he went on a temporary basis to Knight's Chicago Daily News, then returned to Akron. Basil "Stuffy" Walters, who was named executive editor of Knight Newspapers in 1944, made his presence felt until he headed for the Chicago Daily News in 1945. Dale Stafford, who had established a reputation with the Associated Press in Michigan, was made sports editor. He later succeeded Martin as managing editor.

At the editorial page level, Knight stuck with Malcolm Bingay, who had been the key man in Stair's vigorously conservative approach throughout the '30s. Working with Knight, however, Bingay tempered his words; for his part Knight learned to live with a man who tended to be a bit more flamboyant than most. "You need to have the Bingays on a paper," Knight said. "You learn to get along with them." Pointing up his further appreciation of unusual people, Knight added, "You never have trouble with routine people."

Knight told Detroiters something of his philosophy in his first speech to a joint gathering of the Detroit Adcraft Club and the Detroit Chamber of Commerce. He explained that newspapers had a grave responsibility, particularly at that time when war was raging in Europe and the United States was debating what its role should be. "It is up to us (the press) to help people keep their feet on the ground, to try to prevent them from going off half-cocked. We have a free press. The only threat to it of which I know is so-called lobbies of special interest. I know of no other threat. I believe that freedom will never disappear."

He said the Free Press would be an independent newspaper, then added, "By independent I do not mean neutral. We will take a forthright stand on every issue. But we are not bound by party . . . In our news columns we believe in facts, aggressiveness and giving both sides a hearing. We think of our editorial page as a public defender and a builder of causes."

Changes in content gradually became apparent, in keeping with Knight's policy to make changes slowly and carefully so as not to upset readers whose loyalty to a paper and whose reading habits are great assets in building circulation. A full-page advertisement nine days after Knight's takeover announced the addition of two new columns — Eleanor Roosevelt's "My Day" and Drew Pearson and Robert S. Allen's "Washington Merry-Go-Round" — and a new comic, "Smilin' Jack." The two columns were wise additions, indicating, in the heavily Democratic and union city of Detroit, the first moves toward a less doctrinaire posture. A cartoon became a fixture on the editorial page, brightening it considerably.

A major break with the past came Sunday, April 20, 1941, when the Free Press introduced a totally new headline style — Bodoni, the type face it has used ever since. In an editorial, the Free Press added, "The past year has seen many innovations . . . more extensive news coverage, new columns, new features, the Sunday Editorial Magazine, the Sunday

Graphic, more comics and the like . . . There will be more as time goes on."

Knight continued to work with people he knew and trusted before buying the Free Press, but he also forged lasting relationships with people he had found there. C. Blake McDowell, an attorney associated for years with the Knight family in Akron, was an important confidante for Knight at the corporate level, while Kenneth Murray, a delightful, sensitive, longtime Free Press enthusiast, continued, beyond his "temporary" status, as the Free Press attorney. Murray's editor-like approach to handling troublesome stories delighted editors. While many of his counterparts on papers around the country continually warned editors about the legal pitfalls of publishing certain stories, Murray believed simply, "My job is to get it in the paper." So he would suggest a word change here or an idea there to make the story libel-proof. Often, Murray provided more than legal opinions. Asked once to review a series about slum landlords in Detroit, on which the reporter had worked long and written voluminously, Murray gave the stories a careful reading. "There's nothing to worry about," he said as he dropped the stack of copy on the editor's desk and started to leave. At the door he offered a final bit of advice: "But it sure is dull reading" — a clear signal that the series needed more editing.

As a mark of the high regard in which he is held by the news staff, on the occasion of his 70th birthday in 1974, the staff surprised him with a party in the newsroom. On the cake was inscribed: "Happy Birthday, Ken, from those wonderful folks who brought you . . . " What followed — carefully inscribed in frosting — was a list of the more than 20 lawsuits Murray was currently defending on their behalf.

Knight brought in Earl Woodard to handle the composing room and strengthened the circulation department staff but left it in the hands of E. Roy Hatton, only the second circulation manager in the history of the Free Press, who served in that job from 1905 to 1959.

When Knight took over in May 1940, Europe was being ravaged by war. The eight-column headline on the front page May 1 said: "Allies Fight to Avert Rout." The story told of Allied efforts to contain the Nazi invasion of Norway. It was also a time when Roosevelt was about to launch a campaign for a third term — firmly opposed by the Free Press. And the American economy faced wrenching problems of adjustment to defense spending.

While the paper's editorial policy was not changed radically to reflect the views of the majority in pro-union, pro-Roosevelt Detroit, under Knight, a greater effort was apparent in acknowledging a wide diversity of opinion. Knight was apprehensive of developments moving the country inexorably toward war, but he supported a strong defense, with some qualifications. When President Roosevelt asked for a $2.5 billion appropriation for defense for the next fiscal year, the Free Press said, on May 16, that FDR's "outline for the increase of the American defense program . . . is not too much if it is needed to safeguard the interests of this nation. But Congress will do well to follow the suggestion of Sen. Henry Cabot Lodge that before sanctioning such an additional burden of debt, careful study be made of what it is to be spent for . . . The manner in which Mr. Roosevelt airily waves aside questions of costs and of debt and taxation to be created by his demands — suggests that he is acting in haste rather than on matured judgment . . . We should have a great navy, a competent army and an efficient air corps. These are requisite and necessary. The taxpayers supposed they were being organized with the billions (eight in the previous seven years) already voted."

Another major sign of editorial refocusing came June 4 with an unusual, four-column presentation headlined "The Test Is at Hand." That editorial noted, "The depths of Mr. Roosevelt's love for his country and his loyalty to its ideals deep in his heart need never be questioned. It is silly to charge that he has ever had ambitions to be a dictator. Rather he has been an enthusiastic innovator." But the editorial added, "For seven years the Republicans did nothing — and failed; for seven years the New Dealers tried everything — and failed. There need be no recriminations or personal hates now. Both made sorry messes of their allotted tasks. Let the dead bury their dead. A new situation dwarfs the past."

In an editorial just days before the 1940 election, the Free Press said the issue was one of personal liberty vs. personal power and emphasized, "No matter how good he is, how capable, how lofty his desires, how far-visioned, no man should ever be allowed a third term as President." A day later an editorial suggested that Roosevelt's choice of Henry A. Wallace as his running mate was "another good reason why our vote will be cast for Wendell Willkie."

Knight could see the war widening, and wrote in his Editor's Notebook that "Our country will still be here no matter which man is elected." That column urged citizens to give whoever was elected "our undivided support. To do this we need not sacrifice our right to criticize but our criticism should be on the constructive side rather than expressed with cheap little wisecracks that serve only to widen the breach."

That year also provided another major sign of editorial change as the Free Press endorsed Democrat Murray Van Wagonner for governor, crediting him with an "intelligent approach to state issues" during the campaign. Van Wagonner was elected.

As the war in Europe swung strongly in favor of Germany, Knight warned against a policy of "cautious involvement" which "eventually means naval convoys, encounters at sea . . . " The editorials began to take on a more somber tone. Knight's May 25, 1941, Editor's Notebook provided a full-scale analysis and suggested the administration was handling "the country's hour of greatest peril" in a manner "quite as ineffective as the bumbling Mr. Hoover's indecisive measures to end the Great Depression." He said the administration had no understandable foreign policy, lacked management skills and the ability to create unity and had failed to provide a sound method of financing the war program.

The column wound up with a plea: "In the heat of the presidential campaign in 1940, many editors charged that the president was aspiring to be a dictator. The Free Press ridiculed any such possibility for the simple reason that we recognize the president is not of the stuff of which dictators are made. Fully conscious of this high ideal, we are critical only of his lack of administrative ability, his failure to transmit those ideals into a program that would actually work.

"The same criticism can properly be made today. We are not looking for a dictator in this country, but we have a right to demand leadership in critical times. But out of Washington comes nothing but trial balloons by third-rate politicians and favor-seeking columnists. There is a tragic lack of any purposeful action. There is no strong leadership at the top. The people deserve something better, Mr. President."

A few days later, Roosevelt in a speech vowed the United States would fight anywhere to stop Hitler. The May 28 Free Press headline declared:

Full Emergency Is Decreed
By Roosevelt in Fight on Axis

The following Sunday, in a rare signed editorial on Page One, Knight responded with "A Statement of Policy." After recalling his criticisms, he said:

In this memorable address, (Roosevelt) made one thing
quite clear. He told us in the most direct language that we are
embarked on an undeclared war against the Axis powers. Only
a willfully stupid or pathetically misguided person could
construe his remarks to mean anything else. The Free Press is
glad to know where Mr. Roosevelt now stands. His previous
policy of "Saving England" while trying to avoid a "shooting
war" was a type of unrealism which we never were quite able to
understand.

The Free Press has opposed every step leading toward
involvement in a war which was not of our making ... But
NOW the die is cast. We are in this war quite as though our
Congress has made a formal declaration of hostilities. There is
no turning back. To that end, the Free Press pledges its
complete support to President Roosevelt as our commander-in-
chief ...

It is in this spirit of adherence to the finest traditions, and
with every realization of the enormity of the task before you,
Mr. President, that we pledge the loyal support of the Free
Press.

John S. Knight

Knight's statement created a stir among Free Press readers and
across the country. To reiterate his position and clear up any misunder-
standing, he wrote, on June 8: "For the sake of the record, let it be set
down here and now that the Free Press is not 'joining the fold' of (the
newspapers) who have been shouting for war in strident tones for
months upon end. Nor are we endorsing the President's foreign policy
... We ARE accepting the foreign policy because the full national
emergency has made the President a dictator in fact ... Congress may
still have the power to DECLARE war but the President can actually
MAKE war and neither you nor I are going to be consulted when that
decision is made ... "

The truth of that was emphasized in a Free Press editorial following
an August 1940 story by Cliff Prevost, the paper's Washington
correspondent, reporting that FDR and Britain's Winston Churchill
had conferred at sea. That editorial, headlined "At War," began:

"The United States is at war.

"There need be no more qualifying phrases.

"The eight-point declaration of purpose signed by President Roosevelt and Prime Minister Churchill can be construed in no other way.

" ... The destinies of the Republic of the United States and the

British Empire are irrevocably combined 'to achieve the final destruction of the Nazi tyranny . . . .'

"We are in for the duration.

"A new world dawns this day.

"The America we once knew is gone forever . . . ."

On Nov. 30, 1940, the Free Press' headline on Page One said:

Roosevelt Says U.S.
May Fight Next Year

A week later, Dec. 7, came Pearl Harbor. The U.S. was at war. The Free Press headline the next morning said:

U. S. Navy Is Hard Hit
As Japan Opens War

An editorial declared no "room for disagreement when American lives are ruthlessly blotted out and our own soil is violated. That truth is basic. Whatever superficial divisions there may have been were settled with steel by Sunday's events."

The events of that momentous Sunday afternoon caught the Free Press newsroom as unprepared as the rest of the country. Doug Martin, the managing editor, began calling all over town trying to round up a staff to put out an extra. But he found virtually no one at home. Frank Angelo, hired only the week before as a sports writer, was getting off the elevator to begin his 3 p.m. shift when he encountered the frantic Martin. Unaware of the attack on Pearl Harbor, Angelo had stopped by the Newspaper Guild's annual bingo party at the Book Cadillac before reporting to work. He suggested a call to the hotel might get Martin the staff he needed. It did, and the paper produced a "Metropolitan Extra" for Dec. 8.

The willingness to change editorial policy with changing circumstances helped mightily as Knight and his aides began to alter the public's perception of the Free Press in big ways and small. One small way was the paper's offer to have staff photographers take pictures of mothers and their newborn babies to send to fathers in the service who had never seen their sons or daughters.

Both the intensity of interest in the war and a winning baseball team helped the Free Press attract new readers. The Detroit Tigers won the pennant in 1940, and then, as now, a winning sports team in Detroit means people eager to read all about them. As Detroit's economy shifted to the production of war materiel, making the city the "Arsenal of Democracy," its population increased dramatically, heading toward the peak of almost 1.9 million in 1950. Great social and economic changes were underway, with the successful conclusion of the UAW's organizing drive at Ford in 1941 and the influx of thousands of blacks to bolster the wartime work force.

In this booming and boisterous atmosphere, new people and new ideas helped broaden the appeal of the Free Press. One was Jack Pickering, the first Town Crier. Pickering was succeeded in 1943 by Tony Weitzel, a cherubic, happy-go-lucky free spirit whom Jack Knight brought from Akron. Weitzel became the first really hot new newspaper personality in Detroit in many years. His forte was a pleasant, gossipy approach. He was so successful in helping attract readers that, in 1945, the News took a previously unthinkable step — hiring Weitzel away at what was, for the time in the newspaper business, an extraordinary salary — reportedly $15,000.

That move sparked a feud that has become part of Detroit newspaper legend. First, Weitzel found himself shunned by his News colleagues who were shocked that the paper would hire someone at that salary to produce what they perceived as a gossip column. Weitzel could find no space in the News' own bulding and wound up "exiled" to an office in the basement of the News' radio station across the street. A Free Press story in 1946 gleefully revealed that Weitzel was arranging to sell automobiles in the desperately tight postwar market, an obvious conflict of interest with his job as a newspaper columnist. The News was stunned by the revelation, but did nothing. A few weeks later, the Free Press revealed that Weitzel was continuing his practice. The News and Weitzel parted in 1948. (He worked for Knight again, however, at the Chicago Daily News.)

Knight's promise of aggressive news coverage became evident in the handling of two major stories of violence and corruption in 1943. Beginning in the late 1930s but intensifying in the hectic wartime boom, racial tensions were building in Detroit. The migration of blacks from the South had swelled with Henry Ford's $5 day, increasing the number of blacks in Detroit from 4,741 in 1910 to 40,838 in 1920. By 1930, the number was 120,066. Migration slowed somewhat during the Depression, but the humming war plants once again made Detroit a boom town. In the first two years of the war, an estimated 350,000 people, almost all Southerners and 50,000 of them black, migrated to the city. Between 1940 and 1950, Detroit's black community doubled — 149,119 to 300,506.

Blacks were confined to living in clearly circumscribed areas of the city, and the housing shortage was acute. In 1942, the federal government had tried to relieve the shortage by moving black families into the new Sojourner Truth housing project. White home owners living in the surrounding neighborhood mounted demonstrations that ranged from picket lines at City Hall to rock-throwing battles at the construction site. When moving vans appeared, loaded with the belongings of black families, a battle erupted. It took hundreds of lawmen and three months to move blacks into the 200 housing units.

Tensions heightened early in June 1943, when workers at the Packard plant defied UAW officials and staged a wildcat strike because they were "opposed to mixing white and black workers" on the same job. The Free Press — in a notable break with its historic position on racial issues — said on June 3:

> When men throw down their tools and go home because they won't work on the same job with members of this or that racial or religious group, what can either the contractors or the unions do? They can't chain men to their machines.
>
> A good deal more is involved than the utilization of a large amount of manpower now idle. The discrimination against Negroes, for instance, challenges the sincerity of our beliefs in Christianity and in Jefferson's declaration that all men are created equal. We talk about world leadership. Yet in barring Asiatics from the Country, and in discriminating against 13 million Americans because of their color, and other millions because they were born in the Old World, we proclaim a double standard of justice, a different set of rules for men of different races and colors.
>
> The issue is moral. The virus of racial bias must be exorcised from millions of hearts in this Country before discrimination can be eliminated. That calls for a new type of leadership more than for a new executive agency. A renascence of humanitarianism and enlightened self-interest in the South has almost abolished lynchings. A similar renascence all over this country must precede the disappearance of racial and religious discrimination.
>
> We can't expect the world to accept the principles on which this nation was founded until we give greater evidence of respecting and acting on those principles ourselves.

Two days later the Free Press was even more emphatic: "A Negro has as much right to work for a living as any other American. The formula on which the nation was founded — that every human being has a right to life, liberty and the pursuit of happiness — still stands. We recognize the superiority of no class, no race, no creed ... There is no mincing words or dodging the question. That is the one issue which precipitated the strike at the Packard Motor Company . . . The Negro problem is still with us . . . It can be solved only by the leadership of honest and fair-minded men and women imbued with love of God and their fellow mortals."

On the same page, incidentally, in a short editorial commenting on a War Labor Board ruling, the Free Press agreed flatly that "women are entitled to the same pay for the same work as men . . . The basis of wages should not be sex but production."

Through this period the Free Press called attention to the housing crisis. A May 1, 1943, editorial expressed concern that "prejudices (might) be fanned into riotous hate by extremists on either side of the controversy." Agreement among Mayor Edward J. Jeffries, the city council and the housing commission that "to try to change the racial pattern of any area in Detroit now will result in violent opposition to the housing program and could very easily reach a point where war production efforts of this entire community would be endangered" had heightened the controversy.

The Free Press suggested, "The better element among our Negro citizens, in co-operation with that same element among the whites, can come to harmonious agreement over the issue" and added that with "tolerance and understanding NOW, (Negro leaders) have an opportunity to win greater support of their fellow citizens in their long, dreary upward struggle, and further sweep away the fog of bigotry and blind prejudice."

But on June 20, 1943, a warm, humid Sunday, tolerance and understanding turned out to be in short supply in Detroit. A full-page ad in the Free Press that day, signed by a group who called themselves patriotic citizens, apparently felt that if an appeal to brotherhood wouldn't work, maybe patriotism would. The ad read: "Strikes, sit-downs and work stoppages for any reason only hurt Old Glory and help Hitler. War tests men's minds and souls. It unnerves, it irritates, digs in and makes mountains in every day living . . . Let's keep at our jobs, no matter how distasteful, how distracting may be the environment."

By Sunday night a race riot had erupted that left 34 dead (25 blacks, nine whites); 675 hurt, 416 seriously enough to be hospitalized; 1,893 arrested, and more than $2 million in property losses. It had begun when a fight between black youths and white sailors on crowded Belle Isle mushroomed into a free-for-all on the bridge to the mainland. A false rumor swept through the black community that a black woman and her baby had been thrown off the bridge. Blacks began stoning and beating whites who wandered into their neighborhoods. White mobs retaliated by attacking and beating black pedestrians. Soon after daybreak Monday, whites were stoning cars driven by blacks, overturning them and assaulting the drivers. Streetcars were stopped, and black passengers were beaten. Some police attempted to protect the targets of the violence; others did little or nothing. By afternoon, the white rioters numbered more than 10,000 and were attacking blacks along Woodward Avenue from Cadillac Square north to Warren Avenue. Others piled into cars and fired at blacks with shotguns and rifles as they sped past. In Paradise Valley, a black neighborhood, blacks retaliated in kind against any whites unfortunate enough to be caught in the wrong area. As night fell, the first of 5,000 federal troops marched into the city to disperse the rioters.

The Free Press covered the riot thoroughly in its news columns and, on the editorial page, quickly supported a call made by UAW President R. J. Thomas for a grand jury probe to discover "why more drastic action in subduing the mobs was not taken." The Free Press' Malcolm Bingay criticized Police Commissioner John Witherspooon for giving orders "to handle it (any outbreak) with kid gloves." The Free Press saw the police commissioner's philosophy "at the root of the troubles" and added, "This is no time for kid-glove treatment of law violations."

"You will notice," the editorial continued, "that none of those gangsters who swarmed over the streets Sunday night and all day Monday passed on any insults to the soldiers of the United States Army when the troops rumbled into town at midnight. Instead they scurried to their holes in keeping with their rattish nature."

The call for a grand jury investigation, pushed by a young councilman named George C. Edwards Jr., was voted down, as was a second appeal by Mayor Edward Jeffries a month later. Eighteen years later, another mayor, Jerome P. Cavanagh, appointed Edwards police commissioner. Edwards' subsequent racial reforms in the police department rankled many, but he became the first Detroit police commissioner to take any real steps in that direction. Edwards, who later became a U.S. Appeals Court judge, said of his appointment as police commissioner: "My first job was to teach the police they didn't have a constitutional right to automatically beat up Negroes on arrest."

When on Aug. 11, 1943, a governor's committee report placed most of the blame on Detroit's black community, the Free Press called the re-

Weather Report

The Detroit Free Press

CITY EDITION
EXTRA

On Guard for Over a Century

Tuesday, June 22, 1943. No. 49   113th Year   30 Pages   Four Cents

MARTIAL LAW AT 10 P.M.
U.S. TROOPS MOVE IN

Gov. Kelly at 6 p. m. signed a proclamation declaring a state of martial law in Detroit. Military rule of the City will begin at 10 p. m. The streets were ordered cleared at that hour.

The Governor's proclamation read:

I, Harry F. Kelly, governor of the State of Michigan and Commander in Chief of the military forces of the said State of Michigan, hereby declare a state of emergency and the necessity for the armed forces of the State of Michigan to aid and assist, but in subordina-

tion thereto, all duly constituted civil authorities in the execution of the law of the state.

The necessity for such aid and assistance is declared to extend to the following counties of the State of Michigan, namely: Wayne, Oakland and Macomb.

In witness whereof, I have here unto

set my hand and caused to be affixed the great seal of the State of Michigan this Twenty-first Day of June, 1943.

HARRY F. KELLY,
Governor

In addition Gov. Kelly prohibited the sale of all liquor until further notice. All places of amusement were ordered closed at 9 p. m. Monday.

World War II was a tumultuous time in Detroit, marked by a race riot, reported in the June 22, 1943, Free Press, above. The invasion of Normandy, reported June 7, 1945, right.

WEATHER

The Detroit Free Press

METRO FINAL

On Guard for Over a Century   Vol. 114 - No. 41   Five Cents

BEACHHEADS ARE REINFORCED
Only 3 American Ships Lost in Invasion

FDR Says Attack Is Up to Schedule

Reports Small Naval Casualties But Warns of Over-Confidence

First Pictures of Landings on Invasion Coast

Nazi Counterblow Is Expected Soon

Germans Admit Deep Penetrations of France in First Day's Offensive

Allies Smash On in Italy

Troops Several Miles Inland, Churchill Says

Secret Arms Pounding Foe

War Bulletins

Detroit Rushes to Give Blood

Appreciation

On Inside Pages

Bomber Crash Kills 18 Fliers

Dee Day Makes Debut on D-Day

Vets Returned on Grindelm

Report Beck Dead

port a "whitewash" that was "largely drawn up by Police Commissioner Witherspoon, the apple-cheeked boy scout Mayor Jeffries placed in charge of the police department . . . With Commissioner Witherspoon furnishing most of the evidence, it is hardly conceivable that he would suggest an investigation of himself and his department."

While the governor's committee was attempting to end the controversy spawned by the riot, the Free Press was deep into another story that would thoroughly jolt state government and bring the paper, in 1945, its second Pulitzer Prize.

The series began with an Aug. 14, 1943, story by reporter Ken McCormick, involving charges of legislative bribery and political corruption. That kind of story was tailor-made for the rugged McCormick, who had joined the Free Press staff in 1931. McCormick had worked on the Cleveland Press where he started as a copy boy, and later in Indianapolis. He applied by letter to the Free Press and was offered a reporting job at $20 a week by Free Press City Editor Will MacDonald. McCormick, who was not reluctant to punch out some fellow who tried to cheat him in a poker game, was the kind of reporter who made it a point to know everything happening in town. He worked the police beat and on the rewrite desk and did a stint on the obituary desk where he drove the editor bonkers by humming "Ah, Sweet Mystery of Life" as he worked. In the '50s he impressed some of his colleagues, and all the copy boys, by showing up in the newsroom on occasion with a bodyguard, a husky prize-fighter named Hank Postaway who usually leaned on a wall near McCormick's desk while McCormick wrote his stories. McCormick availed himself of Postaway's services any time he was on an assignment where the subjects of his stories might react violently to what he was writing about them. And McCormick more often than not wrote stories about people whose reputation for violence was documented.

A typical assignment came in 1939 when McCormick covered the Ferguson Grand Jury which had been convened to investigate police and political corruption in Detroit and Wayne County in an era when the buying of politicians and policemen was considered less serious than it obviously should have been. The one-man grand jury had been convened, with Circuit Judge Homer Ferguson sitting as the grand juror, after newspapers and the FBI received letters and a diary from a woman who had killed herself and her 11-year-old daughter. The woman had been jilted by her boyfriend, a small-time gambler, and the letters were her revenge. She documented payoffs to police and public officials who were bribed to overlook gambling and prostitution. Her former boy-friend had been the payoff man.

There were 220 bookmakers' establishments operating in Detroit at the time (the dead woman had been a clerk in one of them), to say nothing of the blind pigs (illegal drinking spots) and houses of prostitution. When the grand jury finished its work in 1942, that investigation led to indictments of three councilmen, the mayor and his son, scores of police officers from the highest ranks to patrolmen, the Wayne County prosecutor and a number of prosecuting attorney officials. McCormick recalled the day he and a Free Press photographer were taken to a house where they saw a pile of money sitting on a table. They were left alone for a short time. When their host, one of the so-called bagmen of the prosecutor's office, drove them back to the office, he inquired casually, "Well, I hope you helped yourself to enough of the money." At which point, McCormick let the fellow have it — verbally this time.

The story that brought McCormick and the Free Press the Pulitzer started when John Knight had picked up information of political payoffs in Lansing. In 1943 McCormick wrote that William P. Lovett, secretary of the Detroit Citizens League (a reform group dating to 1912 which published the Civic Searchlight voters guide), had asked for an investigation into charges that a "barrel of money had changed hands" in the state Legislature to defeat a banking bill in 1941 and again in 1943. McCormick followed that story with a series that "demonstrated beyond a reasonable doubt that some legislators had sold their votes to the highest bidder." Attorney General Herbert Rushton, under pressure, set up a grand jury with Ingham County Judge Leland Carr heading the inquiry.

McCormick got an exclusive story from a jailed legislator who broke down and implicated others. McCormick also exposed an effort by Rushton to put the inquiry in the hands of a crony of state Republican boss Frank D. McKay. McCormick then played an active role in getting Judge Carr to appoint as special grand jury prosecutor a Hastings lawyer, Kim Sigler, a man McCormick described as having "the guts of a burglar." A couple of days after McCormick had approached him about taking the assignment, Sigler appeared in Lansing, called McCormick and told him, "I've decided to take the job because it sounds like too much fun to turn down." An hour later, McCormick had talked to Carr, and Carr made the selection public.

A little more than a month later, Jan. 22, 1944, the grand jury indicted 20 state legislators and six automobile finance company officials for plotting to corrupt the Legislature. Subsequent testimony showed that state laws were being bought and sold freely and that slush funds existed to buy every manner of favorable legislation. The story reached its peak with the murder on Jan. 11, 1945, of State Sen. Warren G. Hooper, of Albion, who was a key witness against Republican boss McKay and others in a graft plot. Hooper was shot to death in his car while returning from Lansing to Albion. The murder was never solved although three Detroit men, members of the infamous Purple Gang, were convicted of plotting to kill Hooper, but not of murdering him. They were sentenced to five years in prison.

In all, Sigler indicted, tried and convicted more than a score of legislators and others involved in bribe-taking; in 1946, he rode his popularity to Michigan's governorship. Carr was elected to the Supreme Court, and McCormick and the Free Press were presented with a Pulitzer "for the most disinterested and meritorious public service rendered by an American newspaper during the year 1944."

While those stories were forcing even the war into secondary status on Page One on many days, the tragedy of World War II would soon become a personal tragedy for John S. Knight.

Knight, as a newcomer to the city, was "majoring in Detroit," going to the ballpark and living comfortably in an apartment at the Book Cadillac Hotel when he wasn't at his longtime home near the Portage Golf Club in Akron. Early in 1943 Byron Price, director of the U.S. Office of Censorship, approached Knight and asked him to take on the key job of serving as chief liaison between the U.S. and Britain in improving intelligence flow. Typically, Knight insisted on being fully prepared before heading for his post in London and spent several months training with the Army, Navy and the U.S. Office of Censorship, which he would represent in working out differences with the British Ministry of Information. In June 1943, Bingay ran an editorial to explain Knight's job, because, he said, "There have been those who have misunderstood Mr. Knight's assignment, thinking it a political berth, the purpose of which would be to curtail his well-known editorial independence. It is not. Out of all the editors and publishers in the United States, he was selected by Mr. Price, former general manager of the Associated Press, as the best man to do the job."

Knight returned to the United States in May 1944 and in a few months had bought controlling interest in the Chicago Daily News for

$2.3 million in cash, assuming a debt of $13 million. He was caught up in a stirring newspaper battle in the country's second largest city with "mixed feelings of pride and a sobering awareness of my responsibilities." He continued to spend a good bit of time in Detroit, where Stuffy Walters had been installed as executive editor, with Dale Stafford as assistant to Managing Editor Doug Martin until Martin retired in September 1945 and Stafford succeeded him. Brewster Campbell was city editor.

Knight was supporting Dewey in the 1944 election because, as he said in his Notebook, "He represents the America to come, a nation of great development and faith in the future . . . There is no reason to believe that President Roosevelt is as ill as his bitterest enemies contend but the facts are that the strain upon his energies has taken its toll."

How much a toll was not known until 5:50 p.m. April 12, 1945. Harry Fenton, a Free Press staffer, was standing by the wire service machine. Suddenly, the flash bell began to ring. Conversation in the newsroom ceased; many thought the bells might presage the end of the war. Fenton, the wire copy in his hand and tears in his eyes, told the others: "Roosevelt is dead."

For a minute, everyone just stood there. Then someone yelled, "My God, we've got a paper to get out!" The regular City Edition was just being completed, but within half an hour pages were torn apart; engravings were brought up from the library; clerks from the classified ad department were called in to answer the flood of telephone calls that had jammed the switchboard, making it almost impossible to place an outgoing call. By 6:30, the last copy had cleared the newsroom and new pages were being made up in the composing room. At 6:58, two minutes before the regular starting time, "The reassuring roar of the presses permeated the building, and within seconds the stillness outside was broken by the eerie echoes . . . 'Extra, Extra, Roosevelt is dead.'"

John Knight reacted with profound sadness to Roosevelt's death. It came at a particularly difficult moment in his own life. In March 1945, the eldest of his three sons, First Lt. John S. Knight Jr., was killed in Germany. In his Editor's Notebook on April 22, 1945, Jack Knight provided his readers a glimpse of the man usually seen only by his close associates. He wrote:

> Johnny is gone. The lovable kid who never had a vicious thought in his life is sleeping in Germany because of the mad, senseless ambitions of a demented paranoiac; because in the last 20 years, the "statesmen" of Europe have repeatedly

Franklin Delano Roosevelt dies, reported April 13, 1945.

Atom bomb dropped on Hiroshima, reported Aug. 7, 1945.

sacrificed principle on the altar of power politics; because as his friend and fellow paratrooper, First Lt. Denis Jones of Landisburg, Pa., expressed it: "Johnny was killed just the same way he lived, doing just a little more than anyone asked him to do — giving more than he was required to give." That is one thing nobody will ever forget about him — no matter what he was asked to do, he always threw in a little extra ...

As we strive to fight back the tears, there are memories of his childhood ... There are moments of comfort when we are told of the esteem in which Johnny was held ... (but) the great tragedy of the Johnnys, the Sams, the Peters, the Joes and all the hundreds of thousands of other fine young men who have died for us is that few of them ever had a real chance at life ...

Nearly 300,000 Johnnys are gone.

We must make an appointment with those gallant boys and give them a solemn pledge that we shall never again shirk the task of achieving a peaceful world, free from the bestialities and carnage that have made a mockery of civilization through the ages.

We must guarantee them further that their returning comrades will be given the chance at life which was denied to them, that no one of them shall ever suffer through our selfishness and greed, that our high-sounding promises will never re-echo as a hollow mockery of words.

To the Johnnys who are gone and the millions of Johnnys to come, let it at least be proved by our acts that we sought redemption and endeavored to make atonement for the sins of a shallow, self-indulgent and greedy generation.

Through tear-dimmed eyes, I offer a silent and humble prayer.

May his noble soul rest in peace.

During those hectic years when so many were off to war, Stafford faced the problem of getting the staff pulled together. As wartime city desk assistant Charlie Haun said years later, "I wondered how we ever put out a newspaper. I came to work one day and eight people arrived, and I didn't know one of them. Two weeks later they were gone." There was, obviously, little time for long-range planning during those years. But when the war ended, Stafford had a small but effective nucleus around which to build.

At war's end, the Free Press was poised for the all-out circulation battle to come. In the six-month period ending September 1946, the Free Press held the lead with 417,336 daily to 412,605 for the News and 405,887 for the Times. By September 1951, a few weeks before Stafford left the Free Press to buy his own paper, the News had a circulation lead of about 12,000, with the Times third, another 12,000 behind. The Times had reached its peak circulation the previous year and was beginning the sharp drop that led to its demise in 1960.

Stafford was a hard-news man with an Associated Press background. He was a correspondent for the Lansing State Journal while he attended Lansing Central High. After a stint as sports writer with the Lansing Capital News, he enrolled at Michigan State and, with George Allerton, sports editor of the Lansing State Journal, is credited with tagging MSU teams "Spartans" instead of "Staters." He worked at the Pontiac Press (now the Oakland Press) and as sports editor of the Michigan AP before joining the Free Press early in 1941.

He placed great emphasis on the sports staff, providing it with leadership by hiring Lyall Smith as sports editor in 1945. Smith, a rangy, 6-foot-3½ blond, grew up in Peoria, Ill., where he starred on his high school basketball, baseball and football teams (as he did in college, too). He attended Bradley University for a couple of years, then headed for the University of Illinois where he earned a master's degree in history and political science. He had planned to become a teacher but was hired by the Chicago Daily News in 1937 to write feature stories; in 1940 he was on the Daily News sports staff. In 1945 he came to the Free Press, then, at 30, the youngest sports editor of a metropolitan paper in the United States. He left the Free Press in 1965 to take a job with the Detroit Lions. Smith was official scorer for one of baseball's most memorable events — the perfect game Yankee Don Larsen pitched against the Dodgers in the 1956 World Series. Smith scored the game as part of his role as president that year of the Baseball Writers Association.

Staff changes were frequent in the hectic days following the war, with Jack Sinclair, Duane DeLoach and Art Carstens taking off to launch careers as publishers of weeklies, Bud Guest moving into radio, and others arriving — Mark Beltaire, for many years the Town Crier; Frank Williams, the editorial cartoonist; Hal Schram, who still covers high school sports for the paper in the 1980s, and Tony Spina, chief photographer.

Spina, a graduate of Detroit Tech, joined the Free Press after serving with the Army in North Africa. He has won hundreds of awards for his brilliant photos. In 1958, he made his first trip to the Vatican to cover the election of Pope John XXIII, and in 1960 he was accorded the unusual honor of a private audience to photograph the Pope as he sat for a sculptor. He has returned to Rome for other papal installations and accompanied John Paul II on his trip to Poland in 1979.

Beltaire, a native Detroiter, took over the Town Crier column when Tony Weitzel left for the News (Beltaire had worked as a hockey writer at the News). Beltaire continued as Town Crier 36 years, until his retirement in 1980.

Schram, often called the dean of Michigan high school sports writers, has had a long and fascinating career as a reporter despite

Morgan Oates, Free Press librarian, among the bound volumes of the Free Press, in 1946, before the pages were microfilmed and the bound volumes given to the Detroit Public Library for safekeeping. (Photo by Tony Spina)

having been declared legally blind when he was nine years old. After graduating from MSU, he underwent an operation that restored sight in one eye. His insight and his high school selections have earned him his reputation as "the Swami." One fan, disgruntled over his playoff picks, sent the Swami a box of poison. And on another occasion, when he picked against St. Ignace, a telegram of protest bearing 600 names arrived for him — happily, not collect.

The women's department in the post-war years was led by Laurena

Pringle, with Jean Pearson handling fashion, Grace Barber beauty articles, Kay Savage food, Marguerite Riley the society column, and Pat Talbot, Lettie Gavin and Peggy Monaghan a variety of other assignments. Bill Coughlin was the Sunday editor, and Brewster Campbell the city editor, with a staff that included Art O'Shea as labor writer, Leo Donovan covering the auto beat, Charlie Weber, Jim Ransom and John Murray at City Hall, Hub M. George, Owen Deatrick and Jim Haswell handling Lansing and other politics stories, and Charlie Haun on the

Mark Beltaire, the Town Crier, signing
autographs in 1947.

night city desk. Walt Pierre and Jim Keith ran the news desk, and Don Schram was state editor.

Sunday Editor Coughlin also conducted a post-war veterans affairs column which was getting as many as 2,400 letters a week as it attempted to present the serviceman's side and sniped at infringements on his rights. That column's lighter moments included a letter from a wife who asked what she could do to keep her husband in the Army, "because my daughter and I live much better on the allotment, and he's such a pest when he is home."

Labor, of course, was a major story in Detroit. The competition for exclusive stories was intense and reporters went to great lengths to get the stories and get them first. Early in 1946, for example, when a Teamster local, led by Jimmy Hoffa, was trying to organize independent grocers and meat dealers — a move that produced a lot of resistance and some violence — Free Press reporter Clyde Bates managed to get into a meeting of grocers and meat dealers at which Hoffa was to appear. It had been closed to the press, but Bates hid on a shelf behind a bar. He was stretched out there, undiscovered, for four hours and came up with a story that included Hoffa's dramatic statement: "We've got one million bucks to get the organizing job done." Some years later, during the 1958 UAW talks, reporter Tom Craig climbed to a catwalk high above the stage in the Ford Auditorium to listen while UAW president Walter Reuther outlined strategy for the coming negotiations to top UAW leaders from around the country. Craig's exclusive story of the meeting appeared in the early editions of the Free Press that same night.

The Free Press made some labor news of its own in 1948 in a startling public break with the News and Times over how a contract with the typographical union and the mailers union had been settled. The first of many confrontations, it was important in establishing the Free Press' determination to be what Jack Knight called "firm but fair" in its approach to labor relations. Knight had demonstrated his attitude in Chicago a year earlier when the newspapers there (including his Chicago Daily News) continued publishing despite a strike by printers. Knight also made clear his stand when printers struck the Miami Herald in 1948 and the paper continued publication. Evenutally the Herald became a non-union paper.

In Detroit in March 1948, the publishers had settled with all other unions except the mailers and typographers, and there was agreement, or so Knight believed, that the publishers would be firm against the demands of the two holdouts. In fact, arrangements were completed for establishing an alternative typesetting process in the Barlum Tower downtown to continue publishing in the event of a strike. At the last minute, however, the News and Times unexpectedly settled with the unions. Knight, in a statement to the Detroit Labor News, in which he described in detail dealings with Herbert Ponting of the News and William Mills of the Times through Henry Weidler, said, "The Detroit News simply pulled the rug out from under us without warning . . . So far as I am concerned, Detroit's 'Munich' will not alter my stand in Chicago where I hope publishers are made of sterner stuff."

But in 1955, the Free Press stance proved more acceptable to new

management at the News, and the Detroit papers were shut down by
their first strike. It was not, as it turned out, the last. In the next 25 years,
Detroit's papers were hit with almost two-score authorized and unauthorized strikes.

It was during this period that Knight played a key role in establishing
the United Foundation. And it was a time when Mayor Ed Jeffries and
later Eugene Van Antwerp talked of grand plans for the city's future,
and urban redevelopment — with bulldozing as a major feature — was
being pushed. In 1948 the Free Press, having given all-out support to
Gov. Sigler in his successful bid for re-election, also saw the beginning of
what proved to be the Soapy Williams era, which left the Free Press editorial pages something less than enthusiastic.

Editorially, too, Knight and the Free Press got caught up in the
turmoil that marked the final months of Harry S Truman's first term.
The Free Press' antagonism toward Harry Truman came to a head
during his 1948 campaign against Thomas E. Dewey. In his Notebook
the Sunday before the election, Knight wrote, after 10 weeks "of the dullest campaign since 1936, President Truman and Gov. Dewey are
precisely where they were before this whole thing started. At the
Republican Convention last June, Dewey was the confident, self-
assured candidate as he talked about morality in government, national
unity and the need for a spiritual reawakening.

"He still is.

"In accepting renomination from the Democrats last July, President
Truman indulged in the crudest form of demagoguery. This is the
technique that fans the flames of class warfare by implying that the
opposition candidate is really a Hitler-lover at heart.

"He's still using it . . .

"From the very day he was nominated, Dewey sensed that he was a
sure winner and the decision to keep his campaign on a high level was a
calculated risk he could well afford to take. He will therefore assume office next January without having offended any member of Congress,
regardless of party."

But years later, when asked whom he thought had been the most
effective of all the presidents he had known, Knight unhesitatingly
replied, "Truman, because he was decisive even though some of his
decisions may not have been of the best."

While some newspapers, most memorably the Chicago Tribune,
found it difficult to contain their enthusiasm for Dewey until all the
votes were counted, the Free Press managed to keep the embarrassment

of wrong results off the front page; it did not, however, do so well on the editorial page. On the morning its Page One headlines proclaimed Truman the winner, the Free Press editorial, unchanged since the early editions, somberly — but not unhappily — bade farewell to Truman and offered some advice to the man it had assumed would lose: "The sympathy we feel is rather for a game little fellow, who never sought the Presidency and was lost in it, but who went down fighting with all he had to prove to the leaders of his own party, who tried to kick him aside, that he was a better man than they . . ."

The editorial also suggested Truman ask Gen. George Marshall, then secretary of state, to resign and appoint John Foster Dulles to succeed him thus assuring "Mr. Truman (at the peak of the Cold War) accepting the verdict of the nation and lending authority of his office to the policies of the man who soon will occupy it. True, that is asking a good deal of Mr. Truman. Yet these are times which, with all our unity and patriotism, will ask a great deal more of millions of other Americans."

Editors working in the newsroom that night, realizing the embarrassment that the paper might suffer if Truman won and the editorial wasn't changed, started looking for Malcolm Bingay who had charge of the editorial page. He was located finally in the midst of a party which had convened early to celebrate Dewey's victory. Bingay was told that returns showed Truman ahead and that the numbers strongly suggested that he would win. But it was strict policy that Bingay alone had control of the editorial page and only he could make the decision to change the editorial.

He arrived at the newsroom sometime later, walked over to the copy desk and, in his most domineering voice, inquired, "What's this about Truman winning?" He was shown the figures and the headline planned for the edition which would be going to press in a few minutes. He mumbled a few words, dug his hand in his pocket, came up with a handful of coins, tossed them on the desk, and said, "I'll bet that and more that Dewey wins." Then he spun on his heel, walked out the door without touching the editorial. No one else did either.

Earlier, a call had been made to Jack Knight asking what he suggested be done. He replied, typically, that it was Bingay's page, and he should be the one to do something. His unwavering policy of total control for local editors allowed them the control even to pull sizable boners.

This incident points out another basic Knight guideline — the division between the newsroom and the editorial page staff. In most cases the policy was to insure the separation of news coverage and opinion. But at the Free Press at that time, it went beyond pure journalistic necessity. Managing Editor Stafford and Editorial Director Bingay simply did not get along. Soon Stafford, one of those newsmen who always wanted to own his own newspaper, was quietly looking for a chance to buy one. He had made several trips of inspection to various newspapers prior to the day in November 1951 when he got a call about

Dale Stafford, managing editor, receives congratulations from John S. Knight and the Free Press staff as he leaves to become publisher of his own newspaper in Greenville, Mich., 1951.

the availability of the Greenville (Mich.) Daily News. As he explained, he had to make a fast decision. And he did. Within hours, he had resigned, and soon thereafter Knight asked Lee Hills to become executive editor of the Free Press.

At the time, the rumor was that Knight wanted to sell the Free Press and was bringing in Hills to make preparations for the sale. But Knight said later, "It never entered my mind." Instead, Hills' arrival marked a new era of expansion for the Detroit Free Press.

Knight's newspaper group grew — he sold the Chicago Daily News but bought the Charlotte Observer, the Philadelphia Inquirer, the papers in Lexington, Ky., and Macon and Columbus, Ga., among others, and in 1974 Knight Newspapers merged with Ridder Publications to become the largest daily-circulation newspaper group in the United States. Although he gave up his corporate titles in 1976 to leave his newspapers in the hands of men and women he made sure were up to the job, Knight has the respect of his employees in a way that borders on veneration. He knows an astonishing number of them by name, and reporters have always been special favorites. Once, in Detroit, Knight was being introduced to a group of staff members by a junior executive who was new to the paper.

"This is Leo so-and-so," the junior exec said.

"Hello, Neal," the publisher replied, because that was the reporter's name, and Knight knew it.

In a way that chief executives of other sorts of corporations find remarkable, Knight has allowed — in fact, insisted on — independence among his papers. He frequently limits his comments and suggestions because his words might carry more weight than he intended. "Sometimes it's hard to avoid stepping in with an elephant's foot," he used to say.

The legacy he has given his papers is expressed in the credo he wrote himself to make sure it said what he meant it to:

> The Knight Newspapers strive to meet the highest standards of journalism. We try to keep our news columns factual and unbiased, reserving our personal opinions for the editorial page, where they belong. It is true that we make mistakes. So does every other newspaper that isn't afraid of its own shadow. When our facts are shown to be faulty, we make amends cheerfully and resolve to do better next time.
>
> But our newspapers . . . have never been run by the Board of Commerce, the Retail Merchants Association, the manufacturers, the banks or the labor unions. We do not operate them in the interests of any class, group, faction or political party. As my late father said so appropriately many years ago: "We are ourselves free, and our paper should be free — free as the Constitution we enjoy — free to truth, good manners and good sense.
>
> "We shall be, for whatever measure is best, adapted to defending the rights and liberties of the people and advancing

useful knowledge. We shall labor at all times to inspire the people with a just and proper sense of their own condition, to point out to them their true interest and rouse them to pursue it."

When he sent Lee Hills from Miami to Detroit, there was no one John Knight trusted more to build a great newspaper on that foundation.

"An intensely single-minded man, committed to reaching for journalism's peak."

Lee Hills

Chapter Seven

The Surge with Hills

Chapter 7

O ther newspapers in other cities may have had more exciting periods than the Detroit Free Press of the 1950s, but that is difficult to imagine. For what happened in the years between December 1951, when Lee Hills first appeared on the scene in Detroit, and November 1960, when the Detroit Times faded out of the picture, was the creation of a new newspaper.

The change was from a paper that had built slowly on a great tradition into one that surged vigorously into the new era of the following decades, an era that would bring incredible technological changes and a continuing circulation battle between two of America's largest newspapers.

Under Lee Hills' direction, the Free Press became a bright, highly readable newspaper, adding to its reputation as a vehicle of solid coverage. The paper became known for its aggressive coverage of the growing suburban area, including questionable government practices in some communities. But the Free Press responded to the postwar shift of interest toward personal concerns and good reading. A "For and About the Family" section — a descendant of "The Household" — ran stories on life-styles, recognizing their importance at a time when few newspapers ran such stories. A strong comics section, well known pundits like Walter Lippmann and Roscoe Drummond and advice pioneer Ann Landers became identified with the Free Press. And the Free Press strived for bright appearance as well as bright writing. Graphics were important; the front page looked snappy and inviting. The Free Press sensed, earlier than most publications, that life was growing faster and busier and that readers wanted to get their news and information as quickly and as effortlessly as possible.

The foundation for these changes was laid, piece by piece, through the leadership of Hills, a man committed to reaching for the peak in American journalism or whatever he attempted. Like many of his predecessors at the helm of the Free Press, his career began as a teenager working in a print shop. He won his first job by impressing the editor of the weekly News-Advocate in Price, Utah, with his reporting and writing "of local happenings," and he soon was "doing everything" — setting type, making up pages, writing, editing and "sweeping the floors," he recalled. He was born in Granville, N. D., in 1906 (the year E.D. Stair took over the Free Press). By the time he was 17, Hills was editor of the News-Advocate. After attending Brigham Young University, he convinced a tough-minded local banker to lend him the money for tuition at the University of Missouri School of Journalism. By 1929, he had a job with the Oklahoma City Times.

He studied law at Oklahoma City University at night, earned a degree and passed the bar examination. He decided to resolve any potential career conflict by vowing to himself: "If I hadn't made it to a top job in the newspaper business by the time I was 29, I'd get out." He made it, working in several executive jobs for a decade with Scripps-Howard in Oklahoma City, Indianapolis, Memphis and Cleveland. In 1942, at 36, he became managing editor of the Miami Herald, beginning an association with John S. Knight that lasted throughout his career.

The relationship between Hills and Knight flourished into one of the most mutually rewarding and mutually respectful ones imaginable. Knight called Hills "one of the finest newspapermen in the nation," and supported that opinion in many ways. In 1967, Hills became the first person outside the Knight family to become president of Knight Newspapers Inc. It became a public corporation two years later; four years later Hills was its chairman and chief executive officer. He was one of the major architects of a merger with Ridder Publications Inc. in 1974 and was named the first chairman and chief executive of Knight-Ridder Newspapers, with the largest daily circulation of any newspaper group in America.

Further testament to his leadership among news executives is his election as president of four major newspaper organizations — the American Society of Newspapers Editors, the Associated Press Managing Editors Association, the Inter-American Press Association and the Society of Professional Journalists (Sigma Delta Chi).

Like Knight, he won a Pulitzer Prize for his own efforts — in addition to the Pulitzers given newspapers under his direction. His was in 1956 for his reporting on the labor negotiations between the auto industry and the UAW in Detroit the previous year. Other honors include two awards for Distinguished Service to Journalism from the University of Missouri, and the Maria Moors Cabot Award from Columbia University for his work on inter-American relations.

Hills, who had helped build the Miami Herald into an internationally respected newspaper, with a special air-express edition to South America, had also helped organize the Inter-American Press Association. And during his year as president of ASNE, he led a group of editors to the USSR. After a 2½-hour interview with Nikita Khrushchev, he wrote an exclusive story saying Khrushchev claimed the Russians had an anti-missile missile "that can hit a fly in outer space." His 12-part series on that trip included this perceptive paragraph: "Though ill-housed and fed a monotonous diet, they (the Soviet people) march the street with a purposeful stride that makes you want to come home and tell America to get off its big fat complacency or we won't continue to be No. 1."

Knight, who could give less personal attention to the Free Press after he bought the Chicago Daily News in 1944, had total confidence in Hills. In turn, Hills could seek, and get, total support from Knight. "When Jack asked me to go to Detroit," Hills explained, "I knew that there had been a certain amount of frustration about how the paper was going, so I reviewed with him plans for the future and came to a full understanding of where we would be headed. He told me to 'Go up there and run it' but I still remained executive editor of the Miami Herald."

Unquestionably they agreed on the basic concepts Knight had always espoused. Hills, like Knight, had that rare combination of talents — solid editorial skills, hard-nosed business acumen and the sensitivity to balance them to create a newspaper in the finest tradition. Hills summarized their shared philosophy in a talk to Knight Newspapers editors:

> One important part of our future depends upon business-editorial relationships. For KNI this has grown into a unique and healthy partnership pattern. The key, I believe, is that we frankly recognize the built-in dichotomy of newspaper publishing. By doing so, we make it work dynamically to unify and strengthen us, not to tear us apart.
>
> We have avoided any real problems ... because we talk about it openly. We examine and refine our practices and we try to improve on a set of relationships which are unusual among American newspapers. This special something results in fine newspapers and will, I believe, produce great newspapers.

> ... A newspaper, unlike most other corporations, must reflect the community in which it operates.
>
> And like it or not, a newspaper is inescapably saddled with the proud and exciting responsibility of leading. It cannot lead or influence if it gets too far out of step with its constituency or if someone from headquarters tries to call the shots on news coverage and local editorial policy. The trend toward group newspaper ownership makes local editorial direction even more important.

Thus were spelled out the ideas Hills refined as he reshaped the Free Press in the decade of the '50s and after. While there was never any doubt about the primacy of a newspaper's news function, Hills also devoted considerable energy and ability to the business side of the paper — and to its competitive strategy. The circumstances in Detroit suited Hills well, for he had a winning instinct — and a great impatience with those who didn't. He was quick to delegate authority, yet always managed to keep a hand in whatever was going on.

When he arrived in Detroit, the Free Press was in second place, trailing the News by 12,000 daily and leading the Times by about 9,000 (ABC, September 1951). The circulation growth of all three newspapers was not keeping pace with the growth in the area's population. Hills found impressive Free Press circulation gains in the previous decade, but even larger News gains. The city was changing dramatically, and Hills saw the need for equally dramatic changes in the newspaper.

The nucleus Hills inherited included Henry Weidler, the business manager; Malcolm Bingay, editorial director; Brewster Campbell, city editor, and Frank Angelo, feature editor. Hills quickly made clear to Bingay that Hills would be the final voice on editorial policy and soon designated Angelo as his assistant with primary responsibility for liaison with the news department.

Not only did Hills' arrival mark a new era for the Free Press, but it came at a time when the News and Times also were on the verge of major personnel changes, due primarily to retirements. It was time for a change, and Hills was in charge.

Characteristically, he plunged in on all fronts. He spent long days covering every corner of the Free Press building. As he questioned every facet of the operation, he took notes in shorthand, a skill he had learned in high school. Within weeks, he arrived at two major conclusions — that archaic Free Press production equipment which had barely been touched since it was put in place in 1925 had to be replaced, and that the Free Press, heavily dependent on its early edition sales (home-delivered before 9:30 p.m.), had a great potential for circulation expansion if it became truly a morning paper. The production refurbishing was critical to achieving the circulation goal.

Knight agreed in 1952 to invest in new press units and stereotype and composing room equipment. A second phase of investment in 1953, a third in 1961, then more installations in 1968 helped modernize production facilities. With that first step taken, Hills moved on to a steady stream of innovations at various levels.

The first full-color photograph printed during a regular press run in Detroit — a picture of a duck dinner — ran in December 1953 after the first of the new press units had been installed. Color use was stepped up in mid-1954 as other press units came on line, but the high cost of run-of-press color made regular use impractical. For a while the Free Press turned to the SpectaColor process — a way of printing color in advance of the full press run. That, too, was dropped because it made use of timely news photographs impossible and because of the expense. Not until 1980 and the next generation of equipment — a new offset printing plant — did the regular use of full-color photographs and art work become routine at the Free Press.

Hills brought in Cle Althaus to centralize and organize personnel practices, including the use of pre-employment testing — a practice greeted with some skepticism in the beginning and some controversy later, until the tests were refined to relate directly to job skills. He reshuffled the circulation department, naming Tade Walsh director to work with Roy Hatton, who had run the office since the early 1900s, and he began the use of telephone solicitation of subscribers on a massive scale.

George Nelson, an enthusiastic sales type, was named advertising director to work with a staff that included such dedicated veterans as Cy Cosgrove, Gil Hatie, Elliott Shumaker, Walter Batura, Fred Butler, Charles O. (Tommy) Thompson, Bruce Munro, Fred Hartman and John Patterson. A major expansion of the promotion effort, which had been limited to the work of Lynn West and one secretary, was inaugurated to bolster the marketing effort. Fred Lowe became promotion director, and he soon had working for him Bob McBride, who later became general manager of Detroit television station WJBK, and Fred Currier, who later established one of the country's major polling and research organizations, Market Opinion Research Inc. Long-time

Derick Daniels, executive
editor.

Frank Angelo, managing
editor.

Royce Howes, editor of the
editorial page.

Mark Ethridge Jr., editor
of the editorial page.

employee Gertrude Rumsey handled public service.

The Free Press also became, in 1953, this country's first newspaper to use motivational research to find out how readers felt about the paper, now a common practice among newspapers. As Lowe put it in a presentation to the Inland Press Association, "The survey helped us to see ourselves as others see us." The research warned, among other things, of the need to be concerned about "the emotional as well as the rational needs of readers." The study also provided some information to indicate how news, promotion and circulation departments could plan and work together. Lowe pointed to one example: "An August Festival of Reading" in 1957 which took two months of planning and produced, at a time when the city was going through one of its cyclical recessions, the largest ever August circulation.

The first of several major changes in packaging the paper's news content occurred July 24, 1952, with the introduction on Page Three of a Second Front Page for local news; sports news in a separate section with a section front, to match one previously established for the For and About Women section, and a re-styling of the Sunday magazine. In addition, features were anchored so readers could depend on finding them in the same place every day. With these steps, the Free Press adopted a new promotional slogan: "Easy to Read, Easy to Find."

Hills also insisted on a friendlier attitude in the newspaper's approach to readers. And another slogan soon was being used: "You See the Friendly Free Press Everywhere." Even a corny radio jingle repeating the slogan to the tune of "She'll Be Comin' 'Round the Mountain When She Comes" didn't curb the public's enthusiastic acceptance of the friendly approach. In fact, people began referring to the paper simply as the "Morning Friendly." At least one sarcastic variation of the slogan went something like, "You see the Friendly Free Press everywhere, in the bushes, on the roof, on the grass," a reference to the talent some carriers had for missing large targets — like porches — in favor of the surrounding areas. Though the line hasn't been used in Free Press advertising in years, many Detroiters still refer to the paper in the 1980s as "The Friendly."

One story among many that helped to establish that friendly spirit was developed by reporter Ken McCormick, who heard one day from Warden William Bannan of Jackson Prison that he had finally met the only innocent inmate he had ever known in his 25 years of prison service. It was Willie Calloway, at the time a 28-year-old lifer who had spent nine years in jail after being convicted in the holdup-slaying of a Detroit woman. He had been a model prisoner, "quietly, persistently protesting his innocence." McCormick's eight-week investigation in 1953 led to a new trial for Calloway, and a finding of innocent. It was the kind of story — one that produced results — that people would come to expect from the Free Press.

Hills early recognized the paper was operating with a small news

Willie Calloway, sentenced to life in prison, with reporter Ken
McCormick, whose investigation led to a new trial for Calloway
and his being found innocent.

staff, with very few people paid more than the minimum amounts set in
the union contract. At a staff meeting, he brought up the very welcome
subject of merit raises. And he moved to increase the size of the staff.
Typically, he built on the one he inherited, including Campbell and
Angelo, Walt Pierre as news editor, Don Schram as state editor,
Laurena Pringle as women's editor, Lyall Smith as sports editor and Bill
Coughlin as Sunday editor. The inimitable Helen Bower was handling
movies and books; J. Dorsey Callaghan, drama and music criticism;
Lilian Jackson Braun was covering interior design; Adrian Fuller wrote
about religion. Joe Kalec and Tony Spina headed the photo staff.

In April 1952, Hills made the first major personnel shifts in the city
room, moving Campbell to executive city editor, and naming Royce
Howes, another longtime Free Press staffer, as city editor. Charles
Haun became picture editor, and Fred Olmsted, a veteran reporter who
later became city editor, took Haun's spot on the night city desk. Angelo
remained as feature editor, working as liaison between Hills and the
news staff. More features were added, including the Ann Landers

Dorothy Jurney, pioneering women's editor, and her staff in the 1950s.

column and the Peanuts cartoon; both proved to be instant hits.

Hills, busy in the office, was busy outside, too. He became involved in many facets of community life, making many valuable personal news contacts. Over time he became one of the city desk's best tipsters. Simultaneously, he urged others on the staff to become involved.

Tony Spina, chief photographer, in 1954.

Another key Hills' move was to hold regular management staff meetings, including all department heads, among them Harry Lentz, the composing room foreman; Clark Renwick, the controller, and Don Walker, the cashier. The developing *esprit de corps* continued through the decade and contributed mightily to the paper's surge.

After the first price increase since 1944 (from five to seven cents daily) was put into effect in July 1952, Free Press circulation (ABC, March 1953) trailed the News by about 56,000, and the Times by 3,000. The Free Press then moved to convert from an "afternoon newspaper with a morning paper hangover" into a full-fledged morning paper. Test solicitations by telephone confirmed a great potential for selling more subscriptions. Walsh, the circulation director, had begun to build a home delivery force, particularly in the suburbs, and circulation strategy called for gradually changing certain sections of the metropolitan area from evening to morning home delivery. The goal, later reached, was to end home delivery of the evening edition by the mid-1960s.

A key element in this plan was a drive launched in August 1953 in cooperation with the Children's Hospital of Detroit. The Free Press offered to make a contribution to the hospital on behalf of each new subscriber, taking care to ensure no city ordinances were violated and not to interfere with policies of the Better Business Bureau and the United Foundation.

The response was phenomenal. While the contributions had an appeal, the Free Press also was tapping a pool of people who had never been asked before to subscribe. The success was not lost on the News which in mid-December signaled its concern with a story in which it referred "to another newspaper" that was involved in a promotion which, it implied, wasn't "charity." Hills reacted quickly; a call to Augustus Ledyard, president of Children's Hospital, brought a letter praising what the Free Press was doing. That letter was reprinted in a full-page ad Dec. 30.

The next day's News response was a story saying the Better Business Bureau had "disclaimed approval" of the Free Press effort. It also quoted city officials and the head of the United Foundation as questioning the Free Press campaign. By day's end, those early precautions paid off, and the Free Press response was prepared, including photos of pertinent letters. By this time John Knight himself insisted on including an editorial expressing his feelings about the News' reaction. Knight's editorial was headlined, "Here's Your Answer, Mr. Booth" — and what an answer. After three paragraphs reviewing the situation, Knight wrote:

> Now at year's end ... The Detroit News proposes to find something sinister about this well publicized method of helping little children who are ill and hospitalized.
>
> However, their cheap, petty attacks ... come as no surprise to the Free Press. For several weeks Mr. Warren Booth, president of the Detroit News, has been waging a campaign of threat and intimidation against officials of the United Foundation and the Children's Hospital.
>
> He is known to have told officials of the United Foundation that The Detroit News would not give one cent to this worthy organization unless the Free Press program was "stopped."
>
> When these blustering dog-in-the-manger tactics didn't impress anyone but Mr. Booth, he started an anvil chorus on the Children's Hospital. Here again his threats were to no avail.
>
> The Free Press is happy to be of service to Children's Hospital.
>
> What's wrong with making donations on behalf of our readers to help little children in their improvement and eventual recovery?
>
> In this season ... when men of good faith are rededicating themselves to the teachings of our Creator, we suggest that the hysterical Mr. Booth might try re-reading the Ten Commandments.
>
> If he could generate a little more warmth in his heart and stop acting like a sorehead his distinguished journalistic ancestors, whose name he bears, would think more of him as a publisher and a man.

The exchange drew national attention, and Newsweek magazine devoted more than a page. After explaining the background and presenting Knight's comments, the Newsweek reporter quoted Booth saying, "We did everything possible to keep our stories impersonal. Their personal attack on me is astounding and unintelligent and ridiculous. They must be pretty desperate over at the Free Press." On New Year's Day, the News ran a story with a headline reading, "Ban on Phone Charity Drives Under Consideration by City." Several months later, after public hearings on that question, the proposed ordinance was unanimously brushed aside by the city council which felt the one it had on its book was more than adequate.

The Newsweek story concluded: "With the Free Press strengthening its news staff, the News, boasting a new management team, is set for a hard fight to maintain its present slim circulation leadership. The Times, no mere spectator in the grab for readers, has recently scored several scoops on its evening rival, the News. But the Detroit battle was more than a tussle for scoops. The stake was domination in the field, and somebody was likely to get hurt."

Hills — and a staff whose morale was boosted by Knight's strong editorial — was determined to make certain the Free Press wouldn't be hurt. That the total circulation campaign was effective is reflected by the Free Press' one-year gains of 39,000 compared to about 1,000 each for the News and Times in the March 1954 ABC report. By September 1954, the Free Press had a 13,605 daily lead over the News and 45,600 over the fast-slipping Times. It was the beginning of the surge that carried the Free Press to that moment in March 1960 when it maintained its first year-long lead over the News — which, in turn, led the News to buy and kill the Times.

Hills' strategy, developed in the early '50s to move toward "morning-ness," formed the foundation for the circulation surge of that decade and the next. A major moment of symbolism came June 6, 1966, when Virgil Fassio, then circulation manager, revealed that the "last of 5,000 home-delivered subscribers to the night city edition were transferred to morning delivery."

That crucial decision to go "morning" meant survival. It enabled the Free Press to end a costly dual system that had developed from the days in the early 1930s when it built its evening first-edition strength. Two circulation operations, plus heavy and additional production costs, were required to get papers printed and delivered morning and night. In a time of rapidly rising costs, the old system was sapping the strength of the paper. By solidifying the morning edition, resources became available for what Hills considered of primary importance — the newsroom.

Staff size was gradually increased and so was the space spent on news. The war winding down in Korea and the election campaign of Dwight Eisenhower, who got solid support from the Free Press, were major news stories, as were soon the opening rounds of the school-desegregation story, the Army-McCarthy hearings, Mayor Cobo's administration and the building of the civic center, the city's 250th birthday, the development of the freeways and the continuing story of Michigan's business climate.

The 1954 decision by U.S. Supreme Court banning school segregation was played rather routinely in the news columns, but editorial support was firm:

> ... Human rights, we believe, are not of exclusive state or local concern. They are too fundamental to the well-being of the nation and to the implementation of that philosophy which Thomas Jefferson expounded in the Declaration of Independence ... Had the court ruled other than the way it did, the result would have been to retrograde the steady advance towards full acceptance of the human rights principle.
>
> ... This decision will not be accepted with approval in many parts of the South. Nor will it be put into effect without emotions which will range from honest misgivings to violent anger ... Extreme action now is hardly anticipated and will not occur, even though compliance will be painful. People do not abandon their established way of life and thought just because a judicial decision is signed. But good reason will prevail as it has usually prevailed in the United States, and in time those who regret the decision will look upon it as the wise and decent thing. The South will adjust to it, just as the North over a long period of time also adjusted.
>
> And the world, we believe, will note this decision with approval. For among the millions of oppressed, there must be many who will take new hope that the cherished ideals propounded in America in 1776 are still attainable.

The court decision marked the beginning of a long, sometimes violent fight for equal rights. As Jack Knight wrote in September 1957, after federal troops were sent to Little Rock, Ark., to restore order after attempts to integrate a high school there, "The advocates of reason, education, patience and understanding must and will ultimately prevail but their task has become vastly more difficult since the clash of State versus Federal authority in Arkansas."

The Free Press took a consistent stance on its editorial page critical of Sen. Joseph McCarthy, a man who, it said, "continues to use the tactics which have been developed to a high degree by Communists ... to accuse the enemy of doing what you yourself are doing." But one of its most significant editorial positions was expounded by Knight himself when in a Notebook column May 23, 1954, he criticized the Eisenhower administration's "blustery diplomacy" that had put the country on the verge of intervention in Vietnam. "There was never any moral justification for our proposed intervention in Indochina where the French have been fighting a colonial war for more than seven years," Knight wrote.

He then quoted Sen. Edwin C. Johnson of Colorado: "Whether every one of the 24 million people of Vietnam is a Communist or whether one of them is, is not the question . . . What is to be accomplished by sending 10 American divisions there to make them live as we want them to?"

A couple of weeks later, Knight returned to this theme. With considerable foresight, he said, "The threat of war has not been averted . . . merely postponed." Knight's strong anti-war stance was unvarying, and it was reflected in the editorial policy of the Free Press for years, under the direction of Royce Howes, Mark Ethridge Jr. and Joe Stroud.

By 1955, the groundwork Hills had laid in his first years in Detroit was paying dividends. New presses were in place, and the circulation department had been reorganized and was functioning more effectively. New leadership had been provided in various other departments. It was time now to consolidate the editorial department alignment.

In mid-January 1955, Knight named Hills vice president in addition to his title as executive editor. Hills then named Angelo managing editor and Royce Howes was made an associate editor and put in charge of the editorial writing staff, a function he had been performing since the death of Malcolm Bingay in 1953. About this time Brewster Campbell retired as executive city editor to join former managing editor Doug Martin as a journalism professor at the University of Arizona. Fred Olmsted was moved from the night city desk to become city editor. Olmsted may have been the last of the "old breed" of city editors. He shouted at reporters whose work didn't meet his high standards. Veteran reporters were respectfully wary of his wrath; young reporters were terrified of him. When he was too upset with a reporter to call him by name, he called him "Buster." He terminated unsatisfactory telephone calls by slamming the phone down so hard that it often broke, scattering around the room fragments of what reporters came to call "Western Electric shrapnel."

That management team led the news-editorial departments during the remainder of the decade, with two additions — John Driver, who had joined the paper in 1954, replaced Olmsted as city editor in 1957, and Dorothy Jurney was named women's editor, succeeding B. Dale Davis. Jurney came to Detroit from the Miami Herald where she had gained a national reputation. She was responsible in large measure for changing the look and philosophy of the Free Press women's pages. Davis became feature editor and Olmsted was named auto editor, succeeding Leo Donovan, whose sudden death had shocked the staff, and Olmsted also became head of a new department covering business and financial news.

For Angelo, the appointment was the culmination of a dream that had begun to take shape after his first semester as a reporter for the Northeastern High Review. Angelo was a native of Detroit (born in 1914), grew up on the east side and landed at City College (later Wayne State University) in the middle of the Depression. He had worked for the News as a high school correspondent and maintained that contact thoroughout his college years. In June 1934, after his graduation, he became a part-time copy boy, moved up to a fulltime notch in a few weeks and eventually was a writer and editor in the sports department. In 1941, one week before Pearl Harbor, he joined the Free Press sports staff, managed to stay around for a few months before heading for the Navy and serving in the Pacific as an officer on a destroyer escort.

When he returned in 1945, managing editor Dale Stafford asked him what he wanted to do, and he was quick to tell him, "I want to work on the news-side copy desk because I'm shooting to be managing editor myself someday." Stafford was just as quick to say, "Fine," and to help mightily in the years that followed in providing the opportunities for Angelo to learn. In January 1955, that dream would be fulfilled, and he held the job until April 1971.

The changes were significant for several reasons. For one thing, it clarified roles in the newsroom. For another, relationships between Howes and Angelo were congenial, in contrast to former antagonisms between the editorial writers and the newsroom. In addition, while the paper would continue to develop its tradition of aggressive reporting, Angelo was more a participant in and proponent for the community than an arm's-length sort of editor. He became involved in such organizations as the Urban League, and he would spend many of his evenings at dinners and meetings where his deep sense of wanting to help people achieve goals in education, in solving social problems and in fostering racial understanding were refined.

The paper's slogan, "You See the Friendly Free Press Everywhere," took on great meaning through the efforts and contributions of Hills and Angelo and many others. Those contributions came through clearly in fine, compassionate writing. For instance, there was Jean Sharley, who had joined the paper as a fashion writer in 1950 and produced a steady stream of warm, sensitive stories about people and situations that got good play and excellent reception; she is now a top editor at the Los Angeles Times. Warren Stromberg, a general assignment reporter since coming to Detroit from Chicago in 1932, reported on the problems of ju-

The Free Press newsroom in the 1950s.

Harry Fenton, a fixture at the Free Press, gets a new helmet from Fire Commissioner James Mahon, 1949.

veniles and the elderly and of the mentally retarded. His work led to the convening of a special session of the Legislature that focused private and public attention on mental health.

There were many others, notably Louis Cook, who had come to Detroit from Des Moines with a writing touch that lent a special quality to the Free Press for many years. Cook, a lanky, slow-talking, always thoughtful fellow, was highly regarded not only by readers but by his colleagues. He once watched as a young reporter stared for 15 minutes at his typewriter trying to write the perfect final paragraph to his story. Cook quietly told him: "If you haven't thought of it by this time, you've probably already written it." It was a writing lesson the reporter never forgot.

In keeping with the friendly, personal image it was promoting, the Free Press sponsored a Book Fair for young people and health seminars and seminars for the aging, led by medical writer Jean Pearson; in 1956, the Free Press celebrated its 125th birthday with a series of supplements, focusing on the city and state as well as Michigan industry, most especially on the auto industry. The paper also introduced and sponsored a variety of sports promotions like bowling tournaments and golf and skiing schools. Outdoor writer Jack Van Coevering, who had established the Free Press' conservation coverage in 1931, intensified a campaign to "Save Our Streams" which he had launched in 1947 and would carry on until he retired in 1965.

An important event in building staff morale was the first luncheon, held in 1955, honoring those of long service. There were 249 persons from all departments with 26 years or more of service, led by Eddie Guest, who had 60, and seven others with more than 45 years — Harry Fenton; E. Roy Hatton; Floyd Nixon, art director; William Valentine, pressroom foreman; Stanley Schemanske of circulation; Walter Butler, building manager, and Herbert Collins in the composing room.

Fenton was unique in the city room. His job was never quite defined, but no one really cared because it would have seemed incongruous at the time to have a staff without Fenton on hand. A fire reporter in the early years of the century, he covered his beat then on a bike. One of his early assignments, he recalled, was to call every doctor in the city each July 4 and record the number of persons who had been burned or maimed by fireworks. A half-century later, he still knew the call signals from every fire alarm box in the city. When the fire alarm bell in the newsroom tapped out its code, Harry would shout for all to hear: "Grand River and the Boulevard!" or whatever other location was involved.

It was at this time, too, that the Free Press hired its first black reporter, Collins George. John Dancy, director of the Detroit Urban League, had made the initial approach to the Free Press in behalf of George, who had an outstanding reputation as a reporter on the Pittsburgh Courier. In fact, George had scored a national exclusive when he was the first to report that President Truman was going to desegregate the military services. When word got out that George was joining the staff, Angelo was told some photographers had said they would refuse to go on assignments with him. Angelo made it clear that the first refusal would mean immediate dismissal. There were no refusals, and George soon was one of the more respected and beloved members of the staff. He eventually became the paper's music critic, a post he held until his retirement.

George often laughed about his first introduction to the Free Press news staff. He knew it was an important moment and was predictably uneasy about it. "Lee Hills brought me down from his (fourth floor) office into the (third floor) newsroom. I was determined to make a good impression, but I tripped on the bottom stair and as Hills walked into the newsroom, I stumbled in behind him, struggling to keep from falling. I remember thinking later, 'Well, so much for the light-on-their-feet stereotype.'"

And 1955 was memorable for labor news. The UAW negotiations in 1955 were the ones in which Walter Reuther was making his pitch for the revolutionary Guaranteed Annual Wage (GAW). It was one of the most intensely controversial labor ideas since the UAW had organized the auto industry. Interest was high, not only because of what it meant to the workers but because within the industry itself opinions differed greatly about what to do about the GAW. Hills, caught up in the excitement, returned to the role of reporter. Soon he put together the first of what would be a series of columns that appeared under a standing headline, "A Look Behind the UAW-Auto Curtain," with no byline.

Each day, Hills revealed later, he talked to 18 to 20 people, all of whom supplied bits of information that helped him to give not only some facts about what was happening but also some insights into what it meant to the workers, the companies and the community. His sources covered the range from within the UAW to the top echelons of the companies, particularly Ford and General Motors.

The biggest flap occurred after Ford Motor, as predicted in Hills' column, settled with the UAW on a Supplementary Unemployment Benefits (SUB) plan and it appeared that GM might balk. On

Thursday, June 6, Hills said flatly in his column that there would be no GM strike, and on Saturday afternoon Hills created something of a flurry by appearing at GM headquarters. As he explained later, "Everybody was friendly, and I replied to all those who asked who was doing the 'Curtain' that it's somebody in whom I have great confidence."

It was valuable to the Free Press in several ways. With labor writer Bob Perrin and reporter Ed Winge also providing solid labor coverage during the time the column ran, Free Press circulation rose an average of more than 11,000 daily. The column brought Hills a Pulitzer Prize the following year for what the committee called "aggressive, resourceful and comprehensive coverage." It was the second Pulitzer for Hills who had directed a major expose of Florida crime as executive editor of the Miami Herald in 1949. For Hills, the Pulitzer was, of course, an outstanding personal achievement; yet he appreciated almost as much a call from Jim Trainor, legendary city editor of the Times, congratulating him on his "beat" on the GM no-strike story.

Angelo worked closely with Hills, handling much of the editing, but as he wrote after Hills won the Pulitzer, "Hills literally lived in his fourth-floor office at the Free Press for a week at a time. He sent home for clean clothes; sent out for meals and razor blades. No one but Lee knows how much sleep he actually got. He was up before the morning crew came to work, and he was still at it — on the phone and at the typewriter — when the night staff went home in the wee hours."

For the Free Press, it was the fourth Pulitzer, the third having been announced just a few days before Hills completed work on his own effort. The 1955 award went to Royce Howes for his editorial on an unauthorized strike at Chrysler in July 1954. Howes' editorial analyzed the responsibility of the UAW and the management for a walkout that put 45,000 workers on the street. The full-page editorial also emphasized one aspect of the paper's policy when it said, after discussing the reasons for the strike:

> What troubles us most gravely is the long-range, long-term damage to Detroit as a place to prosper, whether you are a production worker, a management man or merchant. Accumulatively, affairs such as last week's strike hurt Detroit's reputation. And when its reputation goes, hope of an ever-building prosperity goes with it.

The Pulitzer committee said the editorial made "a notable contribution to the public understanding of the respective responsibilities of labor and management in this field."

For Howes, who had joined the Free Press Nov. 2, 1927, as the first person to be assigned exclusively to rewrite, it was a climactic point. He had served as city editor twice and had been in charge of the vast Army News Service as a colonel in World War II. He had written several books, had been a military analyst for the Free Press, a journalism teacher. Howes was named editorial director in 1961; he retired in 1965 and was succeeded by Mark Ethridge Jr., who had joined the Free Press as an editorial writer in 1960. Ethridge served during a particularly trying period — when the Vietnam war and a social revolution were dividing the country. Ethridge, a graduate of Princeton, was editor of the Newsday editorial page when that paper won a Pulitzer in 1953 for meritorious public service, and had also been editor of the Raleigh Times before coming to Detroit. He left the Free Press in 1973 to become editor of the Akron Beacon Journal.

Before long, the Free Press was involved in a labor story of its own — a strike which shut down all three Detroit newspapers for the first time in their history. It began at 4:30 a.m. on Dec. 1, 1955. It lasted 47 days. It involved, at the start, only 116 stereotype employees out of about 4,500 total employees on the Free Press, News and Times payrolls. Ostensibly, the dispute involved working conditions and a demand for extra manpower to handle color plates, but this relatively simple issue masked a more profound problem which management had spelled out but which the 14 unions with which it dealt tended to discount.

As had been signaled by Jack Knight's strong statement in the 1948 negotiations when he accused the other papers of "having pulled out the rug" from under his determined stand, a posture of firmness with fairness had emerged among the publishers; Hills played a strong role in insisting on that stance. A Publishers' Association was made stronger at Hills' urging, and by 1955 Robert C. Butz was the executive secretary. Butz would be the spokesman for all the papers in the negotiations in which management insisted "it was time to regain some management rights that had gone either by default and had been gradually usurped by the unions or had been incorporated in some union-management agreements."

Primarily, as one private report later suggested, "it was time (for management) to insist on running its business mainly in the hiring and firing procedures, posting of work schedules, work assignments and such activity . . . (because) high overtime and other undesirable practices were quite prevalent."

The basic problem was spelled out publicly by the News in a 1962 editorial after a fourth strike hit the papers. "It should be made clear that we do not claim that the present situation (the 1962 strike) is the sole fault of our unionized employees or their leaders," said the News. "Publishers generally have permitted the bad situation to grow.

"In other days of wider profit margins, they accepted any alternative as better than an interruption of regular publication. They permitted gross featherbedding practices. They winked at (some say colluded in) such Taft-Hartley violations as continuation of the closed shop and contracts requiring that foremen be union members, subject to discipline by subordinates.

"Assessment of the blame, however, is immaterial. More important is the collision course being steered . . . The answer must be found between management and its unionized workers. We want such an answer, will go a long way to find it. We hope that the public will understand our efforts, that our employees will join us in them."

It would take a few more strikes — authorized and unauthorized — before some issues were largely resolved. The longest, and climactic, strike came in 1967-68, and there would not be another until 1980. That lasted a dozen days, and was particularly dramatic because it came at a time when the Free Press was about to display the results of its year-long planning to cover the Republican National Convention in Detroit.

But 15 years earlier, in 1955, talk of a strike had been discounted by most observers. As the strike deadline approached, Butz said George Robinson, president of the stereotypers union, had told him there would be a strike even though they had agreed to another negotiating session at 12:30 a.m. Robinson, who was finally located by Free Press reporter Riley Murray in a bar just before midnight, claimed he had simply said there would be a strike if no agreement was reached at the proposed 12:30 a.m. session, which was never held. The Free Press story on the strike the next morning was the first word that anyone in town had that there might be a shutdown. It began at 4:30 a.m. that morning, Dec. 1, and before it was over on Jan. 17, 1956, it had become up to then the longest newspaper strike to close down all of a city's newspapers.

The strike jolted the papers, their employees and the community. It had come amid the heaviest advertising period for newspapers and heaviest merchandising effort by retailers. Later, the Bureau of Business Research at Michigan State University estimated the strike cost Detroit merchants $35 million. The papers joined to set up what amounted to a news bureau at the Fort Shelby Hotel. Staffed by supervisory personnel, the bureau issued one-page news summaries to be distributed around town and particularly to keep other media informed about the strike. Guild employees, with support from other unions, produced a strike paper called "The Detroit Reporter," which started as a four-page tabloid, grew to 20 pages and circulated about 120,000 copies daily. Detroit's Polish Daily News quickly added a section in English and increased its circulation from 40,000 to about 150,000. Out-of-town papers flooded the city and sold for up to $1 a copy. Traffic jams were created in downtown Detroit on the Sunday after the strike started by people seeking newsstands to buy out-of-town papers.

Employees suddenly put out of work managed to adapt, as a Reporter story by Charles Weber, then City Hall bureau chief for the Free Press, pointed out. "Members of the Guild scurried off in many fields to get temporary jobs that would allow them to eat and at the same time carry on 'the work of the soul,' for the Guild and The Detroit Reporter . . . 300 got such jobs or are working on the Reporter . . . a few landed better jobs . . . permanently . . . but then there was a reporter who had been on the City-County beat who turned up as a temporary building guard, one reporter who became a men's clothing salesman at Saks, and a couple who got corners on downtown streets to sell newspapers." Reporters Herb Levitt and Neal Shine went to the city Parks & Recreation Department to find jobs. Levitt got a job as a play leader in a recreation center, and Shine became a guard at a city ice rink, neglecting to tell his new employer that he could not skate. Levitt later became regional administrator of the State Court Administrative Office, and Shine became Free Press managing editor.

The strike, which had started with the stereotypers demanding changes in the number of people to perform jobs, eventually spread to include the mailers and the printers. Woodruff Randolph, president of the International Typographical Union, came to Detroit to help resolve the situation. A $3.75-a-week offer for the first year of a two-year contract and $2.75 for the second year finally ended the strike without the major changes the stereotypers had sought and with some gains by management.

While the strike was on, several Free Press editors managed to maintain complete files of what was happening in Detroit and around the world. When the paper finally reappeared, a package including complete summaries of the news and a 20-page section with a complete rundown on all the comics was included. It was an impressive product, but it was not repeated after later strikes, when the philosophy became, "Let's get on with it."

A Free Press editorial said: " . . . We aren't mad at anybody . . . We're too confident of our future to rankle about bygones. And we think our employees — strikers and non-strikers — feel the same way.

" . . . Management felt that it had no choice but to be very firm . . . and also to be patient. Among the demands were some which could not be met without jeopardizing progress and the long-term welfare of both the papers and those who look to them for their livelihood. But neither firmness nor rhetoric calls for rancor.

"Newspapers are hotly competitive. They meet some rugged competition from other media. To succeed they must advance technologically . . . (Our) wage rates are among the highest . . . but . . . high wages and other benefits are only as good and as guaranteed as the economic health of the papers. A profitless one gives as little milk as a dry cow."

The Free Press and the News rebounded strongly, but the strike proved to be a blow to the Times, which fell far short of regaining its lost subscribers; its circulation continued to slip. During the next 12 years, Detroit's newspapers missed almost two full years of publication because of strikes. Four of them are especially noteworthy for what they may have meant to the city — and, of course, the papers themselves.

On Saturday, Aug. 17, 1957, an unexpected strike at the News occurred when 67 mailers were suspended for refusing to work about one hour of scheduled overtime. Involved, however, was a battle for recognition between two rival mailer groups, one supported by the Teamsters. The Teamster-supported group called the strike, and Teamster truck drivers refused to cross the picket line, forcing a shutdown. Ironically (some suggested a real connection) Teamster boss James R. Hoffa was boarding a plane for Washington almost at the moment the strike began. He was due to testify the following week before the Senate committee investigating labor racketeering.

Efforts that Saturday to get Hoffa to intercede in the strike proved futile. The Free Press and Times agreed to print double-masthead newspapers in their final Sunday editions that Saturday night. Free Press and Times Teamsters refused to handle the papers, as was anticipated, and a citywide strike was on. But no one was laid off, and efforts to settle matters were intensified. Ken McCormick, who knew

Hoffa well, tried repeatedly to reach him but was told Hoffa was "working with his attorneys on testimony." Finally, on Friday, with his testimony completed, Hoffa rushed back to Detroit and dramatically swept into the Publishers' Association office in the Book Building, and within hours a settlement was reached. Sunday papers were published the next day. But Detroiters, limited to the brief segments on television and radio news shows, never got the full story of Hoffa's testimony which most certainly would have appeared in the three newspapers in detail during that week.

A strike hit the Free Press in 1958 when pressmen walked out because of the firing of a union officer for countermanding an order from the pressroom foreman. That firing was later settled by arbitration, but the three-day strike ended with the Free Press taking over from the union the responsibility for hiring and scheduling pressmen.

In 1962, another Teamster strike, this one over economic issues in a new contract, shut the Free Press and News for 29 days. During that time, a city income tax which Mayor Jerome Cavanagh had been urging to help solve the city's financial problems, was adopted.

In 1964, the pressmen and publishers became involved in a battle over manning that led to a 134-day strike that shut out newspaper coverage of the 1964 presidential election. That strike also brought out some intensive public reaction, with civic leaders eventually stepping into the negotiations.

The record set in 1964 was shattered by a strike that began in November 1967, when the Teamsters struck the News just when Detroit was beginning to shake the trauma of the July riot. It became a bitter one, closing down the Free Press as well as the News, and lasted until August 1968.

In testimony he gave in March 1968, before a state legislative committee investigating the strike, Lee Hills said: "The Detroit newspapers, their employees and the public are once again the unfortunate victims of whipsaw tactics which cannot be justified and cannot succeed." He maintained that the newspapers had suspended publication because "unions, who have joint agreements with the News and the Free Press, refused to cross the Teamsters' picket lines . . . (in) violation of the contracts they had signed with both papers." Hills added that for the Free Press to have published under such circumstances "would have conceded that any one of the 14 unions we bargain with could arbitrarily decide which newspaper would publish and which would not."

Hills defended the right to shut down, pointing to court opinions. He decried the fact that the city was being deprived of much needed coverage at a "time of crisis." He also told legislators that some were implying, shabbily so, that "we somehow like a strike, for financial reasons" because of the insurance policies held by the newspapers. He said that amounted to only $10,000 a day for 50 days and compared it to union strike funds.

Then Hills went to the nub of the controversy: "Another complicating factor is that our own productivity is shackled by artificial restrictions that make it impossible for us to make the best use of the great improvements in technology which are now available to the industry . . . Newspapers suffer by comparison with productivity gains in most other industries."

The strikes, not unexpectedly but unfortunately, affected staff morale and longevity. Their frequency became a factor in people's judgments about whether they wanted to work in Detroit. Yet the effort to build a finer, bigger staff continued unabated.

One thing editors learned was how deeply readers were attached to their newspapers. Jimmy Pooler's post-strike story in 1956 quoted one reader as saying, "It's like eating . . . you were left hungry" without a paper. And Angelo recalled the day a frantic reader came into his office asking, "Haven't you some old newspapers I can read?" The visitor got a couple of old ones and left beaming.

The following year, 1957, John Driver became city editor. A demanding but sensitive relative newcomer, he won the respect of the staff with his writing, reporting and keen mind. Driver played a key part in keeping things moving late in 1959 and through 1960 as Angelo suffered heart problems and was out for much of a year. Driver served as city editor until his death at 46 of cancer in 1961.

There was another Driver in a Free Press seat those years. John's wife, Morley, wrote the paper's weekly art column. Her perceptive, gentle but firm critical statements about what was happening at the Detroit Institute of Arts helped to open the DIA to greater public participation. On the last day of 1961, her column noted that "Mayor Cavanagh has a lot of problems but I hope he will take time out for our museum. I hope, too, that he knows that he will not get the 'story' of the museum from those so firmly entrenched in it." It was during Cavanagh's administration that expansion plans for the museum got underway; by the following decade, the DIA was established as one of the country's best art museums.

Morley Driver stimulated Hills' interest in art. In turn, Hills significantly contributed to art in Detroit by serving as president of the Detroit Arts Commission for more than 14 years, longer than any other president in the museum's history (which, incidentally, was established in 1883 with James Scripps of the News providing a major impetus).

If the '50s had been a decade of dramatic change for the Free Press, and for the competitive situation among Detroit newspapers, it soon became apparent that the '60s would test its strength. The social and political trends that had been only dimly perceived in the '50s began to build to full flood and would demand growing attention. A key figure arrived at the Free Press. After John Driver's death in 1961, Derick J. Daniels, who had been executive city editor of the Miami Herald, another Knight paper, became city editor. Daniels, a member of a prominent North Carolina newspaper family, made a significant mark on the paper over the next 16 years as city editor and later as executive editor and finally as vice president for news for Knight-Ridder Newspapers.

If the '60s will be remembered as a decade of revolution throughout the country, the decade also must be remembered as one that revolutionized newspapering, too. Major newspapers came to grips with television and a new world of mobility and communication. The Free Press built on its reputation for being aware of reader concerns and of the influence of the times on reading. Under Daniels, the Free Press became a leader in the journalism of service, variety and new ideas. Daniels, however, believed in the newspaper as a complex assortment of offerings overlaid on a base of exciting, aggressive newsgathering. The paper's coverage of the 1967 Detroit riots is a good example of this. Daniels also believed in packaging the assortment. His favorite slogan was: "A place for everything, and everything in its place." Like Lee Hills, he wanted the newspaper well organized, with features easy to find, stories easy to read. One of Daniels' improvements came with his attention to the financial pages, with David Smith of the Wall Street Journal being hired as business editor.

In the late 1960s, the Free Press re-established a Feature Page anchored by columnist Bob Talbert. Talbert was hired by Daniels and Mort Persky, the Sunday editor, with a strong assist from Persky's mother. She had been sending copies of Talbert's column, which was then appearing in the Columbia (S.C.) State, to Persky, urging him to hire Talbert for the Free Press. Persky was a leader in innovation during those Free Press years. And Talbert's success with the readers grew out of his personal-journalism approach, a long-standing tradition at the Free Press.

Persky was a quiet, witty intellectual who established broader-scale entertainment coverage, started the first full book page and introduced Detroit Magazine to Free Press readers. Before Persky, the Free Press, like all American papers with the exception of the New York Herald Tribune, published a traditional picture-story rotogravure magazine. Persky gave Detroit Magazine a distinctive approach, from the cover to the inside content and layout. It displayed an unabashed love of the urban scene — certainly a new approach in a tough, shirt-sleeves town like Detroit.

The women's section of the time was directed by one of the industry's top innovators — Dorothy Jurney. She furnished basic coverage of such subjects as fashion, food, home decorating and child care and covered them with a professionalism that was not then a hallmark of women's departments at many newspapers. And she added hard reporting on social trends, community activities and behavior problems.

The ascendance of John F. Kennedy, whose election was the big story on the day the Free Press launched the Family Edition as a challenge to the News' purchase of the Times, would help set the tone for the early years of the '60s. In addition to intensive coverage of the development of his administration, a number of series about Kennedy and his family were presented. There seemed no end to the public interest generated by his election, particularly when he quickly faced up to the October 1962 crisis in our relations with Cuba and the USSR.

The Free Press had supported Vice President Richard Nixon because, as Jack Knight explained in his Notebook, "Nixon stands for the kind of America which jeopardizes neither our society nor our freedom." It was a theme which Knight had been striking for years in addition to his constant concern about the maintenance of peace in the world.

In the final weeks of 1960, a series of brutal, unrelated murders created an atmosphere of panic in Detroit that led Mayor Louis Miriani and Police Comissioner Herbert Hart to announce a dramatic crackdown on crime. The Free Press had been reporting in detail on the slayings (four in a few days), on the crackdown which led to 1,165 arrests in a week, and on the protests that followed from church and

John F. Kennedy's election reported in the Free Press Nov. 9, 1960.

John F. Kennedy's assassination reported in the Free Press Nov. 23, 1963.

NAACP leaders who charged that the effort was directed at the black community.

Editorially, the Free Press supported Miriani, saying: "The police campaign is not directed against individuals simply because of their color or race. It is, as the mayor pointed out, a program of crime prevention to protect life and property of all citizens. It was not put into effect simply because an emergency existed, and it should be continued as long as it is necessary."

While the Free Press news coverage had been sensitive in reporting the reaction of leaders, it failed to present as thoroughly as it should have the police actions, particularly indiscriminate street searches, fostering a deep resentment in the black community. Those resentments exploded into impressive action the following November when the almost unanimous vote of the black community for a relatively unknown Jerry Cavanagh helped to sweep Miriani from office. From an historical perspective, the police crackdown was a critical turning point in the story of race relations in Detroit. It revealed the true dimensions of the latent political power residing in the black community. It was not latent thereafter.

The Free Press supported Miriani strongly in the election, charging Cavanagh with making "claims and promises both demagogic and ridiculous." It took note of Miriani's fiscal responsibility, his efforts in creating a fine water system, and for continuing progress in developing a civic center, and then added: "Like many Northern industrial cities, Detroit has been going through a difficult period of social adjustment. Our problem in this respect is no greater or worse than that of our sister cities.

"Utopia may not have been reached yet in Detroit but on the whole our citizens of all classes, creeds and colors have made considerable advances in community relations.

"Wise leadership, fairness and resistance to pressure when it would have been harmful have characterized Mr. Miriani's administration."

A few days later, the Free Press was saying: "We hope that Cavanagh is as good as his word, which in his victory statement were good indeed when he said: 'It is not a time for winners in a hard-fought campaign to forget that the campaign will have been in vain if we do not work hard to carry out the ideas expressed for the benefit of the entire community.'" Cavanagh's victory was such a stunning upset that even the news staff had let its guard down. On election night a Free Press reporter spent much of the evening on the phone frantically trying to get enough information — including the names of the mayor-elect's children — to do a profile on him.

Cavanagh's administration proved to be innovative and sensitive to the developing aspirations and ideas of the black community. And he won its confidence with one move: his selection of a new police commissioner. That choice, of course, was anxiously awaited, and the Free Press was able to get it exclusively, thanks to a tip to Angelo. Tommy McIntyre, a former Detroit News reporter, was one of the first people to join the Cavanagh campaign and had helped with press relations and in opening doors for Cavanagh to the black community. After a month of stories speculating on the selection, Angelo called his friend McIntyre and the next day, after ducking all questions during lunch, McIntyre stuck out his hand as they were leaving, slipped Angelo a piece of paper which turned out to have two words written on it: "George Edwards." It was a surprise since Edwards was a State Supreme Court justice. The next morning, after confirming the information, the Free Press broke the story.

In November 1960, the voters approved the calling of a Constitutional Convention in Michigan, the first since 1908. The Free Press had strongly backed such a move on its editorial page and now, with Jim Robinson heading its Lansing Bureau, it was prepared to provide intensive news coverage. Romney seized on the convention as a vehicle for his next political move. He was elected a delegate, as was Coleman Young, who was moving into a leadership role in the Legislature as a representative from Detroit's east side. It was a long and sometimes bitter convention, with Democrats battling Republicans over many issues and the Republicans battling among themselves over others. Finally, the major break came when Republican conservatives and Romney agreed to compromise during a secret all-day meeting. Robinson managed to get all the details and filed them about 7 p.m., just in time to make the deadline for the Free Press' state edition. The headline said Romney had made "a deal" that produced a new constitution. Romney, infuriated by the suggestion that he had been involved in "a deal," was only slightly placated after meeting with Free Press editors. The story was precisely right. A few days later, the convention adopted a constitution which was passed by the voters, indicating Romney's viability as a political candidate. Romney ran successfully for governor, strongly backed by the Free Press in his race against incumbent Democrat John Swainson.

Newspapers are tested in the way they handle big stories, and none was bigger than the assassination of President Kennedy in 1963. As the flash came on the wire machines shortly after 1 p.m. — "Kennedy shot . . . perhaps fatally" — editors put aside personal reactions to get on with covering the story.

Ann Voss, who had served two managing editors as secretary, got hold of Angelo and Bill Sudomier, the city editor, at lunch at the Sheraton Cadillac. They rushed back to meet with Derick Daniels, assistant managing editor then, to plan the first edition. On a story of this magnitude, teamwork develops automatically — in the newsroom, composing room, pressroom, circulation department. And in the frantic atmosphere of getting the story and meeting the deadline, journalists show their character. Amid that tension-filled afternoon, Art Dorazio, who had been news editor for several years before leaving to teach at Wayne State, walked into the newsroom and said simply, "I knew you'd need some help." He was quickly put to work.

Tommy Blower, the composing room foreman, brought in extra printers immediately. Bill Coddington negotiated with the pressmen for an early starting time. General Manager Henry Weidler made as much news space available as needed. The press run started at 6:03 p.m. (instead of the usual 7 p.m.) Before the night was over, 221,000 more papers than usual had been printed, the largest press run in the Free Press' history. In the days and weeks that followed, Gene Roberts, who had been with the paper only a few months and was its labor editor, provided some outstanding coverage from Dallas. Roberts later became city editor of the Free Press and executive editor of the Philadelphia Inquirer.

During this period, Hills was finding his work with Knight newspapers expanding as the Charlotte Observer and later the Charlotte News were added to the group. The trend to public ownership of newspapers was becoming apparent. It seemed likely Knight would move in that direction, with Hills playing a major role. To provide more help for the Free Press because Hills' attention was being diverted, Hills brought Allen Neuharth from Miami in 1960 to become assistant executive editor. Neuharth assumed the liaison role between Hills and department heads, with Angelo managing the newsroom and Royce Howes in charge of the editorial page. Neuharth stayed until 1963, when he left for the Gannett newspaper chain, where he later became chairman and chief executive officer. At Neuharth's departure, Daniels was given broader assignments by Hills, first as assistant managing editor for news. At the same time B. Dale Davis was named assistant managing editor for features, and Bill Sudomier, who had been with the paper for 19 years, was named city editor.

In the years that followed, while Angelo remained as managing editor, Daniels orchestrated a series of changes as he rose to the executive editorship. Key people in these moves included Neal Shine, who became city editor in 1965, replacing Gene Roberts who had, a year earlier, succeeded Sudomier. Shine's career at the Free Press started in 1950 as a copy boy, advancing to reporter, then to the city desk, then managing editor in 1971. Also involved were Kurt Luedtke, a bright, talented young newsman who had worked as a reporter with the Grand Rapids Press and Miami Herald before coming to the Free Press in 1965, and Persky, the imaginative, innovative editor who ran much of the Sunday and feature efforts at the Free Press. As an assistant city editor, Luedtke was responsible in large measure for the day-to-day coverage of the 1967 Detroit riot. He edited and helped write the massive Free Press effort in investigating each of the 43 deaths in the riot.

Daniels was the son of two prominent Washington, D.C., doctors, and the grandson of famed Josephus Daniels, founder of the News & Observer in Raleigh, N.C., and Navy secretary in the Woodrow Wilson administration. It was Derick Daniels who established Action Line, the feature with the greatest circulation impact of any ever developed at the Free Press. The idea was not new, having been tried in Houston with notable success, but Action Line at the Free Press became the model for all such columns with its irreverent style and its ability to get the problem solved, regardless of difficulty. It was introduced in the Free Press Jan. 12, 1966, with a Page One story under this headline: "Got a Problem? A Question? You make the Call — We'll Get the Action." The story's lead read:

> If you think you can't fight city hall ...
> If you're mad at your neighbor, or your tailor or your school board ...
> If you're curious about soap, or Soapy, or sunspots ...
> Or if you just think something's wrong and want it straightened out ...
> Dial the Action Line ...

They dialed and dialed and dialed until Michigan Bell was forced to

Kurt Luedtke, left foreground, the first Action Line writer when it was started in 1966, later became executive editor. (Photo by Ed Haun)

Action Line introduced with an invitation to call in problems, Jan. 12, 1966. The first column appeared two days later.

shut Action Line down for a few hours that first day because the volume
of calls was fouling up service in the entire downtown area. The first column appeared two days later, Jan. 14. Daniels believed if the column
was going to work, it would have to have a number of things that similar
features on other papers did not have. It would have to have its own staff
with no responsibilities other than Action Line, its own work area, and a
good writer. The first writer was Kurt Luedtke, who set a writing tone
that is still used in the column.

Nothing like this had ever hit the city. Within days, Action Line
became the password around Detroit. On the floor of the Legislature, an
angry legislator said that if he couldn't get the Legislature to act on his
suggestion, then he'd get Action Line to do it. The increases could be
traced to more factors than Action Line, but Free Press circulation
soared from 510,221 in March 1966, just after the column was started,
to 537,302 by September 1966 and 600,803 in March 1968. In fact, in
the week following the introduction of the column, circulation had
jumped 10,000. The gap between the News and the Free Press, which
was more than 200,000 after the News bought the Times, was cut to
100,000, and the News paid the Free Press the ultimate tribute when in
1968 it, too, started its own version of Action Line.

On Sept. 7, 1969, in a signed column on Page One, Angelo saluted the
fact that Action Line had received its one-millionth telephone call:

> You have come up with an infinite number of ways to test
> our promise to "solve problems, get answers, cut red tape, and
> stand up for your rights."
>
> The barber who suddenly developed an allergy to human
> hair has successfully launched a new drapery handling career.
> The young parents who lost the ID tags of their identical twin
> babies had fingerprint experts to figure out who was Terry and
> who was Tracy.
>
> You've sent Action Line to Fiji (to find actor Raymond
> Burr, whose art gallery owed Detroit artist Richard Kozlow
> $800 for two paintings) and Vietnam (to fetch GIs home for
> weddings and funerals) and to Tiger Stadium (to force a price
> rollback by parking lot gougers for the World Series) ...

He wound up the column with a comment from a reader's letter:

> I don't want anything. I don't even have any problems for
> you to solve. I just think you're the most wonderful group of
> people I've ever known, and by reading Action Line every day, I
> feel I do know you. It's an awfully good feeling to know that if

you ever need help, you'd be here for me as you have been for so
many others. I'm sure I speak for all of them when I say —
"Thank you, Action Line, for caring . . . "

Action Line remained a fixture on Page One until 1980, when it was
moved to a new anchored position on the last inside page of the A section.
In 1966, Daniels' original plan had been to run Action Line on Page One
for 90 days and then move it to Page Three. The unexpected and
overwhelming success of the column kept it on the front page nearly 15
years longer than planned.

The Action Line impact came at a propitious moment, since the Free
Press was just beginning to pull out of a slump that followed the 134-day
strike of 1964-65. The momentum continued to build until after the city
was devastated by a riot and before the paper itself was traumatized by a
record nine-month strike. In that interim, it recorded a daily circulation
average of slightly more than 600,000.

Through the mid-'60s the Free Press had given intensive coverage to
the Vietnam war with on-the-spot reports at various times from Jack
Knight, Mark Ethridge Jr. and Van Sauter, who became president of
CBS Sports. The Free Press was, in the early and mid-1960s, a leading
American newspaper in speaking out on the social, economic and
political problems of the day. It reported in detail on the changing mood
on American campuses, the emergence of the New Left, on hunger and
poverty in Detroit, on the poor, on the inequities of the draft in the
Detroit area and the growth of the civil rights movement in the South.
Sauter covered the Freedom Rides, the sit-ins and the voter registration
drives in the South, events that foretold what was to come in Detroit and
other Northern cities.

By 1967, Mayor Cavanagh had begun to speak ominously of growing
racial tension in Detroit; in June, a Free Press series helped to point up
the problems by showing the wide disparity of prices and quality in
grocery stores in the predominantly black areas compared to stores in
other areas. Then on Sunday morning, July 23, the worst happened. A
police raid and some bottle- and rock-throwing that followed triggered a
massive riot that left the city with 43 dead, millions in property damage
and untold scars in social injuries.

It started at 3:50 a.m. when police broke into an after-hours drinking
spot at Twelfth and Clairmount. At 4:45 a.m., when police were
preparing to pull away with the last of those they had arrested for
drinking illegally in that "blind pig," the first bottles and rocks began

flying from among a crowd gathered across the street. Within minutes, people who had been good-naturedly joshing police and those being arrested began to move down Twelfth, still throwing things, and the riot was underway. By 6:30 a.m., the first fire broke out; shortly after, Damon Keith, then co-chairman of the Michigan Civil Rights Commission and later a U.S. District judge, was calling newspapers and radio and television stations, pleading for a blackout on what was happening. The request was honored with the exception of a radio talk show which some listeners called to ask what was going on.

In the case of the Free Press, the request was academic since there would be no newspapers printed in the city until its first edition at 7 p.m. John "Red" Griffith, who covered police, reported to work as usual at 8:30 a.m., and reached Wayne King, assistant city editor, as he walked in at his normal 9 a.m. starting time. Reporter Bill Serrin and photographer Ira Rosenberg were sent to the scene. About 11 a.m. Serrin called and was saying, "Wayne, there's a riot going on out here," when a brick was thrown through the window of the store from which he was calling. King moved quickly to bolster the normally slim Sunday staff, the first call going to the late Jim Dewey, a superb rewrite man who would spend the next four days and four nights writing the lead stories during this crisis. Serrin became an early casualty when a flying bottle opened a deep gash in his head. By noon most of the staff had been mobilized for an effort that would be capped months later with the award of a Pulitzer Prize to the Free Press for its coverage.

The showcase piece was a massive investigation into each riot-caused death and was called "The 43 Who Died." It was written by Gene Goltz, Barbara Stanton and Serrin and edited by Luedtke, who also wrote the lead piece for the 24,000-word report. But it was Serrin who had to convince his editors that it was a story that needed to be done. The editors were reluctant to investigate each of the 43 deaths, feeling that the task was too massive an undertaking. Serrin prevailed, and the story stands as one of the paper's most important efforts. It was Serrin, incidentally, who had earlier written that the Michigan National Guard was probably ill-equipped to deal with any major civil disorder. The story appeared in the Free Press of Sunday, July 23, the day the riot started. The National Guard proved the validity of Serrin's story in the days to come.

There were scores of highlights in the coverage and writing of the riot story which, from the perspective of time, must be considered one of the finest overall performances by any newspaper staff anywhere on any story. The outstanding — often brilliant — writing, editing and reporting helped to keep the story in perspective from the moment it began until the day in November when a strike would preclude further efforts for nine months.

Notably there was the investigation of the Algiers Motel deaths on July 31 that included stories by Luedtke and Stanton and a dramatic sketch by Dick Mayer, the art director. In that case, three young men had been killed in a Woodward motel by police who claimed the men were snipers. An initial investigation by Stanton raised questions about the police claim, and the Free Press began a full investigation. Unsatisfied with official autopsy reports, the paper hired a forensic pathologist and got permission of the families for the doctor to do post-mortem examinations on the victims. The family of one victim delayed his funeral so that the examination could be done. Those examinations showed all three victims were shot at close range with shotguns carrying a "riot load" of buckshot. Three police officers were later indicted for murder but were not convicted.

Another unusual effort was put together by Phil Meyer, of the paper's Washington Bureau, who completed a survey — in cooperation with the Urban League — published less than a month after the riot started. It gave the first and most thorough look at the causes of and re-actions to the riot. One finding of particular interest to journalists, who have always been concerned about being asked to conceal word of a developing riot or any news event, was that more than 50 percent of the people first heard about the riot through a call by neighbors or friends.

Scores of stories deserve mention, among them Gary Blonston's analysis of "How Detroit's Militants Are Changing;" George Walker's story on "The Horror of Violence and Its Trembling Victims;" Susan Holmes Watson's look at a ravaged neighborhood; and the coverage of breaking events by Tom Delisle, Jim Mudge, Griffith, Bob DeWolfe, Jerry Hansen, David Dolson, Larue Heard, Bill Panill, Tom Shawver, Ralph Nelson, Saul Friedman, to name only a few. The photographic staff, led by Tony Spina, Jerry Heiman, Dick Tripp and Rosenberg, produced scores of photos. But a major key to the effort was the co-ordi-nation of all this activity through a series of daily meetings among Daniels, Angelo, City Editor Neal Shine, Assistant City Editors Kurt Luedtke and Tom Wark, Mort Persky, and Walt Pierre, Vincent "Tick" Klock, Joe Miller and Bob McKelvey of the news desk, and the ever-pre-sent and irrepressible Charlie Haun, picture editor. During the first four days, 25 to 40 columns a day were used for pictures, in addition to space allocated for stories. Editorially, Ethridge summed up the situation in his perceptive commentary on the Free Press-Urban League survey when he wrote:

> Our analysis indicates what some observers have been saying all along. This is that the riots sweeping the nation's cities are rooted in deep frustrations but have many similarities to a revolution of rising expectations. Younger Negroes seeing success all about them want it faster than they've been getting it. These are Northern Negroes, native Detroiters, alienated to some extent from both Negroes and whites whom they consider to have made it.
>
> There is an undeniable racial overlay to Detroit's riot, but more than race, class was involved. The rioters come from an under-class.
>
> This does not mean that Detroit has failed its Negro citizens altogether. It means that the city has failed them to some extent. It means that while a large number of Negroes do have a stake in our society, there are others who don't and who consider present channels for advancement too narrow.
>
> And the course of action, while tremendously difficult, becomes abundantly clear. The frustrated and the disenchanted must be given new hope.
>
> This means that education is important but education alone is not the answer. This means that jobs are important, but income levels alone didn't prove the crucial factor. This means that far more must be done across a broad range of activities and that a largely integrated society must become a wholly integrated society.
>
> This means, at bottom, that if the attitudes of alienated young Negroes are to change, the attitudes of the rest of society must change.

There were lighter moments, even in the dark tragedy of the riots. City Editor Shine managed to borrow an armored military vehicle from the Chrysler Corp., and Free Press reporters ranged the streets during the closing days of the riot in comparative safety. Police Commissioner Ray Girardin had requested that the tank-like vehicle be marked with the paper's name so it would not be mistaken for a military vehicle. Months after the riot, people were still calling the paper with statements like: "My wife tells me that she saw a tank on the streets during the riot with 'Detroit Free Press' on the side and I told her she's crazy. Am I right?" After the riot ended, Free Press reporters drove the vehicle down Lafayette and pulled it up on the sidewalk outside the Detroit News building. Using a loudspeaker, the people inside the armored car demanded that Martin Hayden, editor of the News, be sent out as a hostage. While the News people watched in amusement from the windows and a curious crowd gathered outside, the only person to come out of the News was a photographer who took one picture of the car and quickly disappeared back inside the building.

With the effects of the riot still far from resolved, a new crisis developed for the Free Press as negotiations for a contract between the publishers and their unions hit a snag in November 1967. It would be nine months before this one was settled. During the strike Daniels and Angelo spent much of their time keeping in touch with staff members, some of whom had been placed on other papers, and with planning ahead.

When publication resumed in August 1968, the Free Press, as it had at another dark moment in the '30s, got a big helping hand from the Detroit Tigers, who were in the midst of a drive for pennant — with colorful Denny McLain setting pitching records. It was a summer full of good stories — for newspaper people, a good story is not necessarily the same as good news — among them, the dramatic and violent Democratic National Convention in Chicago, the presidential race between Hubert Humphrey and Richard Nixon, the continuing war in Vietnam. These events provided a major boost in helping to rebuild a staff that had not had a paper for nine months. But it would be almost five years before the Free Press would regain the circulation it lost. The News, which had been at a level slightly above 700,000 before the strike, was still far from that mark a decade later.

Thus the two papers headed into the '70s with the Free Press facing still more changes, climaxed by the opening of a new $50 million production plant in 1979 that finally would help complete Lee Hills' effort begun in the '50s to make the Free Press an all-out morning newspaper.

"The type originated in a new electronic text editing system, where reporters and editors worked at video display terminals instead of typewriters." (Photo by David C. Turnley)

Chapter Eight

The '70s . . . and Beyond

Chapter 8

On a bright, breezy day in September 1979, Lee Hills stood before about 400 people gathered outside the new Free Press production plant on the riverfront in downtown Detroit to participate in a ritual of dedication. But it was more than that.

In a very real sense, as Hills spoke of the challenge of the future that would be met with the impressive technology of this new $50-million project, there was also an affirmation of the vision of the Sheldons, the McKnights, the Baggs, the Storeys, the Walkers, the Quinbys, the Stairs, the Knights and the thousands of others who had written, reported, edited, sold ads, carried messages, filed letters, set type, handled stereo plates, made engravings, run presses, carried papers in wagons and horse-drawn carts and trucks and bags and bicycles, and yelled "Extra!" on noisy corners and quiet residential streets. Those others — the people who tend to get lost in an institutional history — are the ones without whom nothing much would have happened. Many gave most of their lives to the Free Press.

Now, the Free Press, with its new computers and offset presses, was once again proving itself equal to the needs of the time — still building on the foundation seasoned by 148 years of fires, cholera epidemics, depressions, riots, strikes, as well as the satisfactions that come from serving a community well. In a more limited sense, this dedication was the climax of another decade during which war, the venality of politicians and the growth of a renaissance spirit in a city struggling to survive had provided the Free Press staff with new tests of its resolve to help build the community to which it was so closely tied. In fact, the downtown location was chosen in part to reaffirm the Free Press' commitment to the renaissance of Detroit.

But on this special day much of the talk was of new technology, new

Don C. Becker, president

David Lawrence Jr., executive editor

Neal Shine, managing editor

Joe H. Stroud, editor

ways to produce a paper that would make it possible, every morning, for the Free Press to deliver the latest news to the great bulk of its subscribers. The move was timely, since the Detroit News, with plans for a satellite plant in Lansing and a shift to all-day publication, was preparing for its own new competitive efforts.

As Detroit's Renaissance Center represented a climactic point for the city, so did the new plant represent a major milestone for the Free Press. Built on 22 acres of prime riverfront property, the clean-looking, brick-lined facility, designed by Smith, Hinchman & Grylls, with its six seven-unit Goss offset presses provided the paper's 1,929 employees with the capability they had needed to produce a highly competitive morning paper — clean and crisp looking, full of color, and printed mostly after midnight with the latest possible news for morning home delivery. When production moved to the new plant, the Free Press became the largest newspaper in the country to be printed by the offset method. It soon took advantage of offset's capability for clear printing to increase sharply the use of color. The new presses also provided the means for continued circulation growth.

Offset was only one aspect of the new technology. Others came to the offices for news, advertising and circulation and the composing room, which remained at the building on W. Lafayette the Free Press had occupied since 1925. After type was set electronically and pages pasted up, completed pages were transmitted to the riverfront plant by laser beam impulse. The type originated in a new electronic text editing system, where reporters and editors worked at video display terminals instead of typewriters. It was a long way from the handwritten copy, hand-set metal type and clumsy flatbed press that gave birth to the Detroit Free Press almost 150 years ago.

Though the times and the technology had changed dramatically, the struggle for circulation leadership had not. The increasingly intense battle had not diminished since 1940 when John S. Knight bought the Free Press. Every indication was that it would continue as vigorously into the '80s.

As the Free Press entered the '70s, it was still showing some effects of the harrowing nine-month strike in 1967-68. It had topped the 600,000 mark for the first time, at 600,803 in March 1968 (the ABC reporting period reflecting circulation before the strike), but still trailed the News by more than 100,000. The figures for the period following the end of the strike showed how devastating the work stoppage had been. By September 1968 the Free Press had dropped to 530,264 and the News to

The riverfront plant opened in 1979, making the Free Press the
largest newspaper in the United States to be printed by the
offset method.

592,616 from its pre-strike figure of 700,321. By March 1970, the Free
Press had moved to within 51,000 of the News, 575,446 to 626,512. By
September 1975 the margin was a mere 3,000 with the News at 626,801
and the Free Press at 623,846.

Again, the News reacted. It added a morning edition in hopes of
hanging on to the slim lead. That edition boosted the News' lead from
3,000 to variously 15,000 to 25,000 through the end of the decade. But
recessions and competitive pressures of stronger outstate and suburban
papers kept both Detroit papers on a relatively flat circulation pattern
into the '80s. And while the Free Press added considerably to its total advertising linage, the News managed to maintain its approximate 60-40
share of the market.

Both papers continued to compete vigorously and would go to
virtually any length to get the edge on the other. The goal, of course, was
to produce a paper that would guarantee circulation superiority. But the
emotional rewards of beating the competition were an equally strong
incentive. In 1967, for example, the Free Press sent reporter Gary
Blonston, later the paper's executive news editor, to the Philippines to

At the dedication of the new plant Sept. 19, 1979, from left, Governor William Milliken; Lee Hills, editorial chairman of Knight-Ridder Newspapers; Alvah Chapman, president of Knight-Ridder; John S. Knight, Knight-Ridder editor emeritus, Mayor Coleman Young, and Bernard H. Ridder Jr., board chairman of Knight-Ridder. (Photo by Tony Spina)

report on a planeload of seriously ill Detroit area people who had gone there to be cured by a healer of dubious reputation. The News also sent a reporter. To ensure Blonston the competitive edge, two Free Press editors called the U.S. Public Health Service in San Francisco, the News reporter's point of departure for Manila, to tell them that the News reporter had a communicable disease and should be quarantined. The plane, however, had already left. Blonston was able to make his own arrangements. In the Philippines Blonston paid an RCA telegraph operator a few dollars extra not to transmit the Detroit News story until well after the Free Press story was sent. The result: The Free Press had the story in the paper a full 36 hours before the News.

The strike and post-strike era saw a number of changes in the management of the Free Press. John B. Olsen and John Prescott had succeeded Henry Weidler on the business side. Later business-side executives included Lee Templeton, Lee Guittar, Lee Dirks and Ralph

Roth. As the Free Press approached its 150th anniversary, it was under the direction of Don C. Becker, who had come from Knight-Ridder's Gary (Ind.) Post-Tribune, where he was publisher. A former United Press International reporter and executive, Becker also had served in Knight-Ridder's corporate headquarters before becoming Free Press president. Becker arrived at the Free Press in late 1979, and his first full year was marked by aggressive, enthusiastic management and a desire to "zero base" (examine) everything.

His chief lieutenants were Ed Engel, business manager; Dave Henes, promotion; Frank Kenny, research; John Kimball, advertising; William Louwers, labor relations and personnel; George Martin, circulation; Larry Strutton, production, and Gerard Teagan, controller. They were the latest in a long line of executives with a special place in Free Press history — Bob Wheeler, Elving Anderson, Elliott Shumaker, Dan Renner and Don Gunn in advertising; Virgil Fassio, Al Korach and Bob Cullinan in circulation (their total years of service not matching Roy Hatton's remarkable more than half-century in that job).

Leadership in the news and editorial departments changed too, bringing shifts in the approach to news coverage and opinion-writing. Top editors at the News also changed, but the intensity of the efforts to reach the minds of readers never wavered. During the '60s, the Free Press was an innovative, well-written newspaper. The '70s would bring sophistication, cleverness, usefulness, rounding out the gains of the previous decades.

Derick Daniels, who had assumed broader interest in editorial affairs of Knight Newspapers (then Knight-Ridder following the merger of the two newspaper groups in 1974), made a major Free Press shift in newsroom management when he named Neal Shine managing editor and Walker Lundy city editor in 1971. Angelo was named associate executive editor and began writing a thrice-weekly column. Daniels was vice-president for news for Knight-Ridder when he resigned in 1977 to become president of Playboy Enterprises in Chicago. And he played a major role in making that financially troubled company a successful one.

In the mid-'60s, Daniels had hired Kurt Luedtke, a bright, aggressive reporter from the Miami Herald. Luedtke was consumed with doing things his way, with great instincts for quality writing and knowing what would interest readers. By 1970, following his successes as the first Action Line writer and in his key role, as an assistant city editor, in the riot coverage, he had been named assistant to the executive editor (dropping the *to the* from the title whenever he could get away with it). The '70s were mostly Luedtke's years. He largely ran the news operation in the early 1970s and in 1973 was named executive editor.

The paper crackled with lively reportage; with gossipy features such as Tipoff, and with a new focus on service, calendars and how-to stories. The four-section open-front pages that came to mark the Free Press of the '80s were Luedtke's parting contribution. He kept the traditional news section and sports section. He renamed the For and About Women section in response to years of complaints from readers and from his sub-editors, who recognized its broader approach. His title: The Way We Live. And he added a fourth section daily, called Extra, which featured a different topic each day. They were introduced in October 1978, the week he announced his resignation.

At 33, Luedtke was one of the youngest newsroom bosses in the country. In building the Free Press staff he emphasized one skill more than any other — fine writing. He was convinced that most American newspapers were poorly written and that excellence in writing could make the difference in a competitive newspaper city. During his years as an editor, the Free Press staff won many prizes for journalism excellence. Luedtke left the Free Press to work as a screenwriter. His first film — a newspaper story — began production two years after he departed.

The examples of Luedtke's competitiveness were numerous. There was the time in 1966 when a ship, the Daniel J. Morrell, went down in Lake Huron with a loss of 28 crew members. The lone survivor was taken to a hospital at Harbor Beach, Mich. The Free Press story was complete except for one thing, an interview with the survivor. Hospital personnel would not permit an interview. Luedtke called the hospital from the newsroom, told the medical director that he was "Commander Whitehead," head of the Coast Guard's Ninth District. He urged that the seaman be made available to the press, suggesting the interview be limited to one reporter — the one from the Free Press. The doctor was determined that no one see the sailor until the doctor decided it was advisable. He told the caller that he resented outside interference and nobody, the Coast Guard included, would change his mind. The rebuffed Luedtke/Whitehead had one parting shot before he hung up the phone: "The next time you want your goddamn lighthouse fixed," he said, "don't come whining to me."

After a series of personnel changes at the Free Press in the late '70s, Joe Stroud, who in 1973 had become editor, in charge of the editorial page, wrote:

"What the Free Press has been for a long time and is still isn't dependent on one or two, or even a dozen, people. What it is — at least in my head — is a spirit, an idea, a sense of a newspaper being forever alive and independent and aggressive and young. Of caring about the news and about this town.

"It's a place with a heart, with a sense of humor, with a feeling of delight in life, in the job we're assigned to do and the camaraderie that role engenders. It is full of spirit and sprightliness, sometimes impudent, almost always open."

David Lawrence Jr., who had been editor of the Charlotte Observer, succeeded Luedtke in late 1978. His arrival coincided with total conversion of the news operation to an electronic editing system. More importantly, Lawrence at 36 conveyed his intense capacity for competition to those around him, telling them more than once that he had not come to Detroit to be part of a second-place newspaper. The energetic Lawrence reacted to news quickly, directing the production of the first extra edition in nearly 20 years in the early morning hours after an aborted attempt by the United States to rescue the Americans held hostage in Iran. Hearing of the attempt shortly after 2 a.m. — what normally would be in the news cycle of an afternoon paper — he roused a sleeping staff to work on an edition that was on the streets by 9 a.m.

He worked hard at adding more minorities and women to the reporting, editing and supervisory staffs; at making the Free Press, in a favorite phrase, "more complete," with the addition of staff specialists and comprehensive examinations of such subjects as blacks in Detroit and the auto industry of the '80s; and at being available to readers, both through occasional signed letters on Page One inviting comments on what they read in the Free Press and through more direct personal contact. He made it a point to meet as many community leaders and ordinary readers as possible in his first months in Detroit. His thoroughness was apparent in the way he, shortly after arriving in Detroit, enrolled in a course on Detroit history at Wayne State University.

Lawrence was raised on a farm in upstate New York but moved to Florida for his high school and college (University of Florida) years. He began his newspaper career at age 15 during summers in the composing room of a Sarasota (Fla.) newspaper. After graduation from college in 1963, he worked as a reporter and editor at the St. Petersburg (Fla.)

Times, then worked two years on the Washington Post. He returned to Florida in 1969 as managing editor of the Palm Beach Post. He joined Knight Newspapers in 1971, was managing editor of the Philadelphia Daily News until 1975, and was editor of the Charlotte (N.C.) Observer until late 1978 and the move to Detroit.

In Detroit, Lawrence gradually made some staff shifts. He named Bill Baker as assistant executive editor, with responsibility for the Graphics, Sunday, The Way We Live, Entertainment and Systems departments. Baker joined the Free Press in 1956 as a copy boy and later, as Free Press Sunday editor, established a national reputation as an expert on newspaper feature and syndicate content, especially comics. He frequently serves as a consultant to other Knight-Ridder newspapers on content and packaging. Scott McGehee, an editor in the evolution of the former women's section to The Way We Live and in the creation of the new Extra sections, became associate editor, with news and administrative responsibilites. Frank Denton, who had been her assistant, took over The Way We Live department. Gary Blonston, who had been Sunday editor and also helped in creating the Extra sections, replaced retiring Vincent (Tick) Klock in 1980 as executive news editor. Alexander Cruden became the paper's first national/international editor with additional responsibility for the new Free Press foreign bureaus — one in Toronto, Canada, staffed by Jim Neubacher, and one with Bill Mitchell covering eastern and central Europe from Vienna. Remer Tyson, who had earned a national reputation as Free Press politics writer for a decade, was named to establish a Free Press Africa bureau in 1981, headquartered in Nairobi, Kenya.

Sandra White was named graphics editor, with veterans Tony Spina as chief photographer and Dick Mayer as art director. Scott Bosley, former managing editor of Knight-Ridder's Akron Beacon Journal, became Sunday and features editor. John Oppedahl, city editor since 1975, became executive city editor, and Susan Watson, a distinguished reporter and assistant city editor, became city editor. Other editors guiding the Free Press into its second 150 years were Louis Heldman, business; Joe Distelheim, sports; and Polk Laffoon IV, Detroit magazine. Ken Clover, for years a key editor in sports, became systems editor, responsible for the operations of the newsroom's electronic text editing system. The Free Press reference library, regarded as one of the best anywhere, was under the direction of chief librarian Michele Kapecky. Alison Oppedahl, who had directed the library transition from an outdated "clips in envelopes" newspaper morgue to a modern, efficient service operation, later became a key copydesk chief.

There was one constant in the newsroom through these years, and in many before: Cornelius J. Shine, or "Neal" as everyone called him. Very much a Detroiter in his knowledge of and affection for the Motor City, he started at the Free Press as a 20-year-old copyboy in 1950 when he was a student at the University of Detroit. In 1955, he became a reporter, covering police, and later served as assistant city editor, then city editor, and then managing editor beginning in 1971.

Lit by an Irish twinkle, Shine was chaplain, counselor, coach and stand-up comedian for a generation of Free Press staff members to whom he regularly delivered everything from dialectics about ethics to dialect jokes about ethnics. Shine was in constant demand as a dinner speaker and perenially in charge of the Detroit Press Club Steak-Out, an annual assemblage of local journalists, politicians and other undesirables for a night of good humor and bad taste.

Shine lent more money, co-signed more notes, attended more funerals, kissed more children and charmed more angry citizens than any ward-heeler ever dreamed of. He also occasionally was inclined to thunderous outbursts of dissatisfaction with the performance of his staff, and at such times could go as long as 35 seconds without smiling.

Shine's contributions to the news operation included supervising the Free Press team that investigated the killings of several students by Ohio National Guardsmen at Kent State University in 1970. That investigation, conducted in co-operation with the Free Press' sister paper in Akron, Ohio, won the Akron paper a Pulitzer Prize, but not a single Free Press staff member doubted who had done the work.

Lawrence also named Clark Hoyt assistant to the executive editor with responsibilities in the news area. Hoyt joined the Free Press in 1968 as politics writer and served later in the Knight Newspapers Washington bureau. It was while he was in Washington that Hoyt, and bureau chief Bob Boyd, won a Pulitzer Prize for uncovering the history of mental illness of 1972 Democratic vice-presidential nominee Thomas Eagleton. That reporting was based on information supplied anonymously by telephone to John S. Knight III, a talented Free Press reporter who later became an editor at the Philadelphia Daily News and was murdered in late 1975. Boyd, a Free Press reporter before going to the Washington bureau, and Hoyt were awarded the 1973 Pulitzer Prize for national reporting.

Hoyt spent 14 months planning and directing Free Press coverage of the 1980 election and the first national political convention ever to be held in Detroit, the 1980 Republican National Convention. It was a major event for a city whose reputation had never quite recovered from the 1967 riot and the crime statistics that earned it in the early 1970s the dubious distinction of being called Murder City. With the spotlight of network television attention turned on the city for a week, it was an opportunity to demonstrate to people across the country that Detroit was really the Renaissance City its civic boosters claimed.

For a Midwestern newspaper, albeit the country's eighth biggest, it was an opportunity to be read every morning by the opinion-makers whose bibles are the New York Times and the Washington Post. Every news department at the Free Press was involved in convention coverage. In addition to the politics writers covering the candidates, one reporter, Gerald Volgenau, spent nearly a year immersing himself in the city's preparations — from the Republican National Committee and the Civic Host Committee to telephone installers and Cobo Hall electricians; another, Laura Berman, spent months profiling 15 people — among them delegates, a candidate's spouse, a taxi driver, a prostitute — in preparation for writing a "Convention Diary" daily during convention week to give readers a behind-the-scenes look at what it was like to be part of this political and civic extravaganza.

The circulation department had made elaborate arrangements to distribute papers throughout the convention area. The production department had worked out new deadlines to accommodate the convention schedule. The promotion department had commissioned special television and radio commercials. The Extra sections were going to forego their usual topics for the week and become Extra/Convention, a feature section led by a cartoon and commentary from Garry Trudeau, the Doonesbury creator who was on special assignment for the Free Press.

The Sunday paper for July 13, the opening of Convention Week, had been expanded to include a 56-page magazine devoted to the convention, with a history of the Republican Party, and a special 16-page section led by a comprehensive account, written by Tyson and filling four full pages, of how Ronald Reagan had won the nomination he was sure to get three days later.

But the Free Press' week was not to be.

Within hours of the presses rolling to print more than 750,000 papers that Convention Eve Saturday, the unexpected news came. The Teamsters had struck. That special Sunday edition, mostly already made up in the composing room, was never printed. Other unions honored the

Teamster picket line and the Free Press was shut down for 12 days, the first five an especially bitter disappointment for a newsroom which had prepared so thoroughly to cover the Republican convention.

In an effort to resist the whipsaw tactics reminiscent of the series of strikes in the 1960s, Free Press management decided to produce a section to be printed by and inserted in the Detroit News, which would carry a joint Free Press-News masthead. Union-exempt supervisors in the news and production departments put the section together for 12 trying days, until the strike was settled with a contract essentially the same as the one which had been rejected.

For the newsroom supervisors it was a good test of the teamwork and camaraderie Lawrence had worked to build. He believed in sharing information and decision-making widely and used a number of ways to establish strong working relationships. One was as simple as monthly lunch meetings away from the office so that newsroom supervisors could catch up on what each department was doing and discuss mutual problems and plans. One such lunch was in Windsor, Ontario, a five-minute ride through the tunnel to Canada. The restaurant failed to provide either the promised quick service or private room. So, after lunch, the group walked a couple of blocks to Dieppe Park, on Windsor's riverfront, to discuss what had been impossible in the noisy restaurant. Clad in business suits or dresses, they were an incongruous sight sitting in the grass in the warm summer sun. The first person to talk was interrupted by an ambulance siren, the second by a jackhammer at a nearby construction site, the third by a horn blast from a steamship in the river, the fourth by a helicopter overhead.

Finally, Lawrence suggested they try to finish the only absolutely essential part of the discussion, some problems with the electronic text editing system. Just as he said, "Ken, tell us about the system," a woman who had stopped nearby shouted, "I'll tell you about the system. The system STINKS!" As one, 15 editors stood up and headed back to the office.

Continuing the separation of news gathering and opinion writing that was a hallmark of Knight-Ridder newspapers, Lawrence, as executive editor, ran the news operations while Joe Stroud, the editor, had responsibility for the editorial pages. Stroud, who did much to provide a sense of editorial stability and consistency through the '70s, had come to the Free Press to be associate editor in 1968 and had signaled his independent thoughtfulness rather quickly with a column in support of Hubert Humphrey in contrast to the formal editorial support by the Free Press of Richard Nixon.

Stroud, raised in McGehee, Ark., was educated at Hendrix College with a master's from Tulane; he was contemplating becoming a history teacher when he was induced to go to work at the Arkansas Gazette, in Little Rock, with famed editor Harry Ashmore and publisher John Netherland Heiskell. From Little Rock, Stroud moved to the Winston-Salem Journal and Sentinel in North Carolina, then was hired by the Free Press in 1968 during the strike.

In the many signed columns which he produced aside from editorials, Stroud shared his feelings for basic values, for family, for country, and for the worth of all people. He was unstinting in his promotion of education, of the merits of the city, and of racial tolerance.

At the time he took over, Stroud reiterated some basic ideas that would guide him, beginning with his belief that "we should have a society that is orderly without being oppressive." He said, "I really believe that while a newspaper has to deal with an awful lot of negatives, you avoid the curse of that by trying to stand for things . . . You must know what ought to be done . . . (and) it's much more important that you know what to say than a few set tricks of how to say it."

Over the years Stroud, while strongly supportive of social service programs at all levels, also warned against the "illusory practice . . . of borrowing from the future to keep from cutting back services. The old practice of holding out the hope that the big Sugar Daddy in Washington is going to rescue us has played out," he wrote in July 1970.

And he was perceptive in his analysis when he wrote after the inauguration of Coleman Young as mayor in 1974, "A big new group came to power in Detroit after years of being on the outside looking in. If only we can understand that such a change means opportunity and not a threat, we will make it all right. And we may even discover that the celebration of our various heritages is going to be a whole lot more fun now that we're all able to get up to the table once in a while." Young had laughingly told a friend that the Free Press' relatively cautious endorsement in the election was better than a kick in the rump.

Even more significant for the Free Press, however, had been its endorsement of Richard Austin in the 1969 race against Roman Gribbs. Austin, the first black mayoralty election finalist in the city's history, lost narrowly to Gribbs.

Stroud's sense of the future came through clearly when he wrote in 1974 about Ted Kennedy's efforts to get involved in future presidential

Nixon's resignation,
reported Aug. 9, 1974.

The failed attempt to
rescue American
hostages held in Iran,
reported April 25, 1980,
in the first extra edition
of the Free Press in
nearly 20 years.

politics. Stroud called Kennedy's efforts "just a dream. Much as the nation loves the Kennedy memory, it just won't work to try to hoist Ted Kennedy to the pedestal his brothers occupied."

In 1976 and again in 1980, the Free Press endorsed Jimmy Carter, whose efforts to control the so-called pork barrel distribution of river and water projects, whose strong position on human rights, and whose handling of the Middle Eastern situation, among other things, drew Stroud's support.

In 1977, Stroud introduced the policy of establishing a year-long focus for the editorial page on one subject. The subjects ranged from a look at the courts that year, to a look at education, the environment and the plight of the cities in following years. In the meantime, Stroud also built a well-balanced staff that included Louis Cook, who contributed some bright spots with his touch of humor and regular columns about Detroiters; Reese Cleghorn, Stroud's associate editor who served a term as president of the National Conference of Editorial Writers; Betty De Ramus and Barbara Stanton, who continued the excellent reporting and writing that they had displayed for years in the city room, and Jean Calmen, a fine copy reader.

Under Stroud, the Free Press endorsed Mayor Coleman Young in his re-election effort in 1977, this time more forcefully than he had been endorsed in 1973 when the Free Press said, "Coleman Young is, despite our doubts about him, the better man . . . to lead Detroit over the next four years. We believe he will have to learn a great deal to be a good mayor, and that he will have to move quickly, if elected, to show that he means to be mayor of all the people."

In a particularly crucial time, when Richard Nixon resigned as president, Stroud wrote in his column, "Men die. Politicians let us down. Presidents fall. But the values of a fundamentally lawful and civilized society endure. There is comfort, great comfort, in that."

And endure they did through quite a decade. There was the political turmoil of the Watergate scandal, Nixon's resignation, Gerald Ford's ascendance to the presidency and his subsequent defeat in 1976. There was the Vietnam war and its tragic climax, the Pentagon papers and the battle to secure First Amendment rights. And for Detroit, moments of deep concern when it seemed that racial violence might explode again, and of exhilaration and pride when court-ordered school busing began without incident. The hope of the new Renaissance Center, built to restore the city's ailing downtown, was balanced by the toll two recessions took on the city, and especially its auto industry.

Editorially, the Free Press was counseling calm, reasoned approaches, decrying infringements on human rights wherever they occurred, calling for more effective courts, and getting angry about Wayne County government which the Free Press characterized as "a running sore"; about the double standard of justice in handling white collar crime; about Coleman Young's penchant to perform poorly on "some of the petty stuff that make people — especially whites — miss the importance of what he has done (on the big things)"; about the insensitivity of society in handling the aged and mentally ill; about Gov. Milliken being "too careful with (his political capital)"; about people who don't understand how important it is to "complete the job of developing a conservation ethic."

Through all these years, as he had since 1951, Lee Hills guided the competitive strategies of the Free Press. He was responsible for keeping the new Free Press plant expansion downtown and he selected its riverfront site. Although he was increasingly involved in directing the editorial and business affairs of the Knight-Ridder group, Hills spent much of his time in Detroit.

The Free Press continued to achieve journalistic successes in its news columns. There was the PBB story, with Kathy Warbelow and Ellen Grzech and Bob Calverley doing a masterful investigation of the chemical contamination of cattle feed, which led to contamination of the food chain. When two Filipino nurses were accused — and later found innocent — of killing patients at the Ann Arbor Veterans Administration Hospital by injecting them with a muscle-relaxing drug, Kirk Cheyfitz provided calm, fair coverage of the emotional, often volatile case. Teamster leader Jimmy Hoffa's disappearance was a major story of the decade, with outstanding coverage provided by labor writer Ralph Orr and reporters Billy Bowles, Jane Briggs-Bunting, Peter Gavrilovich and Jo Thomas. The Plymouth Center story, in which Susan Watson and Paul Magnusson documented the state's neglect of mentally ill patients in its care, was another major investigative effort. And Cathy Trost and Dave Zurawik aggressively pursued the plight of teenage Cuban refugees. The Way We Live section, 102 years after the birth of its ancestor, "The Household," won first place for metropolitan lifestyle sections in the prestigious Penney-Missouri awards.

The Free Press boasted other fine writers. Some were newcomers, but there were those, too, who had given long service in special fields. There was the superlative photography and extraordinary commitment

The electronic newsroom, 1980. (Photo by David C. Turnley)

to the paper of Tony Spina; Tom Opre's conservation coverage in the tradition of a leader in the field, the Free Press' Jack Van Coevering, and Ralph Orr, who carried on the labor beat with the sensitivity that had been demonstrated by Art O'Shea, Bob Perrin, Tom Nicholson, Gene Roberts and Pat Owens. And Joe Miller and Bob McKelvey, who lent a solid sense of continuity on the news desk. And Bettelou Peterson, who started writing about television for the Free Press in 1948 when the TV era dawned. And drama critic Lawrence DeVine, who so ably filled the shoes of such predecessors as George Goodale, Len Shaw and Dorsey Callaghan. And John Guinn, who succeeded the pioneering Collins George as music critic. And Dolores Katz, with her keen appraisal of medical developments. And Barbara Holliday, whose versatility and devotion as book editor was unlimited. And William Grant, who as education writer for nine years covered the nation's most massive school busing case. Hugh McDiarmid, the Lansing Bureau chief with a well-developed reporter's sense of outrage, expressed particularly well in his columns about legislators and lobbyists. And, of course, Tom Kleene, who came to the Free Press at that dramatic moment in 1960 when the Times died. His was the onerous job of covering the automobile industry during one of its most revolutionary periods, and he did it with honesty, and with concern and sensitivity for both the consumer and the companies until his retirement at the end of 1980.

And Hal Schram, the dean of Michigan's prep sports writers, and Ken Kraemer and Norb Siwa who helped to put the sports pages together, and Joe Falls, Jim Hawkins and George Puscas whose trenchant columns delighted and provoked sports fans. And Dick Mayer, the incomparable art director whose contributions were superior in quality and quantity; and Jon Buechel, a sensitive fashion artist who also provided delicate and charming touches on so many other occasions; and long-time artists Roy Beaver, Nolan Ross, Bill Sherb and Dominic Trupiano; and Robert De Wolfe, who gave more than 30 years to the police beat. And Billy Bowles, fabled among his fellow reporters for the thoroughness of his reporting. And Marji Kunz, who for 12 years at the Free Press set the pace nationally for imaginative and inventive fashion reporting. She was lured away by the Detroit News for a salary high enough to garner coverage in Women's Wear Daily; two years later, she died, at 40, of cancer. One of her slew of national prizes was awarded for a story about going to a party in a nightgown.

A group of local columnists gave the Free Press its special personality — popular Bob Talbert, who epitomized "personal journalism"; Judd Arnett, a keen observer of the passing scene; Frank Angelo, with a special touch for the people who make a community tick; Jim Fitzgerald, who put the needle in while he made the victim laugh; the incomparable Nickie McWhirter, whose perceptive commentary was equalled by her fine writing; the irrepressible Shirley Eder with her celebrity tidbits.

The Free Press continues to be regarded nationally as a developer of talent, some of which has gone on to other enterprises. The talent which has been nurtured at the Free Press includes Jim Batten, a senior vice-president at Knight-Ridder, and Al Neuharth, who runs the vast Gannett newspaper chain. A succession of associate editors in the '70s — Larry Allison, J. Edward Murray, Rich Oppel, Vance Caesar — left special stints at the Free Press for important editing and managing positions elsewhere in Knight-Ridder.

Today, 150 years after Sheldon McKnight published that first edition, the Free Press strives to be bright, sometimes brash, risking controversy and criticism, but always concerned to do well by its readers and its community. Columnist Judd Arnett caught the spirit of Detroiters, including the ones who work at the Free Press, when in 1976 he wrote:

... (I) may have lived and worked here during one of the most important periods of all. For these have been the years when the very soul of a great city was tested, when it was necessary to make do with less than was needed, when despair and slander were the daily lot, when the poor came in torrents in search of their share of the dream, and some found it and passed it along to the eager hands of their children.

Free Press people, too, have worked for a share of the dream — to be a great newspaper in a great city. Many found it, or a part, and passed it along to the eager minds and hands of a new generation who begin with eagerness the next 150 years.

Epilogue

On April 13, 1981, the Detroit Free Press won its sixth Pulitzer Prize, journalism's highest award. The prize, for "outstanding feature photography," was given to Taro Yamasaki, staff photographer, for his series, "Inside Jackson." Yamasaki spent 10 days inside Jackson State Prison, the world's largest walled prison, to produce a haunting portrait of the inmates' world. The photographs, most in color, ran in the paper for a week, Dec. 14-20, 1980. Previous Free Press Pulitzers — in 1932, 1945, 1955, 1956 and 1968 — had been for reporting or editorial writing. This is its first for photography.

Bibliography

Books and Articles

Angelo, Frank. *Yesterday's Detroit*. Miami, 1974.

Bald, F. Clever. *Michigan in Four Centuries*. New York, 1954.

Beasley, Norman and Stark, George W. *Made in Detroit*. New York, 1957.

Bingay, Malcolm. *Detroit is My Own Home Town*. Indianapolis, 1946; *Of Me I Sing*. Indianapolis, 1949.

Bowen, N. H. "A Fighting Detroit Editor of Seventy-Five Years Ago: The Career of Wilbur F. Storey Who Made the Free Press Famous," *Detroit Saturday Night*. May 5, 1928, Sect. 2, p. 1.

Bradshaw, James Stanford. The Detroit Free Press in England, an article in *Journalism History* 5:1 Spring 1978.

Burton, Clarence M. *The City of Detroit, Michigan, 1701-1922*. Chicago, 1922.

Catlin, George B. "Little Journeys in Journalism — Wilbur F. Storey," *Michigan History,* October 1926, 515-533; *The Story of Detroit*. Detroit, 1923.

Catton, Bruce. *Michigan, a Bicentennial History,* New York, 1976.

Detroit Historical Society Bulletin, June 1955. Biographical sketch of John R. Williams by Dorothy Martin.

Detroit Public Library. *Detroit in Its World Setting, A 250-Year Chronology, 1701-1951*. R.E. Ripps, ed. Detroit, 1953.

Emery, Edwin. *The Press and America,* Third Edition. Englewood Cliffs, N.J., 1972.

Farmer, Silas. *History of Detroit and Wayne County and Early Michigan*, Third Edition. Detroit, 1890.

Fine, Sidney. *Frank Murphy,* 2 Vols. (The Detroit Years, The New Deal Years.) Ann Arbor, 1975, 1979.

Gramling, Oliver. *AP The Story of News*. New York, 1940.

Holli, Melvin G. *Reform in Detroit: Hazen S. Pingree and Urban Politics*. New York, 1969.

Howes, Royce. Unpublished manuscript on early history of Detroit Free Press.

Katzman, David M. *Before the Ghetto: Black Detroit in the Nineteenth Century*. Chicago, 1973.

Livingstone, William. *Livingstone's History of the Republican Party*. Detroit, 1900.

Lochbiler, Don. *Detroit's Coming of Age*. Detroit, 1973.

Lodge, John C. *I Remember Detroit*. Detroit, 1949.

Lutz, William. *The News of Detroit*. Boston, 1973.

M.E.S., His Book, A Tribute and a Souvenir of the AP. New York, 1918.

Masonic World, Vol. 13, April 1947. Biographical sketch, Joseph Campau.

Michigan, *A Centennial History* edited by George N. Fuller. 1939.

Michigan Alumnus, Vol. 2, Pages 81-83. Biographical sketch and portrait, William Emory Quinby.

Michigan History, Vol. 43, No. 1. The Michigan Land Rush in 1836.

O'Reilly, Kenneth. *M Quad and Brother Gardner*, Detroit Perspective, Vol. 3, No. 2, Winter 1979.

Quinby, William E. "Reminiscences of Michigan Journalism." *Michigan Pioneer and Historical Society Collections*. 1906, 507-517.

Rosewater, Victor. *History of Cooperative Newsgathering in the United States*. New York, 1930.

Ross, A.H. and Catlin, George B. *Landmarks of Detroit*. Detroit, 1898.

Ross, Robert B. *Early Bench and Bar in Detroit*. Detroit, 1907.

Rutland, Robert A. *The Newsmongers*. New York, 1973.

Scripps, James E. "Wilbur F. Storey — Detroit's First Great Journalist — Some Recollections of a Very Remarkable Man." *Detroit Sunday News-Tribune*. Sept. 16, 1900.

Shogan, Robert and Craig, Tom. *The Detroit Race Riot*. Philadelphia, 1964.

Smiley, Nixon. *Knights of the Fourth Estate*. Miami, 1974.

Smith, Anthony. *The Newspaper, An International History*. London, 1979.

Solomon, Louis. *America Goes to Press*. New York, 1970.

Stark, George W. *City of Destiny, The Story of Detroit*. Detroit, 1943.

Stewart, Kenneth and Tebbel, John. *Makers of American Journalism*. New York, 1952.

Stocking, William. "Prominent Newspaper Men in Michigan." *Michigan Pioneer and Historical Collections*. XXXIX. Lansing, 1915. 155-173.

Tiller, James A. "More About Storey." *Detroit Sunday News-Tribune*. Sept. 23, 1900.

Walsh, Justin E. *To Print the News and Raise Hell!* Chapel Hill, N.C., 1968.

Wendt, Lloyd. "The Rise of a Great American Newspaper." *Chicago Tribune*. Chicago, 1979.

Woodford, Arthur M. *Detroit, American Urban Renaissance*. Tulsa, 1979.

Woodford, Frank B. and Hyma, Albert. *Gabriel Richard*. Detroit, 1958.

Woodford, Frank B. and Woodford, Arthur M. *All Our Yesterdays*. Detroit, 1969.

Materials from Burton Historical Collections of the Detroit Public Library

Clarence M. Burton, Scrapbooks

George Catlin Papers

Thomas W. Palmer Papers
Hazen Pingree Papers
James McMillan Papers
John P. Sheldon Papers
Henry N. Walker Papers

Resources from Wayne State University Archives

Prismatic Club Archives
Detroit Newspaper Guild

Theses and Dissertations

Applegate, Margaret J. *The Detroit Free Press During the Civil War*. Master's Thesis, Wayne State University. Detroit, 1938.

Berkowitz, Sidney J. *Content Analysis of Detroit Newspapers' Treatment of Labor Strike News*. Master's Thesis, Wayne State University. Detroit, 1951.

Hamper, Winston M. *The Story of the Free Press*. Master's Thesis, Wayne State University. Detroit, 1942.

Lewis, Charles A. *The Evolution of Modern News Story Form in the Detroit Free Press*. Master's Thesis, Wayne State University, 1938.

Morrison, Joyce P. *An Analysis of Race Labeling in the Local Crime Reports of the Three Detroit Daily Newspapers*. Master's Thesis, Wayne State University. Detroit, 1951.

Permaloff, Anne C. *Political Campaign Coverage by Detroit's Daily Newspapers*. Master's Thesis, Wayne State University. Detroit, 1968.

Rolland, Siegfried B. *The Detroit English Language Labor Press, 1839-1889*. Master's Thesis, Wayne State University. Detroit, 1946.

Index

273